Daryl Benson

THE ASHEN HORSE

The Ashen Horse by Daryl Benson
First Edition
Copyright © 2022 by Daryl Benson
Second Edition
Copyright © 2025 by Daryl Benson
All rights reserved.

Cover art designed by Daryl Benson.
Cover art photo by bmanis87 on iStock (by Getty Images)

All rights reserved. No part of this book may be reproduced, transmitted, scanned, manipulated, or distributed by any means or in any form without written permission from the author.

This includes but is not limited to photocopying, recording, electronic, mechanical, or any other method of information storage or transmission or retrieval.

This novel is a work of fiction. Names, characters, places, and incidents either are the product of the author's imagination or are used fictitiously. Any resemblance to actual persons, living or dead, events, or locals is entirely coincidental.

ISBN 9798424303470

For my parents.

A special thanks to all of those who have encouraged me along my writing journey.

This is just the beginning.

The Ashen Horse

Chapter One

The Cape Cod Saga

The assassin slowly watched the sun set over the coastline. She was patiently awaiting the dark, for it was in the dark when she came alive. The rest of the time, she was just an imposter, but she was her true self in the night. Only in the silence of the night.

She didn't know any others like her. That probably shouldn't surprise her; contract killing was a solitary sport. It wasn't advisable to walk up to the unemployment agency and say 'murder' was the preferred skillset and that 'killing' was the employment opportunity that was being sought.

And so, she waited, waiting for tonight's bloody events to unfold. She considered herself a true master of her craft. In an era of technology and weaponry, she opted to be a traditional artist. Modern weapons were loud and obnoxious, with no finesse. She preferred the slick art of the kill, which could only truly be accomplished with an assassin's blade. She was carrying her standard weapons tonight. The ones she carried on every mission. A sleek sword which she could readily fasten to her back or hang at her waist. She preferred the katana but was well versed in various styles; tonight, she was carrying a custom-made Ronin Katana. She had spent a great deal negotiating the particulars of the weapon with the bladesmith, convincing them it was for a rich collector who wanted it to exact specifications. The result was a weapon of mastery, perfectly balanced, with the exact length for her to carry and swing optimally—a weapon of death.

A medium-sized dagger sat tight on her waist so as not to impede movement. At one point, she had carried shurikens just for nostalgia for the bygone era. She had also become reasonably adept at using them, but she found them slightly impractical and exchanged them for more versatile throwing knives. They were securely fastened to the other side of her waist.

She employed several other standard weapons occasionally, but tonight was a quick in-and-out mission, and she wasn't packing excessive weight. However, her most bloody work was done with her true weapon—the sword. She was also a realist and took the work seriously, and because of this, she carried a Browning Buck Mark pistol. It had a laser sight and silencer, nestled comfortably in the small of her back. It wasn't helpful at any range, but if she put the target under a hundred feet, she wouldn't miss.

The .22 wouldn't do much damage; it was an executioner's tool. The double tap to the skull would be used most effectively for close range. However, this line of work required a lightweight ranged weapon, so she found a perfect compromise in the pistol. The other option was bow and arrow, and although she would have preferred it on so many levels, pragmatism had to win the day.

She had been crouching in the shallow brush for hours, waiting for the depths of night. This is when the art came to its true luminescence. The purest form of the skill was always found in darkness. When she judged it to be the right time, she finally stirred from watching the beach. She hiked a mile along the water to the cozy cottage nestled above the breakwaters—a small summer vacation home for the elite executives of McDouglas Banks. McDouglas Banks was a shady business that owned banks throughout the Caribbean,

The Ashen Horse

especially any island known to be a haven for dirty money. The irony is that the cottage was in quaint Cape Cod, Massachusetts. It was even outfitted with a lighthouse at the corner end of the property.

Her target should be sound asleep as time slowly marched past three in the morning. He was a senior vice president of operations and reported directly to the chief operations officer. Not only had he been swindling money from drug dealers, but he had also been swindling money from a prominent South American dictator. The drug dealers chalked it up as a cost of doing business and keeping the authorities away from their money. However, the South American dictator took it as a serious affront to his honorable sensibilities.

She approached the house in a small crouch, avoiding crossing the shine of the moonlight. As she approached, she could hear the television running on the inside in what appeared to be the master bedroom. The TV must have been left on. Even better—movement, lighting, and sounds wouldn't awaken anyone. She slowly entered the back of the house and went to work.

When it was over, she took the twenty thousand dollars that was bundled on the kitchen table. She had found the custom-made black notebook that her client said she would. Apparently, it held details to various secrets the vice president didn't want to get out. Her client told her expressly that she was to find the notebook and return it to him if she wanted to get paid. And she always got paid.

***

Ron Troder got the call early that morning. As a senior detective, he got called out on anything that might make the headlines, and apparently, today was no exception. They woke him at six-thirty in the morning. He had cursed every obscenity possible at the dispatcher. He only had one rule, only one. Don't ever talk to him before coffee. He thought to himself how there was just no decency in this world.

He swung by the Starbucks on his way to the address the dispatcher had given him. He didn't shower. There was no way he was going to shave. He didn't even change from the clothes he was wearing the previous night when he fell into his bed in a drunken stupor from being out too late with the boys. He drove in a wrinkled, half-undone suit but he had a full cup of joe. Just as the world should be, if they called him before coffee, they were lucky he showed up at all. That's how he saw it.

He rolled up to the beachfront property to see five squad cars blocking the entrances and several cops securing the property. It seemed like a big contingent for a run-of-the-mill homicide, but apparently, the guy was some big shot. No press yet, he said a small prayer of thanks to the Almighty. He knew you had to take every blessing you could get, and no press was a mighty big blessing.

Sally was standing near the front door as he walked up to the house. She had made Lieutenant last year and was quickly moving up the ranks. Quite impressive for a twentysomething hotshot. But then she worked twice as hard as anyone else, and even if her beauty helped her move up the ladder quickly, she never abused it. Her normal shining sparkle wasn't quite there today, her light brown complexion looked a pale white.

"We closed it all off, Troder; we wanted to wait for you and the photo guys to arrive. The first officer on site didn't touch anything but the front door handle. We literally retraced his steps."

"Ms. Sally Escanda, you know, for sure, he didn't touch anything? How could you know? Why tell me this up front?" questioned Ron.

She gulped audibly.

"You can see his steps. He didn't go all the way in; you can see where he stopped, called for backup, and walked back out of the house. We...," she grew silent momentarily as she visibly shivered. "We think it's the Ashen Horse, he struck

The Ashen Horse

again. If it isn't him, well, it's a bloodbath, sir."

Ron didn't hesitate; he turned and shouted at a junior officer in the driveway, "Jackson! Coffee! Get lots and lots of coffee. You better get the frou-frou stuff and the black stuff. Don't mess around here; deliver the goods." Jackson rolled his eyes, but getting away from this place didn't sound like that bad of a deal for him, so he was on his way to his patrol car before anyone could contradict the order.

"Let's go in, Sally. Where are the camera guys? They go in first. Did you get two of them? Stills and video? We aren't messing around on this one." This was not Ron's first rodeo, and he wouldn't have his case against the Ashen Horse thrown out on a technicality.

"We are here, man, calm yourself. Are you sure you really need more caffeine? You probably could jump-start a rig already. Seriously, man, that can't be good for the heart, bro."

These new crime photo 'dudes' were all college photography students. Full-on wavy-haired California beach bums turned photojournalists. They applied for other photo jobs when they realized they couldn't get a gig shooting girls in skimpy bikinis. They landed in Ron's lap as crime scene photographers. Did every one of them have to be this way, though?

"Listen, rock stars. Video first, still photo second. Touch nothing, shoot everything. Video capture, full view, two steps forward, repeat. Slow, steady, calculated, full view. Sally and I will be right behind, and the forensic team will be behind us. We capture everything, we bag everything."

They might not be the state-of-the-art crew or have the best equipment, not like they had in Boston, but this team had rigor and discipline on their side. Even Mr. California could deliver. They quickly started shooting, tagging, bagging, and documenting the entire scene.

It was gruesome. There was blood spatter over half the house. Two victims, apparently a senior bank VP and his young lover. They weren't sure if the girl was hired or a mistress, but they knew she wasn't the VP's wife. It looked like the VP didn't see it coming. He had been hacked to pieces in the bedroom, the blood splatter literally outlining where the Ashen Horse had stood, leaving his frame outlined on the double doors leading outside. Tampering with the lock showed he had entered the house right there. He had picked the lock barely a hand's length away from his victims.

It appeared the girl woke in the middle of it and tried to run. She made it to the next room. She didn't make it much further. She was scattered throughout the room. The Ashen Horse was not so much flamboyant as efficient. He killed with a thoroughness that might have been envied if he applied his skills to a better trade. It looked like the girl had been cut maybe ten times, but that was enough to sever body parts, and they had been loosely kicked out of the way. It was surprising how much blood was really in the human body.

***

The newspapers ran a full report the following day, front page news. "The Ashen Horse Strikes Again!" The first detective in Texas had named the killer what they had been calling the serial killer of the century. The blood and gore drew the press every time; they couldn't get enough. They went out of their way to cover the story. News agencies from halfway around the world descended on Cape Cod to get quotes from anyone who knew anything.

A news reporter finally cornered Ron and asked him what he knew as the lead detective on the case. Ron hated the press. Ron loathed everything about the media, but he also knew that if he didn't feed the beast, the beast would never leave him alone. Out of a horrible sense of obligation, he replied to their questions with the team's agreed-upon answers. It had been a carefully devised decision on what they would tell the press and what they wouldn't. Nothing was going to leak in this case.

The Ashen Horse

The interview was slowly ending, and the reporter was twitching, he had to ask one more question. "If you don't mind Ron, can I ask you why you call him the Ashen Horse? That seems like such a silly name for a serial killer."

"Truth be told, we don't know that it is a serial killer. There's no modus operandi to suggest that's what is going on here. The victims are butchered with blades; that's the only similarity between many of them. This isn't someone who enjoys killing, as most serial killers do, or someone who needs to kill. This is someone efficient at killing. There is a subtle difference. Serial killers make mistakes because they get caught in the moment, that moment of need or desire. We haven't seen that from the Ashen Horse."

Ron was quiet for a minute, and then he looked at the reporter and said, "I can't take responsibility for naming him. Honestly, it most likely was one of you journalists, reporters, or whatever who started calling him that. I don't know who it was, but the origin seems clear." Ron paused for emphasis and then continued, "When the Lamb broke the fourth seal, I heard the voice of the fourth living creature saying, 'Come.' I looked, and behold, an ashen horse; and he who sat on it had the name Death, and Hades was following him."

The reporter asked, "That's why they call the serial killer the Ashen Horse?"

"I'm assuming so," Ron said. "It must refer to the quote. Anyway, duty calls, I have a mountain of paperwork that needs to get done." Ron spun and walked away from the reporter as quickly as he could. He knew they'd have follow-up questions, and he knew he'd have to answer them if he stayed. He walked away, cursing all journalists.

Chapter Two

Feats of Salt Lake City

She quietly chuckled as she read the morning papers from Cape Cod, Massachusetts, online. Brazen stories declared, 'The Ashen Horse Strikes Again.'. She, of course, was on the other side of the country, having left early the previous morning. The stories reported how the killer had brutalized the two victims. She thought that was unfair; she had been surprisingly effective and clean in her work. They barely suffered, all things considered. If half the stories were reliable, he deserved what he got three times over.

She was sipping a white chocolate mocha with an extra shot of espresso. She ordered her particular drink, always with soy and never with the whip, no matter what town she was in. It was a special time in the morning when she sat back and enjoyed a perfect cup of bliss while reading about her exploits in the local papers. Her activities were more and more making national news, which was troublesome and brought unwanted attention. It was hard to be a covert assassin when the news was building her up to become the most wanted serial killer of the decade.

She could change the way she killed. Enter the modern era of guns and distance murder. But she didn't want to work that way. It took the humanity out of it. There was a code that she followed, and she wasn't about to abandon it just because the heat was warming up. She would continue in her methods, at least until she genuinely had to bend. And that wouldn't be anytime soon.

As she savored the taste of her coffee, she toggled on her encrypted email and began to look at the new employment opportunities. Usually, she would wait a week between tasks, but she wanted to deflect suspicions from her last job as soon as possible. If she were going to run a race with the police, she would do it in a manner that would genuinely confuse them.

There were a couple of tempting gigs in Europe. That might really turn the tables on the investigations—if they could put them together. Apparently, some president of a couple of monetary funds had said the wrong things and the stocks had spiraled into the abyss. Now, his head was on the hit list. She was tempted; it had been quite a while since she had been to Rome. But the time wasn't right to reveal to the world that she was an international assassin. Although, it would be evident if they ever put together the last ten years of her career. That meant she would have to stay in the USA for at least a couple more assignments.

She continued to browse her options until she found the perfect match. Yes, indeed, this was the man. They wanted him killed because he swindled over ten million dollars out of the company's pension plan. He had done it in twenty thousand-dollar installments, so the contract was for two payments of twenty thousand dollars. She appreciated the humor. She usually worked for more; her talents weren't cheap, but she liked to do charity work when possible. She might as well save the courts some time and money by eliminating him in a more proper way.

He lived in Salt Lake City and managed the fund out of New York City. She hummed to herself as she booked flights to SLC, reserved her hotel room, and rented a car for the week. She checked the local event pages in Salt Lake City and reserved several shows throughout the week, taking the time to read the reviews. She also found two conferences relating to humanitarian efforts and RSVPed to both events. The one looked interesting; it was all about efforts to drill water wells throughout Africa, utilizing local workers and farmers to build the economy and continue the work at the following location—their catchphrase of a 'long-term vision' hit home with her sensibilities.

She knew the importance of planning for the future and having a long-term vision. Much of it came down to having effective and deliberate alibis and reasons for every plane ticket. Another came from making sure that plenty of other plane tickets showed she was not in the cities when crimes took place. She lived out of hotels, but necessity forced her to funnel funds into various rental properties worldwide.

The game changer had been the rise of vacation rentals and home-sharing services. She didn't need a home anymore. How else could she enjoy the perfect coffee looking out over the ocean in San Diego? It was not to last, however. She would be getting everything ready for tomorrow's flight shortly.

The trip was uneventful as she landed at SLC and quickly made her way to the hotel. She would be off to scout the area rather quickly. The art of avoiding detection, implication, and capture was always preparation. She had avoided being implicated for years, and that was because she was always prepared. The target lived in the Capitol Hill area of the city, and she was off to plan her entry into his home. It was always easier to take the target when they were at home, asleep. It solved a lot of other uncomfortable situations that were best avoided.

He didn't live too far from the Capitol Building, which worked out conveniently. There was always good food where politicians congregated. She was grabbing a quick lunch while evaluating the neighborhood at Café Shambala. She did enjoy the perks of the work.

A solid plan was in place; tomorrow was the night. She

would typically plan for several days. Complex jobs may even require a week or two. But this appeared to be an easy mission. The house didn't have any particular security to be concerned with. It looked like the man lived alone, with no wife or kids. That was always good. It avoided any collateral damage. Information seemed to indicate that he drank too much of late and would often return home late.

The following morning, she grabbed breakfast at a café on 1st and headed to his house. She waited. A large percentage of this work was waiting. She almost considered going in early and waiting it out inside, but that might leave physical evidence. So, she waited. When it was clear he wouldn't return before lunch, she grabbed some exceptional Thai. And she waited, yet again.

The rideshare dropped him off a little past midnight. She was surprised he took a safe route home. Everything about this man suggested he was careless and selfish. She would have sworn he would drive home after a night of drinking. He wobbled toward the front door, and that was when she decided there wasn't a huge need for extra caution on this job. She'd casually knock on the front door and see how that played out.

She knocked, and he opened the door, his eyes growing slightly wide as he saw her. Perhaps it was a surprise to see a young woman. Perhaps it was her mystic beauty, partially cloaked. It was hard to say. She looked shocked and out of breath as she quickly stepped inside and closed the door behind her. She brushed him back when she entered, and he wobbled further into his home as she moved in.

He started to ask a question, a hint of lust glimmering in his eyes. As she partially turned toward him, the throwing knife left her hand with deadly precision. It took him right in the neck. His hands quickly grasped for his throat. His gurgle was accompanied by the woosh of her sword being pulled from over her shoulder smoothly. Spending only a single pull down to orient it into her hands. The return path of the blade cleanly cut through his lower abdomen up to his ribs, where it gracefully exited his flesh. One last swish cut his throat clean to the spinal cord as he collapsed, his eyes already glazing over. He never had time to finish his question.

She stood over the body. It had been clean—well, cleanish. The blood was pooling all over the floor. She quickly recovered her throwing blade and cleaned both weapons on his clothes. Stepping over the body, she quickly searched the house for any apparent valuables that wouldn't be noticed. She debated burning the house down to hide the evidence of her visit, but there were neighbors relatively close, and she didn't want to risk torching the block.

In the den, she noticed a couple of interesting manila folders on the corner of the desk. She flipped through them and discovered fact sheets and photos of various vacation homes. It appeared he was going to inspect them and purchase one. It looked like he had come into a rather lovely piece of money lately. She combed through the desk drawers and found a small black notebook. It was smooth and subtle, with a polished sheen. She paused to admire it in her hands before flipping through it. She quietly chuckled. This looked like detailed information on the money he had stolen from the accounts. What kind of fool would write this down? She carefully pocketed the notebook as she turned to leave the desk.

After collecting some nice pieces of silver and gold jewelry, she would melt down; she decided she had finished in the house. There was one particularly charming piece of art she would have liked to take, but that was not in the cards. As she crossed over his body one last time to the door, she stooped down to carve a strange symbol into his forehead. It was meaningless, but she wanted to keep the cops guessing. Playing the game was becoming as fun as the chase. Cleaning her blade carefully, she stepped out of the house and into the night.

She had a conference to get to in the morning, only several hours away, on drilling wells in Africa in a sustainable fashion. It was the long-term vision that sparked her interest. This could be a game changer for local economies in the region.

Chapter Three

The Fibbie Chronicles

"It has become a national issue, Josie," commented Tim. Tim Burkman, a senior Federal Bureau of Investigation detective, sat flipping through papers. This steaming pile of excrement had fallen on his plate, and although he didn't want to get anywhere near it, he had to defend the company line to Josie, a lieutenant in the Salt Lake City Police Department.

"I assure you, Josie. I don't want to deal with this at all. However, the higher-ups have dictated that this will now be a national investigation. I don't know what everyone knows yet, but there's evidence that at least three or four of these murders are tied together. I was supposed to be going on vacation next week, Josie. Vacation. Do you know how long it has been since I had a vacation?" The exasperation and a hint of desperation were clear in his voice. This was a man who was not far from entirely losing it.

"I know your situation, Tim, but this is my case. The FBI doesn't get to swoop in here and take it. I knew the victim, and he will get justice." Josie Flakes wasn't a pushover; she wasn't going to have the FBI pee in her pond; this was her jurisdiction. "I'm entirely willing to cooperate here, Tim; I'll feed the FBI every ounce of information we churn up. But we will be investigating. Fully."

The Ashen Horse

"It sounds like you should recuse yourself, Josie; that's what it sounds like. You are too close to this. But I'll tell you what. I don't have the energy; I just don't have it. So, you get to do whatever you want; I won't get in your way." He could hear her smile over the telephone at that. Little did she know what this meant. "You might think this is free rein, but it's not. It means I'm staying out of it. But here is the catch: if you ruffle the system's feathers, it escalates to leadership beyond me in the FBI or beyond you in the SLC PD…." He let the silence hang in the receiver for a couple of seconds. "If it escalates, they'll just fire you. Last I heard, your team doesn't mess around with this, and I can assure you the FBI doesn't."

He truly was getting too old for the politics. And he wasn't that old. The constant maneuvering wore a guy down. "My responsibility was to tell you to back off, step down, and turn over your investigation. I've delivered that; I will write a memo explicitly saying that, and I'm carbon-copying you and your boss on it. After that, you do whatever you want. But the beauty here is you deal with the consequences." She wasn't going to listen, and the fact was she would be a total pain in the ass for the coming months. He could tell that this would be a very unhealthy working relationship.

"You do what you have to do, Timmy. I'm going to do what I have to do." Tim hated being called Timmy, not that she could know that, or perhaps she knew exactly how to push a man's buttons.

"Exactly, Josie, exactly. My hands are washed of it. I'll have some guys swinging by your office next week for any relevant files. I'm positive you and the team will show them every courtesy."

"Consider it done. We have most of them ready already if you'd prefer them electronically. Utah has been working on a national crime database. You fibbies should have access, you'd think. Maybe the team isn't up to date?"

That final stab was enough; he was done with her for at

least today. "Thanks, Josie, we'll look into it." And with that effective conclusion, he angrily tapped the 'end' button on his smartphone. He didn't like smartphones. There was no way you could appropriately slam down a phone anymore, and that was a call that desperately needed a vicious hang-up.

He had the pleasure of forgetting about the case for a few days while his team built up all the files and started connecting the dots. The serial killer was a busy one; they had five cases that were awfully similar and suspicious. All the victims had been powerful men or women in the upper echelons of society, many of them suspected of crimes themselves. The serial killer almost appeared to be a vigilante. But where was he getting his information?

The killer wasn't that creative, though, or perhaps he was ultra-creative. They could track most of the cases and tie them together because the victims were all decapitated with a sword. And they were all done in the last six months. Sword deaths weren't that common; they stood out in every investigation. That was the primary running theory on why these cases were the same serial killer—victims decapitated by a sword.

Initial forensic evidence hinted that it could, in fact, be the same sword. Tim Burkman wanted that proof on the table; it would change the game. He had spent half the previous day hounding the medical examiners and lab rats, trying to get them to solidify that it was the same sword at multiple crime scenes. The cowards hadn't committed yet. They kept going on and on about more tests and examinations to lock it in. Tim's frustrations went higher, along with his blood pressure.

Right now, they were running on idle suspicions and coincidence. That wasn't the way to run a case. He needed the facts to line up so he could tie these cases together or kick them back to their local jurisdictions.

After yesterday, the frustration was running high for the entire team. He had assembled his small task force together in a room to go over the merit of the current evidence. "What do we have that's really concrete here, guys?"

"Ashen uses a sword, we know that, if nothing else," commented Josh.

"You guys need to stop calling him Ashen. We don't know yet if we can tie all these cases together. The guy already has a serial killer nickname, and we haven't even confirmed it's the same guy."

Ellie was leaning against the door frame as she often did, never wanting to commit to the room fully and always having one foot out the door, ready to blitz away from any conversation. "Come on, Tim, we know it's the same killer. The bodies are decapitated with a sword. There's not a gang of ninjas roaming around America lopping off heads; this is definitely one guy. One guy with a sword fetish."

"Many of the victims also have other wounds, wounds with smaller knives mostly," Tim pointed out. "The medical guys haven't identified what is causing those. They comment on strange angles with the blades. Not normal stabbing wounds. That makes no sense yet, but Tracy will get to the bottom of that. She always closes the medical loopholes given enough time."

"We also know that there is a commonality in the victims as well," Josh said. He was routinely the guy who said the obvious thing. Tim appreciated Josh for it. Sometimes, the obvious things were the most overlooked.

"That's true," Ellie piped up. "We see a vendetta almost being played out with all the victims. Most of them were under a haze of suspicion of crimes. Some are higher-ups in various financial dealings; others are notoriously shady businessmen. The bottom line is that every single one of these victims had enemies, if we should even call them victims. They had lots of enemies."

Tim scratched his head and looked up at the ceiling. He closed his eyes, and while wishing the day could just be over, he asked the question he knew there was no answer for. "But are any of the victims, and we should call them that, associated or tied together?"

"Nope, not a lick, anywhere. We got all their financial records, dates, receipts," Josh said. "Nothing. Only two of them had even crossed into the same cities in the last year. The rest of them are completely isolated and probably didn't even know about the existence of any of the other victims." Josh enunciated the last word to make sure he was poking the leader of the task force just enough.

"Got it. So, we have nothing except a loose tie between the victims, but we don't know how or why. We don't know what. All we got is a loose idea that they are related because the weapon appears to be the same."

"It is the same; it's a three-foot, deftly balanced katana," replied Josh. "It must be incredibly sharp because the cuts show that although pressure is aggressively applied, it is still slicing effectively and cleanly. At least four of these five cases are tied to that same sword. At least as far as my investigation shows. But I've shared all my conclusions and reasoning with the team; I'm sure they'll get this into an effective report soon."

"Didn't take you for a medieval sword master, Josh," chuckled Ellie.

Josh shrugged, "It's a side hobby. You guys should check out the Renaissance Faire this year; we always need volunteers."

The meeting had been going on for the last several hours, and not much was getting accomplished. They broke it up, and each went off to their desks to start combing through a mountain of files. They were all dedicated to 'The Ashen Horse Case,' as it had begun appearing officially in memos. But they all still had other casework they hadn't finished or put aside yet, which clocked up at least a third of their week. The Ashen Horse Case was rapidly turning into weeks. On the positive side, since they were all dedicated to a single case now, it did allow them to close out all the paperwork on the previous cases slowly. The team universally agreed that they were getting more caught up on their past paperwork than they had in months if not years.

Ellie walked over to Tim's desk with a file in hand. "Tim, you might want to look at this. It looks like they think they might have gotten a photo of Ash."

"What? How is this the first we have heard of this? How was it possible that after two weeks, we are just getting this now?"

"Calm down, we just got it earlier today. Besides, it doesn't show anything at all. Just a cloaked figure in black; there is nothing to go on here. Weird clothes, though. I mean, we joked about ninjas, but these clothes are strange. This image is grainy as hell and doesn't show us much. Captured from either an ATM or street cam, I can't even get those details yet."

"Let's see it, Ellie," Tim said as Ellie handed over the image. Tim looked at the glossy print with a critical eye. "Huh, it is grainy, this would barely hold up in...."

The phone on Tim's desk interrupted him. That was odd; everyone he knew always called him on his cell. "Well, son-of-a-goat, if they are calling my desk, it must be official." Tim knew he better take the call. "Hang on, Ellie."

Glancing at the door, just making sure it was still where she had left it, Ellie estimated her time to exit the room. Then she stared at him on the phone, waiting. In these situations, there is nothing to do but stare, wait, and fidget.

Tim said, "Yes, sir," at least twice. Apparently, he was talking to one of his superiors. It sounded a bit serious; this was all business. Tim wasn't giving any details, so the information must be getting funneled only one way. The senior people always wanted and asked for progress, and it was bizarre that this conversation was all one-sided.

"Yes, sir. Thank you, sir. We'll make arrangements; we'll be in touch." Tim finished the call with a last "thank you" and set down the receiver.

"Anything up?" asked Ellie.

"Yeah. Atlanta. All three of us are booking tickets to Atlanta. There's been another murder, and they suspect it's the same killer."

"Tim, you need to start calling him by his name. The Ashen Horse, Ashen, or Ash. 'Killer' just doesn't have the same ring to it."

Tim's face was entirely blank as he looked at her. "You know I was supposed to be on vacation for the last two weeks? You know that, right?"

Ellie laughed, "Boss, we really need to get you a girlfriend. Someone needs to work this tension out of you."

"You're probably right." He sighed. "Look, we leave tomorrow morning, let's all take the rest of the day to get ready. I'll see you all at the gate tomorrow."

Chapter Four

The Path to Atlanta

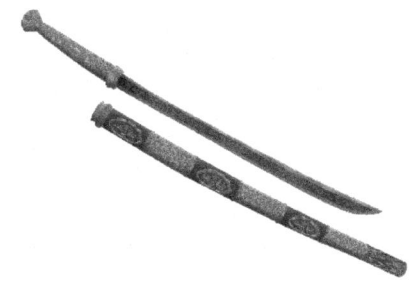

She had flown into Atlanta last week. The week had been bursting with continuous scouting and patrolling. It felt good to be working again after taking several weeks off after the events in Salt Lake City. She had accepted this contract eagerly. It was honestly a sad tale, a religious leader who had been reported to fondle young children. She took her art seriously and never wanted to belittle it too greatly, but now and then, she did take pride in her work. This job would be a masterpiece.

The contract had come in from several victims who had pooled their money. A nice hundred thousand dollars were sitting in an account she would be given access to as soon as the job was confirmed complete. The clients were skittish, which was common in this underworld. However, these clients demanded proof before the account would be turned over, which meant pictures. It was not her style, but the client got what they wanted.

It would be nice if it weren't the typical Catholic priest, but alas it was. He wasn't a priest anymore; he had risen to the prominent position of bishop. It was rumored that the Church fully knew about or suspected his previous deeds, and the promotion was a way to move him out of direct services. She didn't understand those politics. It seemed to her that they should have been proactive the other way around if the Church suspected. But then, the world didn't make sense most of the time. The fact that the Church ignored the situation opened plenty of opportunity for her.

She was unusually excited about this project. The opportunity was just too much to hope for. Ridding the world of someone despicable was not always enjoyable work. But she was going to take great pleasure in this task. There was a moment in there where her conscience moved her to think that it might not be right and that perhaps she was as unbalanced as so many of her victims. But still, she couldn't help but smile as she sat across the street in a coffee shop, watching the Catholic Shrine of the Immaculate Conception. The small deli wasn't anything special, but it did provide a rather sweeping view of the entrance to the cathedral.

When she first accepted the contract, she got the notion that it would be incredibly fitting to do the work inside one of the churches the bishop frequented. She had become a little obsessed with completing it that way. What would be better than doing her tasks at one of the most impeccable Church locations? A premier cathedral in the area. The opportunity seemed too fitting to let it go. She acknowledged that it was foolish and not worth the risk but wanted to do it anyway.

Thus, she silently sipped her coffee, smiling wider than she had in quite some time. It wouldn't have been proper to say she was as giddy as a schoolgirl, although it might be accurate. She had spent two weeks carefully plotting out his movements; tonight was the night. He would be arriving in several hours. She just had enough time to thoroughly soak in the pure aroma of the coffee and let it coat her soul to a state of complete bliss. She took her coffee seriously; it was a nearly spiritual experience.

She was already fully equipped for the night's events. Unfortunately, she couldn't walk around Atlanta with a katana on her back. Unfortunately, she wasn't carrying her blade; this job demanded a sword. But she was always pragmatic about the task at hand. This slime wasn't worth getting caught over, and he wasn't worth taking unnecessary risks. She had carefully taken many precautions. She probably had cameras recording her right now, and because of that, she made sure she was wearing one of her disguises.

The disguise consisted of a long black wig with gorgeous flowing locks. A golden necklace set with a ruby in the center, just enough to distract the observer from taking a good look at the rest of her. She also drew attention away from her by exposing a fair amount of cleavage, propped up by the world's most outstanding sports bra. She had spent two hours on the makeup, reconstructing her face so it nearly wasn't hers. She now had contoured cheekbones, vibrant eyes, and a flawlessly bridged nose. She was naturally beautiful, but with the proper makeup, she became a beautifully different person.

She had knives scattered about her person, an everyday occurrence for this type of night. A long fur cloak sheltered her armed attire nicely. The fur also acted as a minor distraction for people. It wasn't the typical flamboyant fur coat, but it was just a tad over subtle. Enough to catch the eye and then cause the person to disregard whoever was wearing it. The perfect disguise. Just some elitist snob drinking her coffee, nothing more. Although she was a coffee snob, perhaps they were half right. She was carrying a large dagger; it was almost a sword breaker. As large of a weapon as she dared to hide beneath the cloak.

She paid as she exited. She would have loved to leave an excessive tip as the service had been wonderful. But she did nothing to bring attention or remembrance, so it was the standard twenty percent. Forgettable was the goal. She walked to the cathedral and wandered into one of the seats in the middle of the sanctuary. Not in the back, not in the front, slightly in the middle, off to the side. Completely inconspicuous. There were several people in the church waiting for confession. She sat enough behind them so that they didn't see her.

As the sanctuary emptied, she slipped into one of the empty confessionals. Sticking a tiny hidden camera outside the confessional with a wide-angle lens. She flipped open her smartphone and watched the entire sanctuary. She considered this cheating; it made it almost too easy. But using some of the latest technology made the work more dexterous and safer.

She had one other little piece of gear she planned to use tonight. She had attached a small explosive to the power box outside the cathedral where the main power feed came into the building. A cell phone connected to the explosive would set it off. She had attached it to the wall to make it look like any other nondescript electrical box. If someone was standing next to it, they might be in danger, but the electrical connections were tucked into the alley, so it wouldn't do severe damage. It was just enough bang to take out the power to the building. A simple phone call should pitch the cathedral into blackness and, equally, hopefully, take out any cameras and security footage.

Simple plans. She had learned that simple plans usually paid the highest dividends in the long run. Nothing fanciful, just predictable outcomes. This wasn't some flashy Hollywood-style movie. This was just simple, detailed planning executed well. The plan, unfortunately, involved her waiting for the next two hours for the bishop to arrive. She was still smiling when he walked in the front doors. It was all she could do to contain the chuckle that wanted to escape her lips. She was as giddy as a schoolgirl. This truly was going to be glorious.

She was surprised when two other priests entered right behind him. She let out a mental sigh; she was never one who enjoyed the collateral damage. But she also wasn't going to miss this opportunity either. This last week, she had spent too much time carefully scouting his routes and patterns. She was also running out of time; tonight was the night, even now. Besides, they probably knew the type of man he was, right? Maybe they were guilty as well. They probably were. The smile slowly crept back across her face. Perhaps this wasn't an unfortunate event but rather an opportunity.

Still, she would give it a minute to see if they were with him or just arrived simultaneously. They may break off and go about their own business. That might also be dangerous because that risked them coming back in or asking questions when the power went out. Even so, she hated encountering anyone she perceived as a potential innocent. There was a reason she took the contracts she took; they were all guilty of significant crimes or causes, so people were willing to pay extensive sums of money to rid the world of them. No one spent a hundred thousand dollars to get rid of someone that they didn't really want to die.

The men stopped in the middle of the sanctuary and took seats in different rows in a mini circle. They were quietly conversing. She waited. Perhaps the two priests would depart. She didn't want to rush this, but she knew her hand would be forced if all three of them got up together.

A tedious hour passed as they quietly talked. She had considered that she should have put some listening devices in the sanctuary. Then again, she might capture an hour-long conversation about weather and football. Perhaps it was better that she couldn't hear them.

It happened too quickly, as it always does. All three of them abruptly stood up and shook hands, and then, as one, they turned and started for the door. She was almost caught off guard, but five seconds later, she placed a call to her manufactured explosive. A deep rumble echoed through the sanctuary. Wonder of wonder, the bomb worked as planned, and the entire church went dark. Her eyes adjusted quickly, as she had been sitting in darkness for the last four hours; even her camera watching on her smartphone had been dimmed to lessen the impact on her night vision.

She flew out of the confessional. Three blades left her fingers the minute she had cleared the cloth hanging over her hiding place. The two men in front screamed as the throwing blades pierced them.

She sprung onto the pews in a dead run with three more throwing knives gliding away from her. She had time to launch one last knife as she approached them. The dagger was out of its sheaf as she jumped off the pew and crashed into the priest, who was unfortunate to be in the rear.

He had just enough time to turn his head and look at her before the dagger went right through his left eye and into the back of his head. No scream would ever leave his mouth. Perhaps he was aware of what happened, or maybe his brain never fully registered what exactly had occurred before everything went mercifully black.

The priest and her crashed to the floor. She flung herself off his collapsing body and landed on her feet in a crouch with too much speed, causing her to roll and spring back onto her feet in a flying run. Her rise brought her up right next to the adjacent pews, and pushing off them with one leg, she propelled herself at the other two men.

The other priest, scrambling to get a blade out of his side, had watched what she had done to his comrade, and as soon as he saw she was coming for him, he instantly was in a full sprint toward the entrance. Another throwing knife went right into the back of the knee as she charged. His leg unwillingly buckled when the blade hit, and he went sprawling across the stone floor. He never looked back, but he made it up to his knees, still trying to run when the blade went into the back of his neck. His spinal cord was cut; the paralysis dropped him onto the cold floor. He couldn't even feel the three more quick stabs that went into both his lungs.

The last man, the filthy child molester, as she thought of him, was on his knees, desperately trying to reach the knives stuck in his back. No matter how he twisted his arms around and tried to grasp at them, he couldn't reach them. Perhaps

The Ashen Horse

with a little more exercise and a little less gut, he might have made it there, but there was no amount of exercise in the next two minutes that would allow him to reach the knives protruding out of his back.

As she turned from the second priest toward him, the bishop stopped trying to get the blades out of his back. He had gone a ghostly white, and although the throwing knives protruding from his back were quite a bit more than an annoyance, his thoughts were not on the pain. He looked ghastly like he had already been dead for days.

"What are you? What are you doing here? Why?" He quivered as the words came out.

"It is your fault they had to die," she said, gesturing to the two priests that lay on the ground. "I wasn't here for them. Only for you." She looked at the bishop, the contempt rolling off her in waves.

"There are several children that you might know. They all wanted me to say hello. Hello, Charley." She did laugh now. It was just a quick chuckle. Perhaps it was because she was enjoying herself too much. Maybe it was because she noticed the urine flowing down the front of his suit pants. It seemed fitting to her that he should die the coward he was.

As she casually walked toward him, three more blades gracefully sailed into his chest. To his credit, he didn't try to run; he just stared at her. It was like he couldn't accept the reality of the situation. Or perhaps he was immobilized with utter fear. The amount of fear that completely exhausts a man. She didn't know what he was experiencing. But she looked him right in the eye as she swung the long dagger with all her might.

She sighed with frustration. It didn't do the clean work the katana would have done. She had to hack a bit to get the head off. It wasn't her typical clean work, but it got the job done. With all three bodies gracing the cold stone floor, she wasted no time completing her tasks. She returned to the two peppered with throwing knives and recovered all the blades. Cleaning the blood carefully on the clothes of the fallen priests. She left the body of the priests alone, only taking care to make sure everything was recovered. The bishop was not so fortunate as she carved a large X across his chest with the dagger. It was another pointless mark, but it somehow felt right. She was crossing this man off the list in the most literal way. He would never come near a child again.

After carving the X, she placed the head right in the center. It seemed appropriate. The X, it appeared, indeed did mark the spot.

She walked over to where she had left the camera, still stuck covertly outside the confessional. She pocketed it and carefully slipped out a side door into the back alley. Staying away from any cameras, she meandered through back alleys to where she had parked many blocks away.

She drove away carefully.

She stopped in the middle of an abandoned parking lot on a deserted side of the town and selected a couple of options on her smartphone. This started transferring the encrypted video from an unknown account to another unknown account. She waited for the transfer to complete and then popped out the burner SIM card, crushed it with the blunt end of her dagger, and threw it outside her window in the abandoned lot.

She pulled out of the desolate area and started driving to her hotel. The task at hand was completed, and she was now really looking forward to a bath, a glass of wine, candles, and perhaps a good book.

Chapter Five

The Fibbies in Atlanta

The landing in ATL was slick, like glancing on ice. Tim was so impressed that he almost clapped. He didn't travel much but traveled just enough to appreciate the pilot's skill. "Check off flying expertise for this guy," Tim thought. He caught up with the rest of his team at baggage claim.

"I can't believe you are still checking luggage, Josh," Ellie remarked as they stood and waited. "How are you not taking carry-on for everything? We are now just sitting here waiting."

"Equipment, Ellie. Equipment. I can't carry on the good stuff. I got strip-searched after trying it the last time. The TSA didn't even consider the FBI credentials. You would think that would count for something, but no, they went right to probing." Josh didn't finish his tirade before Ellie burst out laughing.

"You laugh all you want," Josh said defensively. "The luggage gets checked." Under his breath, Josh muttered, "Bloody TSA agents."

Tim chortled at the discourse. "I'm good with it; it lets me catch up on emails while we wait. You can grab the car if you want to speed up the process, Ellie. We can catch up with you."

Ellie, already on her phone, made no move to speed up

the process of exiting the airport. "You guys reading this?" she asked and looked around; all three stared at their phones. Additional information had come in overnight or while on the early morning flight. Based on the glazed-over looks, they were all sucked into the same email.

Tim spoke up. "They are throwing knives. The Atlanta police put it together. That's what the small blade wounds are. We should have seen that. The killer took off the bishop's head. This guy is brutal, who takes the time to...." He didn't finish the words, and Tim looked a little greenish under the collar. He swallowed and shook his head; all he could mutter was "sheesh" as he kept reading the details.

The checked equipment had gone around the carousel twice while they read the email. Finally looking up from his smartphone, Josh grabbed the two pieces of luggage containing the specialized equipment he wanted to use to collect evidence at the scene.

Ellie couldn't resist yet another jab. "You know the Atlanta FBI office or the Atlanta police will have all that, right?" Josh's flat stare was proof that he hadn't considered it or wouldn't admit it one way or another. Perhaps he didn't care, but he had his own personal department equipment to gather evidence either way.

"Let's get to the scene, guys. It looks like they are holding it all for us," Tim commanded. "The Cathedral personnel are getting a little cagey about it. That can't look good in the news or within the Catholic Church's internal organization. People have to be going crazy right now."

They quickly got the rental car, piled everything in, and drove out of the Atlanta airport on their way to the Catholic Shrine of the Immaculate Conception.

"Are we going to grab food on the way? I'm starving." To accent his words, Josh's stomach grumbled. "You see."

"Well, we wouldn't want your stomach upset at us, would we?" Tim commented. "But it'll have to be drive-thru; we need to get to the scene."

The Ashen Horse

They arrived at the cathedral shortly after, Josh still stuffing burritos into his face at an alarming rate. He didn't mind that it was drive-thru after all.

"It is somewhat spooky that you can eat like that and not gain weight or just die or something. Where does it go? How are you able to move after eating that much?"

"It's a skill, Ellie, a skill. A rare talent of exceptionalism. I possess it; everyone else envies it."

"It's something, that's for sure."

An Atlanta official was heading for their car. He could have been a detective, maybe a lieutenant; it wasn't entirely obvious. "You must be the FBI agents from Washington?" he inquired. A quick nod from Tim was all he needed. "Let's get right to it; let me explain what we have done already and what you should look at."

They all started walking toward the entrance as he explained what they had detailed at the scene. They had taken pictures of everything, completed initial medical examinations, and logged and marked all the evidence. They hadn't bagged anything yet, waiting for the now special agents on the national case to survey the scene first.

Josh posed the question, "I guess we are the special agents?"

"You've always been special, Josh." It was something Ellie would typically say, but it came from Tim this time.

"That cuts deep, boss. Deep."

Ellie probably would have come up with the same retort if she hadn't been distracted. She was diverted for the time being, and it looked like she was accounting for all the exits and entrances as she entered the building. If you didn't know her well, you probably wouldn't realize that is what she was doing. Still, as she walked into the building, she surveyed the entire scene quickly and calculated all the available paths to vacate or at least possible exit points. It was always unnerving, her focus as they moved through structures. Tim wondered how she would handle herself in tight spaces.

What would she do if there weren't readily available exits?

Their guide, who turned out to be an Atlanta FBI agent named Thomas, pointed to the bishop on the ground. "This is the bishop. He was the target. As far as we can tell, the other two were in the wrong place at the wrong time." Thomas was not entirely pleased with being pulled into the whole debacle.

"How do you figure that?" noted Ellie.

"That wasn't in the report email we got when we landed," observed Tim.

"Yeah, not everything went into that. The killer left a letter on top of his body."

"He did what?!" Josh exclaimed.

"Yeah, we'll get into it, but suffice it to say there was a letter."

Thomas turned out to have better intel than they had received in quite some time on the case. He was carelessly munching on one of Josh's burritos. Josh, as it turned out, hadn't been able to finish them all after all. He had handed the bag off to several agents at the scene. Josh and Ellie approached the body and removed the white cloth covering it as Tim and Thomas continued the conversation.

"The team left the letter, too, huh? This is it?" Josh saw it near the feet of the victim.

"Yeah, that's it. We got detailed photos of it but thought we'd leave it. We covered the bodies with the sheets, though. Honestly, we didn't even want to do that, but we weren't sure about the reporters or news people in the area. Those vultures will swarm in like the black death; you never know when they'll try to get some footage or photos that they can plaster all over the internet or television."

"Your crime scene guys are going to bag everything, right?" Josh inquired.

"Yep. As soon as your team gives the thumbs up, they'll start picking up everything. The Church desperately wants us out of here. The Atlanta police dodged the entire thing by blaming us; the FBI always takes the hit for this kind of stuff." Thomas' face clearly showed the frustration of getting blamed for anything that happened in law enforcement.

"Can't blame them, though; they get to say that the FBI is doing the investigation, and their hands are tied. But my boss is now getting calls from senior members of the Catholic Church, which means I'm getting calls from him. This shit always flows downhill. Let's just say we are all looking to pack it up."

Tim chuckled, "Does that mean you get to blame us now? What could you do? You were waiting for the special team to arrive?"

Thomas smiled. "I see you know exactly how this works."

Josh laughed as Tim said, "Let's say I've also been on both sides of the game. We can take the hit. What were you to do, after all? The FBI was flying in a special elite team to survey the scene, and you had to maintain integrity."

"You guys are the elite team?"

Josh laughed at that. He couldn't resist joking, "I tell myself every morning as I look in the mirror that I'm elite." He continued chuckling, saying, "We'll take the title elite, but really, we are just the special agents who weren't drowning entirely in case logs, so we got snapped up for this special outfit. Ask us in three months how special and elite we are."

Ellie couldn't resist this time. "They are all looking to pack up and to think we have a trunk full of equipment." Josh's chuckling cut off quickly, and he swiveled his head to give Ellie his best blank stare ever. He, at least, was still confident that bringing the equipment had been a grand idea.

Tim interjected, "What's the letter, guys, given it's the evidence we think makes the bishop the target?"

Thomas explained the letter.

"It's an affidavit, signed in court. Apparently, 'unnamed children' had reported sexual abuse to the police against the bishop when he was still a priest. It's an affidavit, and it looks like the children or their guardians, all unnamed specifically here, got it officially signed and sworn and reported in court. The police and the Church didn't do anything about it. We did some research, and it appears he got promoted from priest to bishop shortly after the incident."

Tim whistled, "Well. That changes things. I understand the sheets now. We can't have that information leak to the press."

Ellie commented while looking at the front entrance, "They'll sleuth it out anyway. There's probably a reporter who already knew or knows about his history. It'll be a story."

"Only if they connect the dots," commented Josh. "No one knows Ash's motives here but us on this one. We might keep it out of the press if no one talks about or mentions this affidavit. The press can know that we suspect Ash is the killer, but not his motives. Or at least what we obviously perceive his motives to be."

"Given the letter, I think it isn't perception," commented Thomas. "This dude was killed because someone thought he was a child molester. If it's Ash, then okay, but the perpetrator went for this guy specifically because he abused children."

It was apparent Thomas didn't have any sympathy for the bishop. The team felt that he almost wished he had been the one to slice and dice.

Ellie was looking him up and down. She casually asked, "I don't suppose we should ask you where you were last night?"

Thomas laughed, "Oh, I have a rock-solid alibi with half the city seeing me last night at the local pub. I don't like this man; I'll give you that. Honestly, I've been in this job a long time; this is one of those cases where I think if the facts got lost and the case just got closed, it wouldn't be so bad. Sucks maybe for the other two guys, but this bishop, if anything, he got off too easy."

The Ashen Horse

"You know," Tim called as he approached one of the priests who had been contorted oddly on the ground, "this does match the other killings in that sense."

"How's that, boss?"

"They all appear to be dodgy individuals. Every one of them has something dark in their past. Criminal activity, lurid behavior, angry or cheated business partners, and now apparently a suspected child molester. What's with this body? Why is it twisted? Did you guys move it?"

"Nope, found it like that," said Thomas.

"It looks all contorted. The killer rolled it over, maybe, half-rolled it. Why?"

Josh and Ellie looked at Tim and then at the contorted body. Then they looked at each other. Josh shrugged and went back to studying the bishop. Ellie kept looking at Tim as Tim stared at the body. His eyes twinkled as he thought, his mind churning on the strange puzzle. Ellie started walking over towards Tim to stare at the body closer.

"Knives," Ellie whispered. Tim was startled as he found Ellie standing directly over him. She continued, "The killer recovered knives. Look at the tears in the clothes," she said as she gestured to how the body was contorted just to where the clothing was mangled and was accessible."

Ellie kept staring at the body, and then she went on. "Throwing knives. It must be. That's why the body had to be moved. The blades had to be recovered. The killer has always recovered the blades, which is why we never connected that they were throwing knives. The body was partially rolled over to get to the blades. I don't necessarily see the wounds right now, but we'll find wounds in his back."

Tim didn't need any more cues than that. He pushed the body further over, so it flopped onto its stomach. He stretched out the clothing as best he could.

Ellie pointed, "Yeah, look at that tear in the jacket; that's blood. Ashen dropped him on his back and then had to partially roll him over to get the knives. This also means Ash probably killed him from the front, and he fell backward, then later rolled him over. Looks like efficient work, no energy wasted here."

Still examining the bishop, Josh noted, "There was energy invested here, though. And this isn't the work of the katana." His face went a little green, examining the stump of the neck. "This is spine-tingling." He waited a second for a response. It didn't come. "And that was a good pun. Wasted, apparently." He shook his head slowly and mumbled under his breath, "It's always a shame when a good pun goes to waste." More loudly, he went on, "This is morbid though. His head was, well, might not be hacked off, but, well… Ugh." He audibly swallowed and paused a second. Retaking control, he continued, "Look, it was a different blade used; it didn't sever the head clean as the katana would have. Okay?"

Tim was walking to the third and last body. "Got it, Josh; take a minute, man. Maybe don't keep staring at that." All four of them descended on the third body. "This body looks barely marked."

Licking his fingers after finishing the burrito, Thomas said, "Yep. Granted, we haven't done full medical examinations, but the only mark on this one that we could initially detect is the wound in the face. If you will take a look, it appears that he took a blade directly in the eye."

Josh got a little paler watching Thomas smacking his lips, but Thomas seemed not to notice and continued, "Same blade if I had to guess. We can do detailed forensics on the wounds, but I'm guessing it's the same blade used on both of them. Let's make a note to make sure we get the forensic and medical teams to do that leg work."

Tim had got a good survey of the scene and was getting ready to do some deeper investigation. "So, Thomas. Anything else we really need to know?"

"Well, the only other thing is the bomb."

Josh blinked and looked at the man, "What?"

Tim nearly squawked, "Wait, the bomb?"

"Yeah, outside."

The three Washington agents looked at each other. That definitely wasn't in the morning email.

"All right. Josh, Ellie, you have this, right? Review it all; take a minute. Let's spend an hour trying to model what we think happened, the sequence of events, and order it up. We'll mock it up back at the lab and connect as many dots as possible. Thomas, are you sure your team has photos of everything?"

"Yep, one of the best guys in the business."

"Ellie, do a video anyway. Capture everything you can. Do a full walk-through on how everything is right now. We'll get it on a USB stick and put that in a file. It's after the fact, but it'll give us good context when we review it later with all the details. Let's lay it all out. Let's get to work here. That's it, guys; let's get to it."

Ellie and Josh went to the makeshift table set up by the Atlanta team and started talking and making notes. "Now Thomas," Tim said, "bomb?"

"Yeah, I better just show you. That's why the lighting is set up here the way it is; all the lights are out. I mean, the stained-glass lights this place up pretty good in the day, so we are seeing quite well right now, but last night, it would have been pitch black in here. The bomb cut the power entirely. Another thing the Church is complaining about. We wouldn't let the electrical company or the electricians get anywhere near it until we had a bomb expert go over the whole thing."

"All right, let's go take a look," Tim said, and they headed for the rear exit.

Ellie glanced up, checking off in her mind that the rear right door did in fact exit the cathedral. As Thomas and Tim exited the building, Josh was busy scribbling in a notebook.

Chapter Six

The Backwaters

The banker's body was completely lifeless. Her blood was slowly seeping into the ground. The grass appeared slightly dry and looked like it welcomed the steady flow of blood leaching into it. The assassin watched a flower that the banker had somehow missed when she collapsed. The flower appeared to open its leaves and petals as the blood oozed near it. She found it fascinating. She didn't know if she had ever taken the time to observe the like before.

The banker's eyes had glassed over, her hair a tangled mess, still not dry from the morning shower. She had made it easily predictable. The banker ran in the park every morning. To make it more delicious, she ran at dawn in the morning, when the light was still deceptive. It flickered and wavered, hiding the world in shadow and mist. It was the perfect time of day for a run when everything felt fresh and the ideal time for killing.

And now, the banker lay slain. Her killer stood looking at her, a slight twinkle in her eye. She wasn't sure anymore if she should get out of this line of work or continue. She was starting to enjoy it too much. That couldn't be healthy, could it? This one had been straightforward. The poor woman didn't even see it. She just stepped up and swiped the dagger cleanly into her neck. She collapsed where she lay, slowly pooling blood into the dusty ground.

The assassin stood, carefully posed, just watching the scene. She had on a lustrous red wig and wore a matching highlighted and accented red leather outfit. The outfit looked mythical, which she usually might not have done; an outfit like this people might remember. But it seemed so fitting for the event; the woman should have this grandeur in her end. There are few cameras out here, if any, but it is in a rural park, and she wasn't taking any chances. The buttoned partial cloak finished the ensemble to perfection. Even if someone remembered the outfit, they'd never remember the face, which was always cloaked and shadowed—the perfect mystery.

She sighed; the good times never did last. For all her flamboyance, she had carefully executed this activity in a manner that hopefully didn't trace back to the Ashen Horse. She chuckled a bit as she thought about that. The stupid FBI chasing all the wrong leads was marvelous. Although the banker she had killed was undoubtedly deserving of the wrath of 'Ashen,' as the papers had taken to calling her, she still wanted to keep this one low-key and off the FBI's radar. She almost used a gun because of it, but still, she couldn't bring herself to do it without dire need, so a different short-bladed dagger had been her entirely efficient solution.

She hummed a Christmas tune as she slowly and carefully exited the park, returning to her hotel. The banker had made loans to some very unsavory characters, and those unsavory characters weren't happy at the end of the day. It was not as noble as her standard initiatives, but a girl still had to get paid. She also knew, however, after her quick investigation, that there was a lot more that Alicia Wetherson had done as a Lead CPA of Smith's Bank. If she wasn't directly skimming herself, she was helping quite a few others. And it was evident how many direct cash clients she had; she was laundering money for several other suspicious characters. She was probably laundering money for the very people who killed her.

She laughed out loud at that. She imagined, "I bet they didn't even consider that they were killing their launder." She chuckled as she thought, "Probably didn't even cross their minds." These criminals always made the most basic mistakes. And she always made money off it.

She had fired up her rental car, a brand-new Charger with virtually no miles on it, and was crossing the main intersection when she heard her banking app ding on her phone. Payment received. It was a good job complete. The world was rid of one more elitist snob who was swindling others, even if the others she was swindling were criminals themselves.

She was almost back to the hotel when she saw the small coffee shop. It had a drive-thru, a perfect opportunity. Nothing went better with murder than a white chocolate mocha.

She sipped the holy beverage slowly, eyes closed, pulling in the deliciousness. There was always a slow, glorious moment when that magical beverage first touched the soul. She circled the drive-thru and was again driving towards the hotel.

She parked inconspicuously in the rear of the parking lot. Before going through the drive-thru, she removed part of her outfit and tucked it into her practical satchel. She pulled a very professional, full-length leather jacket over her clothes. She would walk in the front door looking like any other professional businesswoman. Her red wig changed out for a black one. Nothing to see here but a woman who ran out in the morning to grab herself a hot cup of coffee, now returning for a day of long meetings.

Of particular interest was the hotel hosting a series of talks on philanthropic missions in Sudan, which was naturally her reason for being in the city. There was a significant push in the area to revamp local communities and refocus government influence within the region. As it happened, she

The Ashen Horse

had come into some money recently, about an hour ago, actually. She thought she could invest in the program.

There were several key villages in Southern Sudan the talks were supposed to touch on, and the investment was targeted to rebuild the communities from the inside out. She was positive she would hear something about 'give a man a fish, feed him for a day, teach a man to fish....' She almost always heard that cliché. Yet she honestly looked forward to the presentation. Just because it was a cliché didn't mean the cliché was inaccurate.

After the meetings were complete and she had signed a substantial check donating to the program, she returned to her room. She had ordered delivery and was waiting for it to arrive when she flipped on the news. The local news was reporting that a prominent banker had been found dead in the park. She casually listened to the reporter go on at length about the crime but noted that there was no mention of the Ashen Horse. She smiled; at least the police hadn't connected those dots yet. Hopefully, they never would.

She was turning in early tonight; the morning came early when you had to catch a 6 am flight. That happened when she traveled to the middle of nowhere, exclusively 6 am flights. All the small regional airports had to leave at ungodly hours to make it to the hubs for flights at more civilized times. This backwoods city was definitely a 6am flight kind of place. Charming, though, in its own way.

She almost wished she was flying somewhere she could consider home, but she was headed to Miami instead. She had been waiting for months for another truly big score, and this was it. Of course, it involved some insane risks that she still wasn't sure she wanted to tackle.

It was another cliché tale; a prominent drug dealer had angered other drug dealers, and naturally, they wanted the first drug dealer taken out. A smooth million for the job. She had wondered to herself how badly you had to piss someone off for them to pay a million dollars to kill you.

That level of outrage must really be something. But a million dollars was a million dollars; she had accepted that contract immediately.

She probably had accepted it too soon. The devil was always in the details. After accepting, she learned some critical details that weren't in the offer's fine print. The offer was as large as it was because the drug dealer lived in a fortified compound, with armed guards posted twenty-four-seven. Invading the compound, killing or eluding the guards, and killing her primary target, all while living to tell the story was going to be quite the undertaking.

Of course, she would never tell the story, but that was beside the point. Coming out alive was very much part of her plan, though. A million dollars did nobody any good if they weren't alive to spend it. And she wanted to spend it.

She had booked a long-term vacation rental on the beach in Miami. She was planning to take a month to figure this one out. There was no rushing this type of thing. She needed to find out how to get in, get out, and not raise suspicion. She had started putting the plans together, churning ideas, swirling them about, and testing them.

But she had no idea how she would sneak in and out of a well-fortified compound. She was good, but she wasn't suicidal, and she didn't want to take any careless risks. She had stayed alive and out of prison by making careful and calculated moves. Her mind was still bouncing around ideas as she fell asleep that night.

The pesky alarm went off at 3:30 am. She almost put a blade right through it but thought better of it. It didn't help that the alarm was her smartphone, which she didn't want to destroy. But, at 3:30 am, she really did want to destroy it utterly.

At 5 am, she sat at the gate, coffee in hand. A quick shower out of the way, rental car gassed up and returned, checked in and through security, coffee, and now patiently waiting for boarding. Perfect timing. Her expertise in flying was governed by years of practice, much like her other skills. Mastery of her craft took time and precision, similar to how she skillfully navigated the airport bureaucracy. It was as much a matter of patience as it was of skill and equally a matter of understanding the system and its workings as it was about raw talent. Precision, training, craft work, and the willingness to put in the effort all governed where she was today.

She pulled out a book and started to read while she waited for the flight to board. The best time to get quality reading was while waiting in airports; it was where she accomplished most of her reading. She was zoned out for forty minutes until the PA system announced boarding.

It was several airports later when she finally landed in Miami. But she rinsed and repeated the usual scenario of grabbing her rental car and heading for her vacation rental.

After getting situated, she started reading, studying, and evaluating. She had a million dollars to pursue. And there was no way she wouldn't make good on this arrangement.

Chapter Seven

Fibbie Conference

Tim was sweating profusely as he waited for his turn to enter the imposing room. It wasn't often he got called from the depths of his office to report to the senior leadership; it wasn't just one department this time; it was two of them. That was enough to make anyone start sweating bullets. He was sure he could wring out his shirt right now; this was no way to stand before people.

He shouldn't be this nervous; they were making progress. The bomb was a clear signature that they traced through various databases and tried to link to other crimes. So far, it had turned up empty, but they still had quite a few databases to grind through. They also had found at least three more unsolved murders and one solved murder that they thought they could attribute to Ash. Tim scowled as he thought, "Bloody hell, they've even got me calling him Ash now."

Of course, that was a bigger problem, finding a murder that was previously considered solved but now seemed to be the work of Ash. Ash was surprisingly cryptic in his attacks. The political drama of the legal system wouldn't sit well with a whole army of people if his team tried to reopen a solved case. Tim knew he should have never sent that memo. What a disaster. It was a mistake of epic proportions.

He sat, sopping in his sweat. Waiting for the Director of

the Criminal Investigative Division and the Director of the Critical Incident Response Group, hoping he wasn't about to get fired. Well, he didn't think he was going to get fired. But the absolute shitstorm that was going to descend on his team was going to be legendary. The amount of manure he was going to be swimming through for the next month was going to be unbearable.

Why did it feel like he was waiting to go into the principal's office? Oh, because he was. A timid secretary stuck his head into the hallway and said, "They are ready to see you now, Mr. Buckhem."

"Burkman."

"Oh, sorry, sir. Mr. Burkman, they are waiting for you in the conference room down the hall. There should still be refreshments from the earlier meeting, so help yourself."

He started down the hallway, muttering, "Something tells me it won't be the kind of meeting for refreshments."

Tim walked into the conference room to the flat stares of eight men. It was worse than he'd thought; of course, they would bring their army of minions. Naturally, the only seat still open was at the head of the table. He walked to it and slowly started to sit down, all sixteen eyes silently judging. This was a special kind of torture. He was too old for the politics.

Then his nose caught a whiff of something. Was that what he thought it was? He sniffed deliberately, a full nasal inhale. He probably looked ridiculous with the sudden inhale, but he was past the point of really thinking about decorum. He thought to himself, "Oh my." That was definitely a double-glazed bear claw saturated in lightly toasted almonds from Nino's Bakery.

He was half seated, but he carefully rose and checked that all sixteen eyes were swiveling with his motion. He walked around the back of the conference room to the tray with the delicious goodness. He might as well go down with glory if he got throttled. He grabbed one of the marvelous bear claws on a napkin and turned around to follow the instinct for decorum that wanted him to return to his seat. But his thoughts told him to screw it; no bear claw is complete without coffee. He poured a paper cup from the back table and grabbed another claw in his napkin as he returned to his chair.

Finally sitting down, one cup of coffee and a half bear claws later, he looked around the table at the men staring at him. His tongue cleaning the glaze off his upper lip was perhaps over the top, but it was too tasty to let it alone.

It seemed appropriate to make them wait the two minutes it took him to get situated. He had been waiting twenty minutes in the hallway. Plus, a professional never turned down an opportunity to eat pastries from Nino's Bakery. It bordered on blasphemy to do so; they couldn't fault him for following the code.

"Thanks for making the trip in today, Tim. Sorry for the delay; one of the other cases we discussed ran longer than we thought it would." That was Mike Thompsan, Director of the Critical Incident Response Group. "You've probably heard about the explosion that happened in San Diego. It was a suspected terrorist plot originally. But now we aren't sure it wasn't some guy that blew up his garage. The paperwork, though, is endless." He had been in the job for years, steadily making his way to the Director level. By all accounts, he was wicked good at his job—a real slayer. In his late fifties, he had seen and done it all.

"Yeah, I caught it on the news this morning. It's all they were talking about, on an endless loop, of course, typical, you know," Tim said between bites of bear claw.

"Isn't that the truth," commented Darnell Johnson, Director of the Criminal Investigative Division. "Every time I turn on the news anymore, I swear I'm watching something on repeat."

"We will get right to it, Tim," Darnell continued. "Why we asked you here. Although it probably isn't much of a surprise to you at this point, the memo caused a bit of a stir. Do you really think the Kristen Smith case is tied to the Ashen Horse?"

"First, my apologies to the group," Tim began. "We didn't think about the political fallout when we uncovered the evidence that strongly suggested that Ash...." Tim paused mid-sentence when he realized he had done it again. He was going to call him Ash from now on. His team was corrupting him. When did that happen? He blinked a couple of times, realizing he had totally lost his train of thought.

"Uh, yes. The evidence suggested that the Ashen Horse was the killer. My team, myself included, didn't consider at all the politics of the situation. But suffice it to say that we have clear evidence that he killed her. Ash almost certainly did it." He took another bite; this bear claw was divine—a fitting last meal. If you were going down with the ship, you might as well enjoy it.

"You obviously know, Tim, that her husband is serving twenty to life in a federal maximum-security prison for her murder?"

They caught him in the middle of a coffee slurp. Of course, he was the only one eating at the table, which didn't seem fair to him; one of these guys had to want to get in on these pastries. "Yeah, also aware of that," he said between bites.

Mike had been letting Darnell lead with the questions, but it was apparent he was the more irritated of the two, and he piped up finally. "What's the evidence you got that the Ashen Horse is involved?" Tim was expecting this; they would go for the jugular.

"He kills with a sword more often than not. If it isn't a sword, then it's likely a dagger. To immobilize his victims or purely for fun; we can't always tell. He also uses throwing knives. These knives kept us off track for quite a while, but we have finally identified that they are throwing knives. Our medical examiners and forensic teams have identified three precise weapons. Well, four, the throwing knives being one."

One of the lackeys finally broke down, pushed his chair back, and headed for the donuts. Of course, Tim didn't know everyone in the room. This guy could be another director for all he knew. He needed to continue to keep it somewhat professional. Although he realized crumbs were probably smeared on his face.

Mike prodded, "And the other three?"

"Sword and daggers. But very specific ones. The sword is a katana. Based on various victims, we have fairly well-identified the weapon. If we find the sword, we can pinpoint it as the murder weapon in over ten actual killings now." He paused for a moment. "One of which is Kristen Smith. And then two specific daggers. One is, well, one of my team members put it as a medieval dagger, something called an anelace. For practicality, let's call that the long dagger." He felt foolish dropping the tidbit of trivia on them. But Josh had been adamant that he should use the proper terminology. "The other one is unique, called a janbīyah, or more simply a jamb. It's an Arabic type of dagger with a short-curved blade. For our purpose of discussion, it's the short dagger." Again, the trivia. He might as well show them they had been doing their due diligence, though; it couldn't hurt at this point.

"A sword, a short dagger, and a long dagger?" The lackey spoke as he poured coffee in the back of the room.

"That's correct. Plus, the throwing knives. They are also shortish, probably about five to eight inches in length, two inches at their thickest point. We know they are bladed on both sides and potentially bladed on both ends. We aren't sure on that part yet."

Darnell brought the conversation full circle. "And you are sure a katana killed Kristen Smith?"

"Murders with swords are rare enough. And Kristen was killed with a sword. Most people don't own swords. Her husband swore they had never owned one. My medical examiner reviewed the autopsy of Kristen, and she is ready to sign an affidavit that the sword was curved, like a katana. She also compared it to the other victims we believe he is responsible for, and they all align."

Silence hung over the room for a couple of seconds. Tim took a sip of coffee. It was apparent they were going to make him continue. He wanted to be out of this; he didn't want to get into the other details they had uncovered.

It was Darnell to prod this time, "There's more, isn't there?"

"Yes, but I'd rather not get into the specifics."

That lit Mike up. "You don't have that luxury here, Tim. You wrote a memo saying a closed case has the murderer on the loose. That we have falsely incarcerated a man for the last five years. You spell it. You spell it all."

If Tim had ever felt small, he felt small at that moment. They were right, of course. Blast the politics. His team honestly didn't even think about it. They just noticed another sword victim whose wounds showed Ash's handiwork. Of course, there would be politics in sending the wrong person to prison. How did it never dawn on any of them?

Tim sighed, but there was nothing for it. "Ashen appears to be a vigilante of sorts. We aren't just doing forensics and medical investigations anymore on his victims." A couple of the minions appeared to start paying attention after that comment.

"We are doing deep psychological profiling on all his supposed victims now. Well, truth be told, we started doing it on Ash himself, but as we went along, we discovered there was value in pursuing it on the victims. There might be more value, honestly, in examining the victims' psychology profile than our murderer."

He shook his head and thought, "Went off the rails there. Man, keep it together." His mind blended briefly as he tried to get himself back on track. "Uhm. Right. Along with our psychological evaluations, we also conduct deep financial investigations. All the victims have… They have… I don't know how to say it. They have… similarities."

Mike Thompsan at least appeared to be less agitated now, but he wanted the real meat behind the arguments. "Keep going, Tim. What are the similarities?"

This truly was a special kind of agony. He looked down at his napkin on the table. Other than the wayward crumb, it lay desolate. The second bear claw had gone somewhere amid the conversation. Vanished, just like the Ashen Horse. He vaguely remembered eating it. He risked a glance at the back table. Maybe another? A man shouldn't be forced to fall on his sword on an empty stomach, should he?

Tim was stalling; he didn't want to say the obvious answer to the question. He also didn't want to call the kettle black. There was something dangerous in stating the obvious, which always seemed more dangerous the further you went up the corporate food chain. Tim sighed; there was nothing for it but to spill the beans.

"They are all pieces of shit, sir. I hate to put it that bluntly, but that's the bottom line. Everyone Ash kills appears to be mired in the underworld. We have no idea how he picks his victims. But we do have an idea of what the influencers are. Every victim has something very suspicious in their past. And by suspicious, I mean, well…." Tim paused again, trying to use the right words. "I wouldn't say they are all criminals; that's not exactly it." His mind clicked; he found the words he had been seeking for quite some time—finally, an epiphany.

"The words I've been looking for are ethics and morality. They aren't always criminals, but many of them are. But all of Ash's victims appear to be very immoral, or at the least unethical, if they aren't outright criminal." He nodded in satisfaction and took another glance at the back table. There were still maple bars back there.

The blond man spoke; Tim was reasonably sure he was a direct assistant to Mike, "Didn't your team claim Ash killed the bishop? Are you going to say the bishop was suspicious? Kristen Smith was Woman of the Year two years in a row, nominated more than that by several organizations. These are the pillars of suspicion, you claim?"

Tim wanted to know if it was possible for him to be anywhere else. Anywhere else at all? Anywhere but here?

"Yep. The bishop was a child molester or the closest thing to it. That little secret is kept closely under wraps by the Catholic Church. I'd greatly appreciate it if it didn't leave this room. I have enough problems with us internally and the FBI; I don't want to have to start dodging calls from the Church if it's all the same."

A man had a right to die with a full belly. This was his last meal anyway, right? He stood up and headed for the back of the conference room as he continued. "As for Kristen Smith. She was the CEO of Smith Brothers Chemicals. All of you must remember the legal problems they had fifteen years ago. Nearly a hundred were reported dead of cancer in France because of the pesticides spilled both in the river and on farmland. The business might have escaped all the legal trouble, but everyone associated with the case realizes that Smith Brothers Chemicals was liable. Suspicion placed the CEO in direct knowledge of some of the dealings surrounding the incident. Kristen was appointed CEO the year before the fallout. She served as CEO until she was mysteriously murdered 'by her husband.'"

The room did go silent then. He ate a donut while standing at the table, waiting. Then, he grabbed a maple bar and headed back to his chair, with a fresh cup of coffee in hand. This had to be stress eating; he usually wasn't this much of a glutton. Perhaps it had to do with not eating all morning because he was so nervous about today's events. As he sat, he saw a couple of the men looking inwards. They were really thinking about what he said. That was a relief; maybe they wouldn't string him up entirely.

Darnell asked the key question. "They are all suspicious?

The sword deaths?"

"For us to put Ash's name on it now, we have to have deep background that suggests the person had it coming. To put it bluntly again. That's not to say Ash is some hero. He appears to be a monster, and I suspect he has killed people who were a lot less ethically black and white. But the ones we can easily check the box by his name were all suspected of something. Equally, though, that's not to say that the victims weren't falsely accused. All we know is that Ash's victims are universally under suspicion. Keep in mind that Kristen Smith and the bishop weren't suspicious; those two were guilty of sin." He said it bashfully, but the evidence against the bishop and Mrs. Smith were two towering mountains.

"Your entire team will sign legal affidavits and witness statements saying that Kristen Smith was murdered by the killer known as the Ashen Horse and not by her husband?" Darnell must have been a project manager in a former life because he once again put the meeting right back on track.

He looked directly at Tim and added, "Your entire team, Tim. The investigating special agents, medical, and forensic?" It was almost a sixth sense with this guy. Perhaps that's what you must do to make it to the director's level. Although Tim considered that he'd known a few directors who couldn't tie their shoelaces, perhaps that wasn't the case. Darnell appeared to be the real deal, though.

"My two special agents, Josh and Ellie, will sign for sure. I know Tracy, our medical examiner, will as well. I'll have to check the forensic team; they are a reclusive bunch. But at this point, I think everyone would, yes."

It was Mike's turn to sigh. It looked like he had gotten sucker punched. The kind of exhaustion that comes after thirty years on the job and realizing the work was inadequate. The sort of exhaustion that is just deflating.

"This sucks. The egg is all over our faces. It probably wasn't entirely our fault. It's always the husband. Who would have even considered that there was a random sword-wielding assassin on the loose? Still, this sucks." He sighed again, shook his head, and muttered, "It's always the husband."

Darnell agreed, "It is always the husband, or at least usually." Darnell would know; he came up through the ranks. "Not this time, though. Tim, get all the signatures and put all the documentation together. We will start the ball rolling on getting Mr. Smith released. Keep any evidence we don't want the press to know about the Ashen Horse out of the reports, but we need a detailed report on why we are releasing Mr. Smith."

Tim took a minute to consider how much Josh and Ellie would love that.

Darnell continued, "We also need it to be technical and deep enough to show that it is a complete miracle we are uncovering it now. Nothing was missed, nothing was overlooked. Got that? The FBI and the federal government didn't make any mistakes."

"Crystal clear, sir."

Mike said, "Listen, Tim." That was a little too serious for comfort. "We are going to be done here in a second, obviously. Half the reason we invited you up here was for the Kristen Smith memo. And it's a black eye we all would have rather avoided. But if her husband is innocent, obviously we are getting him released. We'd just love to avoid the onslaught of lawsuits with that. The report matters a great deal. I wish we could all be adults and avoid politics, but politics will be a sad reality here. The report can't even hint at liability in any way on the FBI or the judicial system."

"I'm with you."

"Right, anyway, sorry." Mike was still discouraged; he seemed genuinely side-tracked. "Right, so that was part of the reason you are here. The other reason you are here is that we are putting the Ashen Horse case on the ten most wanted list. He probably should have been there before, but we can't identify him. But you should know that it is getting escalated to the highest level. Normally, this comes with a larger task force and more bodies. Regrettably, it usually enters the realm of pop culture as well. But we think you have the case in hand, so we aren't going to change how you or your team is working."

Mike huffed a breath in there and then went on. "If you need more help or agents, let us know. This comes with a promotion of sorts for you and your lead agents as well, for that matter. You're the task force leader now. If you need anything, you can contact me or Darnell directly. Also, weekly updates to both us and our teams; we'll get you a list of people to email."

Tim plucked his jaw off the table. That was quite the shocker. Here, he thought he was going to be fired. Admittedly, he doubted getting fired, but he sure wasn't expecting a promotion, and for the entire team, no less. They were doing something right, apparently. That or they were bribing him for the silence and compliance on Kristen's case. That report would have to be something; all three had better put some serious hours into it. Either way, his team had earned it.

"Uh. Thank you? I appreciate all that; I know my team will also."

A couple of the minions had started to stand; apparently, the meeting was ending just that fast. "Also, Tim. Careful with the memos next time? Perhaps a heads-up first? Something?"

"Yes, sir. We'll clear everything with this larger team from now on."

The conference room quickly emptied. Tim looked at the back table, which had been picked clean as everyone left the room. They didn't leave one single pastry, not so much as a donut hole could be found. Tim chuckled, "Ha, perhaps they all did want to eat them as badly as I did." And with that, he left the conference room.

Chapter Eight

Fibbies Connect the Dots

Tim walked into the team's working area. They technically had an entire half floor now, but they mostly worked in the collaboration space if they weren't sorting evidence in the evidence rooms. As he walked through the front door, he saw Ellie's eyes were watching him. She was always subtle, but she rarely missed anything regarding people coming and going. It was sometimes downright eerie. Josh, being Josh, was totally oblivious to the fact that he had even walked into the room.

Ellie, although always the professional, couldn't wait any longer. "How did it go?"

"Not quite as we expected," Tim said, surprised at how much that was true. "To be sure, they dragged me through the pits of doom and gloom. But in the end, it was rewarding to know they thought we were doing good work."

"Days like today, boss-man, it doesn't feel like we are doing good work." Josh continued to flip through the notes he had on his desk. Perhaps he wasn't as oblivious as Tim had thought initially. "I don't know how we don't have more on this guy than we do. The dude is a smoking ghost. It's depressing."

"We are doing good work, team. We will catch Ash; it's just a matter of time."

Ellie smirked. "You finally calling him by his proper name now?"

"Accidently did it in the meeting, much to the leadership's chagrin, I'm sure. After that, well, I guess it has finally stuck. This vigilante serial killer is called Ash now, at least in this office."

That brought Josh out of his self-induced melancholy. "He's been Ash to everyone here for a long time there, Tim. You are just finally catching up."

"Slow learner, whatcha gonna do."

"What's the scoop on how it went, man? Out with it."

"Well, the big takeaway is that you two are getting promoted. I've been moved up to task force leader, which I guess I always was, or not. Who knows, but they are now giving me the official title of 'Supervisory Special Agent.' And both of you are getting promoted to 'Senior Special Agent,' so congrats. They sent out an official memo as I was leaving their interrogation."

"I thought that kind of thing happened after you caught the guy," commented Ellie.

"Christmas came early, Ellie. Let's enjoy that for what it is." Tim said it flippantly, but he did it with a smile. They would both be pleased with the promotion once they took a minute to internalize it.

"We are also getting more team members if we want them. I'm not sure we do yet; we're keeping up with the documents and paperwork for now. And given that Ash is all over the country, being regional wouldn't help us much. We might add another medical or forensic team member if we have more evidence to comb through. You guys are senior agents now, though, so if you have input, I'd appreciate it."

"Look at that. Change the title, and you will immediately change the man," explained Josh. "See, Ellie, it is Christmas come early."

Ellie smiled as well. "With all this newfound authority, I

The Ashen Horse

might have to solve the case now."

"You are both jackasses, you know that?" Tim said.

"We do, actually," Ellie laughed.

"Badge of pride, really," Josh concurred. "You see, Tim, the key is to wear it like you own it."

"Fine, fine. You both know what I meant. Let me know if you have any input on staffing stuff; we now have the authority to get it done."

"My little sister needs a job."

"Not that kind of staffing, Josh."

"See, you just broke her heart. Not very nice, boss."

Tim just shook his head. He didn't know how he tolerated these two most of the time. If you ever got them both going, and it was like a rollercoaster you couldn't get off of. "The other big piece, aside from all the staffing resources and the promotions, was that Ash is getting promoted to the big time—FBI's ten most wanted. I don't know where on the list he will land, but he's on the list now. I'm still waiting for that email; I'll forward it to everyone when I get it."

Ellie glanced at the door. "That'll draw some attention. Probably unwanted attention."

"Yeah, we discussed that. I tend to agree, but the powers at hand thought the case needed the eyes. They thought some public input might crack something we haven't seen. We will probably have to start scouring through public tips and input. That'll all get screened, of course."

"The attention might be good, though," Josh remarked. "Look, guys, at the very least, we are getting promoted, and we get to put on the resumes that we worked on one of the FBI's most wanted cases. That must be worth a gold star, right?"

Tim smiled; Josh always found the silver lining. "You betcha. Gold stars for everyone."

"As a side note, Josh," Tim continued, "leadership appreciated your insights on the blades. Of course, they are as unsure what to make of it as we are—how is a criminal walking around with a sword and not eliciting comments everywhere?"

"Tracy did most of that work, honestly," Josh admitted. "I just put it together with the right blades. The accuracy and understanding of the cuts and weapons used was all Tracy."

Ellie had been glancing at Josh's notes but piped up again. "She is worth her weight in gold."

Josh was in complete agreement, "Yeah, that's no joke."

"Right, so that was my last two days. The leadership is happy with our work, though. So, let's keep doing what we are doing. We will get Ash; he has to make a mistake sooner or later."

Ellie was still staring at the notes. "Josh, what does this mean here?" She pointed to a section on the page.

"It's just my notes."

"Obviously it's your notes, knucklehead. What does this mean?"

"What?"

"Here, you have written, 'Wealthy.'"

Tim moved over to the edge of the desk and glanced over Josh's other shoulder to read the notes.

"It just means Ash has money. Ash is wealthy. We all realize that, right?"

"I guess I never thought about it, honestly," Tim admitted truthfully.

Josh continued, "He must be flying. Or he drives nonstop. If we are right about attributing all these killings to him, he's all over the USA. Crisscrossing the country nonstop. That means staying in hotels all the time; even if he uses cheap ones, that is a lot of money. As far as we can tell, the equipment is top-notch. Our bomb inspectors swore a long-time professional built the explosive. Perhaps Ash even found a maker to make it for him? We can't find any evidence linking the victims. And we can't find a money trail from those victims to the killer. And the killer travels nonstop, which means Ash has several identities. It takes a bit of money to travel nonstop across the country and to build that much repertoire."

Ellie nodded her understanding. "The obvious question here is where did he get his money?"

They were all looking at each other now. Tim thought out loud, "Inheritance? Josh, there are two things here: not only is Ash wealthy, but he also doesn't have time to work with the time he spends traveling. This is a good line of thinking. Man, we probably should have seen this earlier."

"He might have a traveling job?" Ellie considered further. "There are jobs out there where you travel for the work. Perhaps Ash is just killing when he is on location?"

"That would be very opportunistic. But that brings us to the other question we have had for so long. How does Ash find or know about his victims? All the victims have similarities in that they aren't very good people. Ash isn't just killing random people. Somehow, he is finding dodgy people in society. It makes this guy a bit different than normal serial killers, who are generally opportunistic. Ash isn't an opportunist; he's intentional and carefully looking for his next victim."

Josh added, "It probably means he is traveling more than we think as well. Ash doesn't get caught, and he doesn't leave clues. We have virtually no physical evidence. I don't know how we don't have a video or a camera shot from across the road. We have terrible grainy pictures at best. That means he must be scouting his victims for days, finding the best opportunity and best location to kill them."

Ellie went a little green in the face. "Gruesome."

Tim was right there with her. "Pretty dark, Josh."

"Yeah, it's dark. But how else does someone kill? What is it? —10 people? 20 people? —and not get caught or leave evidence? Ash is careful. Likely way more careful than we realize right now. That takes time and effort."

"So, Ash is independently wealthy," Tim said. "And what, then, killing is his hobby? Killing is the fun thing he does?"

Ellie sighed under her breath, "We need a bloody shrink."

Tim agreed, "We probably do. Right now, I need coffee." He was halfway across the room when he stopped and looked back. "You know, Ellie, that honestly isn't a bad idea. We should get a profiler working on this case. We have the capacity and leverage to make that happen now."

Tim started again for the kitchenette off the main collaboration spaces they worked in. When he got closer, he saw the other two had also followed. It was a sad truth, but coffee was the most critical weapon in the FBI's toolkit.

He poured Ellie the first mug and pushed it over to her as he poured Josh's cup. He was deep in thought. There was something they were missing here. Then he heard a new voice.

"Have you considered…"

It was Roshan Yurka, one of their forensic team members. He had probably been in an evidence room the entire time they talked, moving through paperwork. Roshan did terrific work; he was a proper grinder, putting in the hours to solve cases. Not only did he spend the time to document and catalog countless pieces of evidence, but through the process of staring at the articles of evidence he could put together pieces of information many other junior or even senior agents would miss entirely. He was another member of the team who was worth his weight in gold.

Tim poured him a cup and pushed it over to him. Roshan accepted it and took a sip.

"Terrible coffee, you know," he said.

"Absolutely terrible," Ellie agreed. "I'm going to drink another few gallons of it next week, just to validate the theory, though."

Josh laughed out loud. He wasn't far from spewing the coffee everywhere. Tim was chuckling as he finally got to pouring himself a cup.

Roshan was grinning deeply as he went on. "As I was

saying... I overheard your conversation as I was sorting evidence. Have you considered that killing is a sport or a game for him? It seems like the challenge of it is driving him."

Tim's face, Josh's face, and Ellie's face all went blank. Josh let out a low whistle. "That does fit, I guess. If it is an adventure for him? That might explain why he is so careful. Everything about Ash appears to be careful; he never makes a mistake."

Roshan nodded. "It's a great game. The game is to elude the authorities, or so it seems. How has he never been caught?"

Ellie continued the thought, "It explains the victim count. Most serial killers don't just keep stacking up their bodies. But Ash kills every week, or two weeks, at least once a month, as far as we can tell. We suspect about ten to twenty victims now, but the list could be double that. We keep churning up more as we look back at unsolved cases."

Roshan observed more interesting points in the case as he explained. "The sword is a unique factor. We have found a lot of those victims, but I wonder if we were to start looking at all the stabbings that we would find. Ash appears to use those daggers as often as the sword, perhaps more given the sword is a lot harder to conceal." Roshan had once again proved why half the FBI wanted him on their team.

Tim, his big-picture view coming into focus, chipped into the conversation. "Can you run with that, Roshan? Can you dig up cases involving stab wounds? I guess we'd be looking for any national unsolved cases involving knife wounds. The Kristen Smith case might even bring solved cases into play, but that was a fluke. We can't track all knife cases down."

"Yep, already got the database guys churning on it," Roshan replied. "We should have a list of cases and summaries here in the next few days. It'll be a lot to work, but the paperwork is coming."

"Not sure I should be happy about that," Ellie said.

They needed to run all this down. It was time for the team to get to work. "As always, Roshan, I think we owe you a debt," Tim said. "If you are right—and putting all the strings together in my head, I think there is a good chance you are. But if you are right that Ash is in it as much for the game of it as anything else, then we need to find out how he is finding his victims. We must redouble our efforts to find links between the victims; they must exist. Time to start leveraging every resource we can get to see what we can trace down."

They all headed back to hit their emails and start typing up requests for the digital teams to begin tracking down information. Somewhere, there were links they were missing. The world was one giant chain that interconnected everything and everyone. And links, sources, bridges, data, and information always tie everyone to everyone. It was just a matter of uncovering the information.

Someone in a dark room was handing off a list of instructions or names somewhere. They needed to find the missing links to the chain. The correlation must exist; they just had to unearth it.

Chapter Nine

Surveillance

She sat staring out over the waves of the Atlantic Ocean, enjoying her early morning coffee. The beach house was worth every penny. She could leave the deck and put her feet in the sand. It was simply incredible. Most mornings, she made coffee and walked along the ocean. There were perks to this line of work; waking up every morning to stare at the beach was one of them.

Of course, there were downsides to the work as well. It was always awkward being covered in someone else's blood, watching them gurgle their way out of this life. Awkward indeed. She only had that happen her first few times. As she got more experienced, she learned how to keep most of the blood off her. That was a bit of art in itself.

She had been in Miami for two weeks now. The scouting was not going as well as she had hoped. The drug dealer's house was locked down as tight as a mousetrap. She had learned a lot about Molly Johnson in the last two weeks. The contract had, of course, failed to mention that the drug dealer was a woman. It also failed to mention that her former lover issued it. She had pieced together enough to assume the million-dollar 'reward' for fulfilling the contract was money stolen from Molly in the first place.

It made sense that her house was guarded nonstop. Molly

probably suspected that her ex was coming after her. She lived in a well-fortified compound in the interior section of Florida, on the very outskirts of Miami, if it could be considered in Miami. Half buried in the swamps, Molly's house was an entire gated community unto itself. The guard shack at the entrance monitored everyone who came in and out. The wall around the complex was at least fifteen feet tall. It looked thick, too; God only knew how much that cost. It went around the entire ten acres of the complex.

From the gated entrance, she had gotten a look into the compound. Jungle-like vegetation had grown up and around the interior walls, spanning most of the complex's interior. A pristine cobblestone driveway ran up to the four-story mansion in the middle of the property. A large two-story house sat to the left of the main building, and what appeared to be a six-car garage sat to the right. She hadn't seen behind the house but was reasonably confident she would find an Olympic-size swimming pool. It was Florida, after all.

The house was built in a typical Southern plantation format, which she found surprising and grossly unoriginal. It did afford open outdoor decks that ranged the entire structure on the first and fourth floors, though. Even on her casual drive-by, she counted four guards patrolling the decks. Which, of course, begged the question of how many there were, how many shifts they had, and all the other logistical nightmares.

She was deep in thought, considering the cost of employing thirty, maybe fifty, full-time guards. The numbers were staggering. How much money was Molly moving with her drug business? It must be enough. It also meant that her ex-lover wanted her gone out of spite or because he thought he could encroach on her turf. There were mountains of money involved here. She hesitated even to guess what the property was worth, but it was worth more than she had made in the last fifteen years practicing her trade.

She calmly pondered whether she had gone into the

wrong business. Her line of work was a lot simpler and a lot less dangerous. The drug dealers always had to deal with each other, violent people on the streets, and, worst of all, law enforcement. She only had to deal with the law. Sure, the occasional person might want to kill her, but they'd have to know anything about her for that to pose a real threat. She ensured no one in the business knew anything about her.

Molly Johnson had come up from the backwaters and rose from the lowest ranks in the drug business. A true self-made man, or woman, as it were. She had grown up in the Deep South, the real Deep South. The Appalachian South. She had been poor, the kind of poor where you don't know where your next meal is coming from. Molly's parents had died when she was young, the exact details she hadn't been able to piece together yet. But it was straightforward that Molly grew up in foster homes and finally ran away for the final time at twelve. She had lived on her own ever since. The streets raised her, and that life drove her to gangs before long. Perhaps it was the promise of family or the promise of income, or maybe it was a boy who treated her kindly. Or did he take advantage of her? It couldn't have been easy; most people knew what happened to girls that got initiated into gang life.

By the time Molly was sixteen, she was running her own crew; by the time she was eighteen, she was running twenty and responsible for most of the marijuana and cocaine coming in and out of Tallahassee. By the time she was twenty-one, she was controlling most of the drug trade in Florida. Plenty of other dealers used Florida as the gateway into the country and moved drugs in and out of the state. It was just too convenient a point of entry into the continental USA not to leverage. But at that time, Molly was the major player for the drugs that were moved and sold just in Florida.

That had been a little over ten years ago. That had also been when the cartels started taking note. Once Molly had two cartels supplying her, things changed. Now, she controlled, sold, and supplied most of the Eastern USA. Of course, if the cartels ever found out she was playing both sides, that might spell disaster. That may have explained the need for fifty bodyguards.

She had pieced together most of this about Molly from the word on the street. It wasn't easy digging up this level of intel. She had been busy for the last two weeks, bribing, buying, making deals, and drinking in every dark corner of the city. There was an art to gathering this kind of information. Ensuring no one assumed or made the dire prediction that she was law enforcement was critical. People remembered when people started asking the wrong questions. She had accumulated a lot of information quickly; almost certainly, someone had told important people in the business that someone was snooping around.

Maybe that's why Molly increased her guard count? Rumor was that she had hired another twenty bodies recently. It was interesting that various street thugs coveted the position of being on Molly's guard detail. Rumors suggested that working for Molly was a dream gig and paid better than doing anything on the streets. She thought that was innovative business. Molly probably knew that if you wanted to hire the best talent in the market, you had to offer the best perks and the best pay. Rumors also suggested that Molly got the best, at least the best the streets offered.

She had been trying to find anyone in Molly's employ to talk to, but that had proved tricky. That was her goal for today. She would wait for the guards' shift to change or for any guard to leave the compound. Then, follow that person back to their home and eventually find a way to meet them. It turned out that Molly was an equal-opportunity employer; she employed every race, gender, creed, and affiliation. She could have sworn she simultaneously saw two rival gang members on guard duty. She had no idea how that was even possible. Either Molly was a saint, or she had special voodoo magic that kept the peace. Was the loyalty to the dollar so sweeping in the organization that it put old allegiances and grudges to bed?

After a fantastic morning peacefully breathing in the smell of the rolling ocean, she sat in her rental car quietly listening to 'Miami's #1 Hit Music Station, Y100!' She was parked half a mile away from the entrance to the compound. It probably wasn't far enough, but it did afford the perfect vantage point to see people coming and going. It would be fine. It was a negligible risk, but she made it a point to be aware of all risks. That was how you stayed alive in this game.

It wasn't clear how long she would have to wait. The guards' schedules didn't appear to stay the same—perhaps that was the point. Keep changing it up constantly and keep everyone guessing. So, she waited. It occurred to her that she might have come later in the afternoon, but she was here now. She casually sipped coffee, read news reports on her smartphone, and waited. No one should bother her, but she had several stories and reasons for sitting here if someone came asking. Always have a plan. But for now, she waited.

It took several hours; it was creeping well past midday when a car finally pulled out of the complex. About half an hour earlier, a car had pulled in. She didn't know if it was the changing of the guards, but she decided this was the car she was going to follow, so she slowly merged into traffic several cars back and started to pursue the vehicle that had left the compound.

She had learned a surprising amount while sitting there for half the day. Cars came and went all day. In one car, a young bulky man jumped out in sweatpants; she assumed he could only be a personal trainer. Another vehicle brought in a woman wearing a business suit; she could only assume she was a therapist or lawyer. She had watched one man shuffle boxes in and out of the house; he was wearing what appeared to be chef clothes; he must have been a cook or food supplier. Another one or two, they could be called business associates, had come and gone—probably shot callers or senior lieutenants in her organization. The place was a flurry of activity overall. She thought several guards had also exchanged themselves throughout the day, but she wasn't sure they were the security personnel; perhaps they were the typical street thugs coming and going out the gates.

During her observations, she wasn't just looking for anyone. She didn't want to follow someone with a casual relationship with Molly or, worse, Molly's compound. She was looking for people who worked there every day. That would be her way in.

They pulled onto the larger highway and picked up speed, but her mind was still wandering. She couldn't repeat this exercise in the same way. She had sat there most of the day, and too many people had seen the vehicle. She didn't look particularly suspicious, but most of her contracts weren't seriously suspicious people. This one was. There was a good chance someone noticed her car, and someone likely saw her watching. Perhaps they would misconstrue it as police; that'd be good. But either way, she wasn't stalking the joint again. She also needed to turn this car rental in tomorrow and pick up a different car from a different agency. She had learned never to tempt fate and not to make obvious mistakes.

They had been driving for maybe thirty minutes when the car she was tailing pulled into an apartment complex. She kept her distance and observed. She had wasted an entire day on this; hopefully, it would bear some fruit. A man stepped out of the car. She guessed he was in his late twenties, maybe his early thirties. He had soft brown skin and walked with a confidence that she could relate to. This man knew how to handle himself. He walked to a bottom apartment, 5D, and let himself inside.

She let out a sigh. This ended the day's adventures. She slowly drove past, grabbing a couple of pictures of his car, noting the license plate and apartment number, and snapping a picture of the apartment sign, "Regal Estates." She was developing her future plans. But first things first: getting rid of this car and finding a new restaurant for dinner.

Chapter Ten

Coffee Time

Not only was Molly Johnson one of the largest drug kingpins in the Americas, but she also owned a slew of profitable normal businesses. It was hard to know how much of her normal business profits were legitimate, but all her businesses had reported exceptionally good years—for the last decade. Most of them were cash businesses, naturally. All the easier to launder money through them that way.

She sat in line at an espresso stand, one of roughly twenty that Molly Johnson owned and operated. She didn't manage them; she had people for that, but she owned the lot. It turned out drug dealers really liked coffee, too. It was a great way to siphon money right back into a legitimate business. She could have sworn she saw several rather suspicious customers drive up as she moved up in line. It didn't look like they were doing anything illegal, literally just getting coffee—an interesting phenomenon.

Molly also owned three nightclubs, several bars, and half the coin-operated laundries in the Miami area. It was hard to track down all of Molly's business ventures, and she was sure she had probably missed most of them. Molly had her fingers in everything. One of the major oddities that caught her attention was that Molly also owned two engineering firms.

She pulled out of the lot and moved smoothly into a parking spot across the street from the espresso stand, where she took a moment to enjoy her steaming cup of white chocolate mocha. How was Molly operating with such impunity? She had now spent three weeks investigating this situation, and it was clear that Molly was engaging in numerous illegal activities. How did the police not have this figured out? There must be something else going on here as well. Law enforcement was obtuse, but these flashing signs were hard to miss. If she left evidence and trails the way Molly did, she would have been in prison three times over.

Although not backed up with official money and personnel, her investigations were not casual. She had spent every night for weeks in different shady locations to discover what was known. But still, it hadn't taken her long to find a major player in Miami who was moving massive weight. There's no way the cops didn't know about this. She wondered if they were bought off or trying to build a case.

Her only logical conclusion was that Molly was also buying off the cops, detectives, and senior leadership. She made a mental note to do some further research on this. She would have to track down how Molly wasn't lounging in a cell. If her simple inquiries and internet research had shown how deep the roots went, law enforcement had to be aware.

But now, she had to pay attention to the car that had pulled up to the espresso stand. She'd been waiting for an hour for him to come get coffee. The entire last week, he had coffee every day. She had done the math, and as far as she could tell, today was his day off. This is why it was a gamble on whether he would come to get coffee, but she couldn't keep stalking the apartment complex, even if she had changed out rental cars three times. Being consistent or obvious is what gets a person in trouble. So, she waited at the coffee stand, and here he was, pulling out with his espresso.

She still hadn't figured out exactly how she was going to engage him. A week's investigation had revealed quite a bit about him. She had influenced people she knew to run the license plate and discovered his name, Hector Garcia. He was 29, born in Florida, but additional investigation suggested his parents with his grandparents had migrated from Honduras. After a week of watching him, he appeared to be one of Molly's guards or part of her security detail. She would have noticed if he was running drugs, cooking, or cleaning. He worked Monday through Friday, 9-5, like clockwork. Today was Saturday, so the mystery was to figure out what he was doing today.

She had found him on social media and further discovered that he had graduated with some degree in technology. Perhaps he was doing some of Molly's technical security stuff? She hadn't put together all the pieces yet, but she was still confident that he would be her way to get to Molly.

He eventually pulled into Amelia Earhart Park. She parked on the other side of the parking lot and waited. Hector got out of the car, coffee cup in hand, and casually started for one of the nature trails. It was bizarre that he would come to a random park and walk, but people did strange things for fun. She wouldn't miss this opportunity; this was a perfect place to "accidentally" run into him. She considered her options and decided the damsel in distress was always a winner when meeting new people, particularly men. She had used the trick a few times to slay unsuspecting men. This should work just as well, even if it was a different form of slaying.

She carefully set up the scenario in her mind and then hopped out of her car and walked in the direction that Hector had gone. Looking at the trail map hanging on a post in the park, it took her a minute to figure out where he would end up if he finished the lengthy loop around the park. He could take a couple of different paths, but most of them reconverged in the same area, which eventually returned to the parking lot. She immediately headed there.

Life was a waiting game; she had found this out early. More often than not, you just had to wait for things to happen or for plans to materialize to encounter the right opportunity. She felt like the entire last three weeks had been nothing but waiting. She spared a silent chuckle for herself; she had thought she would have this finished in a month, but it had been three weeks, and she wasn't even close. She was going to earn that money. Of course, the chuckle turned into a croak when she considered whether it was even worth it. She'd have to stay engaged at least another month, maybe two at this rate. That was giving up a lot of other lucrative contracts.

She was musing to herself when she glanced up to see Hector walking in the line to converge where she was. Now, she just had to play it right. She turned and strolled in the opposite direction, allowing Hector to gain on her slowly. She had to wait until he was right next to her or close enough where he was personally engaged when she fell; otherwise, this scheme probably wouldn't work. He couldn't be a bystander to her "sprained" leg; he had to be a direct participant.

As he walked along the side of her, she stepped too close to him, and she started to pretend to fall. She was twisted halfway over when she realized he wasn't even paying attention to her; he was looking out over the water. It was at that moment that he collided with her. She let out a shocked gasp as they both tumbled to the ground. He didn't even manage words until he hit the concrete and sprawled.

He cursed as he smacked concrete and then he followed it by more of a hoarse groan. "I'm sorry." It looked like he tried to get out more, but he appeared to be in a fair amount of pain, another groan escaping.

"I think it was my fault. I'm pretty sure I ran into you," she said while cursing herself for executing the move poorly.

He shouldn't have gone down with her.

"Sounds like we are both to blame," he said, chuckling and wincing.

She laughed, "Perhaps that is the best explanation yet. Are you okay? I think I torqued my leg."

"I'm sure I'll be fine, but my ankle isn't liking me too much right now."

She had been playing the situation, but as she finally looked at him, she noticed he was hurting. She had some experience with pain, and he wasn't faking that twinge in his face.

"Oh my," she said. Perhaps she was putting it on too thick, but it was her experience that men were mostly clueless, so adding on a little more might not hurt either. "You really are hurt. I'm so sorry." She gave it a minute to sink in, then continued, "Let me see if I can stand up quick." She carefully put weight on her leg and stood up, exaggeratedly slowly, and finally stood. Again, it was a little thick, but he was only half paying attention as he massaged his ankle.

"Okay, let's see if we can get you up."

After a considerable amount of grunting, both were standing. He was mostly leaning on her for support, though. Perhaps it was good that she had staged this event so close to his car. She would be forced into half carrying him back to his vehicle.

"You know, you are a lot heavier than you look."

"I'm unsure if I should take that as a compliment or an insult?"

"Uh, let's go with a compliment. Yeah, a compliment sounds better. All that muscle weight or something." She said it good-naturedly; otherwise, it might not have gone over well. He was hard to get a read on, but whatever she was doing appeared to be working, at least a little.

"So, where are we hobbling to?" she pretended to need to know.

The Ashen Horse

"My car is just over there. Although it looks like a rather far way in the current situation."

"Best get a move on then. The best way to travel is one foot at a time."

"I don't know, a scooter sounds pretty good right now."

They shuffled along patiently. It took the better part of fifteen minutes to make it the distance back to his parked car. They exchanged names and other pleasantries as they shambled along. Perhaps they both were moving slower than strictly necessary. She got the feeling he might have been trying to drag this out, which she took as a good sign. He liked her. That was the whole point of this endeavor. She still found it flattering, though. It was nice to know that her feminine charms were good enough to suck in the unexpected.

He hit his key fob to unlock the door as they reached his car. "I feel like I owe you money or something. I would have had to crawl if you hadn't helped me back here."

"True, that would have been quite the sight. Although, if we hadn't collided, you would have just walked here without difficulty."

"Ah, fair point."

"But that said, I feel you owe me as well. I'm a sucker for coffee; there's probably a good coffee shop around here somewhere?"

"I know just the place."

"Oh really?"

"Yep, life-changing coffee. I'm pretty sure I'm not the same man I was before I consumed their beans."

"Now I'm truly intrigued," she said. This was working out better than she could have hoped. "I actually have time right now; this is my day off; I just took a rideshare here and spent the morning reading. Good to be outside, you know?"

"Yep. I was here for pretty much the same thing. You didn't drive? Okay, hop in, and we'll grab lunch. This place also serves excellent food, so it has that going for it."

"Excellent!" she said as she jumped into the passenger side. And she meant it on so many different levels.

Chapter Eleven

The Grind

Roshan sat at his desk, quietly drinking an energy drink. It was mid-morning, which meant he was on his third one. He was twitching a little bit, but that was just a regular event when it was approaching noon. His coworkers in the FBI forensic team told him that being in his mid-fifties was too old for energy drinks. But those kids didn't know what they were talking about. He was as healthy as a horse. Besides, everyone died from something; you might as well go out loving it. Roshan was a big believer in loving it. He took another gulp.

As he twitched, he read countless reports and emails. He paused and thought about how amazing it was, all the information out there. How many unique PDFs were there in the world? How many were just involved in criminal content? It felt like he had read ten thousand in the last week alone. He had sent out significant inquiries to the forty largest cities in the United States asking for information regarding unsolved knife wounds, particularly extensive knife wounds.

A few cities jumped on it, and he was swimming in files the next day. Most of them took their time and sent him partial updates with more cases every few days. The case logs were endless, though. It was surprising how many unsolved crimes there were, all related to knifings, stabbings, or other unknown penetration wounds.

Roshan's eye twitched again as he started reading another case. This was the job. He excelled at it. When he was younger, he thought success came from getting lucky or knowing the right person. Maybe it was marrying the right person? But he learned, mostly from watching others make mistakes, that none of those things determined success. Two simple factors determined success.

First, those who put in the work, the grinders, defined success. He was a grinder. Sitting down and reading useless mounds of paperwork for twelve hours, five days a week. That was the job. There was a beauty in its simplicity. But it was simple grit, the perseverance to do the work. That's how people succeed in life; they put in the work.

Granted, he wasn't always putting in the twelve hours a day anymore. But when he was younger and coming up the ranks, he put in many a twelve-hour day. Age had taught him that it wasn't always about putting in the hours but making the hours productive. He watched many coworkers waste hours in petty drama around the office. If you weren't being productive, taping out after a six-hour day made sense, but if you had the work to do, a twelve-hour day might make sense. But making all of those hours count was the critical point. There was no point staring at a blank screen in the office if it wasn't bringing the business value. He often wondered how much better he might have been at his personal and work life had he learned that lesson ten years earlier. What a difference it might have made.

Success came in other areas of life as well, though. For him, the other elementary factor was living below your means. Live simple, save, and invest. Roshan perhaps took living simply to a minimalist level. He recognized that he probably wasn't healthy either, but he was fifty-four years old and would retire well in just three years. He had three more to go, and then he'd have his final rental property paid off.

Once that was done, he was out. Beaches and rum, that's where it was at.

Until then, though, the grind. Every criminal case broke because some poor sap at the bottom put in the labor. At least, Roshan was convinced that is how it worked. He forwarded another set of emails to the larger forensic team. He started reading yet another case.

His hand, twitching slightly, reached for the energy drink on the desk, then froze. He was mid-sentence in a case, and he started rereading it. He cataloged most of the cases he'd been reading in the last week in a spreadsheet, giving fundamental details about the case. The name of the victim, the date of the murder, the location, and the likely rating, one out of ten, that Ash could be connected to it. The last piece in the database was him adding his name to the log as the one who had done the original analytics—a basic log to track what he had reviewed and hadn't. In any report where he logged at or over a five ranking in possible Ash involvement, he forwarded it to his larger team of researchers. They'd dig deeper, reaching out to the respective jurisdictions and pulling in more files and data to review—the grind.

His role, at least until it drove him to madness, was doing triage on the ridiculous number of cases coming in. His hand still seemed frozen; he looked down, shook it, and grabbed another sip. It was their fault, of course; they had asked for the cases. You couldn't ask people to provide you with all the information and then fail to read it. He read it. Granted, not every case got his full attention, but he was doing solid reviews.

Over the last week, he had found a couple of cases he marked as sevens, which meant he considered it possible that Ash may have been the killer. It was possible Ash had been working the last five years; unlikely but possible.

The case he was reading right now, though, was particularly troubling. The case was explicitly marked as unsolved and cold. The medical examiner noted the murder weapon as a 'sword, katana.' That was something. Roshan skipped around the files and went to the autopsy report on the victim, wondering how the ME had gotten so specific on the type of sword.

"Oh. Well, then. I guess that answers that question," Roshan said to himself.

Stuck in the file were pictures from the scene of the crime and then in the examination room, where they had left, even in transport, the sword buried into the victim's chest. Studying the picture, Roshan observed, "That's definitely a katana, kind of hard to miss when it's blazing right out of his heart."

His train of thought continued, "Well, this can't be Ash, though. This murder was 12 years ago. There's no way he has been operating that long." Roshan was about to dump the file. He had recorded the case as "Brandon Eriks, Seattle, WA," gave it a score of 4, and recorded the twelve-year-old date.

Before he totally ditched the file, though, perhaps he should have seen if anything about the victim stuck out. After all, the murder weapon was a sword, outright found. He should look at it a bit deeper. Before that, though, a bathroom break was in order. It was impossible to drink three energy drinks every morning and not frequently use the facilities. He continued mumbling to himself, "Screw it, I'll review it after lunch, this is a good stopping point anyway." The local deli was too much of a temptation; he frequented the shop almost daily. You couldn't pass up the Reuben, not how they made it.

After returning from his delicious fast-food experience, soaked in goodness, Roshan went right back to it. The grind. He flipped to the digital files that explained the potential motive behind the crime. As they were loading, he cracked open another energy drink. He usually kept it to three in the morning, but today seemed the perfect day to indulge in an afternoon beverage.

The can was halfway to his lips when he read the unforgettable sentence. "The killer appeared to kill Mr. Eriks because Mr. Eriks was involved in a forced prostitution ring." The dude was a sleazeball, Ash always went after sleazeballs. Looking down at the can, Roshan immediately shook his head and took a drink of the elixir. This case did have the likelihood of being their serial killer.

Roshan wanted to go deeper, so he flipped back to the medical examiner's files and read the full report. The victim had minor cuts and abrasions, which the ME couldn't identify. The pictures revealed to Roshan that they very much resembled the throwing knife markings on the other victims. The medical examiner didn't know that's what they were, identifying them as premortem stab wounds.

At that moment, Roshan knew this had to be Ash. It just had to be. "If this isn't Ash, I'll eat my boots. Just how long has this guy been active?"

Roshan quickly changed his previous notes from a ranking of 4 to a ranking of 8 in his spreadsheet. Then, he took all the case files and formed yet another email. Death by emails. The grind. He sent the email to the rest of the forensic team and marked it as a top priority to review this case. Potentially, the single most likely case they'd unearthed that could be Ash. He hit the send button.

He wondered if he should dive deeper into the case and send some follow-up emails to the PD in Seattle or the local FBI contacts there. But then Roshan decided he'd let his team get into the weeds; he'd research the case later once they had done the leg work to get all the information. There was no reason to double up the work; they all had their parts to play. The itch was intense to pursue the case, but he eventually set it aside. He flipped open the next set of files and went to the next case.

He quickly absorbed the next set of files; this one was obviously not Ash. He only spent the better part of ten minutes reviewing this case, updating his spreadsheet, putting it at a score of two, and was about to start the next case. But he stopped.

His thoughts began to race, and he got up and ran out of the room. He ran down the hall and entered the main collaboration room.

Sometimes, a man has to walk away from a task for his subconscious to work out the details behind the scenes. It had happened to Roshan as his mind burned through the Brandon Eriks case in the background.

"Tim," he called, the door still swinging shut behind him. "Tim, we have to talk."

"I've got a call in three minutes. At the top of the hour, Roshan, can it wait?

"Is the call senior FBI leadership?"

"Well, no."

"Then, no. It can't wait, you can blow off everyone else. Hell, you should probably blow off leadership, too, for that matter."

Tim stopped reading his notes and emails. Roshan entirely had his attention now. "What's going on, man? That doesn't sound like your normal self."

"I found a case in Seattle. A real schmuck got himself killed."

"Schmuck?"

"A dude running prostitutes, it doesn't matter. Look, the dude was killed with a katana."

"Sounds like our man. But you wouldn't have come running at that."

"No, probably not. There are three other critical facts. One, the murder was twelve years ago."

"It's not Ash then," voiced Tim.

"That's what I thought and why I discounted it as well. There's no way Ash was in play twelve years ago. The second fact is that the body has what appears to be wounds from throwing knives."

"Seriously?"

"Hand to God."

"A katana sword, twelve years ago, and throwing knife wounds? Wait. How did the ME know it was a katana? They wouldn't have even said sword; they would have just been like 'big knife' or something."

Roshan didn't say anything. He couldn't help smiling a bit, though. Tim looked at Roshan's face while pondering what it all meant.

Then Tim smiled, too.

"They recovered the sword. They have the katana. That's how the ME knew what it was," Tim guessed. "You beautiful bastard. Tell me that thing is in evidence."

"Fact number three. It's ordered, logged, and numbered. It should be in Seattle's evidence lockers. Buried somewhere."

"This is big, Roshan."

"Yeah. It's been a long week of drudging files. Otherwise, I probably would have caught on to the whole thing sooner, but this sure appears to be our man. Pretty big implications, though; it's twelve years ago."

"That changes everything. This guy has been killing for years, then. We have also consistently thought he killed at least every month, if not twice a month. That's a lot of bodies. Look, we are obviously going to Seattle to talk to the police about this case. You uncovered it; do you want to go?"

"Heavens, no. Flying nonstop is a young person's game, and I've spent my time commuting flights. I'll go back to scrounging through files," laughed Roshan.

"I figured, but I thought I'd ask. Looks like Josh and Ellie get to fly out next week. This one is too big to pass up. I'll get all the approvals and get all the communications out. Can you send the files to Josh and Ellie? CC me on all of it. Let's get word out to Seattle that we are coming out there. We must inform them we need to talk about this specific case and see if we can't get the original people working on it in a room."

"Yep, I'll get the ball rolling."

Roshan was smiling as he turned around and headed for his desk. It could be a breakthrough in this case. Who knew what they might discover in Seattle? This could be a game-changing moment.

"Yo, Roshan."

He was at the door, about to leave the collaboration area. "Yeah, Tim?"

"That's epic work, man. You hit a home run today."

"Thanks, Tim. Team effort, let's see what Josh and Ellie can piece together on this in Seattle."

"Great work, man."

Roshan walked to his desk and took a slurp of the energy drink. And started firing off emails to Seattle's PD, carbon-copying the larger task force and the forensic team. After an hour of making sure everything was in process on that case, he cracked open the next one that needed reviewing. It was all about the grind.

Chapter Twelve

Dining Out

It surprised her how much she had enjoyed their lunch outing the previous day. She had been entirely absorbed in the conversation and their time with each other. It was slightly unnerving for her; she couldn't remember the last time she had allowed herself to be as open and carefree with a person as she had been with Hector. Caution was always the leading guide in her decisions regarding her chosen lifestyle. Caution meant maintaining a constant wall of defense and alertness to anyone she encountered.

She didn't feel that type of isolation with Hector. He was candid, open, and carefree. Of course, neither one of them talked about their jobs over lunch. She wasn't about to tell someone she was murder-for-hire; that probably wouldn't go over well. And she doubted he would be upfront about working for one of the most prominent drug dealers in the world. That's another lousy conversation starter.

They did cover all the standard topics, though—music they liked, movies they enjoyed, places they wanted to travel to. They also discussed the innocuous bits of their childhood. His family was from Honduras originally, but he was at least a second-generation American. His degree was in Computer Science, and he used it to do IT security systems.

Their lunch adventure had been so successful that they had agreed to dinner the following day. He was hoping he would be walking better by then. She had watched him hobble out of the restaurant, looking like he was in as much pain as when he was in the park. She had really clobbered him.

Her plan was coming together. She had to get close enough to Hector to leverage him to get close to Molly. She hoped she could maneuver this situation where, in a week or two, she had an opening to get into the compound. But she was troubled by the idea that this could take weeks to materialize. There was a lot at stake with that level of commitment. She also didn't like staying in one place this long. People become memorable if they remain in a place too long. She had learned from an early age that anonymity had tremendous power.

These thoughts plagued her mind as she drove to the Vietnamese restaurant where they agreed to meet. She texted him from her fresh burner SIM card, which she had acquired just for her encounters with him. She couldn't constantly change phone numbers with someone she was socializing with, which put her on the hook to keep this one active, at least periodically.

Hector was waiting for her in the lobby, reading the recent news on his smartphone. She walked in just as he was standing up. "How's the leg?"

"Considerably better, actually," he replied. "Still a twinge, but I can walk now. Sort of."

They waited for the hostess to seat them and continued with small talk. There had been another mass shooting, somewhere on the West Coast this time. They lamented the horrible news. What was the world coming to with this mindless insanity?

The dinner went exceptionally well, and the small talk turned into a deep political discussion on the morality of gun ownership in the modern age. She was on the fence about the value of gun ownership and its negative sponsorship of continued mass attacks. Hector firmly believed that although guns might be responsible for increased accessibility to mass violence, a weapon was only a tool in the hands of a madman.

"You know, ultimately, the gun is just an asset. It might be a powerful tool, but it's just a tool, more or less. A madman can kill dozens with a hatchet, too. It might not be as effective, but it's just as deadly."

"I grant you that, but the 'as effective' is key. A madman with a gun kills twenty-five; the same madman with a hatchet only kills three. That would be the reality of the situation. Is gun ownership in mass quantities worth the lives of those twenty-two people?"

Hector didn't miss a beat, "Yes." Silence settled over the restaurant for a minute. Several other guests silently listened as the conversation continued to evolve, and they swiveled their heads to wait for the continued exchange.

"Nothing else? Just an absolute affirmation?" she pressed.

Even to the onlookers, it is evident that he was hedging his bets. He felt strongly about the conversation, but it was equally apparent that he was trying to make a good impression. Irritating his date beyond reason would turn out badly for him. Hector considered for a moment, then continued.

"There is more...." He paused, choosing his words carefully. "The issue at hand is that guns serve as a vital construct within the governmental framework. The American Founders, our Founders, saw this, and it's the sole reason for the Second Amendment. An armed citizenry prevents tyranny. It is that simple. Throughout history, conquering or would-be conquerors first took away the citizens' ability to be hostile against the ruling class. George Mason said it quite succinctly when he noted that 'to disarm the people is the most effectual way to enslave them.'"

"And every one that gets caught in the crossfire? Just

sucks to be them?"

"I'm not blind to the reality of the issues we face in America, but disarming or removing firearms is not the solution. Proper medical treatments, access to healthcare, mental health initiatives, and clear early warning signs could play a critical factor in changing our approach."

"But the people that died today, because of a madman with a gun, you're good with that?"

Poor Hector saw that he was losing the battle, regardless of the argument or their validity. Death was a hard thing to argue against. "I'm not okay with it. It's a horrible day on all levels."

She finally let him slightly off the hook. "I'm not opposed to your view. I don't know if I ever considered the 'evil government' view, but I have always valued guns as reasonable tools. I think that we can't be blind to the reality of people dying wholesale." Of course, she saw the irony in her saying those words, but it was how she thought either way.

"Fair enough, I think we also have to consider the media's responsibility in mass violence," Hector offered. "They are the sounding board in every American home, and it's very clear they all have an agenda. We shouldn't take that lightly either."

The night went on much like this. Several nearby tables lingered over their dinners, staying longer than initially intended to enjoy the fiery conversation. She and Hector were too enthralled in their conversation to notice. They had arrived at dinnertime and stayed right up to the point where it became apparent that the workers wanted them to leave. One of the waitresses was inching ever closer as she put the chairs upside down on the tables, while the hostess steadily progressed toward them with the sweeping and mopping. They had clearly stayed as long as they could.

She finally commented, "Looks like we are getting kicked out."

The Ashen Horse

"Yeah, we could try going to an after party?"

She laughed, "An after-party?"

"Well, I meant like a bar or something. I don't know, whatever the kids are doing nowadays."

She was truly beginning to find him slightly irresistible. She laughed again. "Well, I took another rideshare here, so I'm game to go somewhere else or head out either way."

"It is late." He looked chagrined right after he said that; clearly, he hadn't meant to.

"Yes, it is, and morning does come early. Look, would you mind taking me home? So, I don't have to use another rideshare?" She saw that he looked disheartened as if he realized he had played that entirely wrong. A split-second poor word choice, and he perceived the night as being over.

Hector picked up the tab and left a hearty tip in a chivalrous move. She assumed he left a good tip based on how happy the waitress became after accepting the final payment. They left the restaurant and got into his car to ride to her place.

Twenty minutes later, they pulled up to the rental house. "Wow, a house right on the beach. This place is incredible."

"Yep, I've been enjoying it. Morning walks on the beach every day. It's really something, actually."

"Amazing. It has that cozy cottage feeling, white picket fence and all."

"Half buried in the sand, but it is a white fence."

"A little piece of Americana right here. This is what makes Florida so great. This picturesque scene is why I truly love living here. The white caps on the ocean glide into the beach, all while sitting on the porch next to a white picket fence. That's the good life."

She chuckled. "That's a little more sentimental than I've gotten out of you all night."

Hector laughed as well. "Yeah, well, I'm just a sucker for the ocean."

The discussion dwindled into that moment of

awkwardness of two people just sitting in a car at the end of the night. He had left the car idling as they discussed the house. He hesitated slightly while leaning over and completely missed the late-night kiss he was angling for because she split-secondly popped the door open and jumped out of the car. His face went completely red.

"Are you blushing?"

His face grew even redder. She laughed outright—the full and rich laugh of truly uncontrolled mirth.

She wanted to push it further and commented, "It was a great night. I needed this, thank you."

Still rosy in the cheeks, he went for the gentlemanly approach again, saying, "Honestly, it was my pleasure. We should do it again soon."

Then she put her cards on the table, continuing to laugh throughout because she couldn't contain herself. "We absolutely should do it again. But for now, are you coming in or not?"

His face split into a genuinely astonishing smile. "Oh, I'm definitely coming in."

"I believe there was something about an after-party we must see to."

The clothes started flying off before the front door was even closed.

The following day was an enjoyable adventure all on its own. In their haste, they forgot to turn off the car. It had run all night, or at least until it had run out of gas.

Chapter Thirteen

Dining In

She was having a proper midlife crisis. The last week had been a blur of emotion, but the overriding feeling was tremendous joy. She had fallen for Hector. Hector Garcia was a simply wonderful man. Gracious, kind, and fun—he was surprisingly fun. They had been having a fantastic time together. Not only was it absolutely amazing in the bedroom—and it was—but they had been truly enjoying each other's company. The long walks on the beach all weekend, where they talked about everything, were entirely new for her.

She had opened up to Hector in ways she had never opened up to anyone. She didn't even realize it was still possible for her to do. She told him about her childhood experiences. She had talked to him in depth about her travels and some of the causes she was passionate about. She was so enthralled with the fun she had been having that she hadn't even thought about her primary mission in tracking down a way to enter Molly's compound. She was supposed to be trying to get close to Molly, but she hadn't thought about Molly all week.

It was an extraordinary time. She started moving money around various accounts and shoring up her long-term investments. She had been living this life for almost fifteen years, and for the last ten, she had been making a killing financially. And literally. She had money; she would never have to work again if she didn't want to. And she was moving that money into long-term investment strategies. It was terrifying in the depth of scope, but she was honestly considered walking away from it all.

Her mind had started considering plans outside of her current occupation. And Hector was the primary reason for that. She had begun to shape her life and her future around the possibility that she could walk away. She could walk away from all of it.

She could build a life here. Couldn't she? Could she leave everything and create a new life here in Florida? Was it entirely irrational to make these kinds of plans after just a week and a half? These questions plagued her for the last several days and why she hadn't slept well the last several nights. It was too soon to be making these kinds of rash decisions, she knew this. But she was making them anyway.

Hector had risen this morning and gone to work for Molly, something they still hadn't discussed. He said that he did IT Security for a private organization. She had spent the morning sipping her white chocolate mocha with soy, no whip. She was sitting on the back porch of her beach house, looking out over the ocean. Her mind was spinning in circles. What in the world was she doing? It had only been a few days. It was too soon to be swooning like this.

They had skirted discussions around her job as well, of course. But she always had several fake careers handy that she could leverage as necessary. In this case, she was a writer who spent her days writing and doing research on her laptop—while drinking coffee. This facilitated several reasonable scenarios of why she didn't have to report to work and why she could also be sitting at a beach house whenever she wanted to be.

Money hadn't come up too much in the relationship, but a couple of things were evident to both of them. They both realized they were financially secure. She didn't know what Molly was paying him, but it facilitated a healthy lifestyle. Of course, she couldn't point to anything she had published, so if the relationship went further, she could say she was a struggling author with a trust fund. Wealthy parents or grandparents could easily explain away her financial means when the relationship went further. Her cautious nature ensured she always thought two steps ahead and needed an alibi and an explanation.

However, the more she thought about it, the more she wasn't sure that it was a good approach. Perhaps she'd change the kind of writer she was. Maybe she wrote product reviews, or she was a technical writer. Many authors wrote for companies and never actually published or had their names associated directly with the content they created. She would have to consider her options; she would need a better background story at some point.

She sat on the porch, developing that backstory. She couldn't have been a failing writer for the last decade; she must have done something else. Writing had to be a new endeavor she was attempting for a season. Her financial knowledge was sound. She decided that she had been a financial advisor in her previous life. Or a senior assistant to a financial advisor who burned out and walked away. That's when she took up writing. Maybe she didn't need the trust fund; perhaps she made enough in the market before giving it all up to sit on a beach.

Her mind wandered for fifteen minutes as she thought about his eyes and smile. His hands. What was happening to her? This wasn't right; it wasn't right at all. His hands, though. The things he could do with his hands. She blushed. She needed more coffee.

She decided to be productive. Well, she decided she needed more coffee. This involved leaving the house to go to the same coffee shop owned by Molly. At that point, she could get some shopping done for the day and start a homemade dinner for when Hector got off work. She would never be the traditional domestic wife, but she enjoyed cooking when the opportunity presented itself. That might be because she rarely did it.

She was on her way to her rental car when she blushed again. Did she really just think about being a wife? She truly was having a midlife crisis. She didn't know how else to think about it. These were things, thoughts, and decisions that she had never entertained. How could she possibly be in this position?

A few minutes later, she was sipping a fresh mocha and on her way to the grocery store. Once she committed to a plan, she committed to it. She had texted Hector, saying she would try her hand at cooking dinner, and he was welcome to come over. His response could only be described as eager. It might have helped if she had any idea what she planned to cook, but she didn't. That part must come later. Of course, in five minutes, she would be standing in the grocery store; that was the later part.

Later came. She was standing in the middle of the grocery store's produce section, slowly reading through a library of online recipes and meal suggestions. There's always that one person buried in their smartphone, standing right in the middle of the aisle. Usually clueless to the world. Today, it was her. Everyone gets to take a turn at being that guy.

It took ten minutes of indecision until she finally landed on a chicken tikka masala recipe that looked to die for. She didn't know how hot Hector liked his food, but he would eat spicy food tonight. Once she had made the decision, she got excited about it. It felt like ages since she had eaten genuinely authentic Indian food and probably longer still since she had cooked it.

She went home, put on her personalized playlist, and started all the preparation. She had several hours before Hector would show up, so she took the time to make a full four-course meal. She wanted the chicken super tender and largely precooked, so it went in the oven for an hour, basted, and dipped in butter and lemon. While that was cooking pleasantly, she moved on to the salad. She opted for nothing fancy with the salad but threw in a host of veggies and topped it off with sliced apples.

While skimming the original tikka masala recipe, she came across a dahl soup recipe and decided to make that as a side. It took a minute to cook on the stovetop, but she finally started prepping the tikka masala once it was in full swing.

At the last minute, she stopped and considered what precisely an Indian meal was without naan. She spent the last half hour before Hector arrived trying her hand at cooking naan. She hadn't realized how tricky the bread could be. It wasn't her best work, but it was a passable attempt.

Overall, she was incredibly pleased with how the meal turned out. And just as she was pulling hot naan out of her pan, she heard a knock at the door. She could hardly contain her excitement as she went to answer it. She would be happy to see Hector but finally get to eat this magnificent creation she had put together.

She opened the door, and there he was—slightly unkempt hair, quirky smile, light brown skin, and barely a hint of accent. She laughed as he sauntered in. He laughed as well. It was apparent he had had a decent day at the office because he was in a good mood. But she had never really found him not in a good mood; part of his charm was a consistent disposition. She paused and just looked at him and realized she was happy. Truly happy. It had been so long since she had felt that inner peace, the calming joy of acceptance, that sincere feeling of home. She felt at home.

As he entered the house, he took a breath in. He paused, then really breathed in. And just for good measure, he did it a third time. "Asombroso! Increíble. This house smells amazing. What have you been doing?"

"Just a little cooking."

"This is more than a little cooking." He took another

deep breath. "I don't know if I have ever cooked anything this extensive in my life."

"I had some time on my hands. I thought I'd whip something up." She snickered a bit at that herself. She couldn't keep up the pretense, although she was tempted to try. "Okay, okay. I'm not going to lie. It's been a while since I cooked anything this extensive myself. I've been tempted to eat half a dozen times waiting for you to arrive. So, let's dive in. I can't wait any longer. Super glad you are here, on time, no less."

They were both chuckling as he said, "Happy to oblige."

He had picked up a bottle of white wine, a lovely Chardonnay. She handed him the corkscrew and started dishing up two plates to put on the table. There wasn't much talking during the meal except the occasional mumble of exultation. The meal had turned out better than she had hoped.

Hector leaned back in his chair and patted his stomach. "Suffice it to say, I ate entirely too much. I don't think I can even waddle right now. And I think I still want thirds. Is it fourths?"

"There's still more."

He laughed. "No, no. I mean, I do, but no. I don't think I can even walk to get it."

She got a very mischievous grin on her face. And with her best possible sexy interpretation, she sauntered up to him, draping a leg across his knee. "Dessert then?"

"Uh. Umm... Yes? Please?"

She pulled away quickly, still flaunting the sultry hip swaying. "Excellent, I'll meet you on the porch with the bottle of wine. Wine counts as a dessert."

"Wait a minute," he growled. "That's not playing fair."

"All is fair in love and war, my dear."

"I've been hoodwinked."

She smiled as she headed to the porch and said, "Yes... bring the wine."

The Ashen Horse

They spent the next several hours polishing off the bottle of wine and enjoying each other's company, quietly talking about life. The conversation would lapse occasionally, and they enjoyed the company and watched the rolling ocean. The pleasant sounds of the water whooshing slowly into the beach and receding, its consistency, almost like a heartbeat. A constant thrumming of the planet, keeping time, capturing the moment.

They watched the ocean as the sunset. The colors played a musical orchestration as they rhymed across the sky. Dancing and playing across the clouds and through the spaces between, changing and pulsing. It was the perfect day. A hush fell over both of them as the sun slowly set, and they enjoyed the marvel presented before them—a perfect moment.

As the light faded and darkness set in, she finally spoke up. "That was wonderful." Her tone was slightly different, and he noticed and looked over. It wasn't her placid and relaxed tone for the last several hours, a tone of contentment. This was more instinctual; there was a craving in it. Her mischievous grin returned. "Now, it's truly time for dessert."

Then, she pounced.

Hector didn't stand a chance. He also couldn't resist. He attempted to move them to the bedroom, but she didn't even let him get inside. Well, the porch of a beach house was as good as anywhere, right? He hadn't noticed anyone on the beach, but he wasn't paying attention either.

After, they finally retreated to the bedroom and cuddled. She lay there, eyes closed, nestled into his arms, slowly listening to his heartbeat. At this moment, she knew that this was the life she wanted. That she would do almost anything to have this life.

She had made a decision. The decision. Molly would live, and she would walk away. She would leave it all to have more days and nights like this one.

She drifted to sleep. The peace and contentment in her

soul were like nothing she had ever known.

Chapter Fourteen

Fibbies in Seattle

It was Tuesday morning, and Josh and Ellie were out for breakfast before heading into the office in Seattle. Josh had opted for the healthy options this morning, some form of gruel, although he didn't look like he was particularly enjoying it. Ellie had the traditional American fare: pancakes, eggs, and bacon.

Ellie chucked, "You really should get an omelet or something."

"Probably. I've been trying to eat healthy, or at least healthier."

Ellie smacked some bacon into her mouth. "Maybe, but how can you not enjoy the pig? He's so tasty."

"I'm not quitting anything, you know. Just trying moderation."

"Missing out on the best things in life, Josh. The best things." She chomped on another bite of bacon.

"So, anyway... my dietary issues aside. What do you think they'll have for us?"

They had arrived in town in the early evening yesterday, had a quick dinner, and then had gone to their hotel rooms. They hadn't discussed the case in four or five days, which seemed like a lifetime. They were both anxious about what they could uncover here. Did Seattle PD actually have a katana in their evidence rooms?

"I've been thinking about it, and I think we'll just have to wait and see," Ellie said thoughtfully. "I mean, they must have recovered the sword. Assuming no one lost it, they should still have it in evidence, right? I hope. I saw the photos; the katana was protruding right from the guy's chest."

Josh waved to the waitress. "It should be an interesting day. That's for sure." Turning to the waitress, he said, "I'm sorry, excuse me. I thought I saw a breakfast burrito on the menu. Can I get one of those to go? Thank you."

"See, backsliding already."

"It was your idea. The burrito can't be that unhealthy."

"And a solidly epic idea it was. Let's get out of here; let's see what these people have for us."

Navigating the city's traffic took a minute, but they made it to Seattle's evidence warehouse. Their team had arranged the meeting location and lined up a couple of the detectives who had worked on the original case twelve years ago. Two of them were still on the job. One was retired, and Roshan was still trying to track him down.

They had arranged to spend the first three hours of the day combing through files and evidence, then they'd break for lunch, which they would most likely have delivered so they could keep digging.

In the afternoon, they had two hours to talk to the detectives. Or however long it took. Depending on what they found, they'd return the following couple of days to keep digging. This case was old enough that none of this information was digital. There were discussions on how much case information they'd convert to digital documentation and then email or upload to the larger team. Depending on where the evidence took them, they might be emailing quite a few different teams.

They pulled in and walked into the warehouse. It felt like a warehouse, too. A warehouse among warehouses, buried in the industrial section of Seattle. It was like driving through a maze of a thousand buildings that all looked identical. The industrial sections of cities always felt the same—working class, rundown but tidily kept, stoic, and always the same bricks and motor, just solidly announcing their presence to the world.

"Hello, we are Ellie Lopez and Josh Dupont, special agents with the Federal Bureau of Investigation. We are here to examine evidence relating to an old cold case, Brandon Eriks."

The front desk officer looked up and made notes in the visitor's log. "Yeah, your team made sure we were expecting you. Not to step on anyone's toes, but they went a little overboard. One email would have done the trick, you know?"

Josh, half speaking to himself, commented, "They are efficient. Maybe to a fault, but they probably wanted to ensure we didn't fly across the country for nothing. At least, that's what we will tell ourselves."

"Sure, let's go with that. Some officers put everything related to the Brandon Eriks case into a conference room. We need your credentials to get you in as visitors, and we should be good. Obviously, and this goes without saying, none of the evidence leaves the facility, ever."

Ellie asked if they had digitizing equipment in the facility. Specifically, a printer that could scan a couple thousand pages if it came to that.

"Yeah, we have a full-scale multifunctional device; we should be able to scan it all and email it directly if that's the goal. We don't digitize all the old stuff. That said, if you digitize anything, email us as well. I'll get you directions. We now put anything that gets digitized in our encrypted cloud, log it to specific cases, and make it searchable. We don't really go back and touch old cases, but if someone is going to be scanning it anyway, we'll get it locked and loaded into our databases."

"Sounds like fun," Josh said sarcastically.

"Living the dream."

"Don't we know it? Appreciate it, man; we'll stew in our conference room."

"One last thing, you're meeting this afternoon; it's outside the security zone, in that conference room. So, we don't have to screen in the two detectives. They set it up, but they both hate logging in. Once you exit for that meeting, we'll probably keep you out the rest of the day, but you'll have to swing by tomorrow to at least box everything back up or continue digging. Logging in and out is as annoying for us as everyone else."

"Got it, thanks, man."

Ellie and Josh didn't expect that much evidence. Perhaps a box or two of effects that were confiscated with the crime. Another box may contain notes and information surrounding the case and the investigation. Probably a special large box to hold the sword and other documents.

Their entire expectation added up to maybe three to four boxes. They had planned a couple of days here to be on the safe side to make sure they could comb through the entire case and talk to everyone. Maybe they would even reach out to some witnesses and get the firsthand details if it came to that.

This meant they weren't prepared for what they saw when they walked into the conference room. The entire back wall had boxes stacked up. There must have been at least twenty, maybe thirty.

Josh's jaw hit the deck as he stared into the room. "What the?" Ellie hadn't made it to the room yet; she was scouting the exits in and out of the conference room, checking the side doors in and out of the warehouse and a couple of paths to each. She hadn't seen inside the room yet, but after quickly scanning the building, she walked up to Josh. Josh was still standing in the doorway to the conference room.

She asked, "What we got that has you in a twitter?" She

The Ashen Horse

finally nudged him forward a bit so she could see around him. Then, she also saw the thirty boxes stacked up. The only response she could utter was, "Oh, good Lord. We had better call Tim."

***

Tim was in semi-shock when he hung up the phone. He really couldn't believe what Josh and Ellie had told him. A quick survey of the boxes totaled forty-eight boxes relating to the Brandon Eriks case. They hadn't even seen the second row when they entered the room. It had taken them an hour to sort and order them to figure out what they had. Tim had expected them to stay in Seattle for maybe a day or two to lock in the evidence and screen the detectives for details. Now, he was thinking two weeks, perhaps more.

He walked down to Roshan's office. Perhaps Roshan knew more than he did about the case; this seemed like a giant can of worms. Maybe they should cut bait now and walk away before it led them down a lengthy, engaged inquiry that no one had the stomach for.

"Yo, Roshan. You got a minute?"

"Just digging through another case." Roshan spun his chair around to get away from his monitors. Then, he spun it back to grab his energy drink and spun back around to face Tim.

"Sure, what's up?"

"How much do you know about Brandon Eriks? Like, really know?"

"I don't know much, only what I skimmed through the case description and the original medical examiner's report. And what I remember from national news."

"National news?"

"Sure, it was a huge case a decade ago; it was all over the news for a week or two."

Tim looked perplexed. "How do I not remember any of this?"

"Might have been busy with something else when it was

going on? Anyway, Brandon Eriks was that startup founder who invented Ishy-Pops."

"The candy?"

"Yep. As far as I know, the product line is still going strong. I invested a couple thousand when they hit the market. Come to think about it; maybe that's why I paid attention to the news. Anyway, Brandon Eriks made a killing when the company went public. Cleared a ridiculous amount of money in the IPO. He didn't leave the company, but the rumors suggested he wasn't involved with it after it went public; he was too busy being a playboy all over the world."

"That's where the prostitution ring comes into play?"

"Something like that. I don't know anything about that. But I do remember it was a huge scandal when it hit the news after he was killed. It probably would have been two days in the national news if he was just murdered, but then a whole bunch of stuff about the widespread prostitution came to light. It was ugly. The media sucked up every ounce of the story. It was the kind of television you can't make up."

"I might remember some of that now that you mention it. I vaguely remember the news reports about the Ishy-Pop founder getting killed." Tim stared out Roshan's window, trying to jar something loose in his mind from twelve years ago. "I have an image in my mind of this young guy in a suit presenting something to a board of directors."

"Yep, that's the story. They showed that stock photo for a week straight. It was Brandon, but like ten years before when he was still getting the company on its feet."

"Then they found him with a katana protruding from his chest. I don't remember that in the news."

"I don't either; they must have kept that piece under wraps. They must have; the media would have been all over that. That's unforgettable television."

"Alright, Roshan. What else do we have here?"

"Hard to say, Tim. The investigation went on forever, I know that. I don't know if the Bureau was ever involved; it might have just been a Seattle thing, but I wouldn't have been surprised if other agencies or cities were involved. Brandon really did get around and travel a lot. He must have been in half the major cities in America leading up to his death. Any investigation must have spanned a ton of jurisdictions."

Tim looked a little queasy. "Great. That's just super. Ugh. This will be a disaster, man. We don't know anything yet, except it sure looks like Ash was behind it. But how do we do this without reopening the entire case? We could get stuck in a yearlong investigation just on this."

"It's going to be a tightrope walk for sure."

Tim often came to Roshan for advice. Roshan had seen it all in his thirty years with the Bureau. He wanted to keep his head down. But he never minded driving cases from the rear. Tim knew the man was anxiously awaiting his retirement and that he kept a calendar with those three years slowly ticking down—just three simple years to getting out. But being a driver of decisions within his sphere of influence had always appealed to Roshan, especially when he could do it from the point of influence and outside the spotlight. Another thing he had learned in his career was that the best decisions were made by team members who weren't in the crosshairs; the real power was always behind the frontman.

"Always appreciate the insight, Roshan. I'm sure we will talk again about this. I want Josh and Ellie to dive in, but at the same time, we must keep our heads above water here. One other thought, though: you knew they were walking into a storm, didn't you?"

Roshan looked a little sheepish. "Yes. But, in my defense, I assumed the team knew something about Brandon Eriks. I didn't think it was so long ago that everyone wouldn't connect the dots. That's why I escalated the case and did the leg work to ensure Seattle was ready for us. Everything about that case fits Ash's MO."

Tim sighed, "It does that. Okay, thanks, Roshan. Let's just try not to get sucked into a two-year reinvestigation of a cold case."

"If we catch the bastard, we get to close it, though."

As Tim turned around, he agreed, "There is that." He headed back to his desk. He sat down and stared out the window for the next ten minutes, thinking about how to keep the case moving forward, while at the same time not getting lost in the minutiae or bogged down in a multiyear investigation that would suck up all of his team's resources.

***

"Ellie!" It wasn't quite a shout, but the exclamation coming from Josh was palpable.

"What?" Ellie asked. They had been digging through boxes for the last two days. It was a mountain of paperwork—evidence, files, transcripts. The detectives who were originally on the case tried hard to find the killer. They had documentation on everything. They had interviewed half of Seattle, or so it felt. Ellie was deep in thought when she heard Josh a second time.

"Ellie!"

"For heaven's sake, what?"

"Look at this," Josh exclaimed again as he waved around a sheet of paper. It flapped excitedly in Josh's hand, almost like it might take flight.

Ellie was reluctant to stand up and walk over, as she was waist-deep in two boxes spread out on the table with papers stacked everywhere. But Josh's flapping paper was still whistling through the air, so she finally inched free of the mess she had created and headed to the other end of the table.

"Is that a composite?!" Ellie sounded as excited as Josh had been. "What is this? We have a composite?"

"Someone saw what the detectives later thought was the murderer walking away. This is the composite drawing." Josh handed Ellie the composite drawing and flipped the page on what he had been reading.

Josh read from the case notes. "It also looks like this,"

The Ashen Horse

Josh paused and pointed to the composite drawing while explaining, "This referring to the composite." Josh went back to reading the case notes, "It also looks like this aligns with a photo of the killer. The composite and the photo closely resemble each other." Josh finished reading the notation and looked expectantly at Ellie.

"We have a photo?!" Ellie, now indeed, was excited. They had a photo of Ash!

"Or so this record reports anyway," Josh explained. "I still haven't found a photo, though. It's buried in these boxes somewhere. Or, well, so the reports say." He lost his train of thought and just stared emotionless at the table. After a moment he kind of jerked and shook his head. "Sorry, my mind is still on the composite, that's pretty huge. It could really crack this case wide open. With Ash being in the top ten most wanted, if we could put an image with that or a photo, that alone might solve this thing."

Ellie was nodding. "This could break the case, honestly. It's a decent composite too. There's a surprising amount of detail. Funny how our two detectives failed to mention this piece of information. It would have been helpful. 'Oh, by the way, there's a picture of the killer in those boxes.' That's the kind of information you generally like to pass along."

Josh couldn't have agreed more. "They weren't that helpful."

"No, they weren't. Surprising though, the documents look in good shape, and everything we have found here looks in order. But no, they didn't like us sniffing around the case at all. They really weren't helpful."

"Probably just turf stuff. Nobody likes us fibbies digging into their laundry. Dirty laundry, generally."

Ellie chuckled, "We usually wash better, though."

"Damn right we do."

Josh flipped the report he was reading, and Ellie continued to study the composite. They both said it at the same time, "We need to find the photo." Then they shared a look. Josh said, "We are thinking the same thing." He chuckled, "Obviously, right?" After the laugh, which Ellie shared with a knowing smile, he went on, "But what's your reasoning?"

"It's just this dude looks like a pretty boy. He also looks like a kid. This can't be Ash. This kid looks like, what – twenty-five, maybe? His features look soft, almost feminine, a true pretty boy." Ellie was still thinking and speaking out loud, "You know, he looks like one of those boys out of the boy bands. All soft features and pretty looks."

"Keep in mind it was twelve years ago."

"True," Ellie said while puzzling out her thoughts. "Do we think Ash was what, mid-twenties, twelve years ago? That would make him what, mid-thirties, now? Maybe late thirties?"

"I don't know if we had enough information at all before to pin dates on anything. But this starts to build a timeline, which sounds right based on what we know about this case."

"Everything we've combed through the last two days. Do you get the feeling this was the killer's first kill?" asked Ellie.

Josh shook his head. "No. This killing might not have been clean, but it wasn't sloppy, either. There appear to be precautions taken; it seems thought-out. The killer, based on the two reports from the beat cops, seems to have known exactly when and where Brandon would be and took advantage of that situation."

Ellie agreed. "Yes. This means that at, let's say, twenty-five, Ash is already a semi-seasoned killer. That's disturbing. This all assumes that many of our conclusions are accurate. But if this picture is of Ash, and right now, we must assume it is. In this composite, this man sure looks in his early to mid-twenties."

"We need to find the photo. See how much it aligns with this composite. It might be all speculation until we put some more meat behind it."

Ellie laid the composite back down on the table. "I need

The Ashen Horse

to get a picture of this." She tried to take a picture of the paper, but the glare and lighting were off. "Blasted technology." She swooped up the paper and walked between the lights to the middle of the table. "Better." She took a picture.

Ellie said, "This is gold, anyway you look at it. If this is Ash, this is the best break yet that we've had in the case." She continued to play around with her smartphone.

Josh had been devouring the report he was reading, still flipping pages. "What's next?"

"I'm starving; I need to get some food or something."

"I meant, like, what are you doing now?"

She stopped working on her phone and looked over at him. He did have an endearing smile. He was too young for her, though, wasn't he? Ellie stopped cold for a moment, then thought to herself, "Shit."

They needed to stop working so closely together. Her mind finally registered his question, and she shook herself out of the blank stare she'd been giving him.

"Oh, right, my phone. Yes, well. I'm putting together an email to the team, including the composite. I want the forensic guys to run it through every database and hit against open cases." They were only like eight years apart, maybe that wasn't too much of an age gap.

"I don't know why I didn't think of that. Nice work, Ellie. Very nice work. So, you said something about food? We should eat. Then try to find this elusive photo."

Her fingers were flying on her smartphone. "Just about to hit send," she said softly as she was still concentrating and blazing a trail across the screen. "And done," she exclaimed as she looked up. Her eyes hit his. She felt both comfortable and uncomfortable simultaneously. Her mind started to race. She thought, "This might get awkward; I have to get this sorted quickly." She mentally sighed, and her mind continued to churn as her eyes locked on Josh's pleasant smile.

"Curse you, Curse me. Blasted feelings and emotions

and… just blah. Curse it all."

What she said out loud was, "Food sounds good; let's go."

Chapter Fifteen

David Smith

Ellie was digging through another box—literally digging. Papers were getting scattered everywhere as she shuffled them out of the box, and then she dove back in for the next stack. This box appeared to hold transcripts of over fifty interviews carried out in the case. Was it one of three interview boxes? Perhaps there were five? They still didn't have a complete inventory in all of this mess, although they were getting there.

They had set up a system, such as it was. They first concluded that both of them should read everything or at least solidly skim everything. Perhaps this defeated the whole divide and conquer approach, but it ensured that they both would have a full view of the entire case, and if one of them missed something, hopefully, the other one would catch it. That was decision number one.

Decision number two was that they should talk about what they learned every day. They had decided that the last hour of every day was carved out entirely just to discuss what each of them had reviewed that day. Of course, they also spent most of dinner discussing the case or the larger Ash case. However, they finally had to branch out to other topics and found they had a surprising number of common interests.

Decision number three was note-taking. They each kept detailed notes of everything they reviewed. Anything particular to the case and anything they wanted to return to and review. Detailed notes about what was present in each box, as well as notes on how to find stuff again between all the different boxes. They were both ten or twenty pages deep in notes and probably only finished with fifteen boxes each.

This directly brought them to decision number four. Inventory everything. They started inventorying the boxes, giving each box a number and cataloging what was in it. Although, to some degree, this was done at the evidence level, they were not happy with the depth of detail in the existing logging and inventory sheets. It hadn't helped them find anything, so they were expanding it in detail.

Josh was flipping through the eyewitness reports. There were several casual impromptu interview notes from the detectives and then at least three official interviews, all transcripts. And, of course, the signed affidavits from at least one witness. Josh wasn't sure how it had made it to a deposition, but in his stack of papers, it looked like an official deposition of the witness's testimony. The paperwork was incredible and largely unending.

Josh glanced up as Ellie grunted. She grunted again as she finally just turned the box upside down on the table. That may be the easiest way to empty them all out. She started at the now top of the stack (the bottom of the box), reading and placing them back into the bottom as she went.

"I guess that's one way to approach it."

"Shut up."

"Yes, ma'am."

Josh put down the report he'd just finished and picked up the next one. When he did, he saw the files underneath it. One of them was a pristine photo. Still glossy. It wasn't a photocopy or some other duplicated effort. It was a full 8x11 printed gloss photo. Beautiful. It was monochrome and looked like a street camera or an ATM camera, but still, it was a full-scale photo. Josh silently mouthed, "Wow."

Still, in a trance-like state, all Josh could do was whisper, "Ellie...."

"I said shut up."

"What?"

"My box skills are sharp and tactful and executed with precision."

"Huh? Oh." Josh chuckled despite himself. "Yes, exquisite, to be sure. One might even say highly refined."

"Yes, exactly. Refined."

"Now that we've established that. Come over here and look at this."

With her head buried in a report, she continued in a joking manner. "You know I can't get anything done with your constant interruptions. If it's anything less than the photo, I might have to hurt you." She kept digging, her head buried in the papers. The silence stretched as she shifted a couple more sheets of paper. She wondered why Josh hadn't said anything; he was always quick with a retort. Finally, she glanced up and saw his face beaming in a wide grin.

Ellie dropped her papers. "No? Really? The photo?" She was shuffling the papers back into the order they needed to be in as she kept an eye on Josh. Eventually, when the papers were in order, she bolted over from the other side of the room to the box Josh was working on.

"Oh, my. That's beautiful."

"It really is."

She hesitated when she realized he was looking at her when he said it and not at the photo. She shook her head and went back to the image.

"Let's get this scanned and take a picture of this on our phones right now. We need to get this over to the team. We need to get Tim on a call, like now. Look at this. It's black and white, but that's a clear picture of Ash, and it looks just like the composite. We got our guy."

She realized she had been rambling; perhaps she was overcompensating. She wasn't even sure. "Get it together, woman," she thought.

"The other interesting thing here, Ellie, in this other report I read earlier today, they mentioned that this individual might have used the name David Smith. They seemed to have some information from a hotel stay or a rental card receipt, which said it was David Smith. I'm also trying to track that down."

Ellie looked amazed. "Wait? You didn't mention that before. We think we have a name?"

"I can't imagine it is real, but I would argue we might have an alias that the killer used. But, yes, that also needs to be circulated with the team. I was trying to track down the actual source of information before we populated it. I have only heard it mentioned; I haven't found the receipts or statements saying that 'David Smith' is the actual name."

"Yep, we need to validate that. But this is definitely worth getting Tim on the phone."

Ellie popped out her cell phone and was about to call Tim, but then she looked up his number and called him on the room's conference phone instead. It seemed to ring forever, but he eventually picked up.

"Tim Burkman, FBI."

Ellie considered messing with him for a moment but thought better of it. "Hi Tim, it's Josh and Ellie. Sorry, called you from the conference room phone."

"Oh. You are lucky I picked up; half the time, I don't pick up numbers I don't have programmed."

Ellie might have been able to resist the temptation, but Josh couldn't. "Somehow, that doesn't surprise me at all, boss."

"Uh-huh. Love you too, Josh. So, what's up?"

"You want to tell him?" asked Ellie.

"Sure, I guess. Are you texting him the picture?" Josh inquired.

"Yep. Photo coming at you, Tim."

"Anyway, boss-man, here's the scoop. We found the picture of the supposed killer in the Brandon Eriks case. Whom we suppose, at least currently, is Ash. The person in the photo, which you should have by now, looks early to mid-twenties. We also have a supposed alias for the killer if the paperwork here is to be believed. A 'David Smith.'"

The line was quiet for a minute. Josh and Ellie stared at each other, waiting. They were about to say something when Tim finally spoke up.

"Do we actually have the bastard?"

Ellie laughed outright. "That was pretty much my response as well, Tim. The photo looks almost identical to the composite. It's pretty amazing, really."

"Yes, this photo is just like the composite," Tim confirmed. "And the eyewitness identified and described the person independently of the photo, correct?"

Josh wasn't sure. It was the working presumption, but he jotted the detail down in his notebook. One more thing they should try to verify. They would need to confirm they were truly independent evidence trails. "That's a good question, Tim; I don't actually know. I'm making a note of it, though; we'll follow up to make sure they are both clean lines."

"Once again, guys, this is fantastic work."

Ellie commented, "Thanks, Tim. We will get out another email, following up on our composite one earlier, that shares the photo with the team. We obviously want to get it run through all the databases. The alias as well; see if 'David Smith' spikes an alert anywhere. Probably will; such a common name is probably all over the legal spectrum."

Josh agreed entirely. "Probably his purpose in using it. With this guy, I wouldn't be surprised if we find a John Doe alias in use for one of his kills. There is probably a John Johnson or Bill Williams in this guy's bag of tricks."

Tim asked the question he had been debating the last several days, ever since the composite photo had been found.

"The million-dollar question is, do we make this public?"

"I'm not sure," Ellie said. "Pros and cons are going both ways, probably. It's also twelve years old. If we make it public, we should take the photo, recreate it digitally, and then digitize it to age it twelve years and release it. This might also protect its origin. Ash might not see it coming or know where he screwed up."

Josh grinned. "That's smart, Ellie. We might finally get a one-up on this guy. Blindside him with a picture; he won't even know where it's coming from."

"That's a great idea," Tim agreed. "I asked the question because the 'Most Wanted' team keeps asking me about a picture. I explained to them that we didn't have any pictures of Ash, hence one of our major obstacles. But now we do, in theory. We could release this. That would make them super happy. They might get off my back. They are bloody predators; you have no idea."

Josh couldn't resist again. "That's why you get paid the big bucks, boss."

"Uh-huh."

Ellie had been considering the options. "Let's make it public. We still don't have a lot. We have a ton of cases tied to Ash, but virtually zero physical evidence. This picture and alias are the first of anything we really have that is concrete. A tip might be what breaks this case. Someone, somewhere, is living next to this guy. All we need them to do is recognize him. People have gotten caught for stupider reasons than that."

"Sounds like a plan to me." Tim was on board. "We just need to ensure a tip line is set up and hopefully screen out the dead ends. We might finally accept the leadership's offer to get more bodies. We must staff that and get a team to follow up on all the tips. That coordination will be a whole thing."

"That's why you get paid...", started Josh—but he could not get it all out because he chortled right in the middle of the sentence.

"Very funny, Josh, very funny."

Josh didn't really jibe at anyone else, but with Tim, it was too easy not to follow through.

"This is good work, team. So, how are you both really doing there? Do you think there is more to glean?"

Josh responded, "Yep, we haven't even gotten to the sword yet. It's buried in here somewhere."

"Another week? Two?"

"Yeah, probably another week anyway. And then it'll only be a high-level survey of the case. Not sure we want to go deeper anyway, though."

"We really don't," Tim said. "All right, I'll look for the email with the details about the alias and the photo, but that's awesome news, guys. Once I have that, I'll respond with the request for the forensic team to age it; after we get that, I'll forward it to the 'Most Wanted' team."

"Sounds like a plan," commented Ellie.

"This is awesome work, guys. I'll let you get back to it."

"Later, boss."

Ellie clicked the hang-up button on the conference room phone. "Back to it?"

Josh smiled. "You know it. I'll get the scan and email this time around; let you get back to being productive on your box skills."

Ellie laughed. "My refined box skills."

"Very refined."

Chapter Sixteen

An Experiment in Writing

She awoke to a bright new day. Her decision to leave the life entirely behind her was one of her best decisions ever. It likely was the best decision. Joy filled her, a smile cascading across her face. She was finally acclimating to what it would be like to walk away from the killing. A piece of her would miss it. The rush, the adrenaline. The challenge, the pursuit. It was a captivating experience to hunt a worthy adversary. Most of her victims hadn't been that worthy, but she had met a couple. Molly would have been one.

Hector was still sleeping. She carefully rolled out of bed and went to get coffee. She usually went out to get coffee as often as not, but that didn't mean she couldn't make a mean cup herself when required. She started brewing a pot, flipped on the TV, and watched the early morning news. The current news segment was two people joking in a kitchen, graciously attempting to cook something. That would probably be over in a minute.

She heard the coffee gurgling that it had finished brewing, and she poured herself a cup. She didn't watch TV often and was about to walk out on the porch and ignore the TV when she heard the name 'David Smith' mentioned by one of the announcers. It was a common enough name; she probably shouldn't have even cared. However, there was a lingering déjà vu in her mind. She had used 'David Smith' as an alias years ago.

She rapidly discovered that the coverage was, in fact, about her. They were presenting breaks in the case of the Ashen Horse. She was surprised at what good work the FBI was doing. None of the other local jurisdictions would have linked as many of her cases as they had. Should she stop using the sword for a while? She hated using a gun, though, no finesse.

She grinned as the realization sank in. She wouldn't need to use either for a very long time, hopefully ever again. Perhaps she was getting out at the perfect time. When the heat starts rising, it is wise to jump into the freezer. The news reporter continued with the story. She took a sip of her coffee and then got deathly still. The newscaster claimed the FBI had a composite sketch of the killer. How was that possible? She was always careful about cameras. She also made a point of never leaving witnesses. Killing innocents wasn't her style entirely, but you didn't stay alive or free if you left witnesses. It was the nature of the job.

The composite sketch flashed up on the screen. She let out a sigh of relief. Whatever the FBI had, it wasn't her. She felt muscles come undone that she hadn't even known she had clenched tight. She let the tension out of her hands, not realizing she had almost crushed the mug between her fingers.

Her eyes focused on the image on the screen more closely. She let out a slight gasp, her eyes going wide. That was her! But in one of her fully outfitted male disguises. It didn't look anything like a woman or her. Something about it was off, though. She'd had that disguise years ago, maybe even a decade or more ago. Her mind churned as she tried to remember when she had used the alias 'David Smith' and when she had used that specific male disguise. There had been so many different looks and identities that it grew harder and harder to keep them all sorted.

Either way, she said a small prayer of thanks. The FBI was doing good work, but they were still clearly miles away from anything she needed to be worried about. Her memory solidifying, she remembered she had used 'David Smith' to kill at least five people before retiring the identity. That must have been just over a decade ago. The FBI must have unearthed one of those old cases; a witness had likely given a statement.

She would have to consider her past work. She needed to know what the FBI was digging into. It didn't make sense that any of those old cases were being tied to her now. Her thoughts wandered as she dived into deep consideration of her past....

"Good morning!"

She nearly jumped out of her skin. Hector was walking over to her, laughing at her startlement.

"You are a brat," she said.

"I do my best," he said, leaning down to give her a good morning smooch. Sniffing the air, he said, "Ahh, coffee. I'll be right back." He headed for the kitchen to pour the delicious elixir of life.

She continued watching the news segment, which was about to end. Her mind churned over and over what the FBI could have found. Then she remembered and startled herself almost as much as Hector had a moment ago. She left the katana. "They found my flaming sword. Stupid child." She cursed herself. She was still young and foolish when she killed Brandon Eriks. She had left the sword as a warning to his partners. "Foolish. Absolute foolishness." She was almost certain, perhaps she was sure, that it was what the FBI had. They tied the cases together because they were unsolved sword cases.

"You are almost in a trance this morning." Hector watched her from the kitchen, leaning against the wall, slowly drinking his coffee.

"Yeah, my mind was in a far-off place. Just watching the

news."

Hector glanced at the screen; they had moved on to featuring the best gadgets and must-have items of the year. "Huh, if electronics affect you, remind me never to talk about my job with you."

"Huh?"

"That's what's on the news. I think I know not to buy you anything electronic."

"Oh, right. Yes, electronics do put me in a trance-like state. One might even say it's meditation. Or it just makes me entirely cross-eyed."

Hector grinned. "Yes, never talk to you about my work. Got it. Look, speaking of work, I have to get going."

"Have a wonderful day. I might plan a special surprise for you when you return here tonight."

"I like surprises."

"You might like this one."

Hector laughed, then walked over and kissed her goodbye. It became a lengthy exploration until he eventually pulled away, much to their mutual dislike. "I'm sorry, I really have to go. Otherwise, I'd love to stay all day."

"You could call in sick?"

"It's a temptation every day." He said it as he was walking toward the door. As he approached the door, he turned around and looked at her. "Literally, every day," he said it while his eyes lingered on hers. "Damn, I don't want to go." He took two steps toward her and then shook his head. "I'm sorry. I really am, but I must go in today. Look, have an amazing day. I'll see you tonight."

She sighed, both in regret that he was gone but equally in contentment with the peace that encompassed her. This was such a new experience for her. The emotions of being wanted, of having something to look forward to. Just experiencing a piece of her full, at its peak, a piece of her that she didn't know what it was or how to describe it. Perhaps it was simply inner peace. It was so unusual. Yet so wonderful.

She had spent a lot of time thinking about it, and she honestly thought that writing might be an avenue for her to consider. She had spent years reading books. It came with the terrain of flying, always sitting for hours with nothing to do except read. She had also learned to love audiobooks, which she relied on heavily when she drove between her contracts. She had told Hector she was a struggling writer in a beach house for inspiration, but she needed a new life. Why not give being a struggling writer a sincere attempt?

That realization had been on her mind the last several days, and today was the day she planned to try it. She didn't think she could do it while sitting in the house, so she planned to go to a new coffee shop she had been driving past lately and conjure up something to write about. Every kid on the street was blogging now. How hard could it be?

She finally got around to showering and cleaning up and headed for the coffee shop. The waiter was exceptionally helpful, and she ordered an americano and breakfast bagel. It was not her usual meal, but she would probably return and order a mocha after finishing this first round. She had hours to kill, after all.

And she did spend hours churning out something. She wasn't entirely sure what it was or what she was even trying to say. It clearly needed work. But she did do something. She had created something.

It was far from Shakespeare, but perhaps there was hope after all. Her goal was to invest more time on it, maybe tomorrow, possibly the next day. One of the great things about her life now was that she had no agenda. There was nowhere she needed to be.

It was around noon, or perhaps an hour later, it didn't matter, when she decided to leave the coffee shop. She thanked the waiter again for his excellent service and headed out the door. The coffee shop was positioned in a strip mall, and she was parked in the center of the parking lot among

The Ashen Horse

the jungle of other sedans that all looked identical.

Her mind was on the work she had spent the last several hours trying to piece together. She wasn't paying attention as she approached her rental car. She beeped the doors unlocked while she was still five or seven vehicles away. She did want to try to write something compelling.

As she reached for the driver's side door handle, thick arms wrapped around her. She felt her entire body get thrown into the cargo van sitting next to her car. More arms grabbed her. She reacted. Her body thrashed wildly as she tried to scream. She couldn't; someone was holding a thick cloth over her mouth. She tried to bite through it. Her arms were held firm, but she jerked and jolted and tried to hit whoever was holding her. Everything was happening quickly; she had no idea what was happening.

Her feet were jerking equally violently. Her body contorted and dipped as she flung herself around, trying to get her arms and legs loose. Whatever was holding her, her hands and feet couldn't move despite how hard she tried.

Her mind galloped, "There must be four men holding me. Two men wouldn't be able to control me in this firmly." She began to be genuinely terrified. She had never allowed herself to be trapped, to be caged. She screamed.

The men holding her just heard the whimper of a woman in desperation. Wheezing into her cloth muzzle. The jerking was annoying them, though, judging by the looks on their faces and the pressure they were starting to apply against the woman's body.

She had only been in the van a moment, and the man who had pitched her into the van was finally crawling in and closing the side door. After the door was securely shut, he put his weight on her flaying body. She kept trying to jerk and swing her limbs, but now there was no give at all. She was petite as it was, but compared to all the men holding her, she could only assume at least five men held her firmly. One on each limb and 225 pounds of raw muscle pushed her down flat.

It had taken so long for her eyes to adjust to the situation; maybe it was just her mind clearing itself out of the fog. But she finally saw them all. Five giant ogres of men locked her into complete submission. Her mind went to the darkest places it could go, and she thought, "They could do anything to me." She screamed again. She felt like all she was doing was screaming.

She instinctively began to struggle again, wracking her body any way she could move. She didn't even twitch; each of them must be over two hundred pounds; she couldn't even budge a muscle now that they all had her securely in their grasp.

Her eyes darted everywhere. Panic and fear ran through her blood like molten lava. Her mind continued to circle to her worst fears, and terror paralyzed her. She was on the verge of screaming again when the hood was flung over her head.

Darkness flooded her. It was not just the darkness of the night or that her eyes were now lost in the blindness. It was the darkness of being alone. The darkness of being a prisoner. The black depths of being chained. She would have screamed then, but her energy was expelled. She just lay there panting into a wet and soggy cloth, desperately trying to get breath that seemed to escape her. The darkness oppressing her.

In that bleak moment, the emptiness brought clarity to the situation. Her terror was so present she could touch it, yet the mask cleared her mind so she could start thinking again. She still gasped for air, and she shivered as the anxiety crept out of her physically.

How could she have been so careless? She always paid attention to the abnormal. "How the bloody hell did I miss a cargo van," she chastised herself, which only fueled her anger. She hadn't felt the anger before, but now her distress was building into rage. And that rage drove her to want to

The Ashen Horse

fight yet again.

She tried to lash out, but once again, it was barely a squirm as she was held tightly. She jerked anyway for all she was worth, her desire to fight resurging inside of her. She would escape; she had to.

The agony flooded her entire being. She had taken a blow to the stomach, which knocked the air out of her. She had felt the brute on top of her shift his weight, and the two quick punches that slammed into her stomach left her spluttering, trying to pull in oxygen that just wouldn't come. Her body went entirely limp, wholly jarred by the pain. She couldn't work any muscle at all. Her body was desperately calling out for oxygen, craving it. What felt like a lifetime passed, and finally, her body spasmed enough to pull in a single half-breath.

Her chest heaved as she breathed in and out, her body clinging to the hope of getting one more cycle in before it was taken from her. She didn't try to struggle again; she knew it was futile. Her anger was shifting from irrational rage to contempt. It still burned white hot, and she knew that she would kill every last one of them.

She felt the needle stabbing into her leg. She didn't think her fear, her terror, could escalate. But panic seized her in a way that she had never known. She felt entirely alone and entirely afraid. The liquid from the needle was flowing into her; she could feel it pulsing. She wanted to scream, to yell, to curse. But her energy and her strength were gone. What little she had in her reserves had evaporated when she took the blows to her abdomen.

She felt the man crawl off her, and then she felt two of the men simply and casually toss her against the side of the van. She thudded against the interior paneling. She immediately tried to spring up, and her hands tried to move to remove the hood.

Her body was double-crossing her. She was desperately trying to lift her thigh or even slightly move her arm, and they both refused to operate. Her mind was growing sluggish; she was losing her concentration. What had they done to her? She could feel her consciousness slipping away from her. She was already entombed in darkness, but she felt like death was coming to join her. The world was dimming; everything was fading into shadow.

The last thing that coursed through her mind was how she had wanted to surprise Hector that night.

Chapter Seventeen

The Pursuit Continues

Ellie and Josh were listening to Tim on the conference room phone. The tip line had been open for a week; nothing was coming of it. They had FBI agents tracking down leads all over the country. Half the country apparently thought that their neighbors were raving serial killers. Ash had been everything from a sixteen-year-old high school student to an eighty-year-old man who peddled excessive amounts of soda to neighborhood kids.

The tension was a little high. "We knew the tip line would be a mixed bag. Although perhaps we didn't think it would go this badly," Tim explained. His exasperation wasn't without cause. Since the release of the aged composite sketch, the case had no significant breaks. That was only a week ago, but his superiors were hoping that something would continue to break given the case's momentum that had come out of the apparent association with the Seattle case. A lot of that optimism was putting faith in the general populace.

"You know how I feel about it, boss." Josh never shied away from pointing out the facts of the situation, at least as he saw them. "Putting your trust in the general population amounts to putting your faith in a rabid zombie rat. It is much the same, honestly."

Ellie asked, "A rabid zombie rat?"

"Yes, devious little creatures that suck the life out of other rats and are also known to rise from the dead after the rabies consume them. Then, they spread their evil, rabid ways among the rest of the population. In this, they are very similar to the American public."

Ellie blinked a couple of times, somewhat in amazement. All she said, though, was, "Wow. You got a whole thing going on there."

"Your faith in our fellow citizenry is awe-inspiring, Josh; I completely agree with Ellie. Aside from our tip line being a fiasco, do either of you have an update?"

Ellie and Josh looked at each other. They had feared this would come up. They had avoided giving Tim any details the last several days. They all were tracking the case closely, and the phone logs were coming in from the tip line. Neither of them wanted to say it, but it was inevitable. One of them had to spill it.

Josh sighed, "Yeah, we have some rather unfortunate news of sorts." He let it linger in the air, hoping Tim would take the sting out. But Tim patiently waited on the other end of the phone, silently lurking. Josh felt the suppression in the air, not a good feeling. But he had to get on with it. Ellie looked at him, giving him a prodding gesture to get on with it. "Fine," he said, looking at Ellie. "Look, boss-man, here is the deal. The sword isn't here."

"What?"

"I don't know what to say; we've now been through all the boxes. We have even revisited all of them, explicitly, looking for the stupid thing. The bottom line, we can't find it anywhere. It's not in any of these fifty boxes we have piled up in the room."

Tim knew he had to say something, he just didn't know what to say. That was the whole reason they had gone out to Seattle in the first place: to track down the sword and see what clues could be leveraged from it. The picture and composite sketch were just a bonus.

"Huh. I don't know what to say. You guys go through all the normal checks?"

Ellie chirped in, "Not entirely. We will, though, of course. We checked with the officer who accumulated all the evidence for us. They swear this is all the boxes associated with the case, so we have everything in this room. We reconfirmed the logs on that, and it does look like these were the boxes filed for the case. We haven't checked the chain of custody yet, though. And we haven't talked to anyone about the sword and if they recall anything about it."

"The two knuckleheads we interviewed first thing didn't have anything on it," explained Josh, flushed in frustration. "Of course, we didn't ask them because we assumed the blasted thing would be here."

Ellie nodded and continued, "We also need to reread the entire ME report and see if there are any notes about what was done with it."

"All good starting places. I wouldn't worry too much about it. I'm sure that blade will turn up; it's just a matter of tracking it down."

"We hope so," Ellie agreed.

"We actually need it," said Josh. "I've been looking at the images of it a bit more lately. They aren't detailed or close. But the one that captures it when it is in Brandon's body looks like it has custom markings. I've also spent some time looking at it. It appears to be a high-quality blade, most likely custom-made or even largely handmade. If it was, and has a marking on it, we might be able to trace it to the manufacturer and the seller."

"That's interesting; it means the sword still could be one of the next big clues in the case. Huh. That's all good work, guys. Anything on the case itself that jumps out at you?"

"Not really," Ellie replied. "Seems like most of Ash's other cases. No personal connection or involvement. It is random killing but with an MO of killing a leech on society.

This case still appears to be Ash's standard way of doing things. We haven't tracked any links to other cases or victims. All of them appear entirely independent. In this case, the detectives also don't appear to have missed anything. They legitimately tried to track down the killer. And I think they would have got their man had the killer had any connection at all to the victim. But there was no connection to anyone the victim knew, so the case turned cold and stayed unsolved."

Tim grinned; his team was the best. He thanked God daily for having these men and women on his team. His grin leaked into his words as he said, "Everything you just said, put that in an official memo."

Josh was confused. "But everything Ellie just said is what we knew already?"

"Yes, true. However, what you have done, at a minimum, is several key things. First, you provided information that Seattle PD did everything right and by the book. That always makes everyone happy. You also have proven that no one who knew Brandon Eriks was the likely killer, which removes questions probably lingering in a lot of his family and friends' minds. But, most importantly for us, you have proven that Ash is, in fact, the likely killer of Brandon Eriks. That's worth documenting formally in a communication we can put into the case file. Also, if you have references and sources from the case material that drives you both to those conclusions, that's worth noting outright."

Josh harumphed. "Why do I get the feeling we just got tasked with a three-hour project summary."

"I knew I could count on you to understand, Josh."

Ellie laughed. "Oh, we get it. We get it. Documentation is part of the job. The evil part."

"Appreciate it, team. Leadership wants a formal review of the case and wants to know what conclusion we have drawn from it. Anyway, I don't need to tie up any more of your day. You know exactly what you are doing; you both make my life easy."

"Here to serve, boss-man."

"One last thing, Josh, Ellie. Do your best to find that sword. There still is probably value there."

"We will start reviewing everything and see if we can track it down."

The conference phone went dark, and Josh and Ellie stared at each other. It might have been his imagination, but lately, Josh swore Ellie was looking at him differently. It was slightly disconcerting. He was going to volunteer to start the paperwork that they had just been tasked with, but Ellie beat him to the punch.

"I'll do it. At least the first round. You can have the privilege of editing it and adding in additional content." She shook her head, a bit of frustration leaking out. "You know, I get that paperwork is part of the job. But do you ever feel like we generate a report no one will ever read or care about?"

"I swear it's half the job."

"Some days, it does feel like it. Anyway, I'll start the report. I've been keeping pages of notes just for this purpose, figured it would come and bite us sooner or later."

"It was an inevitable curse."

"This whole job, some days," grumbled Ellie, shaking her head. "Anyway, look, I'll do that; you want to go through the entire log on the chain of custody and the ME report to see if it mentions the katana?"

"Yep, it's a plan. Let's see if we can't find that sword."

Josh sat there a minute. He watched Ellie as she went digging into her work, busily typing up the report that the boss-man wanted. She glanced up at him and smiled. He smiled back. Their eyes locked for a moment.

Josh stammered, "You know, Ellie, we should grab dinner."

Ellie returned to hammering away on her keyboard and answered, "Sure. I mean, we eat dinner every night, right?"

Josh felt a little sheepish but was too deep to back out

now. "No, I meant, like we should grab dinner sometime."

Ellie stopped typing. Still staring at her machine, she quietly said, "Oh."

Josh didn't know where to go from there, so he let it hang in the air, waiting. It stretched out, and the situation felt tense to him. He didn't know if he had made a colossal mistake or not. He wasn't sure what he was doing. Ellie and he had a great working relationship, and he didn't want to screw that up. Neither one wanted to transfer anytime soon; he knew that for sure.

Ellie started typing again, commenting, "We should grab dinner sometime. Since we planned on doing it tonight anyway, the alternative is sitting in a hotel room bored; we should do it tonight."

Josh was entirely bewildered. He didn't know what kind of response that was. Did she not get what he asked? Was that her sidestep around it, to pretend he didn't ask it? Was that an affirmation? Did he dare ask it again, in a different way? The situation was truly awkward. Josh hadn't moved for several minutes, trying to deduce what happened.

Ellie noticed he hadn't moved and glanced up. Her typing stopped. She immediately saw the bumfuzzled look on his face and laughed. "Oh, for Pete's sake! We should go on a date tonight. An encounter, often at a place of eating, to determine if there is a potential for a long-term relationship."

Josh looked over at Ellie and sighed. "That transparent?"

"Like a polished mirror."

"Ouch."

"Could be worse."

"Uh huh, how is that?"

"You could have missed the clues I've been hinting at for the last week."

It was her idea? There had been clues? Josh couldn't see his face, but if he could, he was confident that the same confused look was plastered all over it. Did he remember any clues at all? Did a single clue stand out to him? This was a trap. He was being tricked.

Ellie glanced over while typing a sentence; all she did was shake her head and laugh.

Chapter Eighteen

A Day in the Life

Molly Johnson woke up at 0500 sharp. She did most mornings. It was her accustomed pattern to be working by 0730. However, most of her work involved oversight and management, now. This is unlike the old days when she regularly carried a bat and used it on more than one occasion. She had a reputation as a brawler and was known to take people out directly if required. She hadn't stayed in the game the last fifteen years by chance. And she hadn't survived by chance either.

By 0515, she was on the treadmill in her luxurious gym. Of course, everything she owned at this point was luxurious. She ran, like always, until 0545. After running, Molly proceeded to weightlifting. Exactly half an hour was spent weightlifting, and her morning workout was complete. At 0615, she was jumping in the shower. After showering, dressing, and putting on makeup, she arrived downstairs at 0705, per usual. Her onsite cook had breakfast just freshly placed on the table. He knew exactly when she would want breakfast, and it was the same time, virtually every day.

She kept her mornings on point because it was the one thing she could regularly control. Her days, being in the business she was in, rarely ran smoothly. And the nights, that was an entirely different matter. Who knew what shady venture would draw her attention on any given day?

Her mornings were hers though, and they ran on an organized schedule. At least until it all got blown to hell. Which happened. Frequently.

It has been happening less and less lately, though. She had reached a point in her career where she provided direction and oversight but didn't have to get her hands dirty anymore. Not like she used to. That was good for business and was also particularly good for keeping her out of prison.

After breakfast, she was in her office, as expected, right at 0730. The first several hours of every day were following up on accounting and business matters. This involved reviewing the books for her legitimate businesses and the not-so-legitimate businesses. She checked schedules and shipments and tracked dates. There were usually a couple of calls with business associates.

She now owned eighteen separate espresso stands, all of which her associates regularly frequented to move money in and out of the business. The coffee stands did enough business in their own right. Who would have thought coffee would be so lucrative? To run the entire operation, she had appointed a manager over the enterprise, and she talked with her at least several times a week. This was mainly to track the illicit funds being funneled into the business, but it was still a necessary conversation.

She also owned three different nightclubs. They were an excellent source of cash flow. Each nightclub had another manager to interface with. She had considered appointing a director over all three and then limiting the engagement to just one person. It was taking up too much time dealing with all three separately. Perhaps she'd start doing conferences with all three at the same time.

Around 0945, her cook brought in a healthy snack. One of the perks of having an onsite cook was that Molly ate fantastic food all day. That was the point. Not just fabulous food, but healthy food. All made from scratch, from the best ingredients that money could buy.

Molly had considered diving into the laundromat and car wash businesses as they were also lucrative cash businesses. But she changed her direction when it occurred to her that having a delivery business might work on multiple levels with her other, more lucrative operations. As a result, the primary companies she had been growing for the past seven years were pizzerias. She had invested millions into growing ten stores throughout Miami and Fort Lauderdale. Seven were entirely legitimate. The other three were staffed by her completely loyal crew that ran drug operations in tandem with pizza delivery.

It was surprising what you could accomplish when teams of people were expected to be delivering food throughout the cities. There was nothing dodgy at all about someone walking up to a door, handing someone a package, accepting payment, and casually walking away. At least, not when the package was a pizza box.

At 1200, Molly usually stopped for lunch. She'd leave her office and head back to the kitchen to a nice spread of food. She didn't necessarily eat alone. She would often schedule business meetings during this time as there was guaranteed to be food. When she wasn't eating with some associates, she'd eat with the chef himself or her security staff. Today, she did happen to be eating alone. A couple of security guards walked through and said hello as they stole food off the counter.

She would have at least ten people working in her home on any given day. Between a minimum of six guards on staff at any given time, from the onsite chef to her IT security consultant, Hector. During the work week, she also had her security director onsite. Employing fifty security guards to work around the clock required a manager or, in this case, her security director.

She would also expect a messenger or two most days. Although her organization heavily used information technology, there were some details and information that would never go into a computer or a smartphone. It was common for runners to still feed intel manually about various pieces of the business.

By 1400, she was usually done for the day, and the last several hours after lunch were mainly reserved for casual meetings. She had made it far enough in her career now that she rarely needed a full eight-hour day. That was a blessing. However, many of her nights were spent meeting in nightclubs to discuss business or the like. It might not be technically working, but it was still a necessary business operation.

Tonight, she was planning on meeting with several venture capitalists who were looking for funds for several startups they wanted to back. All of which, they swore, were the next big thing. She had agreed to a sit-down and promised to hear them out. The problem with having so much money was the constant demand to invest, spend, and move it.

She was constantly searching for more legitimate businesses. It was a serious issue. Molly realized that she couldn't have the most profitable pizzerias in the country without someone starting to ask questions at some point. The IRS was blind and largely incompetent, but red beacons blazing in the night sky eventually got noticed. Her pizzerias were already becoming prominent in their sales as they were some of the best-selling and highest-grossing in the industry. She knew she had to show a significant downturn in the near future to keep questions from being asked. All of these reasons, and several others, drove her need for a more legitimate business to funnel the funds. It was a constant struggle.

She took a break from the day and went for a swim in the pool behind the house. Every Florida mansion needed a proper pool, and she had enjoyed building it precisely to her specifications. Molly felt like she didn't enjoy it enough, but she swam at least three or four times per week. She would do laps, burning off the irritations of the day. She didn't relax in the water; she swam with varying levels of determination. If she wanted to relax, she would jump in the hot tub.

An hour passed as she slowly swam up and down the length of the pool. Today, she wasn't interested in killing herself in the water; she just kept moving, burning off energy. She would enjoy the snack sitting inside the fridge waiting for her. Once again, it is almost certainly a healthy choice. She could always rely on her chef to feed her deliciously healthy food. That was the whole point of having him on staff. For years, she ate garbage, but once she had someone to spend the time cooking correctly, she turned that around. It was a rare gift.

She munched on a sandwich as she was watching the 5 o'clock news. It was an avocado salsa mix spread into the sandwich, further loaded with a multitude of veggies. It was to die for. The chef had made at least ten of them for the guards on shift tonight. She might eat another one; it was delicious.

The news had an interesting story about a serial killer the FBI was desperately trying to track down. Apparently, a crazy man was on the loose doing vigilante justice. The news stated that most of the serial killer's victims appeared to be rich influential people who were doing things under a cloud of suspicion. The reporter commented on how the FBI had used the information to release John Smith from custody, with the new evidence of the serial killer proving Smith hadn't done the killing after serving ten years for the crime. The story was mostly about him; it appeared that he was in discussions with his lawyers about whether he should sue for a vast civil payout for false imprisonment.

In a surprising twist, he appeared to be leaning towards not suing. The newsreel showed him saying that he did not want to penalize the justice system for doing the right thing and releasing him. He did seek a small settlement as it was now unlikely that he could find employment. It was a masterful play of saying he was suing but didn't want to sue simultaneously.

The state could quickly settle and close out the case, the real point of his brazen public address, or so Molly assumed. Molly considered herself a strong evaluator of character, and this man honestly appeared happy to be released, so maybe he wasn't as cynical as she had presumed him to be.

Still, Molly chuckled to herself. Someone was always out there playing the system, even when the system was playing you. There was a lesson for those who paid attention. He might have wanted to do the right thing, but he wouldn't say no to the two- or three-million-dollar settlement that would be put on the table in a plea deal.

She went to get ready for dinner. It wasn't a huge process, but she spent the time to look nice. In her mid-thirties, she could still turn every head in a room, and it was a pity to let that opportunity go to waste. This meant that she put in the effort to turn heads, although she might have been spending less time getting entirely extravagant in the last several years. Some of that might have to do with her ex-fiancé. He had changed her in good ways and bad ways. But the breakup went badly. It still surprised her that she hadn't taken him out. Perhaps a part of her still had feelings for him.

Tonight, though, tonight she was going to turn every head. And she did. When she walked into the restaurant, there wasn't a boy or man, aged thirteen to ninety, whose head didn't swivel and look at her. It did feel good that she still could command an audience. She joined the two suits and their two associates at a table.

Molly was sure she would spend the next two hours listening to drivel. At least once a month, she had meetings like this, and rarely did they turn to anything she was thoroughly interested in. Her eyes fell on the four men sitting at the table, and she couldn't help but smirk. They looked professional enough, but everything about them screamed that they were entirely out of place in these surroundings. Who knew, though? Perhaps these men would be interesting. She doubted these four comical characters would bring something new to the table. But there was always hope.

The night was a well-thought-out business pitch, and it included all the details and logic she asked for. Which was more impressive than most of those who sought her funds. She drilled them for a solid hour on how they would grow, develop revenue streams, and expand, and more on the initial project plan. They had answers for all of it.

This team was ready to go to market on their product. To their credit, they had already raised enough resources through crowdsourcing to start full-scale production, which was underway. They were seeking Molly's investment simply to drive phase two and phase three of the production cycles, after which they should almost be self-sufficient. Revenues should be able to drive both profits and cycles to continue manufacturing.

She was further impressed when they showed her conceptual drawings and logistics of the second generation of the product. That meant they already had R&D invested in improving and making a second release. They explained they would only be doing two production runs of generation one, and then after that, they'd retrofit their manufacturing to move into generation two.

They had also mapped business plans to give existing customers an upgrade path at a significantly reduced rate since generation two was such an improvement and since they had been early adopters of the product. It spoke to the character and integrity of what they were trying to achieve.

It was rare that one of these events impressed Molly, but this one did. These guys were on a clear path to success. She made a rapid decision and bought forty percent of the stock in the company on the spot. It would amount to about ten million dollars; it was an easy investment decision. They wouldn't sell her more, she grumbled about that. But it was smart on their part; they didn't want to give up decision-making in their business, and if she bought anymore, they risked her being able to outvote them entirely. Even in this, they made good business decisions—she begrudgingly gave them the credit they had earned.

They hadn't originally planned to get that kind of buy-in. They were hoping for more than a 10% investment, but they honestly couldn't contain themselves when she committed to buying as much as they were willing to sell. She figured, what was the point of laundering all this money into clean profit and not spending any of it?

They had made a bad mistake, though. Which she, of course, pushed them into intentionally. They each owned 25% of the business or would after they sold her their options. Suppose they disagreed at any point in the future. In that case, she'd be the deciding vote, which meant the potential for more power or an opportunity to acquire the majority of the business at a later time.

When she was younger, she had done some mountaineering. Nothing over the top, but she had learned a critical life lesson in those early days, swinging from a cliff. The lesson she learned was never to underestimate the power of a foothold. It could save your life. Years would pass before she understood that the same principle was critical in business.

After the meeting, she returned to her kingdom. It was late, at least for those who regularly got up at 0500. She called it a night and turned in. She would most likely spend an hour reading before finally going to sleep. Tomorrow was another day to run the empire that she had built.

Chapter Nineteen

The Katana

Josh proudly held up the elusive katana. It was a marvel. He had rarely held a blade that was so balanced, as if someone had measured the weight of the blade perfectly and balanced out the handle. It was lighter than most other swords, as well. He gave it a quick flick of the wrist, and it whooshed, even in the evidence bag it was wrapped in.

It looked entirely customized, though it had the typical katana hilt, spanning about a foot, and it was worked with a flawless Tsuka-Ito. The wrapping around the hilt was graceful. He wasn't sure since he couldn't feel it directly, but he suspected it was finely wrapped silk, over-laced in layers. It was a rich purple, intersected with gold. The blade still looked wickedly sharp. He feared it was so sharp that he dared not mess with it too much, or it might cut open the evidence bag it was held in.

Josh wished it had come with its sheath, which must have been something if the sword itself had been any indication. The quillon or tsuba was exquisite as well; it appeared to be a hand-carved scene of samurai warriors spanning the blade and hilt. It also looked inlaid with gold leaf; perhaps it was even coated with pure gold; it was hard to tell through the evidence bag.

Josh was beaming as he held it, his eyes transfixed, slowly

studying the weapon. "This thing is amazing. Look at the curvature of the blade; there isn't an imperfection in this weapon. It was sticking out of someone, yet it still looks flawless. The craftsmanship is just a wonder. You know," he said, glancing over at Ellie, who was less interested in the medieval weapon, although she was overjoyed they had finally located it.

Josh's eyes fluttered from Ellie and back to the katana as he continued, "You know, I'm not sure this is a modern blade. This could be several hundred years old; it might be a samurai's sword. We should try to get someone to inspect this. I dabble, but we need an antiquities dealer to look into it."

Tim asked, "Does it have the mark you thought it might have?"

They were in a different conference room, the full telepresence room, which allowed them to establish a full video feed. Josh had been examining the blade in front of the camera, painstakingly pointing out every fascinating detail. Tim and Roshan were watching on the other end. They appeared to appreciate it at least as close to the same level as Josh, even if Ellie sat in the back less interested. Perhaps it was a male thing?

"Yep, right here. Although thinking about that, if we can identify this mark, it might point us to an ancient original mark, which, on the one hand, would be amazing. On the other hand, it would be doubtful that we could trace it to a modern dealer."

"Let's see the mark. Can you get it in front of the camera?" Josh held it up and pointed to the mark on the blade near the sword's hilt. "Twist it a bit; the glare on the evidence bag is... there, yeah, hold that a minute." There was a click as the image was captured on the other end. "Perfect, emailing it to the forensic team, and we'll see if they can track down the maker's mark."

Josh tore his eyes away from the blade and looked at the

screen. "Make a note in the email for them to contact Japanese sources. A couple of traditional organizations should be able to identify this quickly. If this is an older sword, as I suspect, some resources at the Smithsonian should also be able to point our team in the right direction."

Tim changed the direction of the conversation. "In other news, team. Since we are all here, the leadership appreciated your memo, Ellie, on how we have sufficient evidence to tack up the Brandon Eriks case as an Ash case. Also, there is still no fruit from the tip line. That has turned into a nightmare. Even if we get a quality tip, we might never know it because of the garbage we have to sift through."

Ellie looked at Josh and said, "Zombie rats?"

"The American public," Josh agreed. Josh asked Tim, "But you put good people on it, right?"

"Yeah, we have them on it now. It didn't start that way, but it might yield results now. It wasn't that we had the wrong people on it per se; I wouldn't want to imply that. They didn't have the experience. We have some big guns on it now: a director-level woman with ten years of experience chasing false leads. She is weeding out the trash very effectively."

"That's what I meant; I saw the one email that there was a shift in personnel," added Josh.

"Yep."

Ellie asked, "Any other news from the top?"

"Not much," acknowledged Tim. "They understand the slow process and that we are digging from a couple of different angles."

"We have found another couple of cases that could be associated with Ash," Roshan commented. "We have discovered some evidence that suggests they are sword wounds. Still unsolved, with all the usual suspects eliminated. All of them following Ash's perceived MO."

"Killing scumbags?" Josh laughed despite himself.

"I wouldn't term it like that in the legal documents, but

more or less, that is the correct sentiment."

"Scattered to the wind, I'm sure as well? All over the country?"

Roshan nodded. "Yes, pretty much half the states now have an Ash case or a suspected Ash case. Some of them have officially moved from 'possible Ash cases' to 'probable Ash cases.'"

An epiphany pulsed in Josh's mind. "Holy cow! Have we tried looking—"

"Internationally," Ellie suggested.

"--out of the country?" Josh finished.

Ellie and Josh looked at each other and smiled. "Great minds think alike."

"You betcha, cowboy."

Josh chuckled, but Tim laughed outright. "Hilarious, you guys," Tim said. "Although that does bring up a huge question. Perhaps we have been too narrow in our assumptions here. Perhaps we should ask other countries if they have evidence of unsolved murders that fit these parameters. God knows it's easier to get these weapons in and out of countries rather than guns. Probably could procure swords in most countries, actually."

"Maybe," Josh commented. "But keep in mind, as this sword shows, Ash is pretty particular about his weapon."

"Fair point."

Tim looked over at Roshan. "Roshan, your thoughts?"

"We haven't utilized any of the international case logs yet, nor have we queried any of our partners or other international agencies. Perhaps it's worth investigating. We might need to assign some bodies to that, though. I'm sure they'd get dumped on just like we did from all the precincts if we asked for some cases to review."

"Maybe reduce the query just to public people?"

Roshan shook his head. "Maybe. Remember that many of Ash's supposed victims aren't necessarily public figures. Many of them have been, but it's not a requirement. Many of them are administrative officials who might have prestige in their circles but aren't exactly public figures. Ash's victims most commonly are either people who have abused their power or have gotten in the crosshairs of criminal activity. Or they are living under a shroud of suspicion surrounding those two things, one or the other."

Tim was still thinking. He usually saw the big picture and drew in the missing pieces; it was one of the things that made him an expert investigator. "That does beg the question if we could lure Ash into a trap?"

Josh followed it up with the obvious question. "The problem, boss-man…"

"You know I hate it when you call me that."

"Only reason I do. The problem, boss-man, is that we'd have to know how Ash picks his victims. How is Ash finding these dodgy characters? Equally, how does Ash know that they are guilty enough to kill them when the, let's say, the 'public atmosphere' is suspicion."

Ellie, studying Josh, interjected, "That's a valid point. How does Ash know more than the authorities? How is he certain these people are guilty?"

Tim looked at Roshan and waited. Over the video conference system, Josh and Ellie looked at Roshan.

"I see how it is. Being thrown to the vultures, am I?"

"You'd be pretty gamy, I think, Roshan," laughed Ellie.

"I'm insulted; I'd be tender and succulent," Roshan laughed. "Trust me, guys, we are working on it. Half of my forensic team is trying to deduce how Ash finds his victims. We have nothing now, but the team is working on it."

"We should analyze what we know," recommended Josh.

"Fair enough," said Tim. "What do we know?"

Josh started the list. "We know Ash isn't like a normal serial killer who knows his victims. His first victims, maybe, but the rest are all strangers to him."

Ellie continued, "We also know they are all over the place. Many cities and states are not tied to the same type of organization or employment. There are no apparent ties to the victims themselves, and few to none of the victims know each other."

Roshan commented, "They must be linked somehow. Given the points you just noted. I imagine the underlying link must be technology."

Tim asked, "What about technology, though? An online group that discusses people within their communities who are breaking the law without prosecution?"

Roshan laughed. "Stupider things have happened. It could be that simple, honestly, Tim."

Ellie was shaking her head. "Maybe, but that would be utterly impossible to find."

Josh, once again, couldn't resist. "Now, now, I thought the internet made everything easy to find."

"Smartass."

"Children, please," Tim admonished. "We all agree it has to be the internet, though?"

Roshan nodded, "Pretty much, something online. There's nothing local that covers this breadth."

Tim winced, but he had to ask. "Don't take this wrong, Roshan, but can I ask if the team is focused on internet-type research around locating the victim links?"

"Probably one of many avenues, but let's type up our thoughts on this, and I'll consolidate it, and we can get it to the forensic team, and you can present it to leadership during one of the next meetings."

Tim nodded. It was something, not much yet, but something. "Baby steps, team. Sometimes, that's all you need to make progress, though. We'll get you a collection of emails, Roshan."

"That's all I got, everyone," Tim said. "Sounds like we are done?" Silence. The natural evolution of the business meeting, from busy chatter to silence. "Okay, guys, we'll schedule something again in a couple of days. Well, we have the team meeting in a couple of days. I'll talk to everyone then if not before."

"Later boss-man, Josh and Ellie out."

"Josh, you know...."

Josh, of course, had hung up the second he said it. And Tim was sure he was busily chuckling away. Roshan wasn't even trying to hide it; he was laughing obnoxiously.

"You know, if you just ignored it, it would lose its appeal, and he'd probably stop."

"Yes," Tim admitted. "Although, knowing it brings him as much pleasure as it does makes me not hate it as much as I used to."

Roshan really laughed then. "Make sure he never finds that out or he'll definitely stop."

"Touché."

Chapter Twenty

The Betrayal

Molly arrived at the warehouse. It was a dark warehouse in an industrial part of Miami, one of five she owned for storing everything. A section of this one was built out for offices. Several years ago, her associates had built a 'holding facility' in the offices. She believed that was the term her team used. 'Holding facility' had a better ring to it than 'dungeon.'

The reality is that it was three distinct prison cells. Prison cells, fully complete with toilets. Bars split each room down the middle, and they went all the way around the walls. From the outside hallway, they looked like any large executive office. From the inside, the rooms were dark cells.

The guard outside the room unlocked the door as Molly approached. Molly walked into the cell. The room was virtually pitch black. The guard flipped the light switch on from behind her. He then exited and closed the door.

Molly looked at the woman, who was lying on the bed. She sat up, her eyes blinking and trying to adjust to the light. She had been in here in the dark now for quite some time. Molly was surprised; this woman must have been about her age. She could see herself in her. She had an inner fierceness unique to those who had grown up tragically, like herself. This woman had seen things, had done things.

Molly sighed, "Has it come to this?"

The woman just looked at her, not speaking but very much scowling at her. Molly quietly nodded to herself. Yes, it wasn't likely she would get anything out of her the easy way. Still, she should try. She always tried. "I had hoped it would go easier this time around. I guess not." She opened the door slightly. "Hector, please come in here."

Hector Garcia walked into the room. The woman in the cage let out a growl deep from within her soul. It might have been a whimper; perhaps it was both. A combination of both rage and devastation wrapped into one. It was rage that showed on her face, though, complete rage.

"Hector, this is her? Yes?"

"Yes, Molly. This is her."

"I know this isn't and wasn't easy for you, Hector. I'm sure you might even have feelings for her now, and that's understandable. Do you want a minute alone with her?"

Hector looked at the ground. It wasn't clear if it was embarrassment, shame, or sadness that surrounded him. But the aura was noticeable. It enshrouded him, almost like a walking grave. "I think, ma'am, it might be best to leave it as it is."

"Completely rational. Thank you, Hector. You may go."

"Thank you, ma'am."

Hector moved to the door and turned to walk out. He paused and looked at the woman in the cell. Their eyes locked. Several quiet moments passed, Molly waiting patiently and watching the exchange. Hector looked down at the ground and left the room, closing the door behind him.

Molly waited for several minutes, letting the air clear. "You shouldn't be too mad at him. He was doing as he was directed. He is the only innocent member in this transaction. I'm certainly not innocent, and you, of course, are the worst type of scum."

That awoke new rage in the woman in the cell, and she spoke for the first time. "You would call me something beneath you?! How dare you."

"Please, save your lies for another day. I don't have the energy. I will do you the courtesy of explaining how this will work. Not that you deserve the politeness."

Molly repositioned herself, finding a chair in her half of the room. She sat, bringing herself level with the woman sitting on the bed. "My security force easily recognized you scouting my estate. That was clumsy work. Of course, my eyes and ears throughout the city also reported you before this when you asked questions all over the city. We knew days before you showed up that you would eventually come by."

The woman's eyes widened. Of course, she was shocked; they were always so shocked when they found out. Molly shook her head. They truly had wasted talent with this one; she could have been something with the right motivation.

Molly continued, "Once we knew what you were about, we knew you would approach someone in the organization you could manipulate. Everyone was, of course, made aware. It was bad luck that you picked Hector; he isn't built for this type of thing. But he performed admirably anyway. His leg was never injured, by the way. As he reported the story, though, it seemed like you originally planned to have yourself hurt. It's a pretty standard trick. Damsel in distress. Tell me, does it work?"

The woman had returned to her previous stoic rage. She didn't say anything, just stared murderous daggers at Molly. She was seething with a rage that Molly had rarely seen. Plenty of people got angry or bitter. Many or most in this situation got terrified, completely paralyzed with fear. She had seen it all. A few got flippant; others went right into denial. She had rarely seen rage; it was as if the woman didn't just plan revenge but was certain of it. Molly sighed again; it was distressing. This woman, indeed, did have potential.

Molly had waited for the woman to respond, but she didn't, her eyes staring death. Molly returned to her narrative, "Once Hector had the hooks into you, it was just a matter of waiting. Of course, any of my men would have done the same thing. It was just a matter of time until we could plan appropriate extraction. Admittedly, we delayed it quite a while, hoping you would reveal more information to Hector. But you didn't, so it wasn't advantageous to wait any longer. So here you are."

Molly waited several minutes, seeing if the quiet would draw the woman out. It didn't work. All she saw was the woman staring hate at her. The fury was a deep burning fire behind the calculation in those eyes.

The woman stood up and moved close to the cell bars. She flexed her upper body and tested the bars. Not speaking, not even looking at Molly. It was almost as if she was testing to see if she could reach her. Molly shook her head. Men three times her size had been securely housed in these cells. It's such a waste. She had no idea how the government agency procured such talent. She could recruit ten people off the streets, and they wouldn't have the talent of this woman. After the woman tested the cage, she returned to the uncomfortable bunk and sat down. Her eyes returned to their murderous stare at Molly.

"That's the backstory. A person in your position should know how they got there. Now, let's talk about what happens next. You will have the pleasure of meeting some of my associates. You have two choices: the easy way or the hard way. The easy way is you will tell them everything you know; they will spend as much time as they need to collaborate your story. They will track it, validate it, uncover it, and ensure you have told them everything. Then they will kill you."

Molly waited, seeing if the stark reality of the situation would spike a response from her. It didn't. She was somewhat disappointed, yet at the same time impressed. This woman had steel for bones and mercury for blood. She adhered to her own code. It was always a disappointment when that code aligned with the authorities; such potential was always thrown away.

"The alternative is the hard way. The hard way is essentially the same tale, except in the hard way, you put my associates in a position where they must extract the information from you. Many people in the cell you are in now have tried the hard way. I assure you that I have always gotten all the information I wanted."

Molly waited again. This time, she was tempted to draw out the wait. She wanted to drive home the point. In almost any other circumstance, Molly would have tried to recruit here. She wanted this woman working for her. She probably would have made her a senior lieutenant immediately. This woman had street smarts, and despite her petite form, it was also clear that she could hold her own in a brawl. It would be interesting to know her story, but Molly didn't have the time these days. Molly waited; the woman would speak eventually. Several minutes slowly ticked by. Waiting always worked; patience was a powerful tool, and its partner, silence, a grand operator. So, she patiently waited in silence.

The woman finally spoke, "It would be a terrible mistake for you not to let me out of this cell. Right. Now."

"When I first saw you, I was fairly certain you would choose the hard way." Molly shook her head. "It's always such a waste. There is no reason for you to suffer unnecessarily. If you provide the information I require, the end can be painless and quick."

She spoke once more, "I won't warn you again."

Molly chuckled, "I am fond of making mistakes; you should meet my ex. That piece of shit was a colossal mistake. I'll risk it with you. Things that you should know at this point." Molly raised her hands and started ticking off her fingers. "One, you will tell us what government agency you work for. Two, you will tell us all the information you have collected about me and my organization. Three, you will tell us where all this information is or where it is stored. Four, you will tell us all the agents and personnel who are also working on the case. This is the one that agents like you have a hard time with; I'll warn you upfront. Again, I'll assure you that we always get all the information. Five, you will fully explain, in detail, the depth and breadth of the investigation. Six, you will tell us all your family members. Seven, we will expect a full explanation of how long you have been undercover. There are probably more things my team and I will want, but for now, that is a succinct list you should ponder."

The woman's dagger eyes continued to pierce at Molly. "You and me, Molly, are going to have a very special time together. Very soon."

"Not likely. I don't like getting my hands bloody anymore. That was for when I was younger. I have people for that now. Those sadistic creepers actually enjoy it. You know, I honestly don't know if they have ever had a woman in this situation. usually, the DEA and FBI send men. Come to think of it, I might feel a little bad for you for what's coming."

Molly stood up. There wasn't anything left to say. She opened the door and flipped off the light. As Molly was leaving, she said, "Good night. Sleep well."

"We'll be seeing each other real soon, Molly."

Chapter Twenty-One

Sky Harbor

The FBI team had their monthly conference call, where all the various components of The Ashen Horse task force came together and revealed where the case was. Tim took in-depth notes, highlighting every team's current work, progress, conjectures, and next steps. After this update, Tim had a shorter thirty-minute meeting later in the afternoon, during which he reviewed all this information at a high level with the FBI leadership.

Blessedly, the case had calmed down quite a bit. This was largely because there hadn't been another stack of bodies. For whatever reason, Ash hadn't killed anyone in over a month, at least as far as any of the federal agencies knew. And as far as they knew, this was the first time in a very long time that Ash hadn't killed in a month. Perhaps they should be reading something into that?

Tim was seriously concerned about where Ash had gone. Why hadn't they found any current cases they could link to the serial killer? Ash had been like clockwork for almost six months, at least one, if not two, murders per month. All of them were high profile in their own way. All of them were usually slimy individuals.

Tim stopped his mind from wandering and pulled his attention back to the call. Sometimes, it was difficult, but he tried to make a point to stay focused throughout these briefings. After all, he was supposed to be the main task force leader in charge, and he had to report everything to the senior leadership.

"Wait," he said.

"Tim?" Roshan asked.

"I'm sorry, team, I missed that part. Can you repeat that, Roshan?"

"No worries. I was just saying how we found the manufacturer of the katana in the Brandon Eriks case. They had a record of the sale and gave us all the details surrounding the sale of the weapon."

Josh asked, "Even from fifteen years ago?"

"Yep. The weapon was shipped to John Millers in Phoenix, Arizona. It was shipped to a P.O. Box. We then pulled the USPS records and got a physical address under a different name—Matthew Smith. Not of Phoenix, though; that one is in Flagstaff."

Tim asked the obvious question. "I suppose this means someone needs to get on a plane to Phoenix's Sky Harbor?"

Roshan agreed, "We need to ask the people living in that neighborhood if they know anything about Ash. Nothing for it but boots on the ground."

Tim paused for a moment to see if anyone had anything to add. There was silence on the line for a time. It was Josh who finally spoke. "I'll go. I have family I need to see in Phoenix anyway. Seattle has been slowly losing its charm now after almost three weeks."

Ellie waited a bit longer, but she agreed to it as well. "Yeah, I'm game as well. It still ties to the Brandon Eriks case, and I think Josh and I are the two most dialed in on this right now—for better or worse." Ellie didn't want to admit that she had been enjoying her time with Josh and wanted to extend that time.

That decided, the call moved on to other topics. Roshan turned the call over to another forensic investigator, who pointed out that some of the cases that they associated with Ash had differing fingerprints from the supposed killers. None of the fingerprints were in any national databases. That had been troubling the forensic team for some time. Either Ash was smart enough to be hiding his fingerprints, or he wasn't leaving any, or perhaps not all these killings were attributable to Ash. None of those possible scenarios sat well with the team.

After the annoying revelation that there was something funky going on with the fingerprints at some of the crime scenes, the updates were over. And with that, team members who hadn't talked in a week or two used the meeting to chat for a few minutes. Other team members who had pressing matters quickly jumped off the call. Even so, rather rapidly, the call came to a natural end, and Tim closed the bridge.

Josh and Ellie heard the line go dead while thumbing through the mounds of boxes still in the conference room. They were slowly packing stuff up. They had spent part of their days digitizing some of what they considered critical documents in the case and ensuring they were in the FBI and Seattle PD databases. Now, they were making sure all their added notes, documents, information, logging, and data cataloging were added into yet another additional box. It would act as a table of contents and directory for everything else in the room.

Ellie asked, "Should I have not immediately agreed to go?"

"No one suspected anything," commented Josh. "You know, for being a federal agent, you are surprisingly bad at deception."

Ellie smiled almost sheepishly. "Ahh, yes, well." She sighed. "No, you are right. I'm just not used to playing this subtly."

Josh chuckled. "You know it doesn't matter at all, right? Strictly speaking, nothing in the department's code says we can't go out. I mean, we looked it up and read the entire employee handbook thingy to confirm. They strongly frown upon subordinates dating their leadership. But as far as either of us could tell, if you are a peer, everything indicates you are good to go."

"I know, I know. Like you said, I'm not good at deception."

Josh laughed again. "Just don't think of it as deception. We aren't deceiving people; we are just currently choosing not to tell anyone what may or may not be happening in our personal lives."

"This doesn't bother you at all?"

"Nope. What I do during business hours is the company's time. What I do during my personal time is my time, and the company can shove it."

"Spoken with such elegance."

"It's a gift, really. Years of practice and expert honing."

"A master wordsmith."

"I'm here all week."

Ellie finally chuckled at that. "It will be good to get out of here. It feels like I've spent a lifetime in this conference room."

"In a way, we have. At this point, we have reconstructed most of Brandon Eriks' life. And his death, for that matter. And thanks to Roshan, we might have a link to the killer."

Josh went on, "I'll be super glad to get back into some hot weather, though. This nonstop rain is killing me. I'll take the heat any day over this constant wall of water."

"Oh, come on, it hasn't rained much here."

Josh's deadpan stare said more than words ever could. He quirked his eyebrows in a very poignant way that clearly indicated just how much rain he thought they had suffered. Ellie just laughed.

However, she changed her entire tone as a new idea popped into her head. "Oh, my goodness! Wait, does this mean we really don't have to come back here tomorrow? Or again?"

Josh got super excited. "I didn't even think about that! We might be free."

Josh stopped his note-taking and stared at Ellie, relieved to be done with this maze of evidence. Then he looked down at the box in front of him and sighed. "We have to make sure this is all finished, though. I think I need one more day to finish that last box on the court depositions."

"Think you'll find anything in there that we missed?"

"Not at all. I'm sure there's nothing in it. But at this point, after reading everything else, I can't bring myself to skip out on the last couple of reports. Did you get everything cataloged for that last box we wanted to compile?"

"Almost." Ellie shook her head. "Blast it all; I thought we could escape. Okay, we will need at least one more day, perhaps two. We have to leave it on a high note; after three weeks of digging through all of this, we can spend two more days to close it out right."

"Yeah, it's only two more. But I'll tell you, I'm not quite as excited as when I thought we could bounce today and not come back. But I'm still excited that this chapter is coming to a close. It'll be good to put Brendan Eriks behind us."

"It'll be even better putting Ash in prison," said Ellie.

"You think so?"

Ellie looked aghast. "What do you mean?"

Josh shrugged. "He's killing some pretty dodgy characters, really. I'm not exactly saying he's doing something good or right. But really, he's eliminating some people who probably should have been in jail anyway. I don't know, there's definitely more critical criminals we could be going after."

Ellie couldn't believe she was hearing this from Josh. "We have literally spent like three months on this case. And you're rooting for him?"

"It's not that I'm rooting for him. I'll be more than happy to lock him up. I don't know; I have a grudging respect for the guy."

"Respect?"

"Fair enough, not the best word choice. I see an honor," Josh looked questionably at Ellie as he said it. "...in his actions. Honor might not be the right word, either. There's something about Ash's methods of choosing his victims; most of them really have it coming."

"I'm not sure anyone deserves to be sliced in half by a sword."

"Perhaps not, although Brandon Eriks, as we have both clearly learned, was no saint. The District Attorney probably should have been prosecuting him for several of his 'ventures.'" Josh used air quotes to make sure the point was carried.

"Fine, he was a royal sleazeball. I still do not wish him to get butchered."

Josh could see he wasn't going to get anywhere with Ellie on this one. Ellie had a rigid view of morality. There probably was no grey area at all in there that would even make her remotely consider the notion that Ash was doing some form of noble work. Although, as Josh pondered it, perhaps that was the right word.

Josh attempted to convey the feeling one more time. "I just see a kind of nobility in Ash's actions. That's all I'm saying. It's like he is acting very intentionally in his choice of victims. All these kills were a choice. That's rare, or somewhat rarer, in serial killers. Usually, they kill out of a pure need and the victim's proximity. Ash doesn't appear to do that. Ash's killing has a purpose to it that is outside the normal serial killer's bloodlust."

Ellie was getting rather annoyed. Josh had a way of getting under her skin. Usually, that was a good thing, but he could be quite irritating at times as well. How could he sit there and defend a serial killer? Who does that? But something he had said kept nagging at her. Didn't it always come down to motivation?

Her mind kept working in circles. There was something

here; she just couldn't put her finger on it. Suddenly, her eyes opened wide, and she had a true awakening. Those were incredibly rare in the business, but she was staring one right in the face.

"Josh."

Josh winced. He knew he had gone too far with her. He wasn't sure he should continue at all. He might just dig the hole deeper at this point. Yet, at the same time, despite his better judgment, he always made a point to try to be honest about a situation, even though it got him into trouble quite often. It turns out that most people really didn't want to hear the truth or anyone's opinion, even if they did inquire about it.

Josh finally glanced over at Ellie. To his amazement, she had a deep internal look in her eyes. It wasn't the disgruntled look he had been expecting. Ellie was thinking deeply about something. Josh finally asked, "What is it, Ellie?"

Ellie looked up and locked his eyes. "Why does anyone do anything?"

"Huh?"

"Motivations, Josh. Motivations. Why does anyone do anything."

Josh still wasn't following. All he could think of were life's normal motivations. "What? Like you mean the big five? Love, sex, money, power…."

"The fifth?"

"There is one… I just always forget it." Josh glanced up, trying to jog his memory, and then he started moving them back again through his mind, ticking them off. "Love, sex, money, power… and… food. Yes, food is the fifth one."

Ellie nodded, "Those make sense."

"I don't understand what that has to do with Ash, though?"

"Everything." Ellie smiled. She was almost giddy, completely unlike herself. "Josh, why is Ash killing people?"

"He's a sadistic serial killer? Trying to make the world

burn?"

"But you just said he wasn't a normal serial killer. We have always assumed he was a serial killer. You just made an argument that he isn't a serial killer. His motivations don't have anything to do with what a normal serial killer would be doing."

"True; Ash doesn't behave like other serial killers. But obviously, he must be a serial killer; this guy is killing one or two people a month."

Ellie asked, "Yes, but why?"

"Okay, out with it already, clearly you have something on your mind."

"Didn't you say Ash's killings have a sense of nobility? That's true of almost every one of his victims. What kind of serial killer always finds a bad guy to kill?"

"They'd have to work really hard for that."

"And he finds them all over the country."

"Even less likely," commented Josh, his eyes squinting. He still wasn't sure where this was going.

"Ash isn't killing for normal serial killer motivations. I highly doubt he is killing for food. And it isn't love or sex. None of the victims are tied to explicit power or politics, and at least none of the victims were related to major political or power structure changes after their killings."

"Money?"

"It has to be money."

They sat there, staring at each other. Josh scratched his head as he rolled the idea around in his mind.

He slowly strung his hands through his hair, thinking out loud. "Huh. I don't think we ever considered that he might be getting paid."

"No, for some reason, we have skipped over this."

"So, what are we saying exactly right now—that Ash is a hitman?"

Ellie clarified, "Contract killer?"

"That makes him noble?"

Ellie nodded emphatically. "It gives him the liberty to pick the person he wants to kill. Outside of some other strange desire we might have associated with a serial killer."

Still playing with his hair and thinking aloud, Josh continued, "We concluded before that the only way to find and locate such a specific and diverse pool of victims was to find them online."

"Yep."

"So, we are saying somewhere on the internet, there's a website to rent a hitman?"

Ellie laughed, "I wouldn't put it quite like that, but I bet the internet does. It might be exactly that."

"I'm not sure, Ellie. But we have two days to assemble a theory before we finish here."

Ellie looked a little dejected. "I'm not sure we should wait that long."

Josh finally looked up and blinked. He could see that Ellie was really excited about this; she thought she was on to something. It also looked like he had deflated her quite a bit. She had looked entirely committed before, but now, a level of hesitation had sunk in.

He nodded to himself and her as well. "Sorry, Ellie. I'm not saying you're wrong; I'm just saying I haven't seen all the pieces yet. But don't listen to me on this. Let's get Roshan on the phone right now if you think you've got something. We can brief him, and he can take it to his team. They might know how to run with it."

"There's something here, Josh. It speaks to Ash's core motivation, something we haven't discovered yet. It must be money. This is a job for him. He's making money doing it."

Josh was scooting over to the conference phone in the middle of the room. He nodded and said, "Let's get Roshan on the phone. If he doesn't know exactly how to dig into this, he should at least be aware of what resources the FBI has that can work on it."

Chapter Twenty-Two

In A Cage

She sat in the dark, dank room. Perhaps to call it a room was optimistic; it was a cell. The air oppressed her in every way, but she breathed deeply, considering all her options for escape and tearing apart her mind in deciding exactly how much revenge she should extract on these people. How dare they cage her. How dare Hector betray her. How could he have done this to her? She had given it all up; she had walked away. In these moments that she had been snatched and caged like a violent animal, in the depths of her essence, she determined that vengeance would be paid. It would be paid in full. The storm she would lay down upon their heads would be incredible. Generations would tell tales of when the Ashen Horse had fallen upon them and executed retribution.

She calculated she would be what they had named her. "I truly will become the Ashen Horse. He who sits upon me will be named Death, and Hades will follow behind me. I will kill with the sword, and I will leave in my wake a trail of famine and plague." In these dark moments, she knew bitterness and anger that she had never known before. The crippling sorrow that came with the betrayal left her devoid of meaning. It was not so much an emotion; it was not a tantrum or burst of anger, but a deep-seated inner burning, a flame that could not be quenched. She burned with a tempest, which would only be sated with blood. She burned for retribution. Equally, there was a hollowness that felt like it would consume her. It bent around her, trying to swallow her from the inside.

Molly had entered the room with such confidence, such assurance. Molly did not even know who she was. Molly thought she was some federal agent. Molly... Molly... Molly.... Molly was not as clever as she presumed. That woman was in for a rude awakening.

She thought, "I will not follow the rules you expect an agent to follow. You are grossly mistaken." The harsh reality of the situation would be revealed in due time.

Hector had been a decoy all along—an entrapment to lure her into the clutches of Molly's organization. In the darkness of the cell, she could think of nothing else. All that crossed her mind was her acceptance when lying in Hector's arms. For her to know it was not real crushed a piece of her soul she didn't even know she had. He had made a piece of her alive that she didn't think she had, and now he had ripped it out just as readily. The wound was not clean; it was jagged and pulsating. She felt infected. All she could think about was that Molly was the perpetrator. She would bring the sword; she would know vengeance.

Her eyes wandered to the windows of the warehouse. The offices in this corner of the building had been designed to look out over the warehouse floor, so she had internal windows looking out into a dark warehouse. Everything around her was dark. She could only see the rare glaring or reflecting light that danced into a seemingly abandoned building.

The bitterness oppressed her, and she felt a gloom encapsulate her. It was almost as if a tangible presence had entered the room; it clawed at her and would surely consume her. She mourned for the life that could have been, the life that she had recently decided upon. A life with Hector. The life that she was willing to and would have forsaken everything for. It was gone; with it, all the happiness and joy that had been so promising. That life that might have been was a wisp in the wind, so fleeting and so mystical that it vanished in a mere second.

She would have wept. But she didn't have it in her, neither the character nor the emotion. She had been scoured to her core, rubbed raw of emotion. Any capacity to feel had been gored entirely out of her. She was but an empty shell of herself, having been raped of the liberty to feel.

Her mind churned, remembering the meeting of an hour ago. She saw in Hector's eyes his shame. He did feel what she felt; he was being manipulated by this monster as much as she was. On the one hand, this gave her some sense of relief, yet at the same time, it inflamed her rage toward Molly. Equally, she knew that whatever Hector and she had together was over now. She would never be with Hector. He was lost to her. But she silently promised that she would also free him from this monster.

She suspected this was naïve of her. In those fleeting moments, she had seen in Hector's eyes that he felt something. But perhaps he was as complicit in Molly's schemes as Molly was. She may never know, but she would afford him the grace she saw in his eyes in those brief moments. He would never know that those singular moments of caring would ultimately be what would save his life. Although her rage called upon her to enact judgment on everyone who belonged to Molly, she equally knew that she could never harm Hector. Perhaps even at the cost of her own life, she didn't think she could raise her hand against him.

Molly's speech had assured her death, either mercifully or horribly. She remembered that part. The initial shock of the betrayal had smoldered by that point of the conversation. She remembered the choice that Molly had shown her. A merciful death if she cooperated, or an excruciating death if she refused. Perhaps she would give Molly the same choice. She smiled. In the darkest shadow of the night, she grinned. The grin may have turned into a snarl, but a croaked laugh still emerged from her lips.

The guard outside looked toward the door, perplexed. Was that laughter? She couldn't possibly be laughing. It must be crying that he was hearing. The poor girl was crying. He felt terrible for her. It was a dirty business, killing federal agents. He didn't want any part of it. He had to stand guard tonight before the more gruesome players arrived in the morning. This was not the kind of guard duty he wanted to have any part of. The poor girl was sobbing.

She laughed and laughed uncontrollably. Perhaps it was the only thing she could do. Her emotions would not allow her to cry, but they allowed her to express mirth. It was not the laughter of joy or happiness but the laughter of irony and contempt. She would bring Molly to her knees, and at that moment, she would extract a righteous judgment from her.

She had been busy planning and executing her escape while she contemplated her plight. She had disassembled the bed. Taking small pieces of metal from the frame, she fashioned a clumsy lockpick. But it should be enough to open the cage. There was only one real way to find out, so she worked on the lock.

She carefully and meticulously slid the pieces of wire into the mechanism. With precision that only comes from practice, she slowly began to work on the internal levers of the lock. She didn't consider herself a lockpicker, and if truth be told, she wasn't an expert. But at the same time, years of breaking into buildings, houses, businesses, and even a bank or two had developed in her a distinct ability to maneuver simple locks. It took some effort and multiple tries, but eventually, the lock disengaged.

The guard was growing tired and restless, so he paced the hallway several times. There was nothing to do except stand in the hallway outside the door. It was a terrible way to spend the night. The poor girl had gone silent about two hours ago. She must have finally given over to sleep. He truly did feel sorry for her. He wondered why the agencies always sent someone undercover. Did they have no other means of getting information on Molly? This was the third sacrificial lamb that would be slaughtered. They must have a better way. He considered it as he walked up and down, making a slow circuit.

He probably should not have been considering the options to bring down his boss. But his guilty conscience terrorized him. She was such a beautiful girl and probably just into her thirties. What a waste of a life to go tracking down one of the most notorious drug kingpins in the Americas. Perhaps the DEA and FBI didn't know how large Molly was. Maybe that's why they sent these simple reconnaissance missions that continuously ended in defeat. He felt the waste of it. Just the pure loss of life and goodness that came from throwing away something that was inherently precious.

The cell was open. The room was still pitch black. Perhaps that was intentional, but it was a mistake not to have a window for the guard to look in on her. She had spent twenty minutes shaping a clumsy blade from the dismantled bed. It's not so much a blade as a spring coil with eight protruding four-inch metal spikes wrapped into it. It wasn't as good as any of her knives, but it was a prison shiv times eight. It should be more than effective.

She pressed her ear to the door and waited a full ten minutes to see what she could hear. It was silent. Entirely silent. She didn't think he was moving around, if he was even out there.

As she sat listening, she pondered all her options. She could only conceive of two. Should she swing open the door in a rapid fury and attack with abandon, or sneak out as quietly as possible, survey the scene, and then take appropriate action?

The Ashen Horse

She had spent a lifetime perfecting stealth, which she was most comfortable with. She silently, impossibly slowly, opened the door. The guard was there leaning on the wall, head tilted down. His head jerked up and then slowly teetered toward his chest again as he teetered on the edge of sleep. He was leaning on the opposite wall from her cell and facing the other way.

It was unfortunate for him, but that would be the last mistake he would ever make. A terrible error at that. A lesson she learned while running the streets was to always keep your eyes on the target. This guard would never have the luxury of knowing the same lesson.

She centered herself. She narrowed her focus and cleared her mind. It wasn't quite meditation but a skill she had developed over the years, a concentration that brought herself fully into her own. She quietly and carefully breathed out and then took in a full breath. Then, in complete focus, she lunged.

She acted entirely on muscle memory. Her body swung in a fury, a weapon in and of itself. Her hands worked methodically, her makeshift shiv penetrating flesh in rapid succession—her hands a fury of motion, in and out.

The guard lay twitching on the ground. She had made a standard kill move, two thrusts to the kidneys in the back, move up, and thrust through the lungs. Use that last thrust to push yourself back enough to leverage another full-strength blow to the throat. Repeat the throat until the victim collapses.

The guard's eyes glassed over in seconds, and he had received sixty-four puncture wounds. His mind barely had time to process what happened before his soul was slowly escaping his body. She stood over his body, fire burning in her eyes. The rage that had been storming inside of her was coming to full life. In this horrible moment, standing over a dead body, she articulated death. With her mind aflame, her thoughts followed, "Molly thought to send men against me.

Against me! They will find me. They will know the Ashen Horse."

Chapter Twenty-Three

Hauling the Mail

Josh and Ellie had finished their work in Seattle. It had turned out to take several more days to finish up everything they both wanted to accomplish. The one nice thing about working on cases like these, being both high priorities yet in a way cold, allowed them to focus on things they wanted to accomplish rather than the normal dowsing of fires as they cropped up in routine investigations.

They had walked out that last day with a sense of accomplishment if not achievement. They had let the evidence officers put it all away, including their heavily documented and reviewed case files and notes along with an entirely documented and cataloged solution. And perhaps a quarter of all the files were now digitized and uploaded into the FBI's database under Ash's case.

They had hoped that something productive would come out of their investment, and it appeared that they were making continued progress on both cases even though there hadn't been any real breakthroughs for quite some time in Ash's investigation.

That was also a barrier to great morale on the team. The team knew the job, the never-ending grind that was good detective work, but it was still discouraging when nothing rose to life through the process. Nevertheless, there was nothing for it but to continue putting together the pieces they could find.

And that's what landed Josh and Ellie in Phoenix. They had spent a four-day reprieve back home, but now they would track down these new aliases of Ash and see if anyone recognized anyone that might fit their photograph and composite sketch of Ash.

Their first actual business stop would be to talk to the Phoenix Police Department and let them know they were poking around their jurisdiction and seeking information on the Ashen Horse case. Then, they'd dive into some cases that might fit the timeline and those with various commonality factors. Obviously, they wanted to see any cases relating to knives, particularly large ones, that might resemble a sword. Equally, they wanted to research victims who were under any suspicion, pretty much for anything. It appeared that Ash killed all kinds of questionable individuals; there wasn't a hard-set pathology.

When they had reencountered the victims' randomness, Ellie argued that it bolstered the view that Ash was getting paid for it. The team was onboard, trying to review options for soliciting a murderer, but that was a slow process as well. Despite the wisecracks about 'Hire a Murderer Dot Com,' it wasn't easy to just solicit criminal activity online. And murder certainly was the hardest to conjure magically out of thin air.

Josh and Ellie had split up on the first day in Phoenix. Both went to the most extensive police facilities in the general Phoenix metropolitan area, diving into cases and engaging the local detectives. They sought to pull out any recollection that might relate to Ash's case. They wanted to find memories to tie into the larger narrative.

It was a painful process, and mostly fruitless. Still, it was worth the attempt to find any unknown cases that they might be able to associate with Ash. That's how Josh found himself taking five detectives out to lunch and reminiscing about the good ol' days.

Ellie wasn't faring much better. She was trapped in a room with two detectives who wouldn't take the hint that she wasn't interested in either one of them. The flirting was embarrassing and dismal, but it continued for almost an hour-long interview.

After the day had ended, Josh and Ellie told each other their stories about the day's events over dinner. It turned out that Josh, although he didn't find anything of particular interest, had enjoyed his time with the team. Ellie wanted to kill all of them; it was a completely wasted day, in her opinion.

"We never know what we might have loosened, though," Josh commented.

"Fine. Maybe. I still say we go back there and taser them all tomorrow. Just out of principle."

"You are a very beautiful woman, Ellie; it shouldn't come to you as a huge surprise that men would flirt with you."

"You never did."

"Yes, well, that's also because I'm stupid. And I didn't know how professional it would be."

"It's not at all!"

"True," he said.

"And that's why we should go back there tomorrow…"

"… and taser them all?"

"Exactly."

"Duly noted."

"So today was a bust, but we might get something out of it in the long run. What's the plan for tomorrow?"

Neither of them were entirely sure how to proceed. They had an address, but they wanted to find more information first. They also had the various elements of their forensic team feeding them pieces of information they should follow up on or investigate. This was built from an exhaustive national search of the two aliases that could be linked to Ash. A 'John Millers' and a 'Matthew Smith' could be false aliases for the Ashen Horse, including the originally discovered

'David Smith.' As a result, the FBI was trying to compile any evidence of the names that could be linked to suspicious activity or behavior. Or anything incorrectly linked to a real person holding those names.

Scooping up some Thai noodles, Ellie said, "We could try the United States Postal Service. The USPS might have something buried in the records regarding that P.O. Box. They might have something about the address as well. I doubt they would have footage or anything like that, but perhaps they have another file or document that wasn't turned over."

"It's worth a visit," Josh agreed. "Anything that they can give us would be beneficial. If they know anything more than what we have now, it would be a benefit."

Josh chopped half the egg roll on the table and pushed half of it toward Ellie. Ellie reached for it and continued, "That's part of the day. What else do we plan for tomorrow?"

Josh stopped and stuttered. "Blast it all. Why didn't we think of that?" He was shaking his head and seemed to be quite annoyed. Ellie waited patiently, assuming he had more to say.

"We need to go back and talk to the police. Ah, bloody, why didn't we consider that? We have the shipment information on the sword!"

Ellie was still confused and not following. However, she wasn't sure that Josh was following his reasoning. She tried to probe something out of him, "Yeah? What does that have anything to do with it?"

"We know when Ash was physically here in Phoenix."

"So? We need to find out where he was living at the time. Isn't that what we are trying to do?"

Josh asked, "What if Ash wasn't living here?"

"Well, why would he have been here if he wasn't living here?" Ellie said it, trailing off into her thoughts. She realized something was there, but she wasn't pulling it together. She realized it should be obvious, but it seemed to elude her.

Josh was smiling, watching her. She glared at him. "You think it's funny, don't you?"

"What's that?"

"That I'm not seeing the connection."

Josh chortled. "Don't get all defensive. You are faster at this stuff than me. We are tired; if you refocus, you'll get it in a few seconds."

Ellie blinked, and then she realized it. "Oh. Uh, yeah, so that is rather obvious, isn't it? We know Ash was here at a specific date and time, picking up a delivery. We need to check all major crimes committed plus or minus 30 days?"

Josh was nodding. "Yeah. We just assumed Ash was here because he lived here. Hopefully, we get lucky, and someone can tell us his life story. But what if he was just here for a job?"

Ellie asked, "So we must return to the police stations tomorrow?"

"Appears so."

"Great! I'm going to taze them all."

"No mercy?"

Ellie smirked. "None. I have a better idea. We'll find those detectives I had to deal with today, and you will make sure you give me a big, sloppy kiss right in front of them."

Josh joined Ellie in her grin. "Now that sounds like a plan I can get behind."

***

The kiss went down exactly like they had planned. Pretty much nothing else did, though. They didn't find any invaluable information, although they did find some cases that were eerily like Ash.

They sent those cases off to the forensics team and told Roshan to contact them if they should investigate further. The entire FBI was going with the presumption that Ash was in Arizona during this timeframe, so these cases could likely be associated. They had Roshan move those case logs to the top of the list; they might as well dig through all of them and get feedback from them while they were still in Phoenix.

The days spent sifting through logs in Phoenix, trying to associate cases to specific dates and times, also moved them to consider other possibilities in the case. The recognition that they might be able to start tracking Ash through time put another spin on things. The team back in the main office in Washington DC was now working on taking every case suspected to be Ash and trying to lay it out on a map and graphing it out over time.

They had already assembled a map of where all the cases landed, but they hadn't correlated the dates into a cohesive picture. They were now working on putting that together in a separate flow document. One of the team members wanted to connect everything with a string to show the passage of time, but it was argued that they didn't have a complete map or timeline. At the very least, Josh and Ellie expected a nice spreadsheet with cases, victims, and timelines.

Just connecting those notes might reveal a silent mystery they had overlooked. The problem with mysteries is that revelations usually come from some of the simplest places. Perhaps there was a timeline that they hadn't noticed. Perhaps there were consistencies in the timing of the cases, if not the geography? Did they have cases attributed to Ash that were simultaneously on opposite ends of the country? Did Ash always kill on the last week of the month? Who knew yet? Only analyzing the details of a complete view might lift the veil of the hidden mysteries in the case.

After the epic kiss, which did turn the heads of half the people in the police station, Ellie and Josh departed. The detectives who had harassed Ellie the previous day at least had the decency to look ashamed. Of course, Ellie had pointedly looked at them, staring death rays at both of them until they had to look away. She wouldn't let the opportunity pass without them knowing they were being called out on the spot.

The Ashen Horse

After they left the police department, they found a large chunk of the day had been sucked up through the course of leg work. It was often a strange experience how the hours slipped away, completely uncontrollable, through the daily activities of life. They only had a few hours left before the nine-to-five crowds would leave their offices. As a result, they opted to head to the post office where the P.O. Box was located and see if they could scrounge up any old data. They weren't hopeful, but it was at least another lead they could put to rest with some leg work. So much of this came down to simply doing the leg work.

Josh asked, "Are you excited?"

"About what?"

"We are going to the post office!"

Ellie looked at him with skepticism. "I'm supposed to be excited about the USPS?"

"Everyone seeking their fortunes in this life ultimately finds it at the post office! It's where all truth and adventure come together to be revealed to mere mortals."

"I don't know if I have told you this yet. But there's something truly wrong with you."

"Maybe. But that doesn't change that our destinies will be revealed at the post office."

"You are going crazy, aren't you? You are this bored?"

"It's a long drive."

"It's like twenty minutes!"

"Okay, just that bored."

The postal service may shed some light on the Ash case. They would find out soon enough. Josh was driving at the moment; they switched it up often as they both had a serious fondness for driving. He pulled in and parked. Then they headed into the building, their fortunes awaiting.

Chapter Twenty-Four

Out of the Frying Pan

Molly's morning had been busy. In typical form, she followed her usual schedule. She had several international calls, fully encrypted, with her contacts in South America. A significant shipment would enter the country in several weeks, and everyone needed to be ready. Early in her career, she moved small amounts, but as she increased in the business, she quickly found that it was better to marginalize your risk with fewer larger shipments rather than many smaller shipments. Even with a well-oiled process and iron-clad system, there were still too many opportunities for the police to catch the prize.

She ran her entire operations with six shipments per year, one every other month. Of course, she had to immediately disperse those containers into smaller shipments to sustain her entire operations, which involved bringing in multiple container deliveries. They then were shipped across the Eastern seaboard. This kicked off the process of smuggling the money and proceeds into legitimate businesses and overseas. The company's operations were full-time jobs for five people, and it was dragging on her as the years went on.

She had often considered retiring; she didn't need the money anymore. The simple truth, though, was that she didn't know if the cartels would allow her to exit the system.

She funded a third, maybe as much as half, of their operations. They might come after her if she stopped the purchases—if the money flow dried up.

Her morning had been busy with these internal questions, as mornings had been of late. The struggle to make the right decisions. She walked out of her office to get lunch; it was, of course, nearly noon. Lunch was fantastic, as always. It was a perfect way to decompress in the middle of the day. Her chef had made a light pasta covered in fresh marinara sauce with basil and nutmeg seasoning. It was highlighted with some kind of cream sauce, which truly complemented the pasta, with fresh squeezed orange juice and a bowl of freshly diced fruit. He also had given her a side of veggies to take back into her office for the next several hours of work.

She stood up to head back into the office to continue several scheduled calls when one of her runners barged through the door. He had a gun in his face in an instant, and he stood there in utter horror until her security staff checked him out and then released him. Two of them stood close, though, just in case. She did hire some of the best talent.

"Sorry guys, I should have known not to come barging in here; I just wasn't thinking," the runner gasped.

"Why are you here right now, Jeremy?"

Panting, Jeremy went on, "I went to warehouse two this morning, as instructed, to see what information they had extracted out of Hector's girl."

"I wouldn't call her that if I were you, at least not where Hector can hear you. He's not taking the whole thing well."

"My bad. Look, Molly. You probably should go there and see for yourself."

"Excuse me?"

"To the warehouse," he puffed, gesturing to an expansive area. "You should go to the warehouse."

"And see what, exactly?"

"You should probably just see for yourself...," he trailed off, looking slightly pale.

"Jeremy, let me just put this succinctly as I can, as I have stuff I'm supposed to be doing right now. Tell me what I need to know, or you may have the privilege of joining 'Hector's girl.'"

That appeared to snap him out of it; his eyes met hers. "Right, Molly – look, I didn't mean any disrespect. I didn't mean to waste your time."

"Jeremy..."

"They are all dead, okay? Everyone is dead."

Molly's eyes turned into dark ovals, a mixture of shock and confusion. "What?!"

Jeremy swallowed, and now he did go entirely pale. "It looks like a massacre. It's nothing like you see in the movies. The blood, it... it was everywhere. The Boxer brothers were in pieces, scattered around. And the other two you sent? I don't even know who they were, or I can't recognize them, they... I mean... they were mostly whole, I think."

"And the girl in the cell?"

"The cell is empty; the cell room was trashed entirely and looked like a storm went through it. She isn't there."

Molly yelled for her security director. She found her way back to the lunch table and took a chair. It took the security director a minute to come into the kitchen.

"What's up?"

"Get all my people in a room, now. They all need to come to the house now. We need an organizational meeting."

"On it, I'll make all the calls."

"Now, not tonight, not in two hours. Now."

He spun around and was leaving the room as quickly as possible. He didn't recall ever being at an 'organizational meeting.' Molly made it a point to keep things segmented. She limited everyone's piece of the pie to ensure liability, incrimination, and criminal knowledge were limited throughout her organization. He didn't want to be around for whatever was happening right now. Maybe it was time to move to Alaska like he always wanted. Something was

The Ashen Horse

going down that would not be good for anyone to be in the way of. Even so, he knew he would make all the arrangements and all the calls. Molly knew it, too.

Her security director left the room, and Molly motioned for Jeremy to take a seat at the table. She then pushed some of the food towards him. He sat but didn't touch the food. He looked like he would be sick at any moment.

"You aren't hungry?"

"Starving, actually, but I couldn't keep anything down right now. I threw up everything I ate for the last two weeks at the warehouse."

"Now, Jeremy, what do you think happened?"

"Me? I don't know. Everyone got killed. That's all I know. Then they, they dismembered them... kind of.... They... it wasn't done clean, ma'am." He looked green, and his hand went to his stomach, the other halfway to his mouth.

"Jeremy, I need to know what is happening. The police wouldn't do this. Do you think it was one of the cartels? Does the girl know people? Was she rescued? Was she among the bodies? I need to know what is going on, Jeremy. Actually, for that matter..."

Molly paused and grabbed her phone. She quickly texted three of her senior leadership, telling them to go to the warehouse immediately. She also texted two of her cleaners. She had found men who specialized in hiding and cleaning up evidence. She affectionately called them her cleaners and was never bashful about deploying them as needed. They were never timid about charging her three times what should have already been a healthy rate.

She shook her head, "I should have done that initially. This whole thing has me flustered. It's okay, Jeremy; I have people going on-site to investigate. How many bodies do you think you saw?"

"Five, the Boxer brothers and two others that were...," he swallowed. "Anyway... And what must have been the guard on the cell; he was stabbed repeatedly but otherwise looked untouched in the hallway. He was the only one of the five that was, well, whole."

Molly's agitation clearly showed. "None of this makes any sense. You might have been right in the first place, Jeremy. I might need to go see it myself." She grabbed her phone again and quickly canceled her afternoon meetings, then went to her car and headed for the warehouse.

***

She smiled as she sipped her white chocolate mocha. She usually preferred the mornings for this, but today, she would make do in the afternoon. She was tired, though; she hadn't slept much last night. She estimated she had killed the guard at around 3 am. She took his car keys, found his vehicle, and went to her storage unit, where she had been storing the tools of her trade. She didn't want them in her beach house. It would not have been smart to have anything where Hector would have come across it. Better not to have any questions that she didn't want to answer. She had also learned early never to have evidence anywhere and never have it where the evidence was in your name. Of course, she never had anything in her name anyway.

After she had picked up her tradecraft, she went to a hotel and took a long shower. She would never go back to the beach house again, of course. It might have to get burned down randomly; that would be sad, but it might be necessary. It was a gorgeous cottage-like house positioned perfectly overlooking the ocean. But even so, it might be unavoidable.

After cleaning, she left the hotel, went to an all-night diner, and ate a hearty breakfast. She thought of it as fueling up; the work that would be done this morning would take a lot of energy. Then, she returned to the warehouse. She figured that must have been around 7 am. She was worried that she was too late, but the place was exactly as she had left it. No one else had been there since she left; she checked the signal she made on the body of the guard to make sure it hadn't been disturbed.

Then, she waited.

And waited.

She had learned patience in this lifestyle. She had spent many hours waiting for the mark to come home. Or waiting for collateral to leave so she didn't have to stack up unnecessary bodies. Intel gathering was also an exercise in laborious patience. So, she waited. They finally arrived around 10 am.

They were two hulking thugs, and they looked similar, probably related. She used her twenty-two, the first time in forever that she could remember, and shot them both in the head from the shadows. They didn't even know what happened. Then she went to work on them.

When she was in the middle of her labor with the two ogres, probably about an hour later, two more men showed up. Those two did not get the same sweet ending, as she was caught somewhat off guard. But, rather opportunistically, she had the tools in hand. They screamed for quite some time until, just for her sanity, she had to end them both. It must have been shortly before noon then; maybe it was eleven thirty, something like that. It became clear to her that she was overstaying her welcome. She finished the message she wanted to make. She thought it had been made emphatically clear. She crept carefully out of the warehouse.

She considered that she was making a terrible mistake but decided to risk it. She returned to the beach house, carefully watching to ensure no one was casing the place. Then she went in and took all her items out of it. She had stashes of cash, various passports, and driver's licenses for several identities, and two other smartphones. They had been hidden in the walls, undetectable unless you knew where they were. She would have preferred to keep these in her storage unit but having IDs and money on hand was always necessary. She never knew when she might have to grab a plane out of the country at a moment's notice.

She didn't dare let anyone get their hands on the IDs and smartphones. She was walking out for what would be the last time, and she stopped. She intended to set the place on fire, but she couldn't bring herself to do it. Some of the happiest memories she had ever had happened here. She couldn't destroy it.

She felt a piece of herself depart from her as she stood there. Standing there, she relived those moments of happiness when she had felt more alive than she had dreamed possible. Her hand rose to her cheek, where Hector often would caress her in a way only he could do. She didn't know how it happened, but tears slowly trickled down her face. She shook herself but refused to wipe the tears away. Then, as a few more continued to flow, she walked away.

As she brought herself back into a constant state of emotion, she continued her plan. Perhaps it wasn't a plan, just a roughly strung-together series of events she must complete. Her next step was to take the guard's car back to his house and leave it there. That should bewilder Molly, it would be the last place they would look for the vehicle. She walked two miles away, wandering through the suburbs, and finally called a rideshare outside a random person's house. They might have noticed her, but she only had to wait a few minutes before the ride arrived. It took her to a hotel that was five hotels further away from hers, and then she walked to her new room. She would only spend one more night here and then move again, probably outside of Miami, maybe up to Fort Lauderdale or maybe south.

It had been a busy morning, but she sat drinking her coffee for now. She had picked it up at the coffee shop in the lobby of the hotel. It was delicious, of course. She sat, looking out the window, planning. What would her next move be? The desired vengeance and retribution were still seething inside her, so she continued planning. She wasn't sure what or how she would do it. But she was confident that vengeance was still looming in the shadows. Her vengeance. She was coming to see it done.

Chapter Twenty-Five

Dark Secrets

Jade had been focused on her computer for the last eight hours, as was typical in a day in the FBI offices. Her mind was glued to piecing together how the Ashen Horse was finding his victims. The entire FBI team thought the internet must be the methodology, but Jade wasn't convinced. However, her task for the last week had been to test the methodology. She was specifically trying to pull out some statistical information that might reveal internet correlations. These connections might point to something of interest, or the correlation itself might reveal the source. The type of work involved an unclear objective and a pipe dream. Just the kind of work she enjoyed, the completely fruitless hope. She took the view that leadership can't get mad at you for not delivering if they give you an impossible task.

Of course, there was no clear roadmap on how to accomplish this. She had been working on several internet algorithms to pull information out of the larger internet. In layman's terms, it might be said that she was writing an internet search engine. The algorithms were designed to query thousands upon thousands of websites all over the internet. She wasn't going to the true depth of rewriting an entire search engine. Still, she was scanning hundreds of thousands of websites and images, data mining them for thousands of keywords, and then comparing that information to specific keywords she entered as possibly having anything to do with Ash.

She and a colleague had been playing with this off and on for nine months for the FBI, but now they were fine-tuning it for Ash's case. Tim and Roshan had approached their department a month ago. Her leadership had sent down the directive and told them to start trying to find links to all the murders on the internet, and that had started a massive motive search. It began by trying to identify the unifying motive behind all the cases. That burned out and didn't reveal anything, mainly because there was no cohesive motive they could tell via the technology or from surveying the cases.

Next, they tried to link the victims, but there was absolutely nothing there either. That was particularly frustrating for the team, but especially for Jade and her partner. She had thought to herself repeatedly, "How is it possible that none of these people knew each other?" It had turned out none of them did; none of the victims were tied together. She had pulled her hair out several times in frustration, slowly banging her head against her desk. That had passed, and now they were trying to find the next big thing that might yield discoverable results.

Ellie had made a strong case to Tim, or so they were told, that Ash was a contract killer. Jade had only met Ellie briefly in one of the team meetings, but the woman appeared competent enough. Ellie's theory, now the leading theory they were working with, was that Ash was simply a gunman for hire. It was ludicrous, of course, but Jade knew better than to voice her opinion to the senior leaders of the task force. The several years she had spent working in the dungeons on computers showed her that keeping your head down and doing the job kept much of the daily drama at bay, which was critical when working in the monster of a bureaucracy that was the Federal Bureau of Investigation.

The drama could drown you if the bureaucracy did not.

All of this led to the next big task—trying to find a way to link the victims to murder for hire. Jade had spent the last two days scratching the internet; that was her new term for her algorithm, the scratch. She had scratched the internet repeatedly and not found anything linking any of the known or suspected victims to any murder plot or similar searches. Which she knew she wouldn't, of course. It was impossible for anyone to put that kind of thing on the internet and not get called out or noticed. Which, of course, meant it wasn't on the internet.

She paused her typing and considered what it meant to have information freely online. Information posted online freely was commonly found and viewable and often in searchable inventory on the internet. But equally, there was more information on computer networks that were connected to the internet which wasn't in the public domain.

Her mind churned in circles as she thought about where information might have been stored all over the world. A connection might exist; it just likely wasn't publicly accessible. It was on the internet, and equally, it was not on the internet. The light bulb flashed through her mind's eye. It wasn't on the internet, but it was on the internet. She stopped and blinked a couple of times. Suppose she explained that to Tim; he would look at her in confusion. It might have made complete sense to her, but they would have been bewildered if she tried to explain this epiphany to leadership.

What was revealed to her in her moment of discovery was simply that she would have to take her scratching deeper. She just wasn't scratching the right places. She would have to go into the cryptic hidden depths of the mysterious jungles that were the more nefarious online communities.

After her moment of enlightenment, Jade was programming the tool to dig into the dark web, that cryptic and hidden underground internet that exists. It was the type of challenge that Jade lived for. To explore the deepest secrets that anyone would dare put out in public but still not so public as for the world to see. It was where everything someone didn't want someone else to know was stored. All the secrets.

Jade stared at her screen, writing, compiling, and running the code. Rinse and repeat. Go home while grabbing some lousy fast-food meal, then burn more hours in front of her computer. Then rinse and repeat. Several days went by as she continued to work with her new theory.

She had been on a few conference calls the last three days, pulling in all the information everyone knew about the dark web from the FBI's perspective. The problem was getting into it and its many different tangents. The FBI could crack into several of the key dark webs that housed a lot of the more suspect content on the internet, but that isn't to say they could gain access to all the small pockets of private communities that might house information. Through various FBI sources, she had found that she could get into several of these darknets. They were small units that made up the collective dark web. She hoped that getting into several of these was enough to uncover something more. Something new. Anything new to support the case was the impossible hope. After days of writing new code and digging, she hadn't achieved any substantial results. At this point, she was yearning to get any type of valuable intel anywhere, about anything.

The dark web was not just some alternative internet, as many suspected. Jade had learned and then spent hours explaining to others that it is a collection of smaller private networks that are kept secret and only allow a specific group of people to gain access. An encrypted corporate network riding on the larger internet might be comparable if different.

As a test run, her algorithm scratched away data all over the darknets, revealing a serious amount of suspicious and potentially illegal activity. She was compiling this and shipping it off to various FBI teams while still trying to focus on collecting something relevant to the Ash case. Which usually meant she had to go back and rewrite a massive portion of code to make it more specific to Ash.

To complicate it, she was trying to do good coding. She was a computer forensic scientist, after all. Sure, she could add one or two lines to an algebraic if-then statement, but there was no finesse in that. She wanted this to scale and expand, meaning she would write an entirely new subroutine to call back into her more extensive program to pull in a new feature or other metadata. Her boss's eyes usually glazed over when she tried to explain it. But the power was always in the details when it came to programming.

Her vision slowly became foggy as the night wore endlessly on. But, being as dogged as ever, she was about to try some new code to see what it would do. She had written a function that would include every victim they had evidence of from the Ash files. She had broken them into their first and last names and cities in a data matrix. The program would screen every page of the darknets they had access to. If any of the words were found, they would hold that in memory, and then the darknets would be rescanned and tried to associate them with any other of the words stored. In theory, this should find any page with any victim's first and last name, tie a first name to a city, or tie two victims together. Before she ran the entire code through all the darknets she could access, her goal was to add a mix of correlating words to screen everything they could possibly tie into the case.

Jade was a little nervous about the new feature, fearing that the return on the data might be too enormous to sort properly. She was trying to search for well over a hundred unique terms. Those names and features could be all over the dark web. It was a gamble.

There were days when Jade truly did enjoy her job. Playing with the toys that she was playing with right now was one of them. Running this on any standard computer would cause it to explode, which is why she was running it on one of the few supercomputers in the world. She had it on loan from the Department of Defense because she required the extra processing power. Just the raw computing power she was playing with was exhilarating. Perhaps that was a bit strange, or it was just her inner nerd showing itself, but she was captivated by what could be accomplished with the right tools.

Before she ran her new code, fearing the amount of data it would return, she built a couple more features into another new function. The primary purpose was to continuously move through the returned results and reduce them to a single entry into a table. The program would then scan the entire table, and if the entry existed already, the program would delete the new entry and add another sequential number to the original entry.

It was a simple method of tallying repeated results. It would cut down on overall returned entries and prioritize the returned data by listing the most common entries with the highest information.

She had tried to explain it to her bosses. They didn't make it very far into the conversation, once again their eyes glazing over as they calmly and respectfully nodded. But she had to justify why it took her the extra time to get some of this work into motion.

Any time she tried to discuss the intricacies of writing good code rather than slapping code together, that's when the eyes rolled, and the chairs swiveled. It was a chronic issue with her leadership. They didn't appreciate finesse.

At the end of the day, it didn't matter that her bosses blinked at her in utter confusion. All that mattered was that they approved her direction and allowed her to continue with what she was doing. Of course, she probably could have told them she was robbing a bank, and they would have let her continue. The FBI bureaucracy sometimes put people in charge who had no idea what they oversaw. Normally, that was okay if they had the right people working for them, although it was a disaster on occasion. Jade had seen both situations firsthand in the minimal time she had been at the Bureau. In fairness, she had also seen it firsthand in the private industries she came from. She wondered if it was just a reality in the modern workforce.

As the night grew truly late, perhaps it was approaching morning, Jade was almost ready to proceed. Her goal was to let it run overnight; at least, that was her original goal before a hint of daylight just might have been peeking into the window. Then she would come back the next day and see what the machine could glean off the dark web, what it could scratch. She had done this before and walked in to find the whole process had crashed. She didn't get anything out of it when her entire program exploded. But it also took hours to run, and she wouldn't waste a day having it run when she could fine-tune the code tomorrow.

After finishing her last-minute additions, she was finally ready and hit the initiate button to start the program. Jade watched the program churn along for the next ten minutes. She was making sure it wasn't going to crash right out of the gate. It appeared to be working; it was collecting correlation data; she had put in some output fields in the program that would show the tallying of data. It was clocking up, showing that information was being discovered, logged, and documented.

As she watched the program churn, her mind wandered, likely from exhaustion as much as anything. She wanted to write multiple functions that would explicitly call out the linkage between all the items she had entered. Further, diagram the links within and between words, phrases, and concepts. And then maybe, just maybe, take it one step further and link it to specific websites. Take all that correlated data and digitally represent it into a flow diagram or a complex word cloud. That was her vision. It would take several more weeks of coding to materialize, assuming she didn't get pulled in a completely different direction.

She shook her head, staring back at the screen. She was getting data, and for now, that was the objective. This program would run for the entire night or several days, depending on the depth of the correlation. But she was hoping she would have data in the morning. Well, it would be afternoon now before she crawled back into the office. It wasn't obvious how good the data would be, but she would have data, hopefully. With a task completed, and hopefully completed well, she was done with what turned out to be a very long day. After one last glance at the running code, she turned off the lights in her office and headed out the door.

Chapter Twenty-Six

Stealth

She had been watching the compound for hours so far. She was physically close in a newly acquired rental car, but she had also spent the last two weeks setting up various cameras monitoring roads in and out of Molly's compound. Her eyes were watching the rear of the property and also the entrance. Having stashed two other getaway cars on opposite ends of the property she was making a triangle of sorts to support fleeing from any direction of the compound.

She was moving in and out of her meditative state, preparing for the night. For tonight was finally the night. After several weeks of planning, tonight was the night Molly Johnson would meet her end. She relaxed and contemplated her entire plan. Quite often, she did not dress as the assassin she was, but tonight, she had gone full garb. She wore finely knitted clothing that fit exactly her physique. It was custom-made, like most of her equipment. It was also entirely silk. It was mostly black but had a mix of colors mingled in to cloak it in any surroundings. Very dark greens, greys, and browns. It was not camouflage, for that was too flamboyant. Although the intended effect was effectively camouflage, it was more skillfully and tactfully done. She would be essentially invisible with her clothing on in the dark.

The outfit fit snugly, conforming to her curves. This, of

course, was by design. Her clothes moved as she moved; they wouldn't catch on anything and didn't stick out or cause an obstruction. They were as much a weapon as her entire body was a weapon.

Her actual weapons were the normal tools she carried on most night missions. However, she would be fully equipped this time, so she increased her standard stock of arms. Her katana was at her side, accompanied by its wakizashi. The two swords were the primary weapons she would use. She had nested in the small of her back her trusty .22 pistol, with two extra clips attached to the outside of her thighs for easy reach. She also had a dagger, like a traditional tanto, but customized for her purposes. It rested on her hip in front. Her throwing knives strapped to her forearms and biceps, six per arm.

Uncharacteristically, she carried two larger-sized daggers on the opposite side of her two swords. She planned to stash them somewhere on the property to have, if needed, close at hand.

She had packed two backpacks filled with various electronics. The big pieces she planned on using were ten small portable wireless cameras and associated wireless access points. These would link back to a tablet she was carrying. This part of the puzzle she had spent quite a bit of time considering. These little devices might make all the difference tonight. Her cameras, which she'd spent days researching and testing in her various hotels, were full infrared and night vision capable.

She waited just up to the point where the sun finally sank below the horizon. It was dark, yet not fully dark. The kind of dusk that lingers for some time in the evening hours. She checked her first series of cameras, looking at the entire outside of Molly's compound, and when she recognized it was safe, or at least that she didn't see anyone who could detect her, she got out of her car and launched her grappling hook over the wall. It hooked and she scrambled up and over the perimeter wall. It was still dusk outside, but the ambient light left from the sun was slowly seeping into the darkness of night.

She would need as much of the night as it would afford her. It was in these hours and minutes when she truly knew she was alive. It was also during these hours that her work began.

She planted the grappling hook into the back of a tree near the cars. It would remain there until she came to retrieve it. She hoped she would retrieve it when her tasks were complete, but she planted it there to ensure her escape route was ready if she had to flee in a hurry.

She proceeded to walk the perimeter of the inside of the property and plant two other grappling hooks that she could use to scale the property back out if she needed to. Having an escape plan was just smart and quite often necessary. While sticking to the far outside edge of the property, she looked for any type of security that would hint that the property was alerted to her presence. She didn't see anything, which she thought was odd. Surely Molly had something on her property to alert her to intrusion.

After securing multiple exit points from the environment, she closed in on the houses. To say it was only a single house was a misnomer, for both the houses on the property were elegant in their way. The main house, in its plantation style, was something out of storybooks, and the guest house stood in a modern rancher style that would be the envy of any middle-class family. She slowly crept in close to the houses, finding angles of observation, planting cameras, and then placing her wireless access points to link them all together.

Creep up close, plant gear, and creep back out. Rinse and repeat. Rinse and repeat. After several hours, she had the entire exterior of all the buildings fully monitored. No one could approach, move, or leave the buildings without it showing up on her cameras. She took several moments to activate motion alerts for the system. If any of the cameras

The Ashen Horse

detected motion, she'd get a buzz on her watch telling her the location. She had planned where every camera would go ahead of time and built her programs appropriately. Not only would she get the notification, but she would also know exactly where the motion was detected.

She hiked back to her preferred exit point on the property and left all the excess equipment. It felt like she was dropping off luggage. It was a relief to be rid of the extra baggage that weighed her down as she moved through the night. She downsized her two large packs into a tiny pack that fit tightly on her back. She didn't like carrying it, but she had no other way to utilize her tablet and a keen sense that she would need to see the cameras. All her prep work would be for nothing without it. She had three small cameras tucked into the pack, which she planned to plant in the house to observe the critical areas inside.

She took time to eat, and she watched all the cameras. Waiting. She wanted to learn more about the guards before she went in. She was sure there were seven of them in the house right now, the night shift. Hoping to learn their patrol areas or where they were stationed, she waited, watched, and munched on the rations she had carried over the fence.

She was all too aware that she might be walking directly into a horrible trap. Perhaps she had set off some alarm, tripped some sensor, or got spotted on some camera. The likelihood of them not being prepared for this was rather slim. She was aware of the grandeur and probably the naivety of her scheme. But she was committed anyway. She was going after Molly, and it was happening tonight.

She had waited long enough to ensure Hector had left and was home; her camera watching his property showed him entering his apartment. Half of her wanted to kill Hector as much as Molly and half of her still loved him. It was a horrible feeling. She hadn't decided yet how she would handle that situation. So, she pushed the thoughts from her mind. Tonight was all about Molly.

Daryl Benson

She had put in some fail-safes in case she didn't come out tonight. The cops would learn everything about Molly and find a pile of evidence that should cripple her or bury her in enough legality to make her life the living hell it should be for the rest of her days.

Her original plan was to leave it at that, but she also put in the details about her past in a last-minute decision. She resented this, but she thought that some of her victim's families might want closure. But it was just a fail-safe; she was coming out tonight. The logic was simple: if she died tonight, it didn't matter what anyone knew about her previous life events.

The fury still raged within her. It blazed a white-hot that other emotions could neither temper nor chill. Whether she lived or died tonight, Molly Johnson would be ended. Whether through the natural selection of the death that she would bring upon her or from drowning in the legal system. On this night, one way or another, Molly would know justice.

She learned a little about the guards' movements as the hours ticked away. It wasn't much, but she didn't expect much. She knew several designated areas where the guards appeared to be. Their command center was probably in one of the three areas she observed. That meant the cameras were probably there as well. She had considered her options and guessed that going in the front or back door would be a bad idea. Those must be monitored; the best solution was to climb the balcony and enter the second level.

The time to choose whether to commit or pull out was right now. She would never have this opportunity again. In the back of her mind, she had already fully committed. She headed for the house. She went to the only side of the building that didn't have a wraparound balcony. Her grappling hook sailed slowly up and tore into the railing on the second floor. Silently, she climbed up, keeping her body on the side of the building where there were very obviously no methods of detection. The house was flush, and the

The Ashen Horse

siding unadulterated.

Rising on the second floor, she pressed her body against the side of the house in the darkest recess she could find and slowly pulled up the grappling hook. She debated leaving it there, but she might yet need it, so she tore it apart to compact its size and slid it into her pack. She pulled up part of her silk outfit to wrap her pack tight against her so it wouldn't hinder or catch. She adjusted her silk also to cover her watch. No part of her should give off light at this stage; she must be one with the darkness. Her face was also covered in black war paint mixed with greens and browns. The white of her eyes was the brightest thing on her.

She inched to the closest window and carefully inspected it for security or triggers. Not finding any, which she still found perplexing, she carefully opened it. Amazed to find it unlocked. She was fully prepared to break it or pop out the glass or any number of different tricks she commonly used, but it easily lifted.

She waited. Then, with a rapidness any professional athlete would have been impressed with, she slipped into the room's shadows. Her heart thrummed; she was inside.

Her speed didn't stop as she spun around and swept her sword free of its scabbard. Her katana was out, blade bare. It would have glistened in the reflecting light, but the blade was a custom black metal. It was one of her customizations and one reason she abandoned her earlier blade so many years ago. This blade appeared to absorb the light, not reflect it. An essential adaptation when stalking. And she now did stalk; she went room by room, looking for Molly and her guards.

She had assumed Molly would be on the top floor, but every one of these rooms was empty. All fifteen. This house was ridiculously huge. She had avoided one guard when he came upstairs and walked the floor casually. It was easy work keeping out of his way. She would wait for the next one to go upstairs. But the guard's circuit was quick; he only spent ten minutes upstairs, giving her a ten-minute window downstairs before the guards would grow suspicious.

Her initial plan would have been to leave a dead body as the guard made his circuit. But she might need more time, so she decided to venture downstairs instead of instantly killing one of the guards apart from the others. She would need as much time as she could have in this situation. It might not be advisable to start the clock prematurely.

Stairs exited at both ends of the hallway, both of which then spun around in the wide hallway and went out on the balconies that rotated around three sides of the house. She had to decide which stairway to go down. Both stairwells looked like they came out at the front and back doors of the house, the exact locations she sought to avoid. But it was also clear that there was no other way to get downstairs. There must be cameras there; if they hadn't seen her upstairs, they would see her on the cameras that must be at the entrances.

She needed to get downstairs, but she took the time to put up surveillance. She quickly positioned two cameras on each side of the hallway, hiding a couple of access points in the house underneath beds inside the many bedrooms. The cameras were hidden and shouldn't be detectable, even if someone knew the house well. One was in a plant on the one side of the hallway. The other one hidden behind artwork on the opposite side of the hallway. With her quick deployment finished, it was time to move.

She crept, like a ghost, down the back stairway. Barely daring to breathe, she maneuvered everywhere, looking for a camera. She finally found it. Positioned in the hallway, pointing toward the back door. If she walked down the stairs and turned at the bottom to enter the hallway, it would definitely see her. But there was a slight chance that if she dropped off the stairway into the hallway underneath it, it might just miss her, or she could do it quickly enough that they might not notice.

The Ashen Horse

Choices. Everything in life was a series of choices. The one in front of her right now was wondering whether to go painstakingly slow and hoping they wouldn't notice her movements if they glanced at her on the screen. The problem is that this left her on the screen for much longer, more time for someone half asleep staring at cameras to notice something. The second option was speed. Did she rapidly move in and then out of the frame? Choices.

She chose speed, though she had no idea if it was the right decision. Perhaps there wasn't a right decision. She crept halfway down the stairs, slowly looked around the railings, and confirmed that the hallway was empty. Then she ran up the stairs and leaped off the railing, landing in the hallway and turning it into a roll to suppress the fall's weight and ensure she didn't land with a resounding thud.

Her ultra-alertness was triggering every sense she had in her body. She needed to be out of this hallway as quickly as possible. She dashed to the first door, which looked like a kitchen. She was bolting as quickly as possible to move inside. She was ordinarily calm during her missions, but her heart was elevated after her stunt work. It was probably foolish, but it might have kept her undetected for a while longer, and every minute mattered. She moved around the kitchen's interior and positioned herself on the ground behind the island.

She considered where she was and realized that all six or seven guards were down there, and Molly's bedroom must also be down there. She knew the house had a parlor or large dining room, and she thought she spied it through an open archway off to her right. She also knew that Molly mainly worked from home, so there must be a den, office, or library. Perhaps Molly had positioned all three in a corner of the house. Then, there must be a security or surveillance room. There might have been a breakroom or a lounge for the staff as well. There were many rooms in this house, but if the top floor was any indication, she knew the general layout and positions of what must be where.

Choices. Can I make it to Molly, kill her, and make it out again without the guards even knowing about it? She didn't know if she wanted to hurt any of the guards. She also didn't know if she cared in this particular case. She usually tried to avoid hurting collateral, but in most cases, they were genuinely collateral. In this case, all these men were guilty of running one of the largest drug distribution networks on the East Coast, if not across America in general. No one was innocent in this house.

Her ears perked up as she heard a sound. Boots were steadily clomping towards her. Not just a single pair of boots but multiple pairs of boots. Her mind raced. It was always in these moments where all the planning was hypothetical, and then there were split moments where everything else became a reality.

She cursed under her breath, "Shit." She realized that she was panicking. She wasn't supposed to panic. She moved, quicker than she had all night, and jumped through another door into what appeared to be a small walk-in pantry. She carefully unsheathed her blade and then poised herself to be ready. Now, the hypothetical would fade to the raw reality. She never panicked, so she spent several seconds calming herself and positioning herself for what would come next.

Four guards walked into the kitchen and headed for the fridge. She heard them laughing about an adventure they had participated in the previous weekend. She heard the refrigerator open, heard them all pass through grabbing out dishes, apparently prepared by the cook when he was still onsite. The microwave churned on and cycled through twice. She thought, "Is it two microwaves I hear? It must be two microwaves." The shadows moved across the room, and she heard all four of them sit at the table, still chuckling and jostling each other.

Choices. Did she wait? Or was now the time to move? Did she move fast or slow? She had estimated there must be around six guards in the building tonight if her numbers and watching had meant anything the last two weeks. "Was it six or seven guards?" she thought. Four of them were right here, and she had a moment right now; she had no choice but to leverage. She sheathed the katana. She checked her pistol and ensured she could quickly grab it, even with the pack on her back. She tightened the pack and checked the ammo on her legs. Then, she pulled out four throwing knives, two in each hand.

She moved incredibly slowly and reopened the pantry door. Precious inch by precious inch. They didn't notice the door being opened; it was hidden behind the cabinets. She slowly peeked her head out and saw all four. They still didn't see her. She slowly moved back so they wouldn't be able to see her. The time was now; weeks of planning came to this moment. She exhaled slowly, concentrated, channeling herself into complete focus. She took a deep breath. Then she flew like the wind.

Chapter Twenty-Seven

Dirty Deeds

"I could go for a burger right now," Josh commented while driving to their next-way station.

Ellie rolled her eyes and glanced over, "You are never not ready to eat something."

Josh chuckled but said, "Usually, it isn't burgers, mind you."

"Something else more appealing to the palate?"

Josh chuckled even louder. "Let's grab some food; we have the time. How does that Mexican restaurant look?"

"Not like a burger."

"I'm hungry enough to eat anything right now, but Mexican food is always good."

Ellie smiled when she said, "You know I eat anything. Mexican works. I can eat right now. It seems like we have been working for days without eating."

Josh thought about that as he was pulling into the restaurant. "You know, we probably have. I think we have been skipping lunch most days; it probably has our metabolisms all screwed up."

"Welcome to life on the road. A whirlwind of sadly displaced expectations."

As they headed into the restaurant, Josh commented, "You got that absolutely right. Everyone thinks traveling is all glamorous, but really, it's just in a different dungeon with new cellmates and taskmasters."

"Well, that got dark."

"I'm living proof there's light at the end of the tunnel, Ellie, you know that."

Their banter continued as they were seated and started flipping through the menu. Their focus collapsed into reading the menu, and silence finally settled between them. However, it didn't last long because the waitress soon took their order.

"You found the opposite thing to a burger you could order."

"Just keeping it fresh; this way, when I eat a burger for dinner, I can be completely justified in all my life's choices."

"You need help, sir, desperately."

"You're just jealous of my supreme rationale on this topic…."

"Oh, I'm jealous, all right."

Ellie's phone started wabbling on the table as a call came in.

Ellie mumbled with a fair amount of disgust, "I should just throw that thing out of the window… Hello? Ellie speaking."

Jade was excited, "Ellie? I'm glad I caught you. Josh wasn't picking up his phone."

Ellie glanced over at Josh, "Your phone not working?" As Josh glanced at his phone, Ellie continued to Jade, "We can collectively make fun of Josh in a moment but let me throw you on speakerphone. We are both here."

Jade's excitement seemed to amplify itself further. "Oh, I caught both of you. That's even better. This is excellent. I've been trying to reach Tim half the day, but he is buried in some bureaucratic meeting that I can't get him out of."

"That important, huh?" Josh's skepticism always surfaced when it came to technology. "You hack the planet successfully, then?"

Jade laughed, "Bitch please, you know I hack the planet every day, all day. Never forget it, either."

"Poor planet."

"She's getting what she deserves on that note."

"Poor Mother Earth."

"Enough, children." Ellie couldn't keep a straight face saying it, though. "Josh just wishes he could hack Mother Earth." Josh nodded his agreement while flashing Ellie an obscene gesture. "What's up, Jade? What's the news from the cybersecurity teams?"

"We rebuilt some of the functions in our web search tool and scratched the internet all night. We targeted very specific darknets we had access to. You know, it is a pretty nifty trick we got to work. The functions pull in data from the websites and compile the analytical works into a dictionary—"

Ellie sighed, "Jade...."

"You don't care, do you?"

Josh was shaking his head. "Not at all."

Jade was exasperated. "You guys have no idea how hard we work on these things..."

"And yet, still don't care."

Jade's voice held a bit of mirth as she said, "You non-techies are heartless monsters. It's all fun and games until your printer doesn't work, then you come crawling and begging. But spend 80 straight hours rebuilding and reconstituting a database, where eight energy drinks had to be sacrificed for the greater good of humanity, and no one cares."

"Yep, still nothing there," Ellie said.

"Pfft, monsters. Okay, anyway. We did some really amazing shit, all right. The result is that we got him. We found Ash, and we found how he operates."

Josh exclaimed, "Wait, what?" at literally the same time Ellie was saying, "Huh?"

"Yep, we got him. He's a contract killer, that piece was rightly guessed. We also put together properly that he's almost more of a vigilante. There's a sense of justice in the contracts he has accepted."

Ellie was mystified. "Wait. Jade, wait."

Josh and Ellie looked at each other, the realization that they were witnessing the most significant break in the case up to this point. This moment might be the moment that led to Ash's downfall. The silence stretched on as the understanding of the situation slowly seeped into both of them.

Hearing Jade twitching on the other end of the phone was virtually possible. The silence stretched on too long, and the twitching became audible. "Guys? You there?"

"We are still processing," Josh commented. "First off, you might have started the call with 'we got him.'"

"No fun in that."

"Apparently." Josh's quip was only half-hearted as his mind was still processing. "Okay, Jade, slow down and walk us through this. What do we really have? And you said Tim doesn't know yet?"

"We are compiling the information into a report for the team, and given its substance, we are putting together some high-level executive summaries. If I couldn't get you two to care about the details, there's no way we'll get a jury to care either."

Ellie agreed. "True dat."

"And, yes, Tim doesn't know yet. He's harder to get ahold of than you two. What did you do, Josh, block my number after our date?"

Ellie gasped.

"She's joking. She wouldn't go out with me." He winked at Ellie. "No, my phone has been on silent all morning. Sorry about that. I should have toggled it back on at some point. Keep going...."

"I might change my mind, given the affection you have for us technical cybersecurity experts."

"Should I take that as an invitation?"

"No."

He winked at Ellie again, "Told you." Then to the speakerphone, "Keep going...."

"Right," Jade went on. "Tim doesn't know. We are compiling a sizeable report, well... like three, actually. One on the methodology and process of the software program, one specific to the Ash case and what we have found and correlated on the case, and a third that pulls pieces together on how we could present the information to the court.

"We haven't been able to tie all the cases, mind you. We only have a couple right now. Ash might be getting his victims from multiple sources, but we have traced some victims that we are convinced were killed by Ash from this specific darknet."

Ellie posed the question, "And will this hold up legally?"

"We think so. We also will have to open a half dozen other cases from other documents we've found in this pool of information, but that will be someone else's problem. I've been downloading documents and shipping them to different remote offices. If the FBI doesn't explicitly use it, they should be able to forward it to the various local jurisdictions."

Jade went on, "But specific to Ash, we think we have four dead bodies that were funded and requested hits on this darknet."

"What kind of darknet is it?" Josh asked.

"You guys wouldn't... Well, you probably would. It's a pretty straightforward community, actually. Invitation only, careful two-person invitation, known IRL invites. It requires...."

"IRL?"

"Both of you are so old. IRL means 'In Real Life.' To vouch for someone, you had to know them in real life. The community required two-factor authentication and a ten-thousand-dollar deposit to gain access to it. It was fairly well-locked down. Once you get through all that, it's similar to a mix between eBay and Craigslist."

"Online shopping for a hitman goes to the highest bidder?" Ellie was shaking her head as she said it.

"Well, in this case, you are requesting a service, so you are seeking the lowest bidder in most cases. The difference is also it's a forum, so more information is provided as questions are answered and more information becomes available."

Ellie tapped her lips, "Pretty dark stuff. Is it only contract murder, or are there other things for sale on the site? Is the murder stuff cloaked and dodgy, and it's not obvious what it is? Or is it blatant?"

"That's a good question. Some of the 'hits' were pretty opaque in their nature. Quite a few of them were blatant, though. One particular one was something like 'This PoS needs to die, $25k.'"

"No ambiguity there," Ellie agreed.

Josh nodded. "Sends the right message."

Ellie continued the line of thinking. "How protected are the requestors? Can we deduce who paid for the hits from the details?"

"Based on what we have seen, it really depends on the poster's intelligence. I think some of them not only did we quickly note who the victim was because, in some of the posts, they also said directly who the target was. But with hints and information in the overall detailed thread, it is pretty easy to conclude who the... the 'requestor' of the service is. However, it also appears that some posts are complex, and detailed information wasn't divulged. The two parties probably made contact off the site once they went far enough along the process. I think we'll get a couple of charges directly, though. The several cases we are attributing to Ash span the gamut of, let's call them, intelligent posters."

Ellie got a huge smile on her face. Then she actually giggled. "We should post a hit."

Jade and Josh said in unison, "What?"

"We should post a hit."

Josh looked skeptical. "Umm."

"It shouldn't be that hard. We need to conjure up a completely terrible person. Something along the lines of what Ash would go after. Child pedophile, corporate mogul destroying lives, chronic rapist, we should be able to find someone that is despicable enough that would draw Ash out of the woods."

She continued, "I mean, wouldn't that be the goal? To draw Ash out into the open. Catch him in the act. After we got our hands on him, we could start tying in the other cases, but getting him into custody would solve half our issues."

Josh nodded, "At least half our issues. That would solve the identity issue, that's for sure. We still don't have a clue who this guy is."

Jade didn't like it as much as the other two. "It seems pretty dodgy to me; it's almost like entrapment."

Ellie chuckled. "Dropping crumbs for children is not coercion. Providing opportunity is also not coercion."

Josh nodded his head. "We should follow up with this for sure. We need to get Tim and the larger team informed. Then, stake out a potential plan moving forward. But I think the idea is a good one, Ellie. It might be one of our best opportunities to bring this to a speedy end; let's bait the bastard and draw him into our web." He waited a couple of seconds for laughs.

"Draw him into our web? Internet? Web? Nothing? Nothing at all?" He looked disappointed.

"Ellie, did he try to make an IT joke just now?"

"Tried," Ellie commented. "Tried rather hard, too."

Josh huffed. "Tried nothing; that was comedic gold. Neither of you have any appreciation for the classics."

Jade chuckled. "They are probably called oldies for me, but you can keep calling them classics."

"Jade, if I had feelings, I'd be offended."

Ellie dived into the burrito that had just shown up. "We

need to talk to Tim. I'm pretty sure I know what our next update call will be about. Either way, Jade, this appears to be some fantastic work."

Josh was nodding. "Yep, it really does. You'll get the report emailed out to the team as soon as it is ready?"

"Hopefully sometime in the next two days. I need to talk to Tim before we email it to the larger team."

"Will it be readable?"

Jade replied in a mock, exasperated tone, "Probably not for you, Joshie, but it'll be fine for everyone else."

"Cold."

"More lukewarm."

Ellie just shook her head. "If you two are done, I want to eat this glorious beast of a burrito."

Jade was finally laughing outright. "Yep, glad I got ahold of you two. I'll talk to you both soon; if Tim reaches out to you, make sure he calls me. I'll talk to you guys later." And with that, she hung up the call.

Chapter Twenty-Eight

It's Just a Party

She moved like a force of nature, a violent stream coursing down the rocks, sweeping through a drainage. An avalanche rolled down a mountainside. Two of the guards sat on one side of the enormous table; two guards sat on the other side. The two closest to her received the first four blades. Two into the man on the left and two on the right. That elicited a shout-out from one of the guards who wasn't struck. And that would do it; the game was afoot.

She had pulled one more throwing knife as she closed the gap; it went right into the throat of the one who shouted. He would never shout again, his hands grasping for his throat. She had closed the distance, and in one smooth motion, the katana ejected from its scabbard, and the return stroke took off the head of the man that was closest to her. He was the one on the left who had taken her first two blades. She kicked his chair with every ounce of strength she had, and it caused his headless body to topple into the man behind it. Currently the only one not injured.

He was stunned at what was happening but didn't waste time. He had toppled to the ground, but he would be up in a moment, and she caught his movement out of the corner of her eye. He was going for a gun. She didn't have time to deal with him, though; she had bounced on top of the table, and three quick slashes had disemboweled the other two guards.

She instinctively knew the last guard would almost have the gun ready, so she swept herself down into a crouch and sprang off the table, her passive hand holding the katana down and away from her body so she could roll. Her dominant hand went for another throwing knife. As she flew from the table, the throwing knife sailed from her hand and landed in the thigh of the guard. He yelped. But he had managed to have his gun ready, and the shots rang out through the house as they followed her flight.

She had landed and rolled, coming up with another knife ready; she released it before she was fully standing. This time, it took him in the shoulder. She dove into another tumble right toward him as he fired more shots. He had fired short of her when she was moving off the table, and now, he shot over her as he was aiming for where she should have been had she stood, but she was rolling towards him instead.

The roll closed the distance, and as she came up, the katana slid up right under his sternum. She jerked it forward, rammed it upwards, and then twisted and ripped it out. She didn't hesitate; she immediately wiped the blade on the guard's clothes and dried her hands in a similar fashion.

It all happened so quickly, and the bodies stacked up as it did. Four men now lay dead in the kitchen. The one guard's head still seemed to teeter back and forth in a strange wobble, the momentum still present from its roll across the floor. One had his head down on the table with his hands, where a quick slash through his throat had pitched him forward, and he had collapsed on the table. The third had sprawled off the table with his hands interlaced on his throat, still holding the throwing knife, his insides leaking and sprawling along the floor. The entire thing had taken moments, but all four guards lay dead, scattered to the wind.

It was not five seconds from the time she cleaned her blade to when she was standing behind the entrance to the kitchen, waiting for the next group of guards to arrive in the room. Shots were fired; half of the house, more accurately, all the house, would have heard them. Everyone was now alerted to what could only be an intruder attacking.

This is not how she liked doing things. Stealth was the method of choice. Gunshots were never the goal; they always brought unwanted attention. Everyone in the house would be awake now. Everyone was on alert now. She let out a quiet sigh. Backup could be called, and more alerts sounded. She was on a strict timeline. She had precious minutes to finish this and evac.

What no one ever got used to was how quickly these moments transpired. The entire fight had barely taken twenty seconds. After these slayings, everything was truly on a timer now. If the next group of guards didn't show up in the next minute, she would have to move and move quickly throughout the entire house.

Her fears were realized as several seconds later, she heard feet running down the hallway. Two sets of shoes. "It must be at least two other guards," she thought to herself. They would be in the kitchen any moment.

"I must wait," she thought to herself. "If I've ever needed to have patience, now is the time." She let the first man pass as he entered the room. The second man was right on his heels, though. And she was on him in a split second as he cleared the door. She had positioned herself in an attack stance, ready for a forward motion. The sword pointed slightly bent away from her leg, angled out from her body, and she swung it up and out. The move was rarely used, but it brought the entire strength of her upper body into play. The blade sliced up on the inside of the guard's leg, glancing up and along the femur right up into his hip. There was no doubt that his femoral artery was severed; he would bleed out in no time. Her last motion of the swing twisted the blade, opening the wound further. The blade was too embedded into his body to make it able to pull it free quickly.

The Ashen Horse

She jerked it as she tried to pull it free rapidly. The blade stayed lodged where it was. She was about to draw and use her shorter wakizashi, but instead, she just threw her entire weight into the guard from behind. His body, already beginning to go limp, went sprawling forward, pulling itself free of the katana.

The events were unfolding so rapidly that the first guard who had entered the room was still trying to take in the scene of the room. There was a lot to grasp with the corpses hacked to various pieces strung out across the scene. However, his attention was diverted quickly as he heard the scuffle behind him. He began to turn to face the noise when the thud of the first man hitting the floor brought his full attention. His eyes locked hers, and they drifted over to the guard lying face down in the middle of the kitchen floor.

His hands instinctively moved towards his sidearm, but there was no way to be fast enough when the blade was already descending on you. The gun never cleared its holster.

Once again, there was no time for hesitation. She cleaned the blade. She immediately turned to leave the room, but she hesitated. Very quickly, she went to the earlier four bodies and grabbed and wiped down her throwing knives. She returned them to their sheathes, promptly moved around the kitchen, and sprinted out.

She knew now that she must sprint for the rest of the night to finish her work. She glanced around, planning her next move. There was only one thing she could do now: rapidly search the entire house and find Molly. Molly was here somewhere. She must unearth her. Her head whipped left and right as she made the calculations of which direction she would go, and then she was off sprinting.

As she left the kitchen, she ran into a spray of gunfire. They scored this time around. A bullet went through her shoulder, and she felt where one clipped her opposite arm and a third dug into her side. She saw enough as she dodged into the next entryway, which appeared to be a second entrance into the dining room, the other entrance coming off the kitchen she just left.

A burning yanked at her being as the wounds tore themselves inside of her. She felt the pain rising across her entire body as she hunched over, breathing deeply, trying to catch her breath between the wheezing and the pain that coursed through her body. Time was still of the essence; it was the only thing that was important tonight.

She quickly tightened her silk straps, utilizing her outfit's built-in tourniquet functionality. Her garb was a series of wraps over a thin silk interior. This facilitated making anything a holding place, a container, a cover, or, in this case, a tightened suppression. She tightened and adjusted the outer wraps, noticing that all three wounds felt like clean through-and-throughs. Even so, they hurt like a flaming inferno. The one wound in her bicep wasn't reducing her movement but the wound on the opposite shoulder was making her dominant arm increasingly difficult to operate. It would be enough, though; it would have to be. The wound on her side was something to be legitimately concerned about. She needed to get out of here.

She grunted. "That despicable woman," she thought. Of course, it would be Molly that would shoot her. She shook her head in disgust and to clear the pain from her mind. As far as she knew, Molly was the only one now left in the house. And it had been Molly wielding an M16, of all things, spraying bullets like a mad woman. She grinned, or it was almost like a grin; maybe it was a snarl through clenched teeth. Someone looking on probably would have described it as a woman in extreme pain. Her mind worked as her body pleaded for rest, but she was surprised Molly went with an M16; she seemed much more like an AK-47 kind of woman.

She knew she couldn't go back into the hallway; she was a sitting duck there unless she wanted to use her pistol. She considered that for a moment; perhaps she should. Molly clearly wasn't a good shot, or she was used to stationary targets. She wanted to reject the idea outright; Molly certainly deserved the sword. However, she had always prided herself on her practicality. She quickly sheathed the katana and pulled out her .22.

She saw that this dining room looked like it opened into a hallway out the other side of the room. That had to be a hallway that was adjacent to where Molly was standing. She walked over and picked up a vase that was on display on a pedestal. She shook her head and grunted through the pain; only stupidly rich people had pedestals just to display stuff like this.

She slowly moved back to the door where she had come into the room. Then she focused, emptying her mind of the constant distractions. It didn't work as she had entirely hoped, the pain sapping her away from concentration. Her ability to meditate was failing her now. Despite the pain, she still had to move, so she focused on slowing her breathing. All the pain that was wracking her body, she exhaled and let it flow out of her. Then, she took a deep and steady breath in.

She flung the vase as hard as she could toward the other exit door on the other side of the room. It was a long way away, but the vase somehow almost made it. It hit the ground and shattered into a thousand pieces, those pieces scattering out the door and into what she was presuming was the hallway.

Immediately after the crash, she stuck the pistol around the doorframe, the pistol balanced and held completely still against the doorframe. She was steady, and then she saw it. Molly's head had jerked with the crash, and the momentary distraction was all she needed. Four shots rapidly left the gun. With the aid of the rest, they were right on target. The first two went into Molly's hands; the next two went into her knees.

She was out of the room the second the last shot was fired, running down the hallway. Her katana swung back out of its sheath as she flowed like a river. The initial pain and shock had caused Molly to drop the assault rifle, but she could probably still fire it if she picked it up again. And it looked like Molly was trying to move for the gun.

She wasn't going to give Molly the opportunity; she simply wouldn't let that happen. She was rapidly closing the distance. Molly was on the ground now; it appeared the pain in her legs was sufficient where she wouldn't stand easily.

She reached Molly's gun and rapidly kicked it backwards down the hallway. The exertion, plus her wounds, resulted in her huffing. She was truly panting from her pain and physical exhaustion. Running might have been a bad idea; it felt like she had ripped open the wounds wider despite the tourniquets. The pain was twice as bad as it had been before. She grunted. Molly was panting, clearly trying not to show her own discomfort, and just as clearly failing.

Molly laughed, which came out as a grunt and a wheeze. "So, it comes to this." Her body shifted on the ground to relieve the pressure on her legs.

"A fitting end, don't you think?" Molly continued. "It seems fitting. I should have died a dozen times before now. This seems appropriate."

Her eyes lit with the same fire in them when Molly stood outside her cage. "Glad I could oblige you. You should know, before I kill you, several things." She smiled then, a smile of revenge, and held up her hand and ticked off her fingers. Molly's eyes tingled, and she noticed the symbolism all too well. The irony of the retribution was not lost on her.

Her hand twitched up a single finger. "One, I accepted a contract from your ex to kill you for one million dollars."

"I'll double it." Molly gasped. Molly's mind was racing to find a way out of this, but she would never bring herself to desperation. Even in the end, her pride would not let her forget everything she had learned in the streets. But still, there might yet be hope. She motioned with her hand and spoke more clearly, "I'll even triple it right now."

"Where's the money?"

"It's in a safe in my bedroom, just over there," she said, swinging a hand once again in the general direction of the bedroom.

The mystery woman's eyes raged, and all she uttered was a straightforward command. "Crawl."

She didn't need to say more than that, but she kicked Molly in the leg for good measure. That caused a yelp, despite everything in Molly's composure trying to hide the pain. Molly still appeared resistant, though, or perhaps it was pride.

She twitched the katana in her hand and slowly tapped it against her side. "Molly. Crawl. Now."

It took five minutes, and she counted every minute. But Molly eventually opened the safe. To her surprise, there were, in fact, stacks of money inside the safe.

"Take it all, it's yours."

"Move over there in the corner so I can see it."

Molly slowly crawled to the middle of the room, clearly and intentionally flaunting the least amount of resistance and contempt she could muster. The mystery woman quickly pulled enough money loose and onto the floor to make sure the safe couldn't be closed or swung shut accidentally. Her eyes and sword never left the target. After the money was sprawled out, she calmly forgot about it.

Molly appeared to have a bit of hope as the woman's attention appeared to be distracted, but then she realized that the woman's attention was all back on her. And the burning fire of anger lit her eyes as it did every time she looked at Molly.

She repositioned herself in front of Molly, and once again, she raised her hand and brought up one finger as she pointedly channeled the hate and loathing she felt at her.

"I appreciate you giving me this. Now, as I was saying. There are things you need to know before I kill you. One, I accepted a contract from your ex to kill you for one million dollars."

Molly's eyes went dark, and they slowly flickered toward the ground. The realization that there never was any hope in this situation slowly rested on her shoulders. This woman had every intention of killing her. The painful realization hit her that money, perhaps for the first time in her life, wouldn't be buying her out of this situation. Molly looked back up at the woman.

"Two, I turned down that contract and left the job after meeting Hector. I intended to leave you alone and build a life with him."

Molly's jaw dropped open. She stared. Who was this woman who had involved herself with Hector just to get close enough to kill her? But had walked away?

"Three, I reaccepted the contract after you put me in a cell.

"Four, of course, I killed all your men at the warehouse."

Molly's expression grew more solemn and reserved as she went along. Molly had genuinely lived in this life; she knew its realities. There was nothing she could say or do at this point. She was sure of it. She had sincerely come to the end. She slowly prepared herself. It wouldn't be pretty; she had essentially promised to rape and torture this woman brutally. Her end would not be much better; she steeled herself for what inevitably came next.

Molly had to know, though. She had to. You couldn't brace yourself toward the unknown. Her speech came out as tempered and mild as her mind was, with her imagination whirling, but she had no choice but to ask. She had to know. The muffled words "How will you do it?" whispered from her lips.

"Unlike you, you piece of shit, I am not a monster. I don't torture people."

In a split-second flash, Molly's entire body seemed to release a lifetime of tension she had built up. Her whole body almost spasmed as the tension flooded out of her muscles.

The Ashen Horse

Her emotions swirled in her in a way she hadn't felt in years. A tear escaped one of her eyes.

She hadn't felt this human in what felt like her entire life. Perhaps she had never felt this human. A whimper escaped her. She wouldn't break in this moment, but she hadn't known this level of compassion in decades. Her exhale was filled with the raw emotional exhaustion that she felt and was centered with all the mental fragility that encompassed her. She felt spent and emotionally drained.

She was close to losing it. The mysterious woman stood over her and waited as if giving her time to collect herself. And it took some time; several minutes passed, and she restabilized herself, and then she thanked the mystery woman. "You do me a favor with this, a mercy I don't deserve. One I certainly would not have extended toward you."

The mystery woman nodded when she spoke. "I am well aware of this. Are you ready?"

"At your pleasure."

The wakizashi took off her head cleanly. Mercifully.

Chapter Twenty-Nine

Entrapment

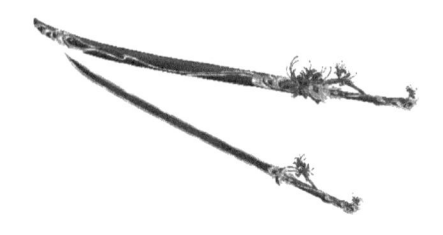

"Great you all could make the meeting today," Tim said. "We have quite a bit to cover. As you all can see, this is a much broader audience than we normally have at these biweekly meetings. That's because the cybersecurity team has some information to present. I don't want to steal their thunder, so we'll let them get into it here in a minute. But that said, we have had a breakthrough and need to take some time to consider our next actions, and that's why I've invited the entire collective to this call."

"Before I turn this over to the cybersecurity team, Josh and Ellie recently returned from their vacation…."

Josh wasted no time retorting, "I wouldn't call it that, boss."

"As you can tell, they immensely enjoyed their time there. Anything to report?"

"Honestly, not much, sir," said Ellie. "We did uncover some interesting anomalies in some old cases, and we did find a couple of new cases that we believe we could attribute to Ash. He is pretty slippery, though."

"The larger team might not know that we have started to try to chronologically order the cases and locations and put them out in sequence," Josh added. "That might be the big breakthrough from our end in the last month. We concluded that we could validate many suspected cases and perhaps correlate some data if we can get everything drawn out on a timeline, so that's in process. We believe we will encounter some inconsistencies in our theories. This will largely be the issue of Ash being unable to be in two places simultaneously. For those cases, we'll have to reevaluate whether we can attribute one of the two to Ash or if they are both a bust. It's a work in progress; Roshan has been drilling away at it for some time now. We help as we can, but special thanks and a sincere golf clap for his efforts."

"Not a problem, guys," Roshan piped in.

Ellie was a little reluctant but eventually spoke up. "We did find one thing. We visited the post office, trying to track down a lead. It's possible we uncovered another false identity Ash used that could be linked to another killing or two. We are just starting to drill into that, though. The lead suggests that perhaps a victim was left alive. I hate even bringing it up because nothing is succinct or known about it, yet. We still aren't sure about the alias and its link to Ash. That said, some local field agents are trying to track down the victim. We think she might be a victim anyway, but perhaps most importantly, she might still be alive."

Ellie's face went a little dark, and she sighed. "Probably shouldn't have brought it up; it's a pretty big pipe dream that any of that might pan out right now. Just a half-eaten biscuit in the oven." Ellie quickly glanced at the doors around the building to verify that secure exits were available. Old habits never die.

Tim thought he mumbled it to himself, but it came out audible, "Half-eaten biscuit in the oven? What does that even mean?"

"Don't try, boss. It's an Ellie-ism. You'll hurt yourself if you try to get into the weeds. Just don't do it, it's dangerous down there."

"Shush, Josh, it makes perfect sense just how it sounds."

"Okay, I believe both of you," Tim laughed. "Now that

we got that out of the way. Let's turn it over to our cybersecurity team. Jade, do you want to cover this, or is it you, Roshan?"

"It's definitely not me," Roshan said.

"We are on different teams," commented Jade.

"What?" Tim exclaimed.

Ellie's response was one more of curiosity, "Really?"

Jade laughed, "You guys really didn't know that?"

Josh just sounded confused. "Aren't you both IT Investigation? Or whatever it is?"

"We are both in the Cyber Division which focuses on cybersecurity and cybercrime, but I'm on the Forensic team," explained Roshan. "I'm mostly focused on information technology analytics, drilling into IT-related data, and tracking information. Other members on my team get more into IT Forensics; my skillset was what your team needed, so I got assigned."

"I'm a programmer," Jade said. "I normally don't work cases at all, or rarely. I'm usually building tools to support either case work or internal streamline systems for the FBI. For the last six months, though, there was a requirement to dig into internet technologies and uncover what is hidden on the internet; I've been trying to drill into network and internet technologies. But yeah, Roshan and I don't even work on the same team. Different reporting structure, different bosses, the works."

Tim was whimsical. "Huh. Learn something new every day. Anyway, sorry for the tangent, everyone. Jade, I guess it's your show."

"Thanks, Tim. I'll keep this short so as not to waste everyone's time today. I've captured everyone on the call and will send out a follow-up email containing three detailed reports that we recently finished. Those reports will have more information than you probably want to know. Of course, if you find any information that you still want to know and that isn't in the reports, please reach out; that way, we can add that as appendixes to the reports, so anything missing or lacking in the documentation, let us know so we can incorporate it."

Jade continued, "That process stuff out of the way. The meat of the details is that we used a custom-built search engine (of sorts) on various darknets we could access. Through this search process, we were able to get some correlation data that, upon further investigation, revealed a strong probability that there were contract killing requests for the lowest bidder on a section of the dark web. Yet further correlation showed that some of the victims could be tied to our known information and therefore strongly suggests that Ash was or is linked to these murders."

Jade paused for a moment while she collected her thoughts. "We think we found him. He bid on some of these murder requests. The cases aligned with several victims we have correlated with, and it's almost certainly the Ashen Horse. We got him."

"The reports will have the technical details?" The others could hear Roshan's expectation echoing in his voice. His excitement riveted through his inquiry.

Josh, being himself, couldn't resist. "It's really that exciting?"

Jade whipped a response at him. "Yes, it is—you, you, marshmallow."

Roshan's more measured response was on point. "Yes, it's pretty critical. There is a lot of value we could use this for outside of the Ashen Horse case. There are many applications for a tool that could prowl the internet and sweep up correlation data. There's probably a market among high schools and colleges to sweep up plagiarism at the minimum. And that's just periphery applications for code like this. Suppose you could bring in deep analytics or machine learning and combine correlation data by concepts; that would have even more power. A lot of business applications and criminal investigations could benefit from this."

"I'll send the team the details, Roshan, don't worry." Jade couldn't help but add, "I'm sure at least you'll read it."

"Oh, I'll read it," Josh said, laughing.

Jade, going for the jugular, said, "I'm sure some of you will understand it."

Josh kept laughing. "No guarantees there. I know my limitations!"

Tim was laughing as well. "A man should know his limitations. But that brings us to the question of the hour and why I wanted the entire team on the call. When she first heard about this, Ellie postulated the theory, saying that we should post a murder and try to bait Ash."

There was silence as the team thought for a minute. Tim continued, "Well, what are your initial reactions to this idea? Should we try to trick our serial killer?"

"How do we know it would be Ash that bites?" asked Roshan.

"Good question," replied Ellie. "But I guess, in a way, it doesn't matter. Anyone we nab was someone who was intent on committing murder for hire. Taking anyone like that off the street must be a good thing. The bonus might be that we get the guy we are after. The potential for a win-win."

Ellie thought a second and went on, "But we also probably can target Ash specifically in a way. We know the types of cases Ash goes after. We can build a profile of a fairly despicable human that needs to be killed, and that's the type of scum Ash yearns to go after."

Josh offered, "We would have to build a fake persona of someone that society feels probably deserves to be killed and that might draw Ash out."

"Exactly," responded Ellie.

Roshan still wasn't sure. "I don't know. If we could capture Ash, there would be no risk of this being deceptive or coercive behavior because we wouldn't even need this occurrence to build a case. It's more about just learning

Ash's identity. If we nab anyone else, this will be rather murky legal water."

"True," Tim commented. "But wouldn't we be more than willing to release a couple of collars if it meant we eventually got Ash in a nab-and-grab?"

"Fair enough," Roshan said. "Let's just make sure the District Attorney is on board with that approach. They often stir the pot on something like this. Ash has always been at least national, let's make sure we set the stage in a friendly jurisdiction where we aren't going to have trouble from the local law enforcement or judicial system."

Tim was impressed. He knew he shouldn't be impressed anymore after all his years of experience and the teams he had worked with. But it never failed to amaze him—when you got the right team together, you could solve major problems. "That's an excellent call out, Roshan. And right on point. Rarely do we get the opportunity to pick a jurisdiction; in this case, we could."

"Out of curiosity, where would we do it?"

Ellie quipped, "Red state."

"Why? Something against us conservatives?"

"Less red tape in red states. They also have judicial systems that are more... uh... rural. This facilitates us doing what we want as long as we don't step on any toes. They are also more appreciative of law enforcement and would appreciate what we are trying to get done if we bring in the local authorities. Pretty sure they'd give us a pass on anything."

Tim had to agree and asked, "Which one?"

"Florida? Arizona? Texas? Montana?"

Josh offered up his knowledge. "Montana is more purple. That might work out, though; some jurisdictions might have values we could draw on from both political perspectives. I did a case in Missoula a couple of years back; it might be perfect for this."

The wheels of his mind continued to turn. "You know,

Missoula is a college town. There's a big university there, the University of Montana or something, I think. If we did do it in Missoula, we could play on that. Something about a bad professor: maybe the guy is molesting students or something. Serial rapist. That would fall right in Ash's paradigm for victims."

"I think this is good," Tim agreed. "Does anyone think we shouldn't proceed with this route? There are some dangers here. Not least of which we might send the Horse into hiding. The last thing we'd want is to put Ash underground for five years. If we mess this up and he suspects we are onto him, it might be impossible to find him. Then, we would still have nothing about his identity. Just like we don't currently. I don't know how this guy stays off the radar, but he isn't slipping. There's still no physical evidence we can detect. Putting him underground is a real concern."

Ellie felt obligated to defend her idea. "He is underground already. We don't have any way to uncover him at all. Unless our random other idea of finding the living victim works out. And that is still a massive pipe dream, unfortunately. But if he stopped killing today, I don't know if we would ever catch him. He's covering his tracks too well. Having an opportunity to draw him out and lure him in might be our best and only chance at catching this monster."

"Just making sure we all agree," Tim said. "When I go before leadership because this turns out to be a disaster, I want to make sure you're all standing behind me saying it was a universally agreed upon decision." He chuckled. "This could go very wrong, as long as we all realize that."

"Not with boss-man on the case. It can't go wrong. It's only success from here on out."

"Did I just hear Josh volunteer to create the entire profile for a false professor at this college? And work with the college and local authorities to start laying the groundwork for a five-year backstory? Did I just hear that?"

"Someday, the boss-man will realize he doesn't have any sense of humor."

"That day isn't today," Tim acknowledged.

"Apparently," Josh said with a laugh. "You know I'm just busting your chops, boss-man. But seriously, I can start the leg work; I'm sure the team will pitch in as necessary. We'll need bios, websites, some newspaper reports of victims, some rumor mills, other seeds planted, and a couple of verified victims that someone could call and ask questions. We probably need to rope in local media contacts to ensure our seeds don't spark some real journalism. This might be a bit of a production to pull this off." Josh was silent momentarily and then asked, "Perhaps Tim is right more than I thought. We all realize the lengths we might have to go to make this work?"

"Sounds like a bit of fun, though, doesn't it?" Jade asked.

Roshan snickered, "You guys will get her in the field yet! Careful about questing after the fun, Jade; it's a lot of late nights drinking coffee in a cramped car."

"That doesn't sound like fun."

"Don't listen to him, Jade," Tim said. "Stakeouts have their moments. Anyway. I think we all have a clear direction at this point. Let's get to it. Let's start laying some groundwork; we'll see where we are in a week."

Chapter Thirty

The Fish Don't Bite

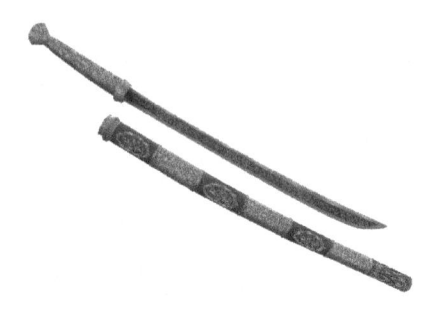

She lay on the ground, slowly bleeding. The physical exertion had taxed her. The pounding of her head made her queasy and woozy. Although she had quickly stopped the bleeding of her wounds, she had still lost a surprising amount of blood, much of which stained her attire. Blood loss also had left her profoundly thirsty. She walked or hobbled to the bathroom and drank as much water as she could. Such a simple act, but it seemed to help immensely.

Molly's compound was quite isolated. If the cops weren't here by now, maybe no one outside the compound heard or cared about the gunfire. She would probably have to risk it either way. As much as she had a clear need to be away from this place, she also had to sanitize the scene.

She was always careful. This line of work had no room for error, and today had been sloppy. Shots were fired, and she was bleeding, scattering evidence everywhere. She thought she had most of it contained, but one could never be too careful about stray droplets of that magical DNA. One drop could be all it takes, assuming the police did their jobs right. It was dangerous to assume they wouldn't.

There was nothing for it but to go to work. Which naturally she did. She found the laundry room, pulled out three bleach bottles, and proceeded to dump bleach throughout the entire area she had been in from the time she got shot to the time when she put Molly down. After that, she took a few moments to truly size up her injuries and properly secure her wounds so there could be no accidental blood droplets escaping.

She collected all her shell casings. Slowly and methodically, she walked the scene, retracing steps and movements. She needed to recover any equipment she had left behind. She thought she had already, but apparently, one of her knives was missed because it was dug deep into the sheetrock in the kitchen. She didn't even recall throwing that one. Everything happened so fast in the heat of the moment.

The sun was slowly topping the horizon as she methodically worked her way through the house. Her patience throughout the night had paid off; she had lived to see the dawn. Something she wasn't sure would be the case yesterday. She leaned against the balcony on the second floor, taking slow, deep breaths and watching the sunrise.

A sweeping range of emotions encapsulated her like an aura. She felt a complex sense of being alive, a combination of sheer relief and joy that she should live to see yet another day. The sense of completing a major task was also a strange satisfaction. Triumph and vindication at ending Molly's control over her. And yet, all of that mixed with the still and quiet feeling of loss that still shrouded her being. Hector was gone, and that loss still cut her to her core. The emotions were enhanced and subdued equally by her exhaustion and physical weariness.

Her consciousness swimming through the complex reality she found herself in made for a confusing moment. Minutes had passed, and the sun slowly crept further up. Not much time had passed as she stared at Molly's estate, but still, time was critical. She shook herself back to awareness and went back to work.

After she had finished in the house, her real work began. And her body was beginning to feel all of it. The stress and movement were becoming more arduous, and her breathing was increasingly labored. But her only option was to continue.

She spent the next two hours collecting all the toys she had scattered around the compound. The wireless access points, the cameras, and the abandoned grappling hooks all went back into her packs. Carrying the packs became so challenging that she had to leave the items at the front door before venturing to collect the next batch.

She continued into the mid-morning hours. Two things dawned on her as she finally began completing most of her tasks. She would have to recover one of her escape vehicles, which would be a difficult walk or climb. And she also realized a mound of money was still sitting in the house. Her entire life, she never let money drive her decisions, at least not entirely. And yet she fully understood that she would not leave the millions of dollars scattered on the floor. That was enough money that she would never need to work again. Financially, she was mostly already there with her past escapades, but there was no reason not to put the cherry on top.

Not believing herself capable of climbing over the perimeter wall in her condition, she started what felt like a five-mile walk to retrieve what she was hoping was the closest escape pod. The events of the night and day continued to exact a heavy toll as she made her way to the car, but it went smoother than she could have possibly hoped, and it wasn't long before she had all her toys and tricks loaded and bag after bag of currency stuffed in the trunk.

The last thing she did was take a photo of Molly's decapitated body. Gruesome work. That was shipped off to the spiteful ex-boyfriend, with some colorful language that he could look like his pretty bride if the funds weren't transferred as promised. That creative license with language usually got those who contracted her to pay what was agreed.

But she knew he was despicable, and it was obvious to her that he would need all the encouragement she could provide to fork over the payment.

Even so, she didn't relish the idea of having to go after him. Best if he just paid and they parted company. She had an eerie feeling that it would not settle so easily, but she never let anyone get out of their debt to her. If he refused to pay, she would visit him, and that visit would be most uncomfortable for him.

She had been driving and didn't even realize it, but she came back to consciousness when it dawned on her that she was at her storage unit and the rental car had been emptied. She stood there blinking several times, the confusion collapsing in on her a bit as she stood there disoriented. She didn't fully remember how she got here. Her exhaustion was finally reaching a dangerous state; she had to get somewhere and sleep.

She shook her head, trying to bring some form of clarity and focus to her mind. She again looked around and was baffled that all the money and tools had already been moved into the storage locker. How did she not remember doing the work? She shuddered and thought to herself, "I must get into a hotel and sleep. I have to sleep."

She didn't want to go anywhere else, and she didn't want to go anywhere permanent. A hotel was the best option. Something that was cleaned thoroughly when you left, someplace where they didn't even know you were there. She was driving again. Finding the right hotel took finesse. Despite what the movies tell everyone, staying at a dive hotel was not ideal. The dive hotels pay a lot more attention to their guests than hotels that don't have a reason to suspect their guests are peddling drugs or doing illicit activities in the room.

What should be sought after is the ability to be forgotten. Just another anonymous middle-class woman walking into a hotel for a good night's rest while on a pleasant business vacation. Perhaps coming from a bar, looking a little worse for wear, had perhaps one too many to drink. Even more forgettable. Just get this crazy lady checked in and out of here so I don't have to deal with her.

Her approach was firmly in her mind, and she found a hotel that would fit the bill. She planned to spend the next several days, if not the next week, perhaps an eternity, just lying in bed sleeping. She was so tired. She parked at the closet bar and had a ride-share on its way while she was still parking. She walked in and ordered a quick shot of vodka to settle the pain and give her planned act some plausibility. A ding on her phone; she was hopping in some poor individual's four-door sedan and on her way to the hotel in moments.

She didn't remember checking in. She wasn't sure she did, really. She woke up standing outside her hotel room door, holding the key card. She seriously started to wonder if she was actually losing consciousness as the tiredness became tangible. She could taste it, smell it. No question was she breathing it in with every breath of her lungs. The key card worked, though, so she figured she had successfully checked in.

Her feet carried her to the bed, and that would be the last thing she would know for quite some time. Her body barely moved over the next two days. Perhaps she went to the bathroom several times, but later, she would not even know for sure if those events occurred.

The days lingered on until almost a full week had passed. She had forgotten to return her various rental cars. The realization of it caused her to finally drag herself from the hotel to make sure they all were handled. She professed confusion and innocence and tried to be a bit snobbish, hoping to be more forgettable. It seemed to do the trick. She would always leave with them loving her, though, professing it was her mistake and 'Thank you so much for your diligent efforts to help me out of this situation.'

She changed hotels several times over the next weeks. Always moving to the other side of town, always using different restaurants, and usually having the food delivered to avoid any human contact at all, if possible. There was no better way to be forgotten than never to be seen.

Two of her wounds, the one in her bicep and the one in her shoulder were predictably straightforward. Clean through-and-throughs, didn't hit any bones, mainly muscle damage. They were painful, scratchy, and stiff. They made moving a cumbersome chore. But ultimately, they were nothing that time wouldn't sort out. The wound on her side was a different matter. It also appeared not to have hit anything critical. She had no idea how it missed a kidney or missed her intestines, but she was sure both were true. But it was festering, perhaps mildly infected and slow to heal.

She was accustomed to self-doctoring, so she had repeatedly recut open the wound to clean it out. Thoroughly scrubbing it, pulling away or cutting away anything that looked dead or festering. She would slowly rip off pieces of her own flesh to make sure nothing was degrading or becoming infected. Nasty work. Rather painful as well. But it was a sure-fire way to keep infections at bay.

Dumping the Russian Standard vodka all over the wound was also not that enjoyable. But she kept the fun going by adding in a layer of hydrogen peroxide just to keep the experience fresh. And rather delightfully painful. Her morbid sense of humor had kept her going the last several weeks as the pain weighed heavily upon her.

As the days drew into weeks, she spent the time deeply reflecting. What did she really want her future to be? Was this going to continue to be her destiny? Was there no other path? Her mind was plagued by questions about the 'What Ifs' that had stacked upon themselves throughout the last several years. Did it really have to go the way it went with Hector? More than once, she broke down in tears at the toll that her life had taken upon her during these years.

She ran down the dozens of men and women she had killed and somehow didn't regret any of them. She had always been careful in her selection of victims. Precisely because they were not the victim but the perpetrator most of the time. She had always made sure that she killed men and women who deserved it. Perhaps it was her version of what they did or did not deserve, but she always picked those for whom the scales of karma were laden with bricks on one end and the other end swinging in the wind. Perhaps she wasn't a righteous killer or an angel of God's wrath. But she never found herself to be unjust in her actions. Those she had killed had stacked the cards against themselves over a lifetime of decisions.

This thinking brought her full circle to realizing she had also made a lifetime of decisions. All of them took her down a dark path. The longer she thought about the choices that had stacked up in front of her over the years, the more she determined that this was not what she would continue to do.

Her life would change. She wasn't sure when, over those weeks, she made the decision. Perhaps it was a slow progression; maybe she made it the first day she awoke after she killed Molly, and she just took time to realize it. It wasn't clear to her. But she had made it.

There was no reason to continue anymore, anyway. The slimy boyfriend had paid the million. It took a bit of convincing; she might have taken a couple of pictures of the six mangled bodies in the kitchen and calmly asked the boyfriend if he had better bodyguards than Molly did. And if he didn't or didn't plan to pay, he should consider spending all the million dollars to hire a security detail. And by the way, it probably still wouldn't be sufficient for what she would bring down upon him. The convincing had worked, and eventually, he had transferred the funds.

She didn't need ever to work again. She would clean Molly's five million. That would take some time and effort. But if she invested what she had now, she could drift

The Ashen Horse

carelessly around the world and never worry about money again. There was no need to ever step into the life again that she now so desperately wanted to leave behind. A new life was calling her, one that had possibilities and opportunities she had never considered.

She dreamed one night of a life with someone that could be special. Perhaps she would never have with anyone ever again what she had with Hector. Maybe that was truly lost to her, and she should abandon that hope. But in the deepest corner of her mind, the slightest bit of longing whispered to her that perhaps she could have that again. Perhaps not all hope of a happy life had abandoned her.

Chapter Thirty-One

Flustered Fibbies

"He's gone underground," Josh observed. "We've barely gotten any interest at all in our profile. And the couple of bites we did get were very obviously not Ash. He's either not checking the site, maybe he's using multiple darknets, or perhaps he's not in the market at the moment."

After a pause, Josh said, "Or perhaps I am missing something?"

They were on their biweekly call, and there was no activity on the fake profile the FBI team had created. They thought it was juicy, all the succulent morsels that would typically pique Ash's interest. However, the profile was stone cold, like a dead and rotting fish. The team was a little disheartened by the lack of any interest in the plan they had spent several weeks putting together.

It's not easy to fabricate an entire person's life. A backstory, a childhood, false pictures, social media profiles, previous girlfriends, educational history, achievements. They even built random false newspaper articles of Dr. Wilson's glory days as a high school athlete. They had made his credentials impressive; he had graduated cum laude from Harvard. His marriage fell apart early on; he had spent too much time working, or so the backstory went.

Tim inquired, "Are you ready to step up and be this guy

in the field, Josh?"

"You betcha, boss-man. I got this on lock. Always wanted to be a doctor, stethoscope and all."

Roshan proceeded to correct Josh, "You aren't that kind of—"

Ellie cut him off with a laugh. "He was joking. He's a nitwit, but he isn't that much of a doofus. He's all too well aware that the character Dr. John Wilson is a Doctor of Philosophy in Religion."

"I wanted a stethoscope. All of you always deny me my dreams."

Now, it was Roshan's turn to laugh. "It's always an adventure when Josh is in the meeting."

"Pain and suffering and regret are more often the case," someone muttered.

Josh made his tone sulky. "Who said that? I'm hurt! I've been wounded unjustly."

Tim, trying to push the meeting forward, said, "You'll live, Josh."

"You say that, but the whole point of this is to get a highly skilled serial killer to come after me."

"You had every opportunity to back out."

"Not a chance."

"Exactly," Tim noted. "Now then. What are our next steps? Do we sit on this for another couple of weeks? Can we do something to increase the likelihood of a hit on this whole endeavor? Do we know how long the other… what would we call them… opportunities?… How long were the other online opportunities before Ash moved against them?"

"I'm honestly not sure," Jade said. "I don't think we looked at that. That said, we should be able to build the data on that; it's a good question."

"It would be good to know," Ellie observed. "Perhaps we are just overly anxious, and it's a multi-month thing. We don't know right now."

"We'll compile the data. I'll get back to you."

"Thanks, Jade, that's helpful," said Tim. "But back to the original observation. What's our next play?"

"I think we need a reason for why Josh isn't actively teaching," suggested Ellie. "Perhaps Dr. Wilson needs to be suspended while the university does an investigation into some charges. We let that churn for a couple of weeks and then have him discharged and have them turn over the case to law enforcement."

"Now you're just trying to send me to jail. I won't go silently into the night! I'll fight!"

Tim inquired, "You done?"

"I'll command legions!"

"Now you done?"

Josh laughed, "Okay, yes, ruin my fun. Now I'm done. But you know the kicker on this whole thing? What might be a turning point for someone who wants justice is if the legal system in Montana decides there isn't enough evidence to take on the case. We panel a fake grand jury, and they refuse to prosecute or something like that. That would be the exact thing we have seen Ash spring on; anytime there is a true miscarriage of justice, there won't be any legal intervention."

They couldn't see Jade's face over the conference call, but it had a sense of wonder. "The jester has a truly exceptional idea. Did he fall down and hit his head?"

"Many times… many, many times. Dr. Wilson, during his athletic youth, sustained quite a few concussions," Josh observed. "Fairly certain we have those doctor visits documented now if those last reports went through."

"You know, you're almost as funny as you try to be," Ellie laughed.

"Almost nothing. I'm exactly as funny as I am. I bet those fake doctors have fake stethoscopes in those fake reports about those fake injuries. It's not fair that I don't get a fake stethoscope."

Roshan had an idea. "Not sure if this is a good idea or

not. But what we need, perhaps, is a victim to decry the injustice. One of Jos... Hmm. One of Dr. Wilson's victims to defame him to the public."

"Right on the courtroom steps, a press release about a miscarriage of justice," Jade giggled. "Wouldn't that be epic? Honestly, it's not far from what would also be expected in this situation. Can the FBI make that happen?"

Tim nodded, which no one saw over the call. "Yes, I think we can make that happen. This thing grows legs. I'll need to engage some of my leadership at this point, we really have expanded the scope of the deception a lot further than we probably ever should have. But to make this continue to work, this is a good next step. I'll give this team credit; we are definitely breaking all the norms on this one."

Josh's customary sarcasm was toned down, and a sense of seriousness entered his voice. He asked the question, "Are you digging a hole with the leadership, Tim? Are we burning any of our credits and capital on this?" It was a sincere question, and the team realized just how serious Josh was if, for no other reason, his typical 'boss' stab at Tim wasn't present.

Tim winced, "I haven't overstepped yet. But we are pulling out all the stops. We will have to get some buy-in from several parties on this. The University of Montana will probably be okay with it, as the blame will shift mostly to the legal authorities of the State of Montana. The school will plan to terminate him, after all. However, the state's decision not to prosecute will make them look bad, especially if we start releasing more evidence. He must look guilty to try to convince Ash he's the scum we are going for. At this point, I'll need buy-in from our leadership, and then we will probably have to get buy-in from the State of Montana, which will probably include a couple of different legal jurisdictions. Then there's the whole issue of whether or not we leave the news media in the dark or not."

Jade didn't hesitate. "Absolutely. Keep those vultures as

much in the dark as possible."

Ellie was intrigued by the amount of venom in her response, but she let it go probably because she agreed with her. "I concur. Let the media spin it out of control, who knows, it might even go national."

"Perhaps," Tim agreed. "We'll have to get some lawyers actually to look at the legality of that. I can't even begin to speak of it off the top of my head. There might be some major complications with deceiving the media in this manner, though. That will cost political capital for everyone involved in the FBI. Thank God that's all above my pay grade. I'll let the senior leadership sort out what surely will be brimstone and fire that collapses on them from the major media outlets."

Josh was back on his game, "Better someone else burns than you." A short moment passed, and then he added, "Boss-man."

"Probably true. Just remember that excrement always rolls downhill in the bureaucratic world. So, when it lands on leadership, they'll also pass on a healthy dose to all of us. That said, I feel good about this meeting, guys. We all have a clear path forward right now. I'll start working with our leadership and see what they will commit us to. The rest of you know the next steps; feel free to start making the necessary arrangements. If leadership balks, we'll return to the drawing board to rethink our next maneuvers in what is turning out to be a rather epic game of chess."

Roshan quipped, "Here's to us getting the first check and the ultimate checkmate."

"Better believe it."

"We'll catch him; this has to work. If this doesn't work, it'll be difficult to figure out anything else to draw this son-of-a-goat out of his hiding."

***

Several weeks later, Ellie stood on the courtroom steps crying before the TV cameras. She recounted how Dr.

The Ashen Horse

Wilson had used his position of authority to take advantage of her, how it had driven her out of her graduate program and turned her into a life of drug abuse. She was only now able to talk about it, having recently come out of a ninety-day treatment facility for drug use. A promising young woman in graduate college driven to the brink of financial, emotional, and spiritual ruin. All because Dr. Wilson had used his authority and coerced her into his bedroom.

It didn't matter that the grand jury thought it was consensual. She was standing here now and exclaiming to the world it was not. The State of Montana should prosecute this man. This was a violation of all moral and ethical behavior everywhere. It wasn't sufficient that he had lost his job. He should be going to prison.

Ellie laid the story on thick. It had been well scripted and well thought out. However, perhaps her acting was going too far because the Montana legal authorities who agreed to the charade were starting to wonder if they shouldn't indict Josh on the spot. Josh, of course, was now tucked away in the lovely two-story rancher home purchased for this operation.

The program was far enough along that most of the parties around the case had to finally commit to operating out of Montana and making Missoula their home for at least the next several months. The FBI had acquired Josh's new home as Dr. Wilson's residence. Another house several blocks away had been purchased to operate as the central command center. Other agents and personnel were scattered in rentals or long-term housing across the city.

Everyone on the team hoped this would wrap up quicker, and they could all return to everyday lives. But they were committed to the hoax now. This strategy had taken a lot of effort from over twenty individuals contributing throughout various FBI departments, and even the senior leadership was on board to play this out. Even if it didn't pull Ash out of his apparent hiatus, it should draw some other would-be contract killers. Perhaps even other serial killers that had completed contracts.

There were several upsides to the ploy. Of course, that also now came with the harsh reality that they were baiting killers to come after FBI agents. Not only was Josh very literally putting his life on the line, but the operation also came with a security detail on guard and watching Dr. Wilson's house.

The risk was not lost on anyone—they were trying to bait lethal and seasoned killers to come and slaughter their numbers. This had caused some heated debates among the team. Initially, they had all been in favor of the plan. As the stark reality of exactly what they were playing with slowly sank in, not everyone stayed onboard. Some of the agents had expressed serious doubts about this approach, not only in its incredible danger but also in the ethics and morality of the ploy. The division in the department was slowly growing and creating more than just mild levels of discomfort.

The core team was still on board with the deception. Josh, Ellie, Roshan, and Jade had all pushed for the adoption of the idea. Tim had surprisingly begun to hedge his bets on the entire thing slowly. The rest of the team wasn't sure why he was slowly turning against the idea, but political influences within the ranks might have been playing a significant role.

To make sure the team was protected from the serial killers they were trying to lure, a complex schedule managing the demand for a constant watch was instituted. There were no fewer than three full-time guards watching Josh's new residence at any time. This involved twelve FBI agents on twelve-hour rotations, running four-on, three-off, three-on, and four-off schedules. It seemed to work well for everyone involved. But it required constant vigilance, especially during the night shifts, the projected most likely time of an assault.

Tensions were high as the days stretched on. Josh was not his usual self, and the continued isolation of being stuck in the house became a reality. One of the major news organizations usually had a van close to the house. The FBI also staged their van, pretending to be another news van nearby. The FBI played a double game: they casually pretended to look like the local news but equally pretended to look like local police. Any suspicious person might realize that they were local police scouting a suspect. A less suspicious person would see them as a news van. The FBI hoped the double agent ploy would thwart further suspicion that the van held federal agents.

The media did their jobs well, finding every scrap of false documentation the team had churned. Their investigations would eventually land the story on national news. The element that would likely turn this into a national news piece was Ellie's performance on the courtroom steps. If the national news was not interested before then, they were interested now.

The national media piece that finally broke pitched the story as a heroic young professor fallen from glory. Playing on the unsure reality of the sexual charges, the news story leveraged the confusion of the case and the gray areas of sexual consent. They didn't quite call out the State for failure to prosecute, but they also didn't defend the State's decision. At the end of the program, everyone looked terrible. The victim looked like a victim and not a victim. The professor looked out of his element and was clearly a beast of a womanizer, if not an outright rapist if an outstanding professor. The few created student reviews had surfaced about how he was the most extraordinary professor on campus. Of course, the media never bothered to find any students who had ever been taught by this mystery Dr. Wilson. The legal system was shown as being an overcomplex and broken institution. The piece ended with B-roll footage scanning the town of Missoula and cutting in on Ellie's defamation of the justice system on the courtroom steps. They played her speech in its entirety and made a mockery of the system.

Tim had worried that the fallout would be worse than it was. He sat by his phone during the entire presentation of the news story, just watching and waiting for his phone to ring. Surely, any minute, senior leadership would be calling him, and he would have to defend this entire debacle. But the call never came. Surprisingly, the team and his boss took the coverage as a matter of course. Maybe it wasn't surprising; they all did have the objective that they wanted national coverage. Perhaps this was the natural course that they were all anticipating.

At the subsequent conference call, the team discussed how no one was aggravated at the coverage. Everyone worried about whether this whole plan would yield any results. If the plan did not bring forward any potential murderers, then the fallout might be severe. Everyone was still optimistic about the potential here. Tim explained that clearly, 'Only time would tell.' For now, they watched and waited.

Chapter Thirty-Two

Just a Short Walk

As the weeks went on, she slowly recovered her strength. The stiffness in her shoulder abated. She had feared she would never stop hearing her blood flow through her abdomen. Perhaps it was a feeling, maybe it was a sense. She wasn't sure, but she was sure it was there, and it was an unnerving sound. She could track the blood in her body as it flowed through her. That feeling had finally also left her. She felt like the curse that had shrouded her had lifted. It was such a relief the first day that she could no longer sense it that she almost felt like she should celebrate.

She started exercising as soon as she was able to. She had learned early that one of the primary keys to her success had been her health. Even if she was leaving the life behind her, she wanted to remain healthy. Her abilities were hard-earned, and they came from good training. She wouldn't throw away her functionality, even after she walked away from what had been her world.

She had been making a point to watch both the national and local news, waiting for the story about Molly to spring to life. It took almost a month before the story finally aired. It had taken that long to discover that she had been killed. That prompted the lengthy investigation into Molly's assets, which led investigators to her other properties.

Her face turned green, and the nausea swept over her as she considered what the state of the corpses she had left in her wake must have been. The news said it more politely as they described that 'the bodies were found in a dismal state of decomposition.'

Given how thoroughly destroyed Molly's entire organization was, the police chalked it up to a significant drug hit, possibly and most probability a direct cartel hit. The police were abuzz about it. They never even remotely suspected the truth behind what had happened. The detective work showed that Molly was working with and linked to multiple cartels. Rumors and the investigation revealed she was integrated with many other key players in the drug business. She chuckled as she watched the coverage. Indeed, each of the cartels assumed the other had taken her out. Not only were the police wrong, but even the cartels' assumptions were flawed with the way the pieces were coming together.

As she watched the report, she was filled with a deep regret that she had left the boyfriend alive. A loose end and also a soul that should not be allowed to breathe air. But he knew better than to ever go to the authorities and talk. Doing so would implicate him as much as anyone else, so her secret was safe with him. She was still filled with regret that he took in oxygen. Oxygen was too good for that man.

She had established the pattern of watching the two news shows back-to-back over the weeks of her recovery, so even after the Molly story had come and gone, somehow, it was a habit that she kept up with. Although she followed the financial markets, she had never been one to keep up with regular news. She didn't know what had changed; perhaps she desired to discover what was happening in the world. Maybe it involved her figuring out what she wanted to do next.

Unfortunately, fate came knocking. She might not have seen it that way, and she might not have known that's what

The Ashen Horse

it was. But it seemed to twist its head and plant its roving feet directly in her path. Once comfortable, it simply sat down. Fate had come, and it appeared it was planning on staying for the duration. She didn't know, but destinies were spinning around her that she could never foresee. A biographer of her life might have described many such times when it appeared the strings of her reality were plucked and pulled by someone other than her. Or maybe her nature was so firmly planted in a fact that she had no control over it; it just was what it was.

Fate crawled next to her one day while following her nightly ritual of watching the news. A brilliant story came on about a professor in Montana, of all places, who had raped countless students, and the courts were declining to prosecute. The story enthralled her. How could this failure of justice happen in modern times? Indeed, this pig should face his accusers in a court of law. Surely? She brooded her head a thundering storm of indignation and outrage at the system's complete failure. Her body crawled with the feeling of helplessness, just like she felt when the men had held her in Molly's van. How could men be allowed to get away with these crimes?

She sat back, slowly stewing at the political and criminal injustice of the world. The coverage went on, describing how Dr. Wilson was an accomplished professor. Then it happened: one of the victims was arguing bloody murder on the very courtroom steps that had refused to prosecute the beast. The woman swore this brute had utterly destroyed her life, and the courts refused to stand up and take action. The victim on the screen made a profound argument that this miscarriage of justice was why women never came forward. She spoke of why women don't want to participate in the legal system; even when they do, it fails them. It is a ship lost at sea, leaking water. The judicial system is faulty and violates the dignity of those who come forward in good faith. In the middle of her eloquent tirade about the utter horror of the situation, she broke down sobbing. Her entire world would never be the same after Dr. Wilson had taken advantage of her. She never said he raped her, but avoiding the word made the accusation all the more compelling.

She snapped off the television. She was shaking, her hands twitching. She hadn't even noticed, but she was leaking tears. Her emotions betrayed her frequently after the shooting, but she'd never been here before. She stared at a blank wall in her new hotel room. Still twitching, still silently crying. How could honest people stand by and watch such injustice in the world? Where was the humanity? Where was the honesty to do the right thing?

***

She stood in the airport security line. In typical fashion, she had already shipped her supplies ahead of her to a hotel where she had set up a single night's reservation. She would pay, collect her shipment, and never even enter her room. She would then travel across town to stay at the hotel she had planned to stay at.

She honestly couldn't even remember why she was standing here. She just saw a show on TV. Why was this impacting her life in any way? She still didn't fully remember how the circumstances brought her to this point.

She just knew that something in her had broken after she had finished watching the special. She vaguely remembered booking an airline ticket to Missoula, Montana. The next day didn't assuage the feelings from the previous days. She was packing her gear and preparing it to travel before her, as she had done many times. The regularity of it, the consistency of it, perhaps even soothed her. The weeks of confusion about where her life would go seemed to subside as she fell back into her habits. She was doing something she knew. She was prepared for this; she was ready.

But oh, how she wanted to stop. She desperately wanted to stop. This was not how she saw her future. Nonetheless, the katana was wrapped with love and care it always was and

The Ashen Horse

put into its faithful pelican case and express shipped. Her hands worked with a methodical logic that had faithfully served them all these years. But somewhere in the back of her mind, perhaps it was in her soul, she was screaming. The screaming was falling on deaf ears, for she didn't stop.

Somewhere in those days between when she first watched the show and the flight, she reached a compromise in her mind. Or she had convinced herself it was a compromise. All she was going to do was inspect the situation.

She was sure there was no way she would get involved in this. It had nothing to do with her. She was going to investigate the situation a bit. Perhaps she could find evidence to help the cops reconsider the case. Her mind had agitated for days for any rationalization she could conjure up that would allow her to go and not fall back into a life she was so desperately trying to walk away from. Her rationalization had landed on going and not getting involved.

She had blinded herself to her own reality. What she refused to acknowledge in the depths of her soul was the burning flame that brewed there. The roaring fire nestled in her, telling her justice had been cheated. For all her convincing that she would go and observe, in her soul, she howled that justice should be done. That justice must be done.

She used every ounce of her strength to suppress that voice, that feeling, to smash it below the waters where it would never resurface again. A cold wisp of air wrapped around her, a quiet and still desire to get on another plane and run as far away as she could go. The other half of her soul slammed the doors shut on those desires just as surely as the others had. Her inner turmoil was not just the devil and angel sitting on her shoulders but an entire rabid pack of wolves fighting amongst themselves inside of her. As any single wolf rose to prominence, the rest of the pack cut him down.

And that's how she found herself sitting at the gate,

having passed through security and now calmly waiting for the boarding call. Her eyes glazed over as her mind drudged in circles while she stared at a handsome man across from her. He seemed to be trying to get her attention to initiate a conversation, but she wasn't even there and didn't notice anything. She just stared with the eyes of death, watching nothing, seeing less.

The flight was uneventful. The irony is she ended up sitting next to the same handsome man. She had come to herself at some point and time, and they had struck up a conversation. She had considered turning on the charm, considering that a quick twist between the sheets might solve so many of her issues. But in the end, she couldn't do it. The guy seemed nice enough, and it seemed to be a cruel road to lead him down. She wondered if she would regret it as soon as she got to her hotel, alone.

She picked up the gear, pretended to check in, and then walked out a back door to her rental car and proceeded to her actual hotel. Repeating the process was as uneventful as the flight, which was always the objective. Be the ghost. Let everyone think you are but vapor in the wind.

As she got situated in her new room, she knew she had to dive directly into intelligence gathering, just like in the olden days. Her plans would come together as she collected information, and she knew the best information hotspot in any city—the local salon. Perhaps if she were a man, it would be the local barbershop, but the salon was a go-to for information consumption for her. It was surprising how much gossip could be found. Most often, it wasn't the salon workers themselves who knew everything but also had the decency to keep the confidence of their patrons. But the other five to ten patrons in the establishment would strike up casual conversations. A compulsion to share details and stories and events that they knew about.

Quickly scanning the best salons in Missoula online yielded a couple of choices. After finishing her customary room setup, she was on her way. As she drove, she pondered how a good manicure and pedicure might be just the thing for her. It might do her good to sit back and get pampered. It had been too long since she had just enjoyed simple pleasures.

She pulled into the parking lot. She was considering her other options as well. She would need as much information as she could consume. The second-best place to get intel was from either waitresses or bartenders. She decided that after the complete workup treatment, she would find the local dive diner and drill the staff on the town's opinion on the situation.

As she sat down in the chair, it didn't take long for her to forget why she had come in. The smells, the quiet and constant chatter, and the relaxation and comfort surrounding everyone brought her a rare and unfamiliar peace. Friendship and hospitality appeared among everyone in the salon. A witty banter and the calmness of true friendship just permeated the shop. She got lost almost immediately in the story of little Tommy breaking his leg at his best friend's birthday party. It was a new experience for her. Perhaps she should have spent more time in rural America, for she was entirely unprepared for this.

She didn't know how to describe what she was experiencing. She could only compare it to the feeling of being welcome. It felt like the community would reach out and hug her and tell her she was home.

Chapter Thirty-Three

Breaking News

"Breaking news!" Jade exclaimed as she walked into the residence Josh had been occupying. "Someone is coming to kill you! How exciting is that?"

"We need to work on what you consider exciting," Josh explained. "Does this mean I should always have one in the chamber?"

"I'm not a field agent, you tell me!" she laughed. "Probably. If it was me, I'd probably have two or three guns on me, and they'd all have a round chambered. Hanging you out like this, as bait, still doesn't seem like a great idea to me."

"I don't recall you objecting during the meetings."

"That's before I had time to think it through. We have encouraged presumably professional killers to come after you. That doesn't seem smart on a variety of levels."

"It'll be okay. I doubt they will ever even get to the house. We'll have Ash at the perimeter before he even gets close. It won't be much of a contest; our guys are the best the agency has. They even brought in some of our seasoned antiterrorism guys to be on this detail."

"I hope you are right," Jade said. "I've gone over some of the scenes on cases we have attributed to the Ashen Horse, and I have to say that it looks like this guy knows how to handle himself in a pinch. There are more than a few literal decapitations in those case files."

"That's one of the reasons I'm not concerned," Josh said. "Ash always uses a sword, or almost always it appears. It's even less likely that he'll get anywhere near me in this house. If it even gets close to that, he'll have two shots in his back. You might not even know that they brought in some sniper teams; they are watching the front and back entrances."

Josh sat puzzled momentarily, then continued, "Come to think of it, I only heard that yesterday. I'm not sure they are here, but they've been deployed for the task anyway. But that brings up the point: What do you know? When did you know it, or when did the FBI know it?"

"Someone accepted the contract on the darknet," Jade explained. "They accepted it late last night, well, more accurately, this morning. My team has no consensus on whether or not it's Ash. The agreement was rather abrupt compared to what Ash would normally do, but it appeared to be just as careful and elusive as Ash, so my team is divided on who the guy coming after you is."

"Do you have odds on it?"

"I'm in the fifty-fifty camp myself; it could go either way. But there is a pretty solid chance we got him. There's no indication of when he'll finish the job, so we can't pinpoint when the hit is coming. But if historical data is relevant, he'll complete the contract within the next month."

"Well, that sounds like an enjoyable revelation."

"Doing what I can to help the cause." Jade laughed.

"What are you doing here, then? This is no longer basic reconnaissance or evaluation; this is an active case with potential shooters in the field at any point. You said yourself you aren't a field agent."

"I pulled some strings. Honestly, it was mostly begging—much begging. I'm always stuck on my computer in a dungeon, busting out analytics, computing statistics, or manipulating code. It makes you twitchy after a while. I wanted to get out and see what it was like to be in the field for a change."

"You got your boss on board with that?"

"I might have told him that Tim needed me desperately, and I had no choice but to get out here as quickly as possible."

"You tell Tim any of that?"

"I might have hinted about it to him." Jade's eyes looked downcast, and she mumbled, "After I was already here…."

"You know I like you, Jade, but you're playing with a bit of fire here," Josh cautioned. "Tim's a good guy; he'll back you up. But still. Anyone else in the agency and you could have been swimming in paperwork for months. And that's not to say you won't have your fair share of it anyway after this."

"Well, I'm kind of already there. Tim was a bit pissed after he talked to my boss…."

"Oh, that's already happened. Yeah, so you're in the doghouse now."

"Yep. Why I'm here is that he has got me in the field kind of fully now. I'll come in and out of this house to bring you whatever you need. I'll have to stay here sometimes overnight. I'm playing the role of your new young squeeze since that's your scene. You, pedophile, you."

"Now, now, all the women a Dr. Wilson was alleged to have slept with, consensually, were of age," explained Josh. He emphatically annunciated the 'alleged' and 'consensual' parts. Josh continued, "Pedophile is not a fair term. Rapist, or womanizer, or philanderer, sure."

"Are you defending your fake persona right now?"

"My fake persona has feelings too."

"Uh-huh. Yeah, so that's all messed up." Jade was rolling her eyes and shaking her head, but she continued. "At any rate, I'll be coming in and out and staying overnight on occasion. I'll bring in food since we don't know how long this will take. I've mostly dodged the press outside, but I'm sure they'll get pictures sooner or later, and that'll be another potential round of stories. Who knows, maybe they'll let it die."

"Those vultures don't let much go. So, you are probably stuck here for a couple of hours today?" Josh walked over to the coffee pot brewed earlier that morning and refreshed his cup. Grabbing another mug, he got Jade a cup of the most excellent joe. "You'll need this. I've been reviewing case stuff this morning and trying to compile reports. We will still be working on that timeline when we have a moment. It's coming together, but there's a lot of data to comb through. Perhaps we attributed too many cases to Ash out of the gate, but honestly, we still haven't found any of the cases that overlap. I thought we would. On the flip side, there's not that many homicides that are committed with long swords, so most of those are pretty easy callouts."

"Yeah, both Ellie and you thought you'd see some overlap. It would be surprising if that hadn't happened," Jade agreed. "I'll be here for a while. I have one of my laptops in the car, along with groceries. I'll bring all that in here in a second. I planned to cook you a home-cooked meal; you have only been eating takeout for weeks now, haven't you?"

"I've been cooking a bit, but it's been a bit of fast food. On the flip side, it allows for a lot of work to get done. I've actually worked on quite a few other cases that some other agents had backlogged that they wanted a second set of eyes on. It's been relaxing not to be actively in the field and just to be able to sit down and work."

"The bonus of being live bait?"

"It should have some benefit."

"Ha. Okay, let me grab all this stuff. You can return to work; I'll work around the kitchen. I'll hit you up when I have some food ready."

Jade had a work location set up in the alcove off the kitchen and was using her laptop to play some island reggae. After that first priority, she went to work dicing up vegetables. It might have been in the middle of the day, but based on the FBI's plan, she would be spending the night tonight. She cracked open the bottle of wine and poured a small glass.

She was planning on cooking with the wine, which was the main reason she pulled it out. But it seemed appropriate, since it was out, to take a moment to indulge. As she finished one vegetable, she threw it in a wok on a low simmer on the stove. She still wasn't sure what she was making, but at some point, hot water got put on the stove, and she pulled out some pasta. Apparently, it was going to be spaghetti.

A little over an hour into the preparation, her phone started buzzing. "Hello, this is Jade."

"Hi, Jade. Tim here."

Her stomach dropped a bit. This could be a very awkward call. "Hi, boss…"

"Stop right there. I tolerate it from Josh just because he'd make it worse if I didn't. But he's the only one I tolerate it from. And only because he's an exceptional agent."

Jade was entirely confused. "What?"

"Calling me boss."

"You don't like being called boss?"

"I hate it from the depths of my soul."

"Josh knows this?"

"Perhaps not the degree, but he definitely knows I don't like it."

"That's hilarious." Jade laughed. Then, she realized what she had done. Still chuckling, she tried to right the ship, "I'm sorry, but that's a little comical. Look, about me being here. I know I put you in an awkward position."

"You didn't even give me a choice. Look, Jade, that piece is done. You wanted to be in the field, and now you are, and you put yourself in direct danger because this is where we need you. I don't know if you have thought this out, but we don't know when Ash is coming to that house. There is a good chance you might be in there when that happens."

Jade sputtered, "I didn't think of that."

The Ashen Horse

"Yeah, I know you didn't. You probably didn't consider yourself as much of a sitting duck in there as Josh is now."

Jade could not think of any response. Her light black complexion was almost turning white as the blood drained from her face as she thought about the consequences.

"Anyway, I need to talk to both of you. Is Josh around?"

Jade was slowly composing herself, with perhaps a much-needed dose of humility and caution. "Uh, I can go get him. Look bos... Tim. I didn't mean to put you in this position. Uh. I just want to say thank you for covering everything with my bos... manager. It means a lot."

"Yeah, just remember that when the bullets start flying."

Jade gulped. "Yeah. Good point. Let me go to Josh." She staggered off to get Josh's attention while seriously contemplating if she had made a mistake with this whole situation.

"Yo, Joshy! Tim's on the phone in the kitchen. He wants to talk to both of us. You got a minute?"

"Yeah, I'll be down in just two seconds; I need to finish this thought, it won't take me a minute to get this email out."

Jade went back downstairs and let Tim know that Josh was coming. She flipped her phone to speakerphone and went back to cooking. Her mind roiled about her choices and her new situation. Most of the meal was complete, but this call might take a while, so she flipped everything to simmer and warm on the stove. It could stew there for the length of the call. She could already tell that it would turn out to be fantastic spaghetti. The secret ingredient would be the diced pineapple and apple. Just that right amount of extra sweetness was going to be delicious.

She had been brewing another pot of coffee and poured herself and Josh a cup each. As she took a sip, she realized that she was content. Even if she was in danger and might have come here by irregular means, at least at this moment, she was content. That isn't to say she wouldn't enjoy returning to her dungeon and doing her code. But at that moment, this was refreshing; it was something new. This coffee was something special.

In the back of her mind, though, a slow and convincing voice told her that she should be afraid. And she was worried. At the moment, she was both content and half scared to death. And that slow voice silently laughed at her, making her unsure of herself.

A few minutes passed, and Tim had refrained from commenting on the reggae music. However, he was considering saying something. Then he heard Josh say that he had walked into the room. Before Tim could get into the details, Jade asked a question.

"What is this coffee? It's phenomenal."

"You like it? It's civet coffee from Vietnam. Stuff is amazing, isn't it?"

Jade had to know. "Civet?"

"Ah, yes, civet. It's a small animal, a mix between a cat and a raccoon or something like that. Maybe if a cat, raccoon, and lemur had a love child. They are cute. Anyway, they let them eat the coffee beans and poop them out, then they make coffee out of those beans. It's incredible, isn't it?"

"You are lying."

"Sure am. But it's a good lie, right? It has a whole lot of texture in there, doesn't it? Anyway, I heard the boss man was on the phone."

Jade snorted coffee out of her nose. She wasn't sure if she had more respect for Josh now or if she was annoyed with him for constantly jabbing Tim.

"This should be quick. Josh? Jade got you up to speed with your two new cover stories. Yours and hers? She's the new girl?"

"Yep. I think the professor could have done…"

Jade's eyes darkened. "If you want to live, I'd choose your next words carefully."

Josh coughed, "Uh, the professor could not have done better. He obviously has great taste." A couple more coughs followed, and he picked up the coffee and drank a couple of sips.

They didn't see Tim rolling his eyes on the other end of the speakerphone. "She'll be in and out for the next month, anyway. We'll try to minimize her exposure, but at the same time, we must make it look somewhat authentic that you are in a relationship. Any contract killer worth his salt should wait until she isn't there if they do any reconnaissance at all. So, with that, we'll amp up security when she isn't there."

"Ten-four."

"You've been here, if not exactly here before, Josh. All the normal stuff is in play. We have snipers on the scene now; they'll rotate in and out but should always have eyes on the building. We have cameras on all streets coming in and out of the house. No car can approach without the cameras getting them on video. We have people monitoring those feeds 24-7, of course—standard stuff. We, of course, picked that house because of the panic room. Get Jade up to speed on that when you get a minute. When anyone approaches the house, we'll sound the alarm in the two rooms. Both of you are to get in the panic room immediately and seal it. No heroism here. If we trap Ash inside, he's never getting outside. There is no reason to put yourself in danger; just wait it out."

"Seems cowardly."

"It might be, but you'll live to tell the tale. Let's start there."

Jade felt the vast world of anxiety she had been carrying since Tim had first warned her of what she faced start to ease off her. Her paranoia and worry that she could genuinely die any minute might have been over the top. She took a deep and steady breath and let it flow out of her. She had put herself in a slightly foolish position but wasn't in grave danger. She told herself that the FBI had everything under control and this situation was clearly in hand.

Perhaps Tim had laid it on a little thick to put her on point for putting him in the position in the first place. Honestly, she really couldn't blame him. She had truly put him in more than an awkward position. He was put into a situation where he might have easily gotten her demoted or terminated had he not lied to her leadership.

"I'm good with being a coward in this case," Jade said.

"That's really all I got," Tim said. "An official email will probably come out tomorrow, or we'll have one of our calls. But a lot has happened in the last 48 hours. I didn't want either of you to be in the dark as this ramps into a major operation. It escalated quickly. A lot changed when the contract got accepted this morning. Jade, you let Josh know that?"

"She was rather happy my head was planned for the pike," Josh replied with a put-on pout.

Jade smirked. "Gleeful, really."

"Boss-man, you know my new girl has a lot of spunk."

Tim smiled. Leave it to these two. A serial killer was literally on their doorstep, and they could still find the humor in the situation. Perhaps it was his turn to throw the joke back at them. "I'm pretty sure that's exactly how the professor likes them."

"Well played, sir. Well played."

"Alright, guys, get some rest. Check the communications and make sure all that panic room stuff works. And don't wing it; do a few drills so you're ready to be locked in that room."

Jade looked pointedly at Josh. "I'll make sure he does it."

"Okay, thanks, guys. Be safe out there. Keep a look out for the emails. I'll talk to you later."

The phone clicked at the end of the call.

Josh took a second to look at Jade seriously, and then, in a rare serious moment, he asked the question. "You still think this was a good idea?"

"What's that?"

Joshed asked, "You wanting to come into the field?"

The Ashen Horse

Jade stood there fleetingly and considered, "Hopefully, it wasn't incredibly stupid. But we have a panic room, right? It should all be fine."

"It's serious business, Jade. We joke around but never underestimate the power of evil in this world. You don't deal with this stuff daily. The files aren't real for you. You haven't stood over the corpses; you haven't smelt the iron in the air from the blood. It's a whole different thing when the bullets are flying. I trust Ellie with my life because she has saved my life. You aren't field trained, and you are largely untested."

Jade swallowed hard and looked at him. "Sounds pretty close to what Tim told me before I came and got you."

"Yeah, well, he also knows what he's about. Anyway, I didn't mean to go off on a tangent there. Just take the time to appreciate the situation. And when I tell you to do something, you'd better react immediately. We might not have time for a discussion."

Jade nodded as she considered his words. She knew she would have much to learn over the next several weeks. The silence stretched a minute, as often happens when a serious conversation comes to its natural end.

Josh's eyes flickered around the kitchen for the first time as if he saw what was happening around him. He was too busy talking to notice before. His eyes lingered on the stove, and the beautiful aroma lingered in the air.

Jade smiled as she looked at Josh and asked, "Hungry?"

Chapter Thirty-Four

To Listen is to Learn

She was supposed to be paying attention; that was why she was here, but she had let her mind wander. She was still thinking about the handsome man she had conversed with on the airplane. She did have his number; she could give him a call. She shook her head. She knew it wasn't so much the interest in him but more simply the loneliness that had consumed her recently. The weeks spent recovering from her wounds had only added to her sense of being alone.

She had been alone for most of her life, and before, it had never bothered her because she never knew what she had been missing. But now, after being with Hector, she knew what it was not to be empty. For the first time in her life, she felt the loneliness creep around her and hug her in an oppressive embrace. She wanted so badly to squirm out of its grip. It was only natural that her mind wandered to the man who had given her his phone number.

"I'm sorry, what was that?"

Of course, whenever she thought about anything romantic, it brought her back to Hector. And then her mood truly turned disheartened. It still felt like her heart was being ripped out every time her mind turned to him. She thought to herself, "Focus, woman, focus! She said something important: focus, blast you."

The Ashen Horse

"Oh, I was just saying that I was a religious major at U of M, and Dr. Wilson wasn't a professor there. The whole story has been kind of weird, actually. I emailed a couple of other students who were in my program as well, and none of us remember him. Did you want me to top you off, dear?"

She nodded, "Yes, please. One can never have too much coffee."

The waitress, still in her early twenties, laughed. "Isn't that the truth? Coffee and being devoid of hope are the only things that got me through college." She winked and smiled as he poured more coffee into the woman's cup. "You aren't from around here, are you? You aren't a reporter, are you?"

"No, nothing like that. I'm not from around here, no. I'm just passing through, really. The last couple of months, I've been a bit of a nomad, to tell you the truth. I'm actually looking for a place to stay for a while. A couple of my friends said some excellent fly was fishing up here in Montana. Thought I'd check it out."

"You and every knucklehead that has ever watched A River Runs Through It. Even worse if they've read the book." She suddenly looked abashed. "Sorry. We get a lot of would-bes and wannabes through here. I wouldn't have said anything at all, but you don't look like that type. But still, my bad. You are just curious about the Dr. Wilson case, then?"

"Don't worry about it. I used to live in New York City, and we saw the same touristy mentality come through there all the time as well. People either thought they could wrestle the city or they thought that the city owed them something. I supposed it's much the same thing here."

She took a sip of the coffee. It was the kind of coffee that could clean rust off a thirty-year-old bumper. You weren't sure if it was acid etching or pure arsenic. She loved it. That small-town diner coffee that could melt lead. It was beautiful.

"This coffee is great."

"And by great, you mean it could kill a standing donkey in its tracks?"

"Yes. Just the way I like it. Yeah, so I'm a true crime buff in my spare time. I mean, nothing serious, but the stories are always fascinating. I probably wouldn't have even noticed this case except it was happening in the town I had booked my flight to. Then, after that, it piqued my interest quite a bit."

"Yep, I get sucked into one of the documentaries about true crime now and then. I definitely can relate. Sorry, I can't help you. I went to most of the religious classes U of M offers, but I never had a class with Dr. Wilson, and I never even heard of him as a professor in the department. The news stories suggest he had been teaching here for years, though. So, I guess I'm confused about the whole thing."

"You didn't know any of the victims either? Well, they probably aren't releasing any of their names, are they?" She was playing the situation calmly. This was exactly the kind of casual conversation that yielded mounds of information. Nothing but a casual chat, but the locals always knew more than they even knew they could know. "Sexual crime a big thing here on campus?"

"Uh, well. I mean. I wouldn't say sexual crime is large anywhere in Montana. For the most part, Montanans still have a strong, chivalrous attitude." The young woman thought for a minute. "Maybe that isn't entirely accurate; we also see post-modernism here. It's almost like men can't be chivalrous anymore without getting in trouble, so perhaps even here, it has subsided substantially. Anyway, cultural mores aside, there has always been a robust drinking culture in our college, and that has led to many walks of shame for both men and women, I think. There is sometimes a very grey line between sexual assault and plain stupidity on both sides of the fence. Lord knows I put myself in plenty of stupid situations when I was in college."

"That either sounds very mature, or it sounds a bit like

shaming the victim. I'm not entirely sure which. Sorry, that's probably forward of me to say."

The young waitress's face showed her disgust with what she had been accused of. The silence stretched on as she thought about it further.

"I probably was victim shaming there a bit." She nodded as the realization crossed her mind. Then she shook her head. "Yet, at the same time, I still think it's true. I put myself in unsafe situations, and I saw my friends do it, too. I never got myself in trouble doing it, but that might have been as much luck as anything else." She paused again, her mind working out what she thought as she contextualized these ideas. "Any man that would have taken advantage of me would have been a monster, and it would have been inexcusable, don't get me wrong."

"That's a pretty levelheaded and analytical response."

"Yeah, sorry. My friends and I have spent some time trying to understand it. It was a different world when my older siblings went to college here. Or perhaps cultures just adjust. We spend a lot of time figuring out what people believe and, usually, just as importantly, why people believe it in my field. Cultural shifts always become a matter of intrigue."

She stopped and filled the cup of coffee again.

"Anyway, just wave at me if you need anything. Those men at the other end of the counter look like they might riot if I don't bring them coffee."

"Coffee this good, it's entirely understandable."

The waitress looked at her cross-eyed. Clearly, she didn't believe that anyone could actually drink this stuff and revel in it. She took another sip; delicious. The waitress walked away, hips swishing for the boys. The girl had talent. The men were almost soothed before she even got there. That girl had the makings of a solid negotiator and tactician. She sat back, wondering if the woman was aware of her potential.

She sipped the coffee, but her mood still somewhat

soured because her mind had wandered to Hector. She'd probably be ruffled the entire day, yet again. Perhaps someday, it wouldn't be like this. Maybe she could think of the good times, only the good times, and not have the heart-wrenching pieces that came with it.

Her mind came around. Something was going on here. Something she didn't understand. How could students in the department who had taken the classes not even be aware of a professor in the department? That didn't sound right. She would have to dig a lot deeper into this situation.

She spent the next hour in the coffee shop, googling everything she could about Dr. John Wilson. Digging up social media profiles, reading all the articles published about the miscarriage of justice, and trying to validate and confirm his athletic achievements. There was a ton of information about him. As she read the articles, she noticed some nuances in the wording that made her question the dating of the articles.

She couldn't put her finger on it, but the tone of the articles felt contemporary. Perhaps it was a delusion, but a subtle voice in her mind made her think that they weren't written ten years ago. One particular article about Dr. Wilson's high school athletic achievements stuck out to her as sounding very contemporary. She sat there reading it repeatedly. It was hard to put her finger on it, but something about it didn't feel aged. She was beginning to think there was a rat in the reeds.

She paid for her breakfast and tipped the waitress three hundred percent. Loose jaws should always be rewarded; that waitress might have saved her life. Throwing a good tip at her seemed the least she could do. As she paid, she made plans and needed to start executing them.

The first wave of her plans involved standard social engineering methods. She'd start calling people and tracking down leads. Which meant she needed burner phones. It also meant she would need to get out of town to make the calls.

The Ashen Horse

She found a cell phone store and walked in with the intention of picking up two burner phones. The standard approach of always deflecting attention came into play. In her life, she was onstage more than she was not, and her performances were always targeted to be forgettable. In this case, she was all excited that she and her new boyfriend would be able to talk on these excellent prepaid phones. The sixteen-year-old behind the counter just rolled his eyes and took her cash. No suspicions there. She shook her head; the kid probably didn't even realize that half the crime in the country was perpetrated on what he was selling. Just skimmed right over his head.

She repeated the stunt at two other locations. After collecting her sixth burner, she was ready to go. She was heading back to her hotel to extend her stay for two more weeks, exclaiming how much she was falling in love with the area and how excited she was to be here. She took the time to ask if the extended stay would qualify her for some kind of discount. The manager said they could do something if she hit thirty days. She extended it to 31 days and said it might go further. "I mean, who knows what wonders I might have yet to find here. This place is just incredible. Have you guys been to the art museum?" They hadn't, which was good for her because neither had she.

She went to her room, threw enough belongings into a backpack that should do her for three or four days, and left out the back door. Then she started to drive. She didn't have plans; she just knew she needed to be a couple of hours away from where she was staying. Burners could still be identified by their number, and they could still be traced to what tower those calls originated from. She wasn't having anyone trace her calls inside her hotel range or even inside the city.

The roads eventually became winding. They twisted and turned up mountain passes, and she was enjoying the curvature of the motion and scenery. Before she knew it, hours had passed. She had gone further than she intended, but at the same time, crossing into a different state was a good idea. She found herself driving along a massive body of water. The signs said that she was approaching Coeur d'Alene. She pulled off the interstate, browsed for a hotel, and was on her way to check in.

She went to bed early that night, knowing tomorrow would be a busy day of jumping around the city making phone calls. As she sat down at the table in her hotel room, she started making a list of people she needed to call and writing out the information she wanted to coerce from them. She doodled out some plans, listing the roles she would play and what she needed to do in each role:

1. Inquiring reporter
    a. Find any current or recent graduate students.
    b. Is Dr. Wilson a good teacher?
2. Previous high school student
    a. Call Dr. Wilson's junior high and high school
    b. Track down his old teachers
3. Inquiring reporter
    a. Call old teachers
    b. What do they know?
4. Current graduate student
    a. Call Harvard staff
    b. What do they know?
5. Inquiring reporter
    a. Call other reporters and ask them about medical records.
    b. Call medical institutions and ask them if they know anything.

Everything about this whole situation felt off. She couldn't put her finger on it. But this seemed like a flamboyant gimmick. Her mind kept going back to the waitress. How could a student in the depth of the program not know a professor teaching in the program? She needed more information, which required further investigation.

Still, it didn't make any sense; all it did was make the legal system, the school, and this mystery professor look bad. What was to be gained from this whole charade if that's what it was? She sat confused, twirling her hair in her fingers. None of it made any sense.

What was making sense was that if this was fake, someone had gone through a lot of work to make it look legitimate. They had serious power and influence and could move many pieces on the game board. Only so many institutions could get that kind of work done. Governments, big corporations, and the big brothers—FBI, CIA, NSA, or Homeland Security; there weren't many other players in the game that could pull off this kind of sweeping intel.

The currents went too deep for just something casual. A lot of legwork went into building a persona. She knew she had several, made dozens, and retired all of them. And as far as she could tell, Dr. Wilson wasn't a professor at the University of Montana. Not from what she had been able to casually dig up from talking with locals. And they would know or should have known. The media appeared either fully committed or they were being duped as well. She spun her hand around her hair, intertwining and untangling her hand as her mind swirled. She added another item to the list.

6. Contact every reporter who did a piece to get their sources. How did they do their legwork?

She scratched down one more line, "Where are they getting their information?" and then underlined it twice for emphasis. Her mind boiled as the night grew late. She hadn't encountered a situation like this before. In every other circumstance it had been straightforward; the victim was apparent, and the perpetrator was clear. She was in uncharted waters, and that made her nervous. She wondered if she should call it off and put this one behind her.

Initially, she wanted righteous justice for the victims, but now she was intrigued. Perhaps something significant was behind the curtains. What major power player was trying to pull these strings? Something or someone was manipulating heavily if Dr. Wilson wasn't who he was. That made her want to know why. An entire city was being skillfully manipulated. What was the point?

She wanted to know.

Chapter Thirty-Five

Tough Act to Follow

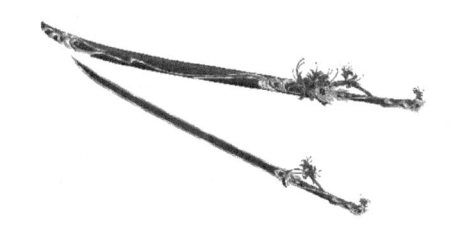

The drive back from Coeur d'Alene was not as enthralling as the drive there had been. She had learned too much to feel comfortable. She had driven around Northern Idaho and Eastern Washington, bouncing off various cell towers as she talked to everyone she could track down. Dr. Wilson was clearly an artificial character. Although the cover story was good, and someone had put a lot of time and effort into it, it was definitely a cover story.

She very simply had gone down her task list. All the current graduate students, current TAs, and graduate students that had been finished for the last several years, to a one, none of them knew Dr. Wilson or had him for a class. None of them could speak to his teaching skills or his philandering. If he had been a womanizer, no one could say one way or another because none of them knew him.

One of the students she cornered on the phone tried to play it up like he knew all about him. He wanted to get in on the story, spelling all the gossip to a reporter. But it didn't take five minutes of questioning to discover that he knew nothing. He just wanted to play himself up. She had been hopeful that he did know something. Then, this aching pain that was causing her severe discomfort could be alleviated. But her spidey senses were in full swing, and she would keep vigilant as she uncovered more mysteries.

She tracked down some old junior high and high school teachers who would have been teaching in the era when Dr. Wilson would have been going to his reported high school. He was an academic star, but no one knew him. Further calls pointed to the fact that there had only been two coaches spanning fifteen years at his theoretical high school. She very carefully reached out to both of them. This was tricky; whoever built the cover story might have had previous contact with these two individuals to ensure they would validate the story.

The first one she called from a local coffee shop, not even using her burners. He didn't know any John Wilson and swore he remembered all his students, even the ones who weren't all-stars. The second she called from a Home Depot, where she had pulled into to buy other, more nefarious supplies. He also didn't remember any John Wilson. The cover story went broad but not very deep.

She could have called it quits right there; clearly, this was a sham. But due diligence sometimes paid dividends, so she continued making calls. And continued to take every precaution. The Harvard story was a little better built. There were attendance records for John Wilson and an academic record that showed him graduating with honors and attaining his PhD. But for the most part, the trail stopped there. She had a lot harder time getting any professors on the phone. They all screened their calls, and none wanted to talk about anything. The information dried up quickly outside of what the academic office was willing to report.

Once she got the actual reporters on the phone, some casually dogged conversation also led her to more insights there. Every time she got one of her supposed colleagues on the phone, it was a cagey conversation. Two leopards were pacing in circles, snarling at each other and sensing each other's weakness, but neither was willing to back down. None of them wanted to reveal their sources or information.

But she soon discovered that what they had was handed to them on a silver platter by some legal advisors doing deep background for the grand jury.

This let her know that all the information was coming from someone in law enforcement. The question was who was feeding the people in the legal departments. That ruled out any mafia activity, major crime organizations, cartels, or probably other national identities. At least, she hoped that ruled out major crime syndicates. As she had found with Molly, the criminal networks ran deep into law enforcement.

At least it was safe to assume this wasn't Venezuela or Iran pulling the strings. That still meant the big brothers or some corporation with serious clout behind them. Her suspicions didn't seem to feed a particular theory just yet. Perhaps it was the local law enforcement, but she couldn't see what they'd have to gain by playing such a sweeping game.

She continued driving as her mind spun a web. Whose game was she stuck in the middle of? What was the game? Some corruption and questionable legal maneuvering were happening here. What plagued her mind the most was what was there to gain. Why set up a man to bring him into a spectacle just to let the charges go? What was the point?

She had been putting together a theory. "They are going to kill him," she thought. That was the only thing that made sense. The man was a fabrication, brought to elite status, then brought low. There is no evidence, and no one would know if he vanished. They'll throw an unidentified John Doe in a casket and claim it's Dr. John Wilson. "The goal must be to kill him, but why?" She truly wanted to know the why.

Her mind was still going in circles as she crawled into her bed in Missoula that night. It was strange, but crawling back into her regular hotel bed felt good. There was some normalcy to it. Which meant it was time to change hotels. She wanted to stay here a bit longer, though. This was the closest thing she had felt too comfortable since Molly had shot her. There was something about this place that brought her a margin of peace.

She had found a local coffee shop she was starting to enjoy also, which is where she found herself in the morning. Sipping some of the best morning chai she had ever had. She felt like she was cheating on her coffee though, especially her standard white chocolate mocha.

"Ma'am. Can I get another one of these to go? Better go with the 24-ounce and two extra espresso shots. That would be fantastic. Thank you so much."

She sat there cradling her current cup, cherishing it like a new mother might hold her child. A warmth flowed through her, the kind she sometimes swore could only find her with a cup of hot liquid, usually some caffeinated coffee.

Her distraction helped her make the hard decision. She wanted to know more, and knowing more meant continuing her digging. She had done all the remote investigation she could at this point. Now, it was time to get her hands dirty at the scene. She needed to start seeing what was happening at Dr. Wilson's residence. The address was a piece of information she had uncovered by talking with reporters. To their credit, only one flapped his jaws and gave up the information. Giving up the goods was an amateur move, but it would make her job slightly more manageable.

The waitress brought her the cup to go, and she handed over her credit card, one of several, all under different false identities.

"Thank you," the waitress said.

"Oh no, the pleasure is all mine. Or it's all going to be mine. This stuff is amazing."

"Glad you like it."

"I'm coming back tomorrow to see how you guys do your white mochas."

"If you like the chai, you should like those as well. We use a special ingredient you'll never find at the big chains. It gives us something special, truly unique."

The Ashen Horse

"See, now I'm all excited. I'll see you tomorrow. Thanks again!"

She left the coffee shop and drove around the corner into a dark alley. A few minutes were spent putting on her false wig and changing her makeup to create inflections on her nose and cheekbones. Twenty minutes later, she looked nothing like herself. It was time for her first drive-by of the house to see what there was to see.

She set up six cameras in her car. Two out of the front at slightly overlapping angles to give her close to a 160-degree view out of the front. The same setup went out the back window. Then, one pointing directly out each side. All the feeds ran to a laptop in the rental car's trunk. The program was going to record them all in sync and would display and play them all in sync later. She'd have close to a 360-degree view of everything around the car, saved and recorded.

She chuckled to herself. Where was this technology ten years ago? Back then, she had to trust that she would see what she needed in one pass. There were no opportunities to analyze stuff later. You either caught what you needed to or missed the advantage forever. She was getting spoiled by the new technologies.

She powered up a secondary laptop and connected various peripherals, including barely noticeable antennas outside the car. She fired up an application that would go through every conceivable radio frequency and digital communication media and document what the frequencies were. If any feed is found, it will start actively recording. The antennas had over a hundred active receptors, which meant the application could, in theory, record close to four hundred active frequencies simultaneously at a degraded rate. Given that it would probably pick up the fifty to seventy radio stations that it would be able to detect, that number wasn't as high as she would sometimes like it to be.

A few more hidden tricks and tools were set up, and she was ready to go. The next piece should be the easiest part.

She punched the rough area into her GPS on her phone and headed past the good doctor's house.

She considered going up and down the road, but it was probably best to do a single pass. She was being so careful about everything else; it would be stupid to get greedy. Patience and due diligence won the day.

She decided that there may be a different way she could get some additional information. If the news van was there, she might stop and try her hand with these reporters to see if she could get any information from them. That would allow her car to spend more time collecting more data. Collecting data was the reason for the maneuver. Any delays also could give her more time to see something. If patience and due diligence won the day, then observation saved it.

She approached the news van, drove slightly past it, and parked her rental car. She parked so the side camera had a clear view of the house. Swinging the car door closed, she started heading for the news van. As she approached, she became aware that there appeared to be four suits inside. It looked like three burly men and a woman, but it was hard to tell for sure. Her projected path changed slowly as she walked and moved to the other end of the sidewalk.

She rapidly changed her persona to appear like any other woman on the street. Just another woman walking down the street; she had no interest in anything in this neighborhood. She knew she had to keep walking with intent to avoid looking suspicious. She quickly searched up and down the offices and businesses along the sidewalk; she just crossed for some purpose for being here. Eyes lit up as the idea sprung to mind. She shifted gradually, making it look like she had always intended to walk into the dental office.

She ducked into the dental office. She was more nervous than she probably should have been. She shivered as the cold reality washed over her. No news station was going to waste four bodies sitting in a house where nothing ever stirred. Those men were agents.

The Ashen Horse

There was nothing for it; she didn't dare turn around and walk out any time soon. Internally sighing with frustration, she engaged the front desk receptionist in idle chat. Her options were limited, so she started filling out the new patient forms. It probably wasn't all bad; her teeth could use a good cleaning. As she worked on the paperwork, she asked the receptionist what the news van was doing out front.

"Oh, those boys aren't newsmen. I have no idea who they are; they look like feds to me. They are here every day and have been for weeks now."

"Oh? You think? Feds? They aren't being very subtle if it's so obvious."

The receptionist laughed. "Oh, they aren't trying to be subtle, darling. They want that rapist monster to know they are out here watching. If our courts aren't going to prosecute him, the big guns are coming after him. I hope he's over there shitting himself. Pardon my language, but we shouldn't have a trial if you ask me. Give me a get-out-jail pass right now, and I'll go over there and just handle it myself."

"Rapist monster?"

"Are you new around here?"

"Kind of. I used to live on the other side of town, and I've only been here a little over a year, so fairly new, I guess."

"You aren't from California, are you?"

She fake laughed. "No, Florida, actually. I vote red."

"Good, we got too many of these young kids here that think everything should be rolled out to them on a golden carpet. The 'rapist monster' is John Wilson. He raped at least ten to twenty students at the university while he was their teacher."

"I think I heard something about that. Isn't it that he allegedly raped a woman?"

The receptionist shook her head. "The coward raped a bunch of them. He should be drug out in the street and shot if you ask me."

"And you think the feds — the FBI? —are investigating

him?"

"I can tell you this much, honey; those aren't news reporters in that van."

"Not very subtle of them, though."

"I'm pretty sure their intention isn't to be subtle. Didn't I say that already?"

"You must be right. Anyway, here is this paperwork."

"Good thing you came in today; we normally never have walk-in openings. We are booked out for two months, but we had a cancellation this morning. You are truly in luck. Jessica will be right with you after she finishes with her current patient."

"Thank you. You have my curiosity up; I'm just going to sit over here and casually bat eyes with our news reporters, who are not news reporters."

"Careful honey, with those eyes, one of them might sweep in here and make you his."

She laughed. The woman was crass and sweet at the same time, an odd combination. She sat down casually and subtly watched everything over the magazine she pretended to read. This may work out better than she originally planned. She watched for ten minutes, cataloging all the information in the back of her head. She watched everything.

A flicker of light or motion caught her eye, and her head swiveled slowly to look. In the furniture store next to the dentist's office, a man was also too casually watching everything. He didn't notice her; his attention was also thoroughly scouting the scene. Her eyes drifted back to scanning everything around her. She froze.

Her head jerked back to the man. Showing sudden movement was such a rookie mistake, but she had done it anyway. And then she honestly looked at him. He was the handsome man she sat beside on the plane.

Cold chills swept up her spine. She slowly and casually turned away from the window entirely. She buried her face into the magazine as her nerves tingled. Head down and engrossed in deep reading, she stood and moved away from the window.

She heard the receptionist chuckle. The mockery was evident in her voice. "Lost interest in those hunks of man flesh already?"

"They seem pretty boring to me."

The receptionist laughed again. "Maybe, but that one strapping fellow. I'm pretty sure he'd never bore me. I've considered going out there a couple of times and asking him if he needs his teeth cleaned."

"You never know; he might be looking for someone just like you."

"Oh, they are all looking for someone like me, darling. Look, Jessica is ready; you can go back now."

The magazine was set down carefully, and her eyes and face turned away. Very carefully, she maneuvered so that her side profile never faced any window. It might have looked strange when she walked back to the exam room, but she had to make sure no one from the street could glance at her, even accidentally.

It turned out that her teeth did need a thorough cleaning.

Chapter Thirty-Six

In the Raptor's Clutches

"Yes, sir, I've got eyes on him," the sniper reported. "Yes, sir. He's in the furniture store. He's in my sights, sir; I could take the shot."

"Good Lord, man. Stand down!" Ellie chirped over the radio. "We don't even know if it's Ash." Ellie was a little exasperated by these new team members. They had spent too much time in the field dishing out harsh measures in antiterrorist campaigns. They didn't have the finesse for these cat-and-mouse games.

The mic went hot. "Standing down, safety on."

Ellie glanced at the other guards with her in the news van. She knew she shouldn't call them guards, but that's what they felt like. "You guys know the goal is ideally to take this guy alive, right? The man has a list of murders an arm long, and there's probably another arm we don't even know about. It would be nice to close some of those cases legitimately. I'm pretty sure we'd make a lot of local jurisdictions happy to get a notice that we captured their killer and closed their case from a decade ago."

"Don't blame us for Johnson. That man has an itchy trigger finger. Normally serves him pretty well."

"No kidding, he's saved my life several times with that twitch."

"Always scratchy, but never dashing."

"To twitch is to live."

Ellie rolled her eyes, "Now you guys are just making stuff up."

"You'll never know."

She couldn't help but chuckle. They were morbid men, but they had humor on their side. Perhaps that was the best you could hope for after being through what she was sure most of these men had been through. Sucked into the FBI's elite team was half of their story, it didn't even begin to cover that most of them had extensive military special forces experience. Johnson, the man getting the brunt of the jokes, had served eight years, which included four tours. Ellie had read all their files. Most of their military service was redacted; she swore she saw more blacked-out content than readable material.

One of them looked at her. "Ms. Lopez?"

"Ellie."

He stopped and then blinked. Continuing, "Ms. Ellie Lopez. Do you think it's him?"

"Yes. I think that's our man. He fits our understanding of the man and is aligned with our profile. He must be in his early forties. He looks adequately distinguished; he'd have no problem getting into any venue. Not dressed to be flashy, he's subtle and easily forgotten. Just the regular guy next door. That's exactly the person we think we are looking for. We might catch this guy. I would have expected him to look a bit more like the composite or photo after we aged it, but he slightly resembles it, so that's further proof if you ask me."

Ellie looked puzzled, though, as she went on. "I would have suspected it would have been harder to pinpoint him, though. He is being careful, but the Ash we know doesn't normally make any mistakes at all."

"I don't know, Ms. Lopez."

Ellie was about to interject and correct him again, but he continued before she was able.

"Ms. Ellie Lopez. I'm pretty sure he knows we are some kind of law enforcement; you'll note he's standing well out of our view there. He avoided us easily. We wouldn't even know he was there right now if Johnson didn't have eyes on him and we didn't have our cameras set up. He doesn't know we got snipers on the buildings, but he scouted everything else out. And he did it quickly and with what can only be described as military precision. I don't know if you have military training in your profile of the Ashen Horse, but this man looks and feels like he has substantial military experience."

Ellie was nodding. "That's good feedback. So, he isn't being particularly sloppy?"

"No, ma'am. We just got lucky to get eyes on him. We started running his face through all the facial recognition, and as soon as we got it on feed, we shall see if it springs anything."

Ellie didn't look hopeful. "I doubt we'll get an identification. Maybe if we are lucky, but something tells me this guy has stayed off the books. Unless... If your military theory is correct and the facial recognition combs through twenty years of military records."

The men exchanged glances amongst themselves but didn't offer any further comment. "Typical," Ellie thought. She wasn't sure if she meant that about men or if she meant that about military men. She decided it was much the same either way. Both were troublesome nuisances to all decent women everywhere.

The news van was acting as their remote command center. It held four people comfortably and ensured they were onsite if anything was going to happen. They were also overshadowed by two snipers on the roofs of opposite buildings from Mr. Wilson's residence. Usually, they wouldn't have four of them in here, but a shift change was approaching, so two were coming, and two were leaving. Ellie didn't usually take a rotation but she felt disconnected

The Ashen Horse

in the command center, so she volunteered to spend the evening onsite. In contrast, one of the other military brutes spent some time ironing out personal issues.

The command center was in a house two streets over. The FBI had bought both of the houses at the same time. It was a solid setup; the command center was entirely out of view and behind another row of houses. Agents could come and go and work out of it without any detection or anyone noticing, as long as they weren't entirely flamboyant with it. It was far enough away for no connection between the houses, yet quickly close enough for any radio communication and video feeds.

The only slight negative with both the houses they were running the sting out of was that they were close to other homes buried in modern urban suburbia. They also had a fair bit of foliage around them on the interior sides of the properties. Dr. Wilson's house faced a city street lined with businesses, including the furniture store and dental office.

This was also why it was decided early in the process that snipers and cameras would supplement the entire operation. There is good visibility throughout the area and enough openings to have solid coverage. Plus, the panic room should make this as secure an operation as hoped. Ellie had voiced many of these thoughts out loud.

The men looked at her, then looked at each other. Then, looked back at her.

"Well?" she said. "What are your thoughts?"

One of them finally spoke. "The plan is sound. The location is secure and well-covered, with a solid perimeter. The people inside have a solid escape plan, or in this case I guess it would be more cover. It's safer than most of the operations we normally do. This guy doesn't look like anything special anyway."

Another man was still watching him on the feed. "I don't know, Jolly. I'd wager he has seen the devil. He walks, acts, and has a smoothness that only comes from when a man…."

He glanced at Ellie. Then shrugged. She leaned back in her chair, casually waiting for him to continue. But he just left the statement hanging. She was twitching, desperately wanting to ask who the devil was. But she thought she better let that one lie where it was. Instead, she approached a different angle. "Jolly?"

"Yes, ma'am. That is a nickname given to me from my time in the military. It is 'Jolly Roger,' strictly speaking, but it has been shortened over the years to Jolly."

"Jolly Roger?"

"Uh, well, yes, miss. The pirate flag, the skull and crossbones."

Their nicknames weren't in their files. However, she had gotten the sense that they weren't as much nicknames as aliases for these men. She suspected that they probably went by their aliases more than their native name in most of their circles. She wanted to ask more questions, but again, she realized she was out of her element with these men. That made her nervous, but she also welcomed the opportunity that she really might learn something gratifying over the next several days or weeks.

A lightbulb flashed in her mind. She could use them. They thought just like Ash thought. Why hadn't she gone and talked to the right people before now? She sprung the question too aggressively, but she couldn't help herself. "If you were him, what would your next move be?"

"That's you, Golf," Jolly said. He saw her bewilderment and added, "He's the group's tactician."

Before Golf could answer, the radios squawked.

"Negative on any ID, team," Tim said. He was drinking coffee in the command center.

"It can never be easy, can it?" Ellie said over the radio.

"It would take all the fun out of it," Tim said. "Although, a break in this case wouldn't be remiss. But, I guess, we can't complain, we might have eyes on the man. Are you guys still watching the feed?"

"Yep, we have eyes on him. He's still watching, although he's browsing more now and tactfully watching. Whenever customers come around, he pretends to be interested in the merchandise."

"Good deal, we have it up on one of our twenty monitors here. And it's recording and going into the case logs. Reach out to us if you guys need anything or see anything. Over and out." Tim put the radio back on the desk, scanned monitors, and sipped his coffee.

Ellie glanced back at the men in the van with her. One looked like a meathead, all muscle and no brain. But that one was apparently Golf, the strategist.

Jolly was clean-shaven and had solid lean muscle; he looked like he could fit in any boardroom anywhere. But she had seen him handle a gun on the range before they took up their post weeks ago. He could drop a man at eighty yards with his pistol, and from what she saw, he could get it done on the draw. His file implied he had earned the nickname, but there had been quite a bit of redaction about what went down in Kabul. But being a pirate might be the least of it.

The last man looked like a homeless delinquent. He hadn't said much the entire time she had been around him. But every single one of the men deferred to him whenever he was going to make a point. Occasionally, one of them would look at him, and he would casually shrug or nod or simply say "Yes" or "No." She sensed he would be their leader if he wanted the role, but he appeared to shy away. She suspected this man had saved all their lives on multiple occasions, and the respect was so apparent that it almost had a tangible presence.

He noticed her staring as she was lost in thought. He guessed what she was thinking, and although he was wrong, his comment was enlightening. "Jolly Roger, or Jolly," he said while pointing. His hand motioned to the other man, "That's Golf." He pointed to monitor one and continued, "Johnson is on Roof A. Beaks is our other sniper," gesturing to monitor two. "I'm...." He paused for a moment, considering his words. "Please understand that we didn't pick these names; they take shape over time...." He took another moment and ended up shaking his head. "Let's just say they take shape over time in less than desirable conditions." He looked intently at her until she nodded her understanding. He nodded in return. "Anyway, I'm Ghost."

Jolly laughed, "Every time you tell it like that man, I can't help but remember Coup." All three men laughed. Jolly grabbed the radio, "Beaks, you remember Coup?"

Johnson was heard laughing. "What lies are you telling in that van?"

"No one could ever forget Coup." Beaks put in. "Dude was insane. Who's crazy enough to count coup in modern warfare?"

Johnson was still chuckling, "You remember the one time he slapped the one's ass? He tore out of there like a banshee from hell was flying after him."

Beaks laughed, "If that hajji could shoot, he would have died ten times over just that one time."

It was Golf's turn on the radio. "Oh, I'm pretty sure that hajji could shoot. Coup just knew how to run. As I recall, a couple did graze him that day. That dipshit zigzagged better than a snake greased in oil. How many times did we see him dodge bullets?"

Ghost agreed, "It was more than a few. More than what was healthy."

The men went silent, all of them smiling and shaking their heads. Remembering the best memories. Ellie stayed silent. Something told her she shouldn't rush the moment, and she had enough self-awareness to know that she shouldn't ask what happened to Coup. In this case, it seemed better not to know.

She did want to know the answer to her question, though, so she asked it again. She was going to ask Ghost; perhaps he wasn't the tactical man, but something told her she would value his opinion. She stopped herself from changing the group dynamic, though, and instead, she asked the group of all three men. She stated, "So if this is the Ashen Horse, and you were him. What would you do?"

Jolly went first. "Probably walk away."

"Huh?"

"He knows we aren't news people. He might not know we are federal agents, but he knows we are some kind of law. If Ash is as good as you all think he is, then there's too much heat here. I wouldn't risk anything; I'd be driving out of Dodge as fast as possible and not looking back."

Golf nodded. "Perhaps. But you assume that he thinks we are here for him. It's as likely that he thinks we are here for the professor." Golf nodded to the screen. "That man thinks we are watching the house. He's making sure we don't notice him, but he's not suspicious of us and fully knows we are here. He's written us off already. How often does he even care about the van? No, he's only paying attention to the house and its surroundings."

Golf looked at the monitors and scanned the scenery that could be seen from the monitors they could view in the van. "He's planning his entrance right now. No, this man isn't going anywhere. He'll enter. There are two options: he'll sneak in through that shrubbery at the back of the house and go in the back way. Or he'll play it casual, walk right up to the front door, and quickly gain entry, like breaking the door glass and unlocking it swiftly. It would be barely noticeable even if someone were watching him do it. If he did it quick enough."

"We'll have him if he continues as he is going the way he is," Golf concluded.

Jolly nodded to Ellie. "Our tactician," is all he said.

Ellie wasn't going to let this opportunity slide away from her. "What are our areas of compromise? What should we be concerned about?"

Golf didn't hesitate. "Johnson and Beaks."

Ghost nodded and added, "The cameras."

Golf glanced over to Ghost. "Yes, those too."

Ellie didn't understand. "Our snipers and cameras?"

Golf was nodding. "Well, it's more than that, but those are the quickest visual cues. If Ash detects anything that suggests something is afoot, such as we are monitoring the outside of the house or that there is surveillance or personnel, that wouldn't make sense. If he detects anything that doesn't make sense or can't be easily rationalized or mentally explained." He paused. "We are in trouble if he notices anything that doesn't make sense. The obvious two in our current environment are our well-hidden cameras, and if he ever spotted Johnson or Beaks, it's over. He'll bounce immediately."

Ellie considered for a minute. "How well hidden is well hidden?"

"He won't find our cameras, and he won't see our snipers," Ghost said.

"You think he is one of you, or at least you suspect," Ellie said. "And yet, you are sure he wouldn't see what you would see?"

Ghost laughed. "That's how I know he won't find our cameras. None of us could find these cameras."

Finally, Ellie understood. "Ahh... well then. Good news for us, I guess."

Jolly smiled. "Very good news indeed."

Ellie was filled with a deep sense of curiosity. These men really knew each other. By all appearances, they had all known each other for a long time. "How long have you all worked together?"

"We all served together in the Middle East, some of us in different teams," Ghost replied. "Johnson and Beaks are Green Berets. Well, now ex-Green Berets. They covered us repeatedly while we went on missions or guarded them. The three of us are, or were, Army Rangers. We are now somewhat of a unit and stay together because we work well together. But we know the guys on the other shifts as well and have worked with them overseas and stateside. There's also a mix in those units: a couple of Navy Seals and two Marine Recons, which are their snipers."

"Isn't Gypsy a Raider?" asked Golf. Then he corrected himself, "Wasn't Gypsy a Raider?"

Ghost nodded. "I do believe so. Wide range of diversity in the team." He smiled. "I'm pretty sure Gypsy would say he still is a Raider and would knock out anyone's teeth if they said otherwise."

Golf summarized the sentiment. "Once. Always."

All the men nodded.

Ellie thought she understood, but the confusion on her face must have shown more than she suspected.

"The three of us, plus our attached snipers," Jolly said, pointing to the cameras that showed the two men entirely hidden in their surroundings. "We were all part of Team Raptor. Once a member, always a member."

Ghost looked at each man in turn. "Once a brother, always a brother."

A nod was exchanged between the men, and then they went back to watching the mysterious man in the furniture store.

If Ellie didn't understand before, now she did.

Chapter Thirty-Seven

Cat and Mouse

She had faithfully returned to the same coffee shop and ordered her usual white chocolate mocha. The barista hadn't lied; they had a special ingredient that made it exceptional. She thought it was a mix between nutmeg and cinnamon, but she couldn't entirely place it.

Now, back in her hotel room, she was watching the FBI camera feeds on her monitors while sipping her coffee. Three laptops sprawled over the desk, each extending to three additional monitors. She had to bring in two folding tables she picked up from a local hardware store to set up her own observation post.

Four nights ago, she had snuck near the rear of the professor's property, deep in the shrubbery of one of his neighbors, and planted a device to relay all radio signals onto the internet, dumped into her personal cloud repository. That turned out to work great. The device intercepted all the radio traffic and uploaded it to the internet. What didn't work great was that all the audio content was scrambled.

At the time of her failed audio attempt, she figured that whoever these guys were, they were using some detailed end-to-end encryption. That meant the team was using real hardware, not the stuff bought at the local electronic stores. It ruled out most corporations, who would have gone for a standard commercial product, which she probably could have worked around.

It surprised her how much she had learned in four days. She now knew it was the FBI; she knew the big brother was watching.

"You must be ultra-careful," she told herself for the tenth time. After failing to get audio, she started scouting all the surrounding streets and roads. It had taken two days of making careful observations and driving through with multiple rental cars and several different disguises before she found the house that had to be their command center. No one was guarding the house, and she observed the same men from the news van come in and out. For all their care in being circumspect around the van and always putting on a good front in monitoring the home, they weren't guarding their command center at all. She watched it for two days, tracking every person to go in and out, and when an opportunity presented itself where no one was inside, she snuck into the back of the house.

They might have protected the communication when it was in flight, but once it landed on the wire, all their encryption was shed. She installed three small devices rapidly. One device replicated everything that was existing on the network. One was a simple, compact computer, which was encrypted in no less than 10 different ways. The third was a cellular router, which transferred all the data into the cloud over a standard cell connection.

She tucked her goodies in with the rest of their gear in the mass of equipment and cables stuffed under the desk. It was such a rat's nest of cabling; it would be impossible ever to decipher her added equipment until they went to break it all apart.

She smoothed her hands together, rinsing off the dust from the cables as she completed tucking in the final box behind the maze of wires. It felt good that at least this phase of the operation had gone smoothly. A resonating exhale shuddered out of her as she took a moment to relax and take in a minor accomplishment that she knew would pay exceptional dividends.

A scratching came from the front door, and her head swiveled. Every muscle in her body tensed as she moved like a jaguar. The key twisted in the lock as she slinked for the rear door. She had left it partially open so she would be ready to slip out. Years of training had taught her never to close or block an exit.

She wasn't breathing as her ears picked up the front door opening and the casual chatter of the two people entering the house. There might have been moments in her life where she had exhibited more stealth, but she swore she closed that door more carefully than any door she ever had.

Her body carefully slithered into the backyard and around the side of the house. She bounced between the outside wall of the house and the fence to the neighbor's property. Her feet leveraged the momentum to fling herself over into the neighbor's side of the wall. The following minutes, what felt like hours, were spent carefully extraditing herself from the situation.

But now, several days later, she sat back, watching the camera feeds that the FBI were watching. And she casually listened to the chatter between the snipers and the van crew. However, to their credit, they kept the conversation to a bare minimum—another slow and savory sip of the coffee. The command center and the van crew talked a whole lot more. Then again, they thought everything was entirely encrypted and secure, so there was no reason to communicate openly.

She learned more intel in the first hour watching these feeds than she might have in a week casing the place. She hadn't realized how lucky she had been to avoid getting noticed by the snipers. Indeed, if they were paying more attention, they would have gotten some insights into a strange woman's multiple sightings. However, her disguises may have ultimately paid off. She looked entirely different every time she went near the professor's house.

"I shouldn't think of him as the professor anymore. Yet, I still do. Perhaps he will always be the professor."

She learned they were looking for her. This whole ploy was to bring down the infamous Ashen Horse. It was an insane amount of setup to take down one person, especially someone who usually only took out people who had it coming. Her blood had boiled the entire first day when she had discovered she was the target. The rage was still a razor wire, and it burned white hot. Bellows worked slowly and constantly to keep the anger at a steady white heat.

"I just took out one of the largest drug kingpins in the Americas, a kingpin these apes didn't even know was a player. Now they think they can eliminate me."

The anger was fueling upon itself and kept blazing hot. After Molly, her anger seemed different. Before Molly, it would have been a loose cannon, ready to blast asunder any that stood in its way. But now, now it was a simmering boil, a steady heat that raged but was closely controlled and tempered.

Or perhaps it was the information that had been learned. What had tempered the fires of her anger to a manageable level was when she discovered they thought this mystery man was Ash. Watching and taking in information over the last day, she had learned they had no idea who Ash was. Who she was! On the one hand, it was incredibly rewarding and encouraging that they were entirely clueless. On the other hand, it was surprisingly insulting. This whole stunt was a blind Hail Mary, trying to catch any mouse they could with a broad trap.

Just a couple of hours ago, she found out who the mystery man was. It was the same handsome man she sat beside on the plane. The same man she had later seen in the furniture store. It appeared to her that he was very carefully and with a high level of suspicion investigating the house.

Interestingly, it looked like he discounted the news van.

It was odd to her that he so readily ignored it, as the people in the news van were very obviously not news people.

The piece that didn't make sense was how, in the world, the feds thought this trap would spring on her. Or rather, how this would catch the Ashen Horse. They had taken to calling her persona Ash, but it still didn't make sense that this trap would attract Ash.

There's no way that a randomly published news story pulls in a random killer; worse still, it was for a specific killer they were looking for. There was something she was missing here. She was supposed to be here, but there was no reason she should be here. That would keep her up at night; it had been keeping her up at night. It also made her wonder again if she shouldn't get on a plane and leave this situation as fast as possible.

She finished the coffee and looked at the bottom of the cup with sadness. It seemed like such a shame whenever any cup of coffee became empty. She took a shameless attempt to slurp just a little more out. Alas, it truly was gone. It just meant she had to get some real work done. At least the project for today would be fun, and it would be safe. Safe was going to be the critical word moving forward.

She spun away from her new monitoring station to the hotel bed and started unboxing the two full-feature paintball guns she had picked up at the local hobby shop. It took a minute to get them together and functional.

As she worked, she grumbled to herself, "Some assembly required, my foot. Practically had to fabricate this thing." She hefted both up like machine guns and let a few rounds fly out over her balcony. "Little buggers got some kick to them, though; these should do nicely."

Having the guns unboxed, she went to the next component. Darts. She removed the darts from their packaging and started doing some initial shaping. Hands working methodically, she began to do minor fabrication work on the darts. Then she did go on to some fabrication on the paintball guns as well. Somewhere in her work, she started to hum a random child lullaby.

She worked quickly but carefully, now and then stopping to listen to any new chatter coming through the network. Her eyes continuously drifted to the monitors, and she checked to ensure there weren't faces she didn't recognize. She mentally cataloged every person that moved through every frame. She would need to note any anomalies or abnormalities.

There was no room for mistakes on this job. It wasn't like other assignments she had delved into. Usually, the worst thing that could happen was that she didn't successfully kill her target, or perhaps she didn't get a clean kill. On this assignment, the stakes couldn't get higher.

Her mind tossed as it often did as she worked, but eventually, she shot the paintball gun into a pillow in her room. Observing the result, she went back to tinkering, making more adjustments. Her mind wandered to life choices and how every road leads to every decision. Could her life have moved her somewhere other than right here and right now, at this moment? She fired the gun again. She nodded, picked up the other one, and started tweaking it. Did she have a choice, or did fate put her here right now? Was walking away really an option, or was that just another delusion of choice that didn't really exist? She didn't know.

She fired gun number two. She cursed audibly, grabbed a new dart, and went to work. Perhaps she was trying to rationalize her decision. She wanted to know if that was indeed the case, though. She had realized consciously or maybe even subconsciously that once she discovered they were here to take her down, she had decided to end them all. Was that unjust, or was that deliberate justice? She didn't know. The decision had been made that she would bring her namesake to bear. Was that her decision, or was it simply fate? If they sought the Ashen Horse, she would let them have him. He would ride forth.

She fired gun number two again. It went better, but the alterations have not been entirely done yet. She glanced up at the monitors again; she spoke to herself softly while she stopped to look at them.

"When the Lamb broke the fourth seal, I heard the voice of the fourth living creature saying, 'Come!' I looked, and behold, an ashen horse; and the one who sat on it had the name Death, and Hades was following with him. Authority was given to them over a fourth of the earth, to kill with sword, and famine, and plague, and by the wild animals of the earth."

She was somewhat saddened to realize that, for the first time ever, she was preparing to go to war. She would bring every inch of her skill, fire, and passion against these people. She fired the paintball gun again and the dart flew true. They would die. All of them would die!

Her work continued as she fiddled with the weapons, attaching her wireless cameras to the paintball guns. Then, she worked on the remote controls for both of them. That piece was a little trickier, but she needed to fire them simultaneously and directly on target. And, perhaps most importantly, entirely remotely. After several more firing sessions and several cameras for firing adjustments, she finally had two working remote-controlled blow guns.

She ideally wanted to be able to load two or three darts in each, but with her time constraints, she would have to make sure she didn't miss the one that would be loaded. She took the four darts she had shaped and all her throwing knives and dropped them in the prepared mixture. It was a mix of elephant tranquilizer and a sleep powder, and just for a certain amount of spice, there was a bit of heroin mixed in. She had hollowed out the darts, so they should be full of the poison. A full-grown horse might live through getting injected with the amount these would be carrying, but it wasn't likely a man would.

Tomorrow, she would put them in place to be able to hit

the snipers. Her remote-control apparatus would give her some functional mobility. The range she achieved should allow her to deploy them outside where the snipers might detect her approach, or at least that was the goal. She didn't want to put them out yet, but she knew she had to be ready. The FBI seemed convinced this other man would try to go after the professor, and when he made his move, she had to be prepared.

Her mind still worked as she moved on to her next project. Did it have to come to this?

"Did I choose this path? Could I have walked away? Could I walk away right now? What if I let the FBI catch this man, and they pin everything on him?"

She shook her head; he wouldn't know anything. Eventually, the truth would come out. Unless they could get him to confess to dozens of killings, which he knew nothing about. Eventually, even the cops would know there would be too many holes in his stories. And that's assuming they could even lead him down that road.

She shook her head. No, there wasn't any choice here. The path was a single path, one way. The forks she kept trying to find did not exist. There was a clear direction; it only had one outcome of any relevance. Either they would be dead, or she would be. Perhaps it was destiny; maybe it was fate. Possibly, something was pulling her strings, something outside of her control. She wasn't sure, and she didn't understand. But she was trying to.

She was being persuaded that her path was set before her. She would do what she could do, what she must do. That was flowing forward and being decisive. And as she did so, she was riding the winds of her destiny.

Chapter Thirty-Eight

Goodnight, Sweetheart, Goodnight

His planning had been exceptional. He had waited for the night when the news van only had two people in it. Their shifts were stupidly predictable. Of course, he had spent two weeks confirming the schedule. Only two of the cops would be in the van tonight, staring blindly at the house, bored. Wasting their time and everyone else's tax dollars. He shook his head, amateurs from end to end, these people.

He had initially wanted to just walk in the front door. It was always his preferred approach and usually the safest way. But with the van having a clear view of the front door, that wasn't an option. So, he had ensured he understood the available routes, including escape routes. The easiest way to avoid the van's prying eyes was to go in the back.

He snuck along the hedges, well out of sight and encased in greenery. He moved slowly, eyes alert and scanning everything. No sound, no noise. Pressure stepped every foot pace to ensure no leaves rustled, and no twigs snapped. This whole thing would be a waste if he alerted people. Otherwise, he should have just gone with the front door approach. A pizza or package delivery guy was always a perfect way to get someone to come to the front door. It was sadly predictable.

It felt like it had taken him half the night to get to the

The Ashen Horse

door. But his slow patience had only taken twenty minutes, which was still excruciatingly slow through the very short transition between the two streets and the lines of houses. His progression finally paid off as it brought him to the back door. He bent down slowly to pick the lock.

His body frozen, he paused to listen. Best to make sure no one was up and moving in the house. Silence. His hands moved to pull out his lockpicks, and he went rigid yet again. He thought he heard something. He knelt and pushed his back against the side of the house. Like a phantom, he melted into his surroundings and waited, his ears and eyes straining for anything.

His mind must be playing tricks on him. He thought he might be getting too old for this. It might be time to hang up the guns after this one. His nerves were usually a bit more stable than this. He felt edgy. He rarely had a bad feeling about these jobs, but this one, he had an unnerving premonition turned on. His hands moved to the door to start his work for what seemed like the third time. The door handle turned blessedly soundlessly and opened into a pitch-black house.

He picked up his jaw, which he was sure was flopping in the wind. Who leaves the door unlocked? He shook his head and thought, "These Montanans are crazy. Why would they not lock their doors? What madness is this?"

The walk through the house was as painfully slow as his approach had been. It looked like he was entering the dining area attached to the kitchen, which was itself off the living room. It was the living room that held the front door access. He moved to the island in the middle of the kitchen, crouching down to listen. He closed his eyes and gave his eyes time to adjust to the new, thicker darkness. The worst possible thing would be to ram into some furniture and alert the entire household of his presence. So, he waited.

He knew she would be in here. She was here more than she wasn't. The young skirt was the new toy for the professor. She had come to the house late that afternoon, and he was certain she hadn't left. He didn't want to kill the young, presumably innocent girl. But there was nothing for it. She would be collateral damage. He could not fathom what would possess a young woman to get involved with a man who was under suspicion of rape and womanizing. He didn't understand it, but then he often found people's passions and delusions to be a mystery.

The search of the house continued. He looked down the hallway and identified what he presumed to be two bedrooms and a bathroom. That must mean the master was upstairs.

Spinning to move for the upstairs, he slowly stopped and considered. "Better make sure," he thought. "They should be empty rooms, but best to make sure." He turned around and started for the bedrooms on this level.

He had opened the door to the first room, and now he silently stared at her. She was sleeping soundly on the bed, just wearing her bra and panties. It's probably how she slept every night. Some of the blankets had fallen off, leaving her half uncovered; it looked as if she had tossed and turned during the night. The full moon glistened off her black skin and lit the room in a light hue. He kept watching her, mesmerized by how at peace she looked.

"She is remarkably beautiful," he thought. The scene and the moment, its tranquility, had taken him. He twitched his eyes and chastised himself, "Beauty is in the eye of the beholder; perhaps I've just become taken with her over the last weeks of watching her."

He slowly pulled out his silenced pistol. He kept watching her breathe in and out, a soft and steady rhythm. "I could just leave her," he considered. "She won't hear me upstairs. I'll be gone before she ever knows anything happened. She is sleeping down here. The professor is in the doghouse even with her. She'd never even know anything happened until tomorrow. There's no way she'd ever know

The Ashen Horse

I was here. She can't identify anyone."

As he watched her sleep, his mind ruffled through more and more reasons to walk away and leave her be. He tucked the gun back behind his belt and slowly started moving to leave the room. As he was slipping out the door, he hesitated mid-step. The breathing rhythm had changed. "Shit," was all he thought. He whipped out his pistol and had three shots fired into her chest before he finished putting his foot down.

His mood darkened in an instant. It was sadness or anger that pushed against him. He felt something, and that was dangerous. He took a deep breath and let out a sigh, the only noise he had made in the last hour. His head shook, and all he could think was how wasteful it had been.

"Too young to die like this. An entire life ahead of her. The love and joy she could have brought to someone. The love and joy she brought to others. And now the sorrow of those who will be deprived of her. Such a waste."

His mind was angered. He knew that wasn't good. "Gotta get ahold of myself," he thought. But really, all that kept going through his mind was that this was just such a waste. He walked up to the young woman and checked her pulse. She was gone, which was expected. He grabbed the blankets that had slipped off her and brought them up to cover her. "The least I can do, poor girl."

The disappointment ripped a piece of his heart away. He truly hated collateral damage. It was always like this, just throwing lives to the Grim Reaper. How many times had he seen it in war? He had long lost count. The civilians always got caught in the crossfire. They died or sometimes lived the worse for it. Their lives were almost discounted more readily than the soldiers. Worse still, the civilians were just as likely to try to kill you as trained soldiers in modern urban warfare. He might have lost count of the civilians he had killed, but his dreams never had.

He took a few moments to knead his hand threw her hair and straighten it out. His mind repeated how it was a waste and how it was just the least he could do for her. His head shook one last time, and he let out one more muffled sigh. Then he turned and abruptly left the room.

He took another moment in the hallway. He knew he had to get his head on right; this was no time to be sentimental. He was here to kill a man, and he always completed the mission. He knew in his soul that it would have been so much easier if it wasn't a woman. The women and children stayed with you; they always stayed with you. He would never forget this girl's face. He knew he never would. Another mystery he would never understand was how the faces of the dead could haunt a man.

His eyes were closed as he wanted to adjust to the dimmer lights of the interior once again now that he was out of the moonlight. As he waited, he was utterly silent; the loudest thing he could hear was the beating of his own heart. His methodical search continued as his eyes came alive again in the darkness.

The second bedroom was empty. He said a small prayer of thanks for that. He had been terrified that there would be a child or something in there. His mind still was not where it needed to be. His relief was so palpable that it significantly restored his fortitude. Standing in the second bedroom, he took a moment to take stock, resolving to the task and returning to a state of focus. It was time to get this night's work complete.

He moved like a specter, wisping through the house—slow and steady, like a mist drifting across a barren landscape. A silence went with him, almost as if he absorbed the sound that should be there. He stalked his prey, a leopard preparing to pounce at the turning of midnight.

He took in a breath as he approached the stairs. Stairs and their squeaking could always cause problems. He knew absolute care had to be taken on stairs. Each step was an act of extreme care as he cautiously ascended each stair, choosing the weight and force applied at every pace. It added

The Ashen Horse

to the delay he didn't want to tolerate. But as he reminded himself, this moment was not the time to give up the caution he had been deploying throughout the night.

It took some doing, but he ascended the top of the stairs. He could see a short hallway to the bedroom. The bedroom door was slightly ajar. At least that should make for an easier entrance. He continued his cautious approach, finally reaching the door.

Shifting the force of his motion, he put minimal pressure on the door that he could muster, and slowly, it began to open. The sufferance he showed was impressive. Everything hinged on not making noise. He was controlled and ready. His left hand pushed the door open, and his right hand pulled the pistol out. The door opened just enough that he could slip in silently.

As he entered, his pistol came up and leveled on the center of the bed. His finger twitched, ready to fire, as he slowly got closer. The moonlight must be cloaked behind the clouds as the room was not as light as the other. He still could not clearly see. But an eerie feeling, the same that he had felt throughout the night, let him know something seemed off. His hand lowered slightly, shifting the pistol out of his line of sight so he could see more clearly. He wasn't sure what he was seeing; in his confusion, he brought the gun down to his side.

Moonlight glistened into the room as it bent its rays around the cloud that had damped its shining. The room glowed with a soft hue. The luminescence tinged the bed. He finally saw what was on the bed. He stood, shocked. He didn't understand.

The professor lay there, uncovered, in his boxers. He was well-muscled for a professor; it was clear this man had exercised regularly for years. But he didn't notice that as much as the gaping wounds that were across his midriff. The blood was splattered across the bedsheets. His eyes were struck with just the gore of it. It took him a moment to scan the rest of the scene. Dr. John Wilson's throat was sliced cleanly to the bone.

His mind worked frantically. What was he looking at? "She must have killed him. That's the only thing that makes any sense. The girl killed him, that's why she was sleeping in the other room. But why was she even still here in the house? None of this makes any sense. Surely she would have left if she had killed him?"

He stood there staring at the body. There was no need to check his pulse; the professor's heart would never beat again. He didn't understand what had happened here, but he did understand the job was done. There was no point in lingering, which just put him at undue risk. It was time for him to make a timely exit.

He looked at the baffling scene one more time and then started to turn to leave the room. As he turned, he caught movement out of the corner of his eye. Years of muscle memory kicked in, and his body moved. He immediately started to raise his weapon on the flutter of movement.

"Stop." One simple word, but with it came a command that held the weight of an army. The voice came with a surprising amount of force, issued in a quiet, muffled tone. It was a woman's voice. She didn't whisper, but she also didn't speak normally. It was a hushed tone, but it resonated with complete command.

"I said stop. I'd do so if I were you. If you twitch a muscle, you die here and now. I assure you, you will envy the man on the bed."

He became rooted where he stood and slowly lowered his hands.

Chapter Thirty-Nine

The Ashen Horse

"Who are you?" was all she said.

Right over the top of her, he said, "What do you want?"

"I want to know who you are." The heat in her voice was palpable.

"I'm not going to tell you who I am."

"I recall you being much more friendly on the plane."

He blinked a few times, then really looked at her. No, it couldn't be. "You?" He looked harder. "It might be her or you. We sat next to each other on the plane. You've done something; you look remarkably different."

"Who are you?"

"Listen, I'm flattered you want to know who I am, but honestly, I think it's best neither of us know anything about the other person now. I also think we should get out of here. There's no point in staying now that the target is dead." He started to turn to leave the room.

"You move, you die."

"You don't intend to kill me. What would it do for you?"

She very carefully leaned over the bed and fired a shot past his face into the wall behind him. The silencer on the gun reverberated a small shockwave into the room. Her voice was utterly calm. "I highly recommend you don't question my motives here. You will answer all my questions.

You won't move again. If you desire to see the light of day again, you will not begin to underestimate me or believe you can disobey me for a minute. I will not give you a second chance; there will be no other warnings. Move again and die."

The blood drained a bit from his face. He was controlled, though; this was just another obstacle to overcome. He felt a little helpless in the situation, making him uncomfortable. He was used to storming the fort, breaking down the walls, and solving the issue. To be paralyzed was not his style, nor was it fitting. He flinched; he wasn't paralyzed; he was captive. The worst thing imaginable.

"What do you want, then?"

"Who are you?"

"I'm not going to tell you who I am."

"Why are you here?"

"My objective was to kill the sleazeball professor. He's dead; I don't need to be here anymore."

She was getting testy. "You are making this harder than it has to be. Why was killing Dr. Wilson your objective?"

"I accepted the contract to kill him. Is that not also why you are here?" He stopped a minute, and then he did get genuinely concerned. He had never encountered another killer on a job before. She wanted the gig; she definitely would kill him for the promised two hundred grand that was on the table for eliminating the professor. "Look, I don't need the money that bad. You can have the contract. Feel free to submit the claim. I have no issues walking away from this one. Besides, it looks like you did get here first."

"Awfully generous of you. What contract?"

"Now you are just wasting both of our time."

She steadied her aim.

"For the love, fine," he said. "I accepted the contract on the darknet group, For Hire something. I don't go there often, but this particular contract was getting some circulation like it was being... I don't know what you'd call it. It was like it was getting promoted."

"For Hire Cleaners?"

"Yeah, that's it."

"Promoted?"

"Like I said, I don't know. It was getting some chatter; it seemed like a couple of different areas of the internet, private groups were mentioning it. It was kind of hard to miss."

"That wasn't suspicious to you?"

"No one else was looking at the opportunity, it seemed like an easy and quick deal."

"What do you know about the guys in the van outside?"

"The news van?"

"Now, who's wasting our time? You scouted them for days; you knew their schedule. You are here tonight because you knew they were understaffed. It was easy to know when you would strike. You know they are cops, at least; you spent too much time tracking them not to know that much."

"How long have you been following me?"

"Days after we exited the plane, I found you scouting this site. After that, it was easy to tail you to your vehicle. I've had a tracker on you ever since."

He appeared genuinely surprised. "Damn."

"How much do you know about our friends in the van?"

"They are cops; they appear more than staters or the local variety. I'd assumed they were potentially feds, local Montana agents, trying to build a case or catch him in a slip-up."

"Entirely incorrect, but fair enough. They are here to catch the person who tries to murder the professor."

"That's impossible; they were too obvious at watching the professor as a suspect."

"As it turns out, it is simultaneously a pretty obvious and clever disguise. You walked right into their trap and didn't question it. So also quite effective, wouldn't you say?"

He nodded. "If half of what you said is true, then touché. I was played for sure. Then why aren't they breaking into this place right now?"

"Not your concern." She thought for a second. She did need to know who this man was. She figured she would try one more time. "One more question: who are you?"

"You think we are friendly enough now to be on a first-name basis."

"I'd really like to know who you are," was all she said.

"Well, I have no real desire to share that information."

She moved quickly. She swung her body around the bed as much as possible without disturbing the bed and fired four times. The unknown man wasn't prepared or ready. He had relaxed as the conversation had carried on. He had not suspected it; at the end of the conversation, he believed they were both walking out alive.

She spoke quietly to herself, "Poor soul. You were a dead man the minute you walked into this house; you just didn't know it. Certainly, after you saw me and knew me, there was no way you would live."

She stood there a moment and checked her firing angles. They were a little sloppy, but they could do. She shoved the professor's body around on the bed. It now looked like he had moved around and tried to move, potentially off the bed, but didn't get far with his head almost severed.

She had used the professor's gun to kill the unknown man. She had recovered it from the nightstand immediately after killing him. After inspecting it, she knew it would get the job done for this. The silencer made for a charming touch. She would have to work quickly, but hopefully, she didn't have to scramble. It would be a great benefit if the weapon were the agent's service weapon. Small details mattered.

She didn't know the professor was a federal agent for sure but suspected he was. They had tried to bait her, very specifically. This whole endeavor was a trap for her, making this man most likely a specialized, trained agent.

She looked at the body on the bed and whispered, "You

put too much faith in your snipers, sir. Now you are all dead for the folly." She fitted the gun she had used to kill the unknown man into the professor's hand. She checked the angles from where she had positioned him now on the edge of the bed. She nodded. "This is better, a lot more aligned," she thought to herself.

She pulled out her katana, which she had placed off to the side, and carefully positioned it in both hands of the unknown man. Looking at the situation, it was a bit off. The professor had to shoot him, but during or immediately after getting slashed. The unknown man needed to be pulled up closer. She hefted him onto the back of the bed, where the katana could rest out in front of him at the foot of the bed. She repositioned the sword so that it looked slightly abandoned after the shooting but was still clearly just out of the man's hand.

She took off her sheath and removed her wakizashi. She attached both to the unknown man's waist and quickly checked him for any intel. The crazy fool had his wallet on him. "I'm not going to make it that easy for the feds," she thought. His wallet went into her custom outfit. She slipped two of her throwing knives into his boots and two others in his back pockets.

She looked down at the scene. It was believable. People saw what they wanted to see. This should work. This should once and for all close the Ashen Horse case.

She then started to once again carefully examine the scene. It truly meant it was at an end. She would officially be in forced into retirement when she walked out of the door.

Her eyes lingered on her katana and wakizashi. She had owned multiple swords over the years but she loved these two. They were like an attachment to her body. To abandon them, to leave them to the unappreciated bastards that would recover them, seemed almost a crime. They would be locked up in an evidence room for years, wasting away and never appreciated. "I'll miss you," she thought, taking a moment to look at their intricacies one last time.

She had already wasted too much time in here. It was time to be gone. She checked the room over, yet again, making sure there was no evidence of anything unusual where she had knelt and hid on the side of the bed. Assuring herself there was no evidence of anything out of the ordinary, she nodded to herself and proceeded to slip out of the door. She made a point of opening it wider than strictly necessary. Then she stopped, went back in, and checked where her test bullet had landed in the wall. Then, she closed the door sufficiently to ensure the test bullet had a clear line of sight into the wall. The door was still way open. All was right. She finally left the room.

She quickly checked the entire house to make sure there was no residual evidence that she had been there or that anyone other than the killer had been there. She completed a full sweep of the house. She was shocked that he had killed the girl.

Previously, she had decided to let her live. But now, with the other killer's revelations, she was sure she was also a federal agent. As she approached the room where she knew the girl would be lying, she was still undecided on whether she was going to kill her. The decision had been handled for her.

"One less thing to worry about, one less loose end. Probably all for the best. Troublesome, she was shot, though. That doesn't fit the narrative. Likely, it won't matter; they'll see what they want to see."

She closed that door on her way out. It was proper for them to know that she was killed first; the story would never work otherwise. If the door was open, the killer left it open after killing her, but if the door was closed, she was dead first for sure, as the killer never left the master room. The FBI might miss the implication, but a good investigator would understand the timeline, and that was just one less thing to even suggest there were any other players in this situation.

Enough was happening outside the house that the timetable had to be locked in—no loose strings, no loose ends, one grand finale.

She slipped out into the night. She would walk several blocks to where her rental car was parked. She had put on fake plates and covered the VIN with a phony sticker that looked like a normal VIN. Getting it to line up on the dashboard in such tight quarters was a painful process, but for this particular night, she figured there was no margin for error. She would drive this car to the airport and turn it back in, just in time and in line with every other shmuck trying to catch a 6 am flight. She wouldn't be hopping on a plane, but getting lost in the shuffle was always the best way to ensure invisibility.

She arrived at the car and realized it was approaching 4 am. She hadn't intended this to go on so late. She had planned to get a shower in before she disposed of the automobile. But plans had to be able to shift as the situation changed, so it didn't take but a moment, and she was on her way, driving through the city.

After going several miles, she removed all the false identifications and returned the car to a standard rental car. She changed out of her special attire into comfortable shorts and a shirt, which were the perfect travel clothes.

The car drop-off was uneventful, and she taxied from the airport back to a false hotel. After getting dropped off, she got her second rental car and drove to her hotel. The several minutes it took her to get situated after arriving found her showering.

Throughout the last hour, her mind had flipped and reverted and flipped over again. She struggled to grasp where she was. She had wanted out so bad. But to be forced out seemed wrong to her. It was more perplexing because her architecture forced her out. She had designed this exact scenario to play out. She had abandoned, quite literally, her craft. She had chosen this, she had opted for it, she had designed it. Yet it still didn't feel right to be forced out. The struggle continued as her mind swirled repeatedly as she dressed.

She wanted nothing more than to crawl into bed and sleep. But she also knew that today, of all days, it was important to keep up a front of normalcy. So, she made a point to walk down and engage the front desk staff. Then, she got back into her car and drove to what was still her favorite coffee shop in the area. It might be the best one in Missoula because she had tried to sample many of them.

Coffee in hand, she sat in the back of the coffee shop, staring out the window. Confused about what the future would be, she stared lifelessly out the window. One thing was sure: the Ashen Horse had died. He could never resurface again. The FBI would do a significant news story and press release saying they finally got him. It would be interesting if they reported the whole story. At what cost did they bring down this beast? Would they speak of the deception and loose morality they had deployed to bring him down? Would they report all those who died with him? Her mind wandered and wondered as she sipped her favorite white mocha.

The Ashen Horse was dead.

Chapter Forty

The Day After

Another boring day. Tim was getting frustrated—all this effort into this entire fiasco, and still no bites. Once again, another night had come and gone, and no one had reported anything. He had quickly glanced at the monitors when he walked through the living room on the way to the kitchen in the command center. Nothing unusual there.

It was early, probably six or seven in the morning. He had avoided looking at his phone yet. It was unusual for him, but he would get to it soon enough. He only wanted five things this morning and was on his way to the last ones. He wanted to use the bathroom in complete peace, have a clean shave, shower, wash the night from himself, eat a delicious breakfast, and spend ten minutes alone with his coffee with no disruptions.

He had coffee brewing, which was way too thick and heavy for any common mortal, but he took his morning coffee to a spiritual level. Perhaps not always, but today, he wanted the entire experience. He was brewing straight black tar and looking forward to that more than breakfast.

A couple of eggs were in the pan, cooking merrily. He went to flip, and in typical fashion, the yolks broke. Scrambled it is. He chuckled to himself. "Never cry over spilled milk or broken yolks." He took life lessons from his mother, and he took them to heart. A quick swirl of eggs and he heard the toaster pop. Butter, jam, scrambled eggs, and bacon, which he had finished first. This allowed for the best way to cook eggs.

He poured the coffee, and the aroma permeated the moment. He sat back and smiled. He knew today was going to be a great day. He sat back, enjoying his breakfast. Looking out into the backyard, he watched a chickadee and squirrel fight over the bird feeder. The hummingbirds were flittering in and out of their feeder. He listened to the chirping and chittering of the birds. He was in the city. He thought to himself, kind of. He was in "the city," but it felt like a little paradise. In mornings like this, he loved his job, even when frustrated at the lack of progress.

After finishing breakfast, he felt charged and ready to tackle the day. He headed to the monitors and was getting ready to sit down when he noticed Ellie was still in the van. That wasn't right; she should have come off shift at 5 am or something, or maybe they changed the rotations again. It was hard keeping track of who filled in and where. He picked up the mic and called out, "You still in the van, Ellie?" It was a stupid question; he could see her, so obviously, she was there, but there wasn't a better way to ask why she hadn't hit shift change. He sat back and waited for her response.

He checked the snipers, and it was Johnson and Beaks. They should have swapped out when Ellie had. She had been spending time with that crew, bonding with the quiet one, Ghost. Quiet wasn't a fair assessment of him; it wasn't that he was silent, which is what everyone said. It was more that he stayed out of the banter and avoided pointless small talk. He spoke as readily as the other men when the conversation turned to something of substance.

But right now, it was Ellie and Jolly in the van. He watched, and Ellie wasn't moving toward the mic; perhaps she didn't hear him. She and Jolly looked like they were engaged in a rather humorous discussion. Tim grabbed the mic again, "Ellie. Anything to report from last night?"

She didn't twitch at all, like she didn't even have her radio on. Tim checked his mic; it appeared to be working. He called out, "Hi, team, anyone care to report?"

The silence was all that answered him. Something must be wrong with his mic; Ellie and Jolly were still going at it in their lively discussion. But still, she wouldn't ignore him. His radio must be having issues. He stood up and stretched. He had left his phone at his bedside upstairs. He trotted into the kitchen to get cup number two of the tar. Then, he headed upstairs to recover his phone. He'd do this the old-fashioned way; he'd call them directly.

Ellie and Jolly looked like they were having fun, so he thought maybe he'd give them a minute and call Josh. It was getting close to 8 am; Josh would have been up early doing some athletic nonsense. He punched in Josh's name and flipped it to speaker as he walked down the stairs to get back in front of the monitors.

It rang and rang. And rang. And rang.

Was Josh showering or away from his phone? Tim had often sworn he took his phone into the shower; the man always picked up his phone. The phone hit Josh's voicemail. Tim hung up and then called Ellie. Déjà vu, the truly eerie kind. Voicemail. He hung up.

Something caught his eye and he looked back at the monitors. Ellie had done that gesture a couple of minutes ago. Tim thought, "I thought that looked like what she said 10 minutes ago." He started watching the monitors and then saw the timestamp on the monitors. Tim spun into a panic. These feeds were from 10 pm last night. He was running for the door before he even realized it. Somehow, his senses and years of instinct calmed him, and he stopped his mad dash.

His head was spinning. No one could do this; someone had tampered with their cameras. They were encrypted; there was no way anyone could filter or corrupt the feed. Yet it became increasingly evident as he watched Ellie make the same joke again that they were compromised.

What did this mean? The cameras were hidden; he couldn't see what was happening with his team. His team wasn't responding. He started moving for the door again, his hand clasped around the doorknob. He desperately wanted to charge out like a running bull and get eyes on what was happening.

He cursed himself. Protocol. If there was ever a time to do something right and follow protocol, it was in this moment. Something was direly wrong, and he had to report it. He sent an emergency text to his boss, and the other leadership was on the team. He also added his boss' boss to the text for good measure. This would go right to the top, but it was either that or he ran into the street like a madman. He waited. He would give them one minute, and then he'd start calling people all over Washington, D.C. if he had to.

Twenty seconds went by, but for Tim, it felt like an entire lifetime. He got a reply text. Surprisingly, it wasn't from his boss but the other leadership on the team. What a quandary, what a disaster. He read the response, "Conference call, now," was all it said. A second later, the personal meeting room came through. He wasn't sure what he would even say, but he clicked the link and his smartphone started kicking off the application.

As he joined the call, he slowly walked back to the command center with the monitors taunting him. He saw Ellie make the same gesture that caught his eye the second time. He was sweating now. This was bad, oh so very bad.

"Sorry, I'm late. Tim, thank you for jumping on. Let's wait a minute. I know your boss is jumping on in a second. I joined the meeting that he was on and told him to end it immediately and jump into my room. He'll be here."

As he was still talking, Mike Thompsan got on the call.

Darnell Johnson continued, "Oh, he's here. Now, Tim, tell me we didn't just make a massive mistake interrupting three critical meetings today. You just said, 'Emergency

Action Required,' and I surely hope that means this truly is an emergency. Do you have Ash?"

Tim was sweating, bleeding water from places he didn't know he could. He didn't care about his leadership, but he didn't know what was going on with his team and was in a near panic. He was using every force of his will that he could muster to hold himself together. "I don't know the status of anything, honestly, sir. I got up this morning and came to look at the monitors. I tried to reach out to my team members, but I didn't get a response. After trying on our local radios with no success, I tried cell phones. All of that took some time, maybe ten or twenty minutes. I had no reason to suspect anything, but after no one picked up, I noticed the feeds in more detail, and the feeds looked like they were on a loop from last night. It looks like a ten- or fifteen-minute loop."

Mike Thompsan interrupted him. "Our cameras? Right now? Are they on a digital loop? In our isolated command center, where you slept last night?"

"It appears so. Yes. I was in a desperate run to leave our post here, but I realized I haven't got a hold of anyone this morning, and I figured before I fly out in the field, I better follow some basic protocol and issue this up the chain."

"We don't know what's going on at all?" asked Darnell. "Just no communication, and the cameras are dark? No one responded to radio or cell phone?"

"All correct, sir."

They were all quiet for a couple of moments, and then one of the leadership finally asked, "Tim, where's your head at? What is going on?"

"It's in the worst possible place, honestly. Ash never leaves evidence. There are never witnesses. I'm not sure any of them are alive right now. I'm losing my mind; I gotta get out of here."

"Stand down. Stand down right now. It can't be that; if Ash knew everything, he would have come for you, too. If you are still alive, it's likely your team is fine; maybe it's just a cell tower down or something. Let's not jump to conclusions."

Tim nodded. "My mind is in a bad place right now. A downed cell tower doesn't explain the loop. Nothing but something malicious explains a digital loop."

Darnell and Mike both knew Tim was right. Nothing explained the loop except something very dark and sinister. But they also saw that Tim was on the edge of hysteria, and they had to bring him around.

"Call the local police; they know we are at that residence. Get two squad cars to come to your house, secure that area first. Then have one stay sitting in our safe house, and then take the other one in your unmarked car and do a casual drive-by. See what you see, then let's go from there."

Tim dialed the local dispatch on the desk phone before Mike finished his proposal.

Darnell commented, "We will let you go, Tim. We don't want to waste any more of your time. Tim?" He paused, no response; Tim was distracted, waiting for the police dispatch to pick up. "Tim?" Nothing. "Tim!"

"What, yes? Yes, I'm still here."

"Tim. Text that group chat every 30 minutes until we find out what's happening."

"Yep, I can do that."

"Tim. Every thirty minutes."

"Will do."

"Okay, let's break. Get ahold of the local police; let's leverage all our available assets. Every 30 minutes, Tim."

The call went dead. Tim was about to abandon the local dispatch and run out the door anyway. Dispatch finally picked up. His exasperation was getting the better of him. He quickly explained the situation and said he immediately needed two squad cars at his location.

The operator sounded like she smacked her lips with bubblegum and said, "I don't have them right now. Yes, I

The Ashen Horse

know you are the feds, and I know you think we should be at your beck and call, but all my units are dispatched right now."

Tim lost it. The words that flew out of his mouth were some of the harshest words and language he had probably used in his career. But he was going to get to his team, and he was going to get to his team now. The situation was not negotiable. The tirade went on for quite some time until she finally broke down and started moving the chess pieces on her board.

"Yes, sir. I'll make it happen. I can pull two of my men off what they are doing; I'll get them over there. Sorry, sir; I'll try my best to accommodate this. I might have a lieutenant I can also get dispatched over there. He won't be happy, but I'll try my best."

Fumes were coursing out of his ears, and he almost shouted at her, saying how he better see cars in the next ten minutes. "They better not have any lights or sirens on, or so help me, I'll have your job."

"I'm making calls; I need this line if you want me to do it quickly."

Tim said the harshest "Thank you" he had ever said and hung up the phone.

He was exhausted. His knees were knocking against themselves. His exhaustion drove him to the knowledge that he needed to sit down. But he was sitting down. It was impossible to focus or concentrate; he only wanted to get out of here. He was going to go for the door. There was no reason to wait. He tried to stand, but his legs wouldn't cooperate. Their lungs were pounding, and the pain that seemed to be gutting him from his chest made him wonder if he was having a heart attack.

He rolled off the chair and lay on the floor. His breathing was out of control. He was hyperventilating, probably on the verge of shock. Years of training told him that he had to get his breathing calmed and slowed. Using every ounce of concentration and self-control, he started taking slow and measured breaths.

He lay there, staring at the ceiling and breathing steadily. Was this a panic attack? Better than a stroke or heart attack, he assumed. It wasn't much comfort knowing he might be okay in a minute. He knew he wouldn't be fine in a minute. That simple thought threatened to spiral him out of control again.

He heard a serious thumping on the door. How long had he been on the ground? Ten minutes? Madness, there was no way. He texted the bosses. "Local police at the post, proceeding." Then, he finally rolled over and headed for the door.

Everything happened in kind of a blur. He told the story again, lined up the officers, and was in the car riding to the professor's residence, Josh's residence. He didn't trust himself to drive, so the local beat cop was behind the wheel.

The world was rushing by him, and he didn't know how to slow it down. It all happened so quickly. He and the cop were standing outside of the news van. And Tim was puking his breakfast onto the sidewalk. The lieutenant who had come along with the other cop shook his head. "She's cleaved in two; how does that even happen?"

Tim's worst nightmares had not been this bad. He collapsed to his knees and dry heaved until his back spasmed to the point where he had to fall onto his side. He lay there a moment and crawled himself back to a sitting position.

While he sat there, he croaked out, "Lieutenant."

The lieutenant finally pulled his eyes from inside the van and looked at Tim. He jolted himself in surprise as he saw Tim. "Do you need help? Are you okay? Man, I'm sorry, you know them, don't you? I'm sorry, man."

"Lieutenant. In a minute, I will ask you to help me stand. But for right now, can you see the monitors? Do you see the snipers on the monitors?"

The lieutenant looked and then nodded. Realizing Tim

didn't see his nod, he gave an affirmative response. He saw the snipers prone on the ground, appearing to watch the house.

"Great, one of those snipers is located on the side balcony of that second-story house over that way." Tim waved his hand. "Do you see the house?" He didn't wait for a response. "The other one is right over here." He pointed in the opposite direction. "Second story, you see the white railing there?" This time, he heard the affirmative response. "Get me up, and then you go check those locations, look at the cameras again, and look where I told you, make sure you got the right places. Grab a radio and radio check, make sure our radios work." The lieutenant reported he got it. "Great, now help me up."

The lieutenant ran off to check on Johnson and Beaks. Tim didn't need his report to know what he would find, but he needed to know definitively. He also needed to get rid of the man. Tim stared at Ellie's body. She was cleaved in two, from the right shoulder down to the left hip. A clean sword had cut her in half. His body dry heaved yet again, but even his body appeared to lack the strength to be successful.

It looked like Jolly tried to shoot, but the tight quarters of the van worked against both of them. Ellie had been closer to the door; she experienced a deliberate end-to-end swing. Jolly had two throwing knives in him, one in the knee and one in the right side of his throat. Then it appeared like the katana had gone right into his chest in a clean thrust.

Tim shuddered. At least it had been quick for both. Tim's eyes glanced over at the policeman who was standing next to him. "Any remarks from you as well?" This man looked at Tim and shook his head. Tim thought he understood and asked the question anyway, "Combat?"

The man Tim had discounted as a simple beat cop answered him, "Afghanistan and Iraq, multiple tours. This is messy, but it's not an IED. We'll leave it at that."

Tim nodded. "We can leave it there. Look, we'll

probably see worse. But I must know. This should take priority over anything else you or the Missoula police might have going on today. I can safely assume that, yes?"

"I should think it would, yes."

"I might have burned all my goodwill from your dispatch. Can you get on your radio and get everyone you can here? Would you do me that favor?"

"Not a problem. Give me a few." He started to turn to walk away to give Tim a minute and then turned back. "Sir?" Tim looked at him. "I know you'll have the urge, and it's none of my business. But don't touch anything, okay? Just take a step back, and let's let our teams process the scene."

Tim nodded; the policeman stared intently at him to make sure, then slowly walked away to place his calls. Emptying his stomach or perhaps wrenching his back had cleared Tim's head. He felt empty, soiled, and defeated. But his mind finally discerned that it might be working for the first time since he realized something was greatly wrong. He felt like he could function, or perhaps he felt like he must function.

Even so, his soul had left him. It was plucked away and left but a hollow hole in its place. Every instinct in his body screamed to run over and hold Ellie. But he also knew the man was right. He shouldn't touch anything. Perhaps if Tim had the energy, he could have screamed in frustration, sorrow, or sadness. But his emotions were so excavated that he didn't have the capacity. He had been gutted end to end.

Tim had lost it for a moment; his body had entirely betrayed him. But somehow, he was now holding it together. He wasn't entirely sure how. The radio in his hand squawked. He looked down at it and stared blankly. Then he picked it up.

"Go ahead."

"I'm behind the white railing, just above you, and... you know where I am. Sorry. The sniper is here. He has no pulse. It doesn't look like anything is wrong with him. He does have, well, it looks like a dart, from a game of darts you might play at a bar, stuck in his back."

"Checked his pulse?" Tim shook his head, trying to clear it; the lieutenant had just told him the man had no pulse.

"Yeah, he's gone. The neck is cold, too; he's been dead for quite some time. Hours."

Tim nodded and then realized the man couldn't see him nod. "I'm sending you on a fool's errand, but do you mind checking the other one? I'm sure you will find the same thing. They probably shouldn't touch anything except checking the pulse. Sorry about before, too; this is going to be a rough day for me. It will be the worst day of my life, to tell you the truth."

"I understand. Sorry about my comment as well; I was just… Honestly, sir, I was mesmerized by the situation. That sounds terrible, I'm sorry. And I'm sorry about my reaction."

"It is what it is. Thanks for doing this. Jump on the radio when you confirm the other sniper."

The policeman was walking back up to Tim; he waited for Tim to wave him up. "You didn't have to wait; it's your guy on the radio."

"Force of habit, maybe. I got dispatch. They are pulling in all personnel, even people on their day off. This place will be swarming shortly. I assume that's the goal?"

"As long as they all can do their job competently and don't destroy evidence."

"They know what they are about."

"All good, then," Tim said. "You ready to go into the house?"

The policeman looked at him suspiciously. "Are you? No disrespect, but you sure you don't need a minute?"

"Let's go."

"Should we wait for the teams to get here?"

"I can't. You are probably right, but I just can't."

Out of nowhere, Tim's phone rang. He was about to send the call to voicemail but then saw it was his boss. "Hello?"

"Tim, it's both Darnell and Mike in the meeting room. We said every 30 minutes, Tim. It's been 50 minutes since your text about the local authorities. Where are we?"

Tim blurted it out, "They are all dead." He would have said more, but there wasn't anything else to say.

Darnell said, "Tim." Then paused. He wasn't sure where to go with this either. "Uh, Tim. Can you expand on that? Exactly what does that mean?"

Tim shook himself. "Sorry. We are at the news van right now. Ellie and one of the special forces' antiterrorist operatives were in it. They are both dead. They were killed with a sword. I have a local officer checking our snipers; at least one is confirmed dead, apparently by some kind of lethal dart. I assume we'll find the same with our other sniper. We are about to go into the house. But I don't expect to find anyone inside alive."

"Tim, maybe you should sit this out?"

"I'm going in," Tim asserted. From his perspective, it wasn't up for discussion.

"Now that we know the situation, we'll start all the escalation on our side," said Darnell.

"I appreciate it, I guess. Sorry, I'm not feeling much right now."

"Tim, this is first entry?"

"Yes."

"Phone out, record everything. Another cop or someone with you, then? Make sure you have them do it, too."

"Okay."

"You won't sit it out?"

"No."

"Tim, call us when you're done in the house."

"Okay."

"Tim, call us. Don't make us call you again."

He was getting frustrated now. "I said okay!"

"We are giving you some extreme latitude right now, Tim, because we know how close you and your team are. All we are asking of you is to keep us informed so we can ensure we are moving stuff properly behind the scenes."

Tim took a deep breath and centered himself. "You are right. I'm sorry. It's been, well, it's been a day."

"We are all too aware, sadly. Just call us, okay?"

"Will do."

"Okay, go do what you need to do."

The phone went dead, and he swooshed his hand in front of him to signal to move forward. The police officer fell in line. "You hear all of that?"

"Enough. Record everything with our phones is the part I think we care about at the moment."

Tim nodded to him. This was the kind of man he would have looked for to join his team. Street smarts for miles and just the right amount of none-of-my-business to be successful. They pulled out their phones and started recording as Tim approached the door. As his hand clasped the door handle, he let out an exasperated sigh. The door opened; it had been unlocked. They walked inside.

Daryl Benson

Epilogue

She was on her layover in Doha, sipping coffee from Soho Coffee. The Hamad International Airport was on the water, facing east into the Persian or Arabian Gulf. She was enjoying the relaxing view gazing out over the waters.

The beauty of the water was always pleasing to her. It took her back to her days in Florida, where she had watched the beach for hours. She remembered the times that she and Hector had walked on the beach and had been with each other to the sounds of the waves lapping up on the shore. She smiled and took another sip. Those were good times, memorable times. She rested her head back on the airport bench, closed her eyes, and relaxed.

Perhaps she'd come back here for a bit after finishing her current destination. The Middle East had a certain appeal. Doha was an option, but maybe Manama, or Dubai, she had wanted to go to Baku for quite some time. She decided that she might go to them all in several months.

Right now, she was waiting on a flight to Bali, where she planned to enjoy the fullness of the beach experience. The tourist visa was good for thirty days but could be extended once before they kicked out those who overstayed. She planned to live there for thirty days in the vacation home on the beach. After that, she would decide where the winds would float her. Perhaps she'd stay another month; perhaps she'd be right back here in Doha.

She didn't have objectives in her current frame of mind. Perhaps that would change; maybe she'd open a small store somewhere and live a quiet life. She didn't know. More critically, she didn't want to know right now. Right now, she wanted to sit back, drink coffee, enjoy a bright and glorious sun, and admire the ocean in all its wonder and splendor.

It was good not to have a goal, a mission, or a project. She was usually on constant alert, constantly researching a new tool or software program, always checking what was around the corner. The constant tension had grown on her; she didn't know when she had put it down, or maybe it had just eased over time. But after that night, she felt different. She was different.

She heard her flight get called out and echo across the airport. Having spent much of her life in airports, she always thought there should be a better way to do that. Being in an airport was a nonstop screeching session of a hundred things trying to grab your attention. She maneuvered for the gate that would eventually get her one leg closer, this one being Jakarta.

As she crisscrossed the string of chairs in the airport, her mind took her to the last several weeks. After that night, she hadn't watched the news or paid attention to anything happening in Missoula. She stayed in town long enough to make sure a quick departure wasn't suspicious. Then she drove down to Yellowstone National Park and spent some days casually meandering through the sites. Old Faithful didn't disappoint, but perhaps her favorite part had been watching a grizzly lumber through a forested meadow. There was something spectacular about that, just watching him live his best bear life.

Perhaps a week had passed before she decided it was okay to leave the area. That was when she booked her flight to Bali for a week out. As her mind wandered, she did the math in her head. It was two weeks ago, precisely from the night that everything had changed. The night the Ashen Horse had finally been killed.

She had zoned out through the safety announcements, still pondering the events from the last several months. The plane was soaring high above the Arabian Sea through a perfectly clear sky; the ocean was the only thing that could be seen, spanning the horizon. They were high enough that she could see the curvature of the earth, the slight bending of the horizon line over hundreds of miles. It was accented by the sunset cascading across the waters. It was not yet a spectacular sunset; the lack of clouds did not give it the reflective qualities one might look for. But the sun's rays did sparkle across the water, and as the sun dipped into the horizon, the glow was a thing of mastery. The setting was starting to pan across the sky. Who knew the beauty it would hold as it went onward?

Her eyes swept in all the marvel that was before her. Her thoughts stayed on Hector for a time, her eyes looking out the window in awe, captivated by the beauty. A single tear slid down her cheek, but all she could do was smile.

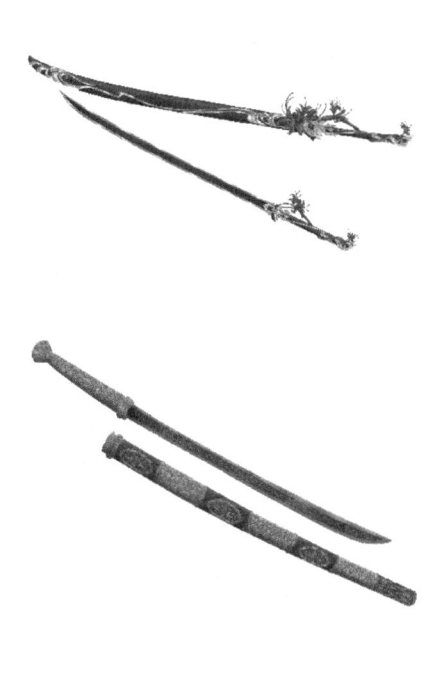

A SPECIAL THANKS

Many people in my personal life, from family members to lifelong friends to acquaintances, encouraged me in this writing journey. To all of them, I have to say a huge thank you!

This story started as a short story submission on Vocal Media (https://vocal.media/), a platform by Creatd, Inc. A creative outlet that I started using when I had a spare moment.

I wrote several other short stories that appeared to form natural chapters in what could be a book. Before I stopped to consider what was happening, I had the foundations of what could be a novel. Once the core was there and I realized it, I started writing what would become The Ashen Horse earnestly.

While writing this book, I learned about Reedsy (reedsy.com), an organization that allows editors and writers to connect. I found my editor, Lisa Findley, on the platform. A huge thank you for her efforts in fixing my words and sentences and reducing my excessively redundant writing style (and you thought what you read was redundant; imagine the first draft!).

The initial short story was originally and entirely inspired by the cover art, which I randomly found on the internet and then eventually traced it to iStock Photo (www.istockphoto.com). I would eventually purchase the rights to use the photo so I could utilize it as the cover photo simply as a tribute to the owner ("bmanis87") and to say 'thank you' for the inspiration.

The cover art was designed casually by using ShutterStock in a relatively simple decision to let the original photo hold most of the attention.

At least for now, I have opted to self-publish this book on Amazon. I am grateful that such a service exists and am indebted to Amazon for bringing this solution to anyone who wants to self-publish—such options were not available even a short while ago.

I also want to extend a huge thank you to my artist. I'll use her internet name, 'BabeLast'. The beautiful artwork throughout this book is her doing, and she does exceptional work.

These are just some of the platforms that made this possible. I am humbled and grateful for all of them as each contributed to completing this work.
https://www.istockphoto.com/
https://vocal.media/
https://reedsy.com/
https://kdp.amazon.com/
https://www.shutterstock.com/
https://babelast.com/

Thank you to everyone who supported me along this journey! As the dedication says, this is just the beginning.

ABOUT THE AUTHOR

Daryl Benson was born and raised in Northwest Montana in the United States. He has lived or worked throughout most of the United States, and his travels have taken him to many parts of the world.

He works in IT (Information Technology) and spends much of his time working with computer networking.

Hiking and wildlife photography in national parks are significant adventures when he isn't pondering his next creative outlet. His photography is available at www.videnphotography.com and features extensive landscape, panoramic, and wildlife photos.

He is working on a fantasy series expected to be released in late 2025 or mid-2026.

He currently resides in Northwest Montana.